The Basel Formula

Being Part 1 of The Basel Trilogy

Ian H. Lane

This is a work of fiction. Names, characters, organisations, places, events and incidents are either products of the author's imagination or are used fictitiously.

Copyright © 2015 Ian H Lane and Jennifer E Lane

All rights reserved.

Ian H Lane asserts his moral right to be identified as the author of this work in accordance with the Copyright, Designs and Patents Act 1988.

ISBN-13: 978-1519293114

ISBN-10: 1519293119

No part of this book may be reproduced, or stored in a retrieval system, or transmitted in any form or by any means, electronic, mechanical, photocopying, recording or otherwise, without the express written permission of the copyright holders.

Printed by CreateSpace. An Amazon.com Company

Dedication

For Jenny, who has persisted in prodding and encouraging me into going on-line and into print with The Basel Trilogy.

Contents

Acknowledgements   Page i

Chapters 1 to 34   Pages 1 to 492

And what next?   Page 493

About the author   Pages 494/495

Acknowledgements

With grateful thanks to:

The staff of the Polyclinique Ambroise Paré, Tournon-sur-Rhône, France for giving me a guided tour of their clinic.

The Revd Dr Jeanette Meadway for guidance on the hospital treatment for suspected meningitis.

Dr Dennis Dell whose work in pharmaceutical research in Basel suggested elements of the plot and who, with his wife Sonia, hosted us on many visits to Basel, some during Fasnacht.

And, of course, the comments on the décor of the Hotel International, Basel are merely the opinions of Elizabeth and Eugene. The dissatisfaction of the night porter is also a fictitious device and no reflection on the hotel as an employer.

Chapter 1

Monday 12th February 1996

Gentle rain had been falling all day and the weak light of the February afternoon was fast disappearing. Peter Lewis paused from his work, interrupted by the sound of a train rattling past on the Euston main line a couple of streets away. His mind had not really been on the paperwork on the desk in front of him. He looked at the piles - letters, invoices and catalogues - he knew that he wasn't the tidiest or most ordered of people. A reasonably successful businessman and good at practical matters but office organisation was not his strength.

There was a knock on the door and Tom his warehouse manager came into the office. 'The order for Hong Kong has just been collected by the shippers, Mr Lewis'.

'Well done, Tom, you've saved our bacon once again. That order means a lot, they'll want more if we treat them properly.'

'That's what I'm here for and that's what you pay me for, sir.'

'Yes, but you always give 110%, Tom, and I'm grateful to you.'

'Thanks, Mr Lewis, you're never slow to say, 'Thank you' and the lads like that. They tell me that there aren't too many bosses around now who take time to show their appreciation. Not that I'd know, having been here all these years.'

Tom returned down the bare concrete stairway, back into the warehouse which was stacked with boxes of glassware and other scientific equipment. Always formal and old fashioned, that was Tom. Lewis had tried to get him to call him Peter but Tom didn't like such casualness and stuck to 'Mr Lewis'.

A minute or two later there was another knock on the door and his secretary came into the room wearing her coat and carrying a shopping bag.

'I've not forgotten, Mrs Nash. You collect Bob from school on Mondays. I'll see you tomorrow morning.'

'I'll make the time up tomorrow evening, sir.'

'You'll do no such thing! If you can't take the odd half hour off now and then when you need to, then I'm not much of an employer!'

She nodded her thanks and left. Despite what he had said, and he had meant it, he knew that she would make up the time in the next couple of days. Like Tom she was one of the old school and he knew that in her eyes he was too soft with his workforce He thought back, it must be six years since she had come to work for him when her husband had had his first spell of sickness. Lewis had been about to disappear under the weight of paper at the time and she had sorted it out and restored some organisation to his office. Together they had struggled with a computer system until they had more or less mastered it: she had brought some order to the paperwork of his business life, and as things at home had begun to show signs of stress, he had been particularly grateful to her.

Lewis returned to the matters that had been on his mind for most of the afternoon. The previous week he had asked his solicitor, an old family friend, to commence divorce proceedings. Separation from Ruth had been a reality for over a year but the prospect of the legal formalities had brought home to him the emotional implications of the impending end of their marriage. Even though his lawyer was a friend or perhaps because of their friendship, Lewis had felt that he was intruding into a private situation, a private failure. To get to this stage was another step towards finality, drawing a line under the past. He was experiencing a paralysis of the will as they faced ending their relationship. Their fifteen years of marriage had begun blissfully in July 1980, he had been nearly 28 and Ruth had been 26. It was only in the last two or three years that their happiness had been dissipated by the tensions that had been gradually growing up between them over the years Their absorption in their separate business interests, with both of them away from home a lot, had in one way caused them to drift apart, though in another, as they hadn't seen too much of one another, it had eased things. When together the difficulties and tensions had in recent years surfaced very quickly. And Lewis' short fling with one of Ruth's staff, which had embarrassed her at work, had certainly not helped matters. The woman, before leaving Ruth's employment, had taken pleasure in publicising their short affair. And Lewis had never been really sure that Ruth's eventual protestations of forgiveness had really come from the heart.

It must have been just over three years before, yes that was right – it had cast a shadow over Christmas 1992. It had been the low point of their marriage. Ruth had been away in France on a business trip and the opportunity had presented itself, or rather Kay had presented herself and he had made the most of the opportunity. The affair had lasted just a couple of weeks and that had been that – or so he had thought. Then one evening he had been confronted by Ruth in a state of icy fury. Their exchange was etched into his memory:

'I hear you've been enjoying yourself while I've been away, Peter.'

'Fine chance! Business here's been pretty hectic, you know.'

'Well, in France the word for business is *affaires* and I understand that you've been having *an affair* in my absence. *An affair* is bad enough but when I hear of it by *whispers* from my staff ... '

He remembered the ensuing silence as he had struggled for the right words, 'Ruth, I'm very sorry that she has let out about it ... '

'But not sorry about what you were doing together?'

'Well, yes, of course, I regret the dalliance, I really do.'

How that word had found its way to his lips he didn't know but he immediately regretted it.

Until then her anger had found expression in a cold, controlled fury and she had kept her voice low and deliberate, now that was cast aside and she erupted, '*Dalliance*, Peter, *dalliance*! How nicely put! How very ... *courtly*, you've been watching too many costume dramas on the box. I suppose it's a mere *peccadillo* in your eyes. Well what you were doing was screwing one of my staff and it was all round the office even before I got back. Your performance in bed really must be good news for someone! In future keep your hands off my staff — look elsewhere if you must. Understood? Good. Just check you haven't caught anything from her, you can't be too careful, Peter! You move into the guest room from tonight! Subject closed.' That had been three years ago but he was still uncomfortable at the memory.

Lewis' thoughts turned to their son Michael. He was twelve, born in September 1983 three years after their marriage. At one and the same time he was a source of their problems and the bond that had kept the marriage together. During their engagement and in the early days of the marriage they had spoken of a large family - Ruth had a sister and three brothers in California and she had enjoyed their companionship as a child. But a difficult pregnancy had been followed by a very unpleasant delivery: although neither mother nor baby had been seriously at risk, the experience had left mental and emotional scars that Ruth still felt. She had been adamant and totally unyielding, 'I won't face that again! I love Michael, and I'm glad that we've got him, but never again, thank you, Peter!'.

At first they had argued over the matter but Ruth had always had the final word, 'Which of us is the one who carries them and has to give birth to kids? Me, isn't it? Well I'm the one who decides and the answer, Peter, is 'No!' And that was that. After a while they had ceased to discuss it any more and if friends raised the topic the conversation was firmly directed in other directions. Lewis had idolised Michael and this had made him feel particularly vulnerable, aware that the loss of his only child would be devastating. Michael's childhood illnesses, though none of them very severe, had been a cause of concern to both his parents. To Ruth, Michael was a source of unresolved tension, at one level she resented the traumatic experience of his birth and on another she was sometimes over expressive in the love that she showed him, feeling that she must blank out her darker memories and assure him of her affection.

Lewis' reverie was broken once again by Tom who showed signs of agitation, 'Sorry to trouble you, Mr Lewis, but there's a policeman here who wants a word with you urgently.' He showed a tall young Constable into the office. Somehow his presence made Lewis aware of the untidiness of his desk and the smallness of the room, 'Was it about Michael or Ruth?', he wondered, aware of the tension in his chest and of the cold sweat on his brow.

'Are you Mr. Peter Lewis?'

'Yes. Is something wrong?'

'Would you spare a moment, sir, and come down to the end of the Mews, please. There's a woman who's been knocked down and we wonder if you could identify her for us. People down there thought that she might work here.'

Lewis' feeling of relief was followed immediately by the horrified thought that the woman might be Vera Nash. As secretary and office manager she was all that stood between him and paper chaos and, more importantly, she was the breadwinner for a son of eight and an invalid husband.

The young policeman watched him as he put on his raincoat. Almost automatically he took down Lewis' details in his mind: height 5 foot 10 inches, hair black with just a trace of gray, medium build and probably once athletic though now he probably didn't take enough exercise, brown eyes and a fresh complexion - nothing to indicate a heavy drinker and he was a non-smoker, no smell of tobacco about the office and no staining on his fingers, a tidy but not an extravagant dresser with a mid-gray double breasted business suit, seemingly with a taste for bright though not garish ties ... Lewis broke into his mental note taking, 'OK I'm ready to go.'

He followed the Constable down the stairs, pulling up the collar of his coat against the rain as they left the building.

'This way, sir' - the Constable was shepherding him to the right and towards the end of the mews a couple of hundred yards away.

Lewis could see ahead of him police cars and an ambulance, their lights reflecting off the wet road, and a knot of people awaiting their arrival. He gritted his teeth and fought against the feeling of apprehension and fear that he could feel building up in the pit of his stomach. A small group of onlookers watched their arrival and those in the way moved aside to let them approach a blanket which covered what was evidently the victim. Lewis now knew for sure that he was being asked to identify a corpse and felt numb at the prospect.

'You don't have any heart problems or anything of that kind, do you, sir?'

'A bit late to ask', went through Lewis' mind but he just said, 'No' and looked down as one corner of the blanket was raised by another policeman to reveal the face of a woman in her early 50's. There was a pause, the policeman looked at him and Lewis, almost as a bystander, heard himself say, 'It's Vera - Mrs Nash that is - she's my secretary'. He knelt beside the policeman and looked at the lifeless face with a gash on the left cheek, the face that only a quarter of an hour earlier had been full of life and energy was now disturbingly empty.

'How?' was all that he could manage to say.

'Hit and run we think, they certainly didn't stay around to help or own up.' There was silence and the Constable continued 'You had better get up, sir. You're getting wet and the road's muddy, you'll ruin your suit.'

'Damn the suit. She has an invalid husband and a youngster to support.'

'I'm sorry, sir, but perhaps you could give us the details about them and where they live. Here in the police car or back in your office, whichever you prefer.'

He looked down at the blanket which covered her body.

Around it the wet cobblestones seemed to glow despite the dullness of the late afternoon light. His head began to swim and nausea swept over him. He was aware of the young Constable taking hold of his arm and being guided back up the mews to his warehouse. Once there the Constable took over and organised hot sweet tea - Lewis loathed sugar in tea but he drank it nevertheless and waited for the policeman to ask his questions. This didn't take long and once he had confirmed that the woman was Vera Nash and given her address and details of her son and husband the Constable rose to leave, 'I'm sorry to have given you a nasty shock, sir. Don't worry we'll send a Woman PC to collect the son from school and another to tell her husband. Shall I let them know that you'll be round to see them?'

'Yes. do that, please? And thank you for looking after me out there. How did it happen?' he asked again.

'I quite understand. It isn't nice to see your first violent death.' He spoke like an old stager though he was only in his early twenties. 'Don't know for sure, some kind of hit and run job. People at that end of the mews heard a car racing along, then a bang as the old girl, sorry your secretary, was struck and her shopping flew around. When they found her the car had gone. Odd that anyone should have been driving at that sort of speed here ... almost makes you wonder whether it was intentional. We may have to come back in the morning and ask you and your staff about her, whether she had enemies and that sort of thing.' Picking up his cap he set off down the stairs just as Vera had thirty minutes or so before.

Down in the warehouse Lewis called Tom and the other employees together, broke the news to them and sent them home. Tom saw that the doors were locked and offered to stay with Lewis until he was ready to leave and then drive him home. Lewis declined and they agreed that Tom should telephone him in an hour to make sure that he felt fit enough to drive.

He sat at his desk in the grip of inertia and emotionally drained. His mouth was dry and seeing the empty tea cup he decided to make another, only without sugar this time. To the tea he added a substantial slug of whisky and gulped the mixture down. 'Better let Ruth know' he thought and picked up the telephone. Ruth's secretary showed an exaggerated civility when she heard Lewis and put him through to his wife. 'Thank God you're there. Vera Nash has been struck by a hit and run driver', he paused to organise his words and thoughts into a coherent form, 'She's dead I'm afraid. ... I had to identify her body. ... Oh, Ruth why *her* with a youngster and a sick husband?'

'Poor souls! And Vera was such a conscientious worker and so caring. You don't sound too good, Peter. You must feel dreadful. I'll be along to collect you right away. I'll be there in around half an hour.'

Despite his protestations that he was all right and able to look after himself he was relieved at her insistence that she would come and accompany him on a call at the Nash's flat nearby. He sat back and poured some more whisky into the tea cup and knocked it back, then realising what he had done, he got up locked the bottle in the filing cabinet and turned to the Business Section of *The Times* and tried to read, but without any real concentration. In the distance another train rattled by, full of people going to their destinations. Where was he going? he wondered. His family life had unravelled and now Vera, who had brought order and stability to the working of his business, was dead and chaos threatened.

***

Less than a mile away in West Hampstead a telephone rang and a terse message was received, 'Old Duck safely out of the way.' The message was passed on by the man who took it to a well groomed man in his mid-thirties who responded with a smile, 'OK I'll give him a day or two to begin to get into a muddle and then offer him Elizabeth's secretarial services. Then things will be under way at last!'

***

Ruth's arrival was in fact rather sooner than she had said and Lewis hurried down the stairs to meet her. She looked at him, taking in his shaken appearance and his drooping shoulders and detecting the smell of whisky on his breath. 'Go easy with the bottle Peter,' then she corrected herself, 'OK I know it's an emergency and you've had a horrible experience. I'm not ticking you off or accusing you of being a secret tippler!'

'I know', he responded, 'You've always been good at looking after me and you still care enough to come round here at short notice. I'm grateful, you know that.'

'What else do you think I'd do? You clearly need help at the moment and I hope that you still regard me as at least your friend, to be called on for help when you need it.' Put like that it sounded as odd to her as it did to Peter but both knew that friendship was something that they might salvage from their marriage and ought to do so for their son's sake.

'Tell me exactly what happened and we'll sort out what

needs to be done and when.'

And so for the next few minutes Lewis told of what had begun as a very ordinary afternoon and ended so tragically. The need to find a replacement for Vera immediately identified itself and Ruth mentioned an agency she used and offered to call them to get a temp. 'Their standards are high but they don't charge the earth. Getting in a good temp will let you find a really suitable replacement at leisure. I'd lend you one of my girls but after the business with Kay ... ' and she immediately regretted mentioning her, 'I know you won't like the idea of putting someone into Vera's job tomorrow but if you don't do something right away you'll only get into a muddle and it'll be more trouble to dig you out!. I'll get her to come here mid-afternoon tomorrow and then she can get started properly the following day. And, Peter, the next thing is to call on the Nash family. It will be easier to do it sooner rather than later and I'll take you there on the way home - it will help both you and them to have a woman around.'

Lewis was not disposed to argue, in his state of shock he was happy to let Ruth organise him.

The visit to the Nash home was quickly over, inadequate words were exchanged and Lewis noted that Ruth's more physical approach to comforting father and son - she hugged them with a naturalness that came from her American background - was somehow more appropriate and effective than his constrained Britishness. They promised to call late the next morning and to assist with the funeral arrangements.

'You just can't realise how much help that was to me', Lewis sat in his wife's car and looked at Ruth. He saw the tear that had trickled down her cheek and wished that he was as capable of letting out the grief that he too felt deep down inside. 'It wasn't easy in there was it?'

'Death never is easy. The loss of my young brother taught me that.' Lewis knew that she had been deeply moved - she had hardly ever referred to that brother during their years of marriage.

'Now home for some decent food, and for you a bath and an early night.'

'Just drop me off at the flat.'

'Certainly not. You'll occupy the guest room in what is still *our* home. In any case you stay there when you look after Michael when I'm away. You are *not* going to spend the night on your own!' And that was that, Lewis was happy to be cared for, cosseted and pampered and he knew that Ruth was pleased to be able to help and, in doing so, try to salvage something of their shattered relationship and establish a supportive background for their son's adolescent years.

***

Elizabeth stood back to admire the wallpaper in the sitting room of her apartment. She was in her early thirties and of mid-height, wearing a white overall and with a scarf over her hair. She slipped off the scarf and shook her head to let her long dark brunette hair fall into place. It was strange how restricted she felt with her head covered but she hadn't wanted to have to wash the paste out of her hair. One more room to be done and the decorating would be complete. For a number of years she had moved regularly from place to place, never spending much time anywhere, and this was the first time that she had been able to have things just as she wanted them.

She had insisted on this apartment and Moscow had agreed, they had been willing to let her have her way. After all she had been very successful in her assignments in north America and there had been time to spare before this assignment got under way. Besides they could use it for their friends afterwards, they would somehow lose the expenditure among other items in the accounts and have a pleasant London apartment to be used for unofficial purposes, a hidden perk.

She looked around the sitting room, pleased that it felt so right. She had wondered whether it would be as good as the virtual reality display in the shop had suggested and she was delighted to see that it was even better. At several points she had resisted the shop assistant's advice and she was glad, as she looked around, that she had done so. The clock in the next room chimed six - time to tidy up from the papering, vacuum the floor and get the furniture back. She could hardly wait to see the total effect. The clearing up complete, she made a cup of coffee and contemplated the task of moving the furniture. It was just then that the apartment's door bell rang and she heard Eugene's voice on the intercom. 'Shall I let him in?' was her first thought but, realising that he would have seen the sitting room light from the street, she replied to him and pressed the button to open the street door - after all she would need help with moving the furniture. A minute later she opened the door of the apartment and admitted Eugene. He kissed her on the cheek and evidently was looking for the kiss to be returned, however Elizabeth showed no sign of doing so. Instead she took his coat and hung it on a peg in the hallway. He wore a suit she hadn't seen before, it was very well cut in a light gray tweed flecked with the odd spot of maroon. He sported a maroon silk tie and matching pocket handkerchief. 'New operation, new suit?' she enquired.'

'If I'm to play the part of a prosperous business man I need to dress appropriately. I'd always wanted to see what a Savile Row suit would look like on me and this seemed the right time to find out.'

'And very fine it is too, Vladimir - sorry I'll have to get used to your being Eugene from now on.' She led him into the sitting room, 'Welcome to the refurbished apartment! What do you think of it?'.

He noticed the smell of damp paper and looked around him. 'Well you'll have a trade to fall back on when Moscow has finished with your services. I have to admit that it looks good. Where did you learn how to do it?'

She smiled contentedly. 'From a book, so far as the technique is concerned, but for the rest I used my judgement and colour sense with a little help from the shops. It's been fun looking round John Lewis and the other stores to find papers, fabrics and things.'

Eugene studied her closely. He had never seen her so relaxed and contented.

She continued, 'Right then. I'm grateful for your social call and the help that you're about to give with moving a few things around. I want to see how the room looks with everything in place.'

'All in good time, I'm not only here on a social call. It's just as well that you've almost finished your decorating as you could be starting work in a few days or a couple of weeks at most.'

A look of disappointment crossed her face. 'A shame but that's what they sent us here for. I'm not very excited though at the prospect of working in some crummy dump in Kilburn for some second rate business. In the States I was working for real blue chip concerns.'

'It needn't appear on your CV just as this needn't either,'

and he kissed her. This time she responded but without much fervour.'

'Nice, but you had more fire in California, Elizabeth.'

'Did I? The weather was hotter and you helped to relax the tension. Here it's different, I'm far more relaxed, after all this is going to be a pretty low key operation. We've gone through all this before, you have a family in Moscow and there isn't any mileage in our relationship.'

'But at any rate you can be civil to an old friend.'

'Friend? I don't know about that,' she teased. 'Colleague, yes. And a colleague that I've enjoyed working with over the last eight years. Here there and almost everywhere. We've certainly had an interesting time. But you know it's very unsettling - never time to put your roots down, always living with a false identity and back home you never know who's running things or what will happen next. Take this new job, is it for Security or for the Moscow Mafiya? No certainties any more for us or for anyone else! When it was the KGB it was clear at any rate why you were out in the West and you knew who would be paying your pension!'

'Elizabeth! Surely you aren't thinking of retirement yet! But I take your point. It's all a bit vague and uncertain, I agree. Private enterprise rules! But who benefits is another matter. Yes I do have my family in Moscow and I hope that I'll be able to maintain them when our bosses have decided that my Western working days are over!'

'I need the job to support my mother, her pension is pitiful. Forget all that for the moment though, I've some work for you now, Eugene. You can practise as a removal man and help me move the furniture back into the room. I want to see how it looks after all this work. Off with your expensive jacket and roll up your sleeves!'

The next thirty minutes were occupied with shifting an assortment of furniture back from the other rooms of the apartment into the sitting room. Elizabeth took her part in the manual work and wasn't satisfied until all was arranged precisely to her liking.

'Well done Eugene. I would have had to wait until tomorrow if you hadn't called. I'll give you a reference as a removal man if you ever need one! You deserve a drink - what would you like? What are you on at the moment?'

'Whatever you like to offer.'

'See what you think of this,' She poured an inch of golden liquid into a heavy cut glass tumbler.'

He took a sip, 'Smooth, different - what is it? Apple?'

'I brought it back from France last week. Calvados from Normandy. Yes, they make it from apples and it can be pretty rough but not this bottle, it's had time to calm down a little, they call it *Tres Vieux Calvados* - I thought that you would appreciate a little treat, something different.' She looked at him and smiled, 'The truth is that I'm still fond of you but you must treat me as a friend and no more. And now you, my good friend Eugene, are going to take me out for a meal to celebrate my finishing work on this room. Tomorrow I will cook you a celebratory meal here. So just relax while I change out of these work clothes into something more suitable.' She put a disc on the player, surveyed the room with a look of satisfaction and left Eugene to contemplate the décor by himself.

He looked around and took in the sitting room. He had seen it when they took over the place. Then it had seemed cold and unfriendly. Now it was transformed. Walls, carpets and upholstery were all in pastel shades and the lighting, from table lamps, was gentle and relaxing. Elizabeth could make a career for herself as an interior decorator, that was clear. He relaxed in the comfort of the sofa, closed his eyes and listened to the piano music which Elizabeth had put on. Probably Chopin, she enjoyed his music a lot. He sat there, took another sip of the Calvados letting it roll around his mouth. He liked the apartment, he liked Elizabeth. In fact he liked everything about her ... but now she persisted in her determination to be no more than a friend. That hurt but he would have to put up with it - or at any rate make the most of her friendship ...

His reverie was interrupted by Elizabeth's laugh, 'If Sleepy Head will wake up we can go out for dinner'. She knelt beside his sofa and kissed him, 'Colleagues can be friends and friendship can still be fun, you know!'

He looked at her quizzically, 'I hope so.'

She looked superb in a little midnight blue cocktail dress that came to just above the knee. He could smell her perfume, subtle and distinctive. She was sure to attract quite a few glances from other interested males that evening, he would enjoy that. It really was a pity that she had cooled towards him.

***

Their departure from the building did not go unnoticed as he unfurled his umbrella against the rain and she took his arm. In a van across the road two men, were watching. 'There they go, a very attractive couple indeed. Ex-lovers though, by the sound of it, with a bit of tension between them. They tally well with their descriptions on the file - so far as you can see in this light. Both in their mid-thirties, the woman - 5 foot 5 inches, longish dark brunette hair, good figure and carries herself well. The man 5 foot 9 inches, medium build and short fair hair. His hair style wouldn't be out of place in the Marine Corps would it?

We'll leave them to themselves, there's no point in following them tonight as they're only going out to eat. Seems they're about to take the bait. You heard him tell her that she'd be working in Kilburn very soon. Once she starts work at Lewis' place we'll keep a close eye and ear on them. One thing though, I wonder if one of the bugs isn't on the blink. If it is we'll have to go in there again and replace it, it's a nuisance but not impossible. You can have a night off Buddy, we may well be busier when things get going.'

'You to your books, Sam, me to the pub.' And the van moved off in the rain towards its base just around the corner.

Chapter 2

Tuesday 13th February – the next day.

Ruth pulled up outside the warehouse and Lewis turned to her as he opened the car door, 'I appreciated your help yesterday, I don't know how I would have managed without you.'

'And, as I told you earlier, I'm here today as well, I'm not leaving you to sort things out for them and for yourself on your own.'

'No, you've done enough and you have your business to deal with.'

'First of all, the business is looking after itself: I've been giving Sally more responsibility lately and it will do her good to carry on without me being around all the time. I know that doesn't sound like my usual attitude to things but I have been thinking about how I want life to shape up and some changes seem to be overdue.' She noticed the look of mild surprise on his face but did not elaborate. 'Secondly you and Vera's family need to have a woman's sensitive and practical approach to what has to be done. Sally has been told to run the office for the day.'

'But you're always so unwilling to lose time!'

'I don't regard this as a waste of time. You and they need help. And I've brought you back to Kilburn - I couldn't come here without seeing them, could I?'

'Well ... your help is very welcome.' He was surprised at Ruth's changed priorities but decided to accept the situation and not to probe into the reasons for her changed attitude.

In Lewis' office they discussed the business and the need to find a permanent replacement for Vera. 'Don't you think that I could leave it to next week? Replacing her now, not even twenty four hours after she's dead seems positively indecent.' It was clear that the idea didn't appeal to Lewis.

'No you've got to get someone in now, on a temporary basis, just as we discussed yesterday,' Ruth was insistent, 'You'll only get into a muddle and it'll be more difficult to get up to date. What would Vera have told you to do?'

'Find someone double quick.'

'That's your answer. OK, if you agree I'll 'phone the agency and get them to send a girl over by taxi after lunch.'

The atmosphere at Lewis' warehouse was heavy with gloom, there was little of the usual chit-chat going on. The business had a small staff who got on well despite their different ages and backgrounds. To have one of their number killed and so near to the warehouse hurt deeply. It was like losing a member of the family but with the added problem that access to Vera's son and husband wasn't easy. If they really had been "family" it would have been straightforward to go along and grieve with them. They weren't "family" and they looked to Lewis, as boss, to go there as their representative.

'Do tell them, Mr Lewis, that we're thinking of them ... and, of course, if there's anything that we can do to help ... ,' Tom's voice tailed off.

'Yes, of course we'll tell them. We'll let them know how you all feel and deliver your card'. Ruth nodded her agreement and they left. Lewis noticed how, as always with his business, she didn't intrude. She knew that it was his show and she had always avoided upstaging him. It was his workforce and it was right that he should be the one who faced and shared their inarticulate grief.

They sat in Ruth's Mercedes. 'What has to be done, Ruth? We ought to make a list of things to cover when we see them, don't you think?'

'Yes but you'll probably find that the Police have given them quite a hand. Let's see ... Coroner - they won't be able to have the funeral until he releases the body - the mortician, sorry the undertaker, church for the service - I remember you saying that she was a churchgoer - and if possible refreshments afterwards, they need to meet people even if it's difficult and there will probably be relations coming from a distance. Your staff will want to speak to them. You know it's far easier when you live in a community that has formal rituals for this sort of thing. Formality, customs and so on they help and give people an opportunity to grieve together. Without something like that it isn't easy. When my brother died we had a lot of folk who dropped in to share our sadness - that helped. It isn't good for people to be left alone with their grief for too long at a time.'

'Round here they probably go in for wakes,' Lewis observed. He noticed that she had mentioned her brother for the second time in two days but he didn't comment on it.

'Better that than nothing, it involves the community. No grief should be wholly private. You'll have to help your troops to get through it.'

'Right let's go. We'll walk, if you don't mind - it's not far and your car would stand out a bit outside the house, and there's not a lot of space in the road with parking on both sides, we don't want it damaged by a passing lorry - besides it's a fine morning.' The crisp sunny weather seemed only to sharpen the sense of sorrow at what had happened.

Two hours later they left the Nash's house. Lewis had been surprised at the length of their stay but it had been Ruth who had taken the lead, knowing that it was not a question of having to keep off her husband's territory. Here it was not a matter of being in charge and commanding any one's respect. Lewis was impressed with the way in which she was able to draw them out and get them to talk about Vera.

'Thanks Ruth, you did us all a power of good. You should have been some kind of therapist!'

'Let's say common sense and humanity. Heaven preserve us from therapists!'

'That place was as clean and shining as a bright new pin and it had a real feel of home about it.'

'And it ought to stay like that, Peter. What will they get from the firm's pension scheme?'

'Well, six years' service won't give a huge pension but there is an accidental death insurance that will give them £100,000 or so and there should be something from the Criminal Injuries Compensation people. I would like to get my hands on the bastard who killed her! Some young thug I expect, joyriding in a stolen car.'

Back at the warehouse Lewis organised some food from the Kilburn High Road and he and Ruth told the staff about their visit to the Nash family. The funeral was to be in a Catholic Church just off the High Road, probably the next Wednesday, and they would close for the day.

After lunch Lucy arrived from the agency and Ruth left Lewis to tell her what the work involved. Lewis liked what he saw, a lively young thing in her late twenties with a strong Essex accent - Estuary English as it had become known - and a smile which kept breaking through however much she tried to restrain it as the circumstances demanded. She seemed happy with the facilities and told Lewis that, as she lived in Cricklewood, getting to work would be no trouble. Despite himself he was glad to be able to hand Vera's work over to her. Ruth chatted to the warehouse staff who were pleased to be able to talk about their dead colleague, Lewis had asked her to do so.

'You don't know how grateful I am to you for yesterday and today,' Lewis was showing Ruth to her car later that afternoon.

'Glad to be able to help. We're still married and even if we weren't I would still want to be supportive. I'll be here for the funeral and do whatever needs doing.' She kissed him on the cheek, 'I'm still fond of you, Peter.'

He was going to reply but found himself lost for words and choking back emotion. 'Thanks,' was all he managed.

'Won't you stay at home for one more night? Michael will be back tonight.'

'Thanks for the idea but I really have to look after myself. Besides it did seem odd, with you there in residence, spending the night in the guest room of what was once my home. Tell Michael that I'll be in on Saturday around eleven, we're going to the football.'

Ruth smiled, 'I see that you still notice a good pair of legs! Lucy's a good looking girl and probably a lot of fun. But do take care. And they say that moderate alcohol intake cuts down the risk of heart attacks! But remember *moderate* is written on the prescription, just as well that it's not on the National Health, though a reasonable bottle of wine is cheaper than a bottle of medicine. Do look after yourself Peter, promise me won't you?'

'And wine's much more pleasant ... and on the other point you have my promise,' Peter added and they laughed, the grief had been shared and its intensity lessened - for the moment anyway.

As she drove off she asked herself why she had warned Peter to take care with Lucy, after all they were heading for the dissolution of their marriage, no one could say that it hadn't broken down irretrievably. And yet .... and yet, it did matter to her what Peter made of his future – they had shared a large slice of life together and Michael would continue to link them together. And those words, 'I'm still fond of you, Peter' were true.

***

Not far away Elizabeth stood in her bathroom admiring the wallpapering that she had just completed. The work on the entire apartment was finished and the place was looking good, no that was not the word that she was hunting for. She thought, 'It's warm, its friendly, it looks and feels right, its what I've planned and done ... it's me.' She smiled to herself in the mirror and then the thought hit her, Eugene had said that the job for which she had come to London would be starting in the next few days. But how long would it last and what then? Back home to who knows what. 'Well I'll enjoy it while I can, I wonder what the crummy dump in Kilburn is really like. Nothing like Silicon Valley, that's for sure!'

She had asked Eugene about the boss in Kilburn and been told, 'Lewis? I'd describe him as a buttoned up Englishman. The sort who keeps his emotions in a bank vault.' She knew that he exaggerated but it didn't seem a very exciting prospect. Still he didn't sound like the predatory over-sexed males she had worked for in North America. And whatever the work was like she had the apartment to return to as her oasis of taste and comfort. Besides there were plenty of concerts and similar events to go to in London. She would have to limit Eugene's visits though, the way he had taken to looking at her was making her feel uncomfortable and he had recently taken to patting her on the bottom as though she were his property. It would be safer to keep him off the premises as much as possible.

Chapter 3

Monday 18th March 1996

Lewis looked around his office and marvelled at its tidiness. Five weeks had passed since Vera's death and Lucy had taken no time at all to reorganise him and the way in which things were done. He appreciated the orderliness but at the same time resented her for achieving this. He felt that it was, in some way, an indictment of all that Vera had stood for and that in showing gratitude to Lucy he was being disloyalty to Vera.

'Some more letters to sign and you have a meeting at 2.30, that's in twenty minutes' time so I'll be back to collect them for posting in ten minutes, Peter,' she looked him straight in the eye and gave one of her warm come-hither smiles and turned to leave the room.

'Thanks, Lucy, you're doing a great job getting things organised when I don't feel very dynamic,' despite himself Lewis knew he must praise her.

She turned back towards him, 'You know it's been a pleasure to be able to give you a hand especially as you were in a fix. As for not being dynamic, I bet that you've got energy for all sorts of things.' Another penetrating look in the eye for Lewis. 'There's quite a lot of urgent work still on hand but don't worry I'll be able to stay on until late this evening, Vince, that's my boy friend, is away in Milan so I don't have to rush off home.' She smiled again and left.

'My, she knows how to project herself,' thought Lewis, contemplating the short skirt and tight jumper that left little to the imagination. Her perfume lingered in the room. 'Watch yourself, Peter', he thought, 'you don't want to make a fool of yourself. And, it's odd, you've spent a lot of effort trying to persuade your staff to call you Peter and when one does so it doesn't seem right. Must be because she's only been here for a couple of weeks. Better do as she says and get this lot signed.'

***

'... that's a fair price and your delivery dates are pretty good. If you can meet them it will be more than a pleasure to do business with you, it will be profitable as well. If you can mix profit with pleasure then you are doing well, don't you think so?' The Canadian looked pleased. 'I've only known you for a month or so and I think that we're going to get on well together. I was sorry to hear about your secretary being killed, that must have been a nasty blow for you and the business.'

'And not just here, she had an invalid husband and a young son - you can guess how they feel, Eugene.'

'I can imagine that they're pretty distraught. Have they found the driver yet?'

'Little chance of that with the number of cars there are in London. People heard the impact but no one actually saw it happen. I doubt whether they'll catch anyone for it.'

'How about the office side of things? It looks pretty well organised here at the moment. That's a neat young thing you've got looking after you!' he smiled knowingly.

'Only for a few weeks, she's a temp from an agency'.

'And then?'

'Find a permanent replacement - which won't be too easy. It can be harder finding the right staff for a small set up than for a large one. We need someone who fits in with the people we've got here rather than someone who stands out too much,' Lewis smiled, 'Lucy's fine, she is a very good secretary. She organises herself, the work and myself extremely well but the staff are a bit dubious about having a pert sex kitten around the place, they find it something of a strain. The lads in the warehouse feel safer with their pin-ups than with the flesh and blood article.'

'And you?' Eugene smiled again, 'I think that I could stand the strain but then I'm not married.'

'Safer with a rather less turbocharged version.'

The Canadian paused, 'I wonder ... my niece is over from Canada and is looking for a secretarial post. She's been in a variety of firms, some big corporations and some quite small businesses, she might fit in here. No, she's not just going to flit off back to Canada, she's a Brit, though you wouldn't know from her accent, and she plans to stay here for a while.'

'There's no reason, I suppose, why we shouldn't talk about it together,' he wondered whether it was wise to have said this but he hadn't wished to offend this potentially profitable new customer.

'OK then, I'll see whether she's keen on the idea and ring you to let you know - probably by Thursday.'

'Thanks, that's kind of you. More tea?'

'You Brits, you would float in the stuff. Bourbon's my drink but I bet you've none here.'

'No Bourbon but we do have Scotch whisky, a more than decent single malt, if that takes your fancy at 3.45 of a March afternoon.' Lewis opened the top drawer of the filing cabinet and took out the bottle that reminded him of the afternoon of Vera's death. 'Not much in this one. Hold on, there's a bottle in Lucy's room.' He called her on the telephone, telling her where it was.

Lucy swung into Lewis' office, 'Here you are, don't make too wild an afternoon of it! I won't feel safe here if I have two inebriated lusty males around the place, especially as I'm working late tonight, don't forget that, Peter.' She smiled teasingly and left them to the whisky, a 12 year old Caol Isla.

'Turbocharged is about right.' Eugene lifted his glass, 'To plenty of business between us and to your finding a non-turbocharged secretary. I think you'll like Elizabeth ... how should I describe her? Not demure, that's not the word. Not really. She's a good looker who doesn't flaunt her sexuality. She's not like that one, though she's a very efficient secretary, she's helped me out at times and I've been grateful. I think you'll like her.'

***

Later that afternoon Eugene called on Elizabeth to find her arranging books and a collection of CD's.

'Lewis looks ready to take the bait. I'm 'phoning him on Thursday to tell him that you're interested in the job and to fix for you to see him. He's got a temporary replacement for his last secretary. Oh, by the way, it seems that we were a bit too effective in putting her out of action, she was killed by the car that hit her. So there's no chance of her getting fit and wanting her job back.' Elizabeth's look killed his smile as it began to form. 'OK it's a pity that it was necessary but that's life ... or rather death - we all die and she just died a little earlier.'

'I don't like the way we're still going about things,' Elizabeth looked at him with a puzzled expression. 'OK people got killed when the West was the enemy but now ... '

'There has been no change, the West is still the enemy, they want us weak and subservient they don't want us to forget that they won the Cold War. Our job's harder than it was. Once we were seen to be a leading power and people feared us, but just look at it now! Who's in power, I ask you. What do the Americans think of us? President and Duma at odds. Most of the Union gone, rebels in Chechnia making fools of us, McDonald's in Red Square. Worst of all it's as bad on the streets of Moscow as in an American city - what a place for my kids! Damn I've said too much.'

Elizabeth was surprised at the strength his anger and reassured him, 'No, what you've said won't go beyond these walls. We've worked together for some time now and you can trust me to keep my mouth shut. You can count on my loyalty.'

'Yes, I know I can trust you - you know I'm grateful for that.' Eugene's gratitude was sincere but he knew that he should take more care about what he said. Not all his colleagues would be as ready as Elizabeth to forget his opinions.

Elizabeth was reflective, 'Once you could rely on things being predictable. Now our President has his tired and emotional phases and nips lady interpreters' bottoms. Our illustrious old boy Andropov knew how to stay sober and keep his wits about him.'

'Yes, you could have some confidence in our leaders when it was just one step from Head of the KGB to General Secretary of the Party. Those were the good days.'

'Yes for us, if you kept your nose clean! Still, we haven't much choice. Once you're prepared to work away from home this is better than some town in Siberia or security duties on some dangerous nuclear reactor. I like it here in London, the shops, the theatres, the galleries ... there's a lot to do. What about a concert this evening? It's nearly five o'clock so there's time to eat and then go out.'

'OK so long as your choice of music has got some decent tunes. That was one thing that Stalin had going for him - he liked a good tune, not the miserable, soul searching stuff that some of them were churning out!'

'Right. Stay here while I get some food. A drink? Calvados? You liked the sample you had the other day? OK, there you are. And some music ... how about Shostakovich 5 - *that* pleased Stalin!' She found the CD and put it in the player.

'That's fine! We Georgians know what we like in music and drink ... I wonder if he ever tried Calvados? On the other hand he would probably have sent me to the gulag for cultivating deviant foreign tastes! Perhaps we are safer when the worst that the President does is to nip a woman's bum!'

Elizabeth closed the kitchen door and turned on the radio. Good, the 5.00 p.m. news programme was beginning. She found the Brits interesting, especially the things that wound them up and got them writing, telephoning or faxing in to the presenters. She wondered how such listeners would have got on in Stalin's Russia. They would probably have been given free tickets for a very cold holiday.

Eugene lay back in his arm chair. This wasn't a bad life at all but what future was there for him and his family? Make the most of the present, that was what he had to do. If only Elizabeth were more co-operative! If there was no mileage left in that relationship he would have to see what he could find locally. At any rate Elizabeth could introduce him to the English social scene. He finished his drink, closed his eyes and listened to the music. Good full blooded stuff he'd call it, proper Soviet music from the good times. People took notice of us then ... gave us proper respect ... feared us ... that's what we could do with now, a decent bit of fear ... it gave you a purpose in life ... Eugene fell asleep.

***

In a house just around the corner two men sat at a table listening in on the conversation in Elizabeth's apartment.

'More work to do, replace that bug that's on the blink.'

The other nodded, 'Yes, we'll have to wait until we can be sure that they're out for long enough for us to do the job properly. Turn that confounded Russian music down, they may like it but I don't. I'm keen to have a look at the place and at her interior design skills.'

'We could get her to do up this dump for us, Sam'

'The Institute wouldn't pay for that sort of luxury ... this is going to tie us down for some time and be expensive enough without pandering to your tastes.'

'You don't seem to notice your surroundings. Give you a book and you're happy anywhere.'

'A book, a worthwhile job and a warm corner and I'm happy ... or as happy as memories allow!'

***

Lewis knocked on the door of Lucy's room, 'It's gone 8 o'clock and you've done quite enough work for one day. I'll give you a lift home, I know you don't live far away but it would be on my conscience if you were attacked on the way home, besides it's raining,' he nodded towards the window.

'That's nice of you, I'd be glad of a lift. Just give me five minutes and I'll finish this letter and get ready.'

A few minutes later he followed her down the stairs and out through the dimly lit warehouse. Her perfume, freshly and liberally applied, hit him in the pit of the stomach. 'Well the girl's willing', he muttered to himself as he set the security system, 'but I wonder if I am.'

'How about a bite Peter, I'm sure both of us are hungry and it's a bit late to be cooking at home.'
'Where do you suggest, Lucy, you know Cricklewood and I don't.'
'There's the Galteemore Club, the food's good and filling and I'm a member.'
'OK, I'll be your guest but promise to let me pay.'
Filling was indeed the word and after Irish Stew and a pint of Guinness hunger had been well and truly banished.

They pulled up outside her apartment block. The heavy rain had increased to a downpour. 'Well, here we are, just hold on - I'll get an umbrella from the boot. He opened the passenger door to Lucy and looked down at her as she emerged from the car all hair, legs and a smile. She took his arm and guided him to the awning over the entrance to the apartment block.
'Now Peter you *will* come in for a coffee, *won't* you?'
He thought of his own place and the prospect of the rest of the evening alone. 'OK you've persuaded me,' he replied. 'On a night like this a haven from the storm is very welcome.'

She sat on the sofa adjusting her underwear – green, she had told him to celebrate St Patrick's Day, adding that she didn't know what St Paddy would have made of it.
'Perhaps we should have limited it to coffee, Peter – we don't seem to have been very successful. You did say that you were in the throes of a divorce and I'd assumed

you'd be willing ... '

'To go all the way? I'd thought so too but I'm in a bit of a muddle emotionally, I must admit. Just when we seemed set to wind up the marriage I find myself having doubts. It must be the shock of Vera's death. So, sorry Lucy, I've disappointed you, though you've helped to release some of my tension this evening but I'm not the best of company at the moment. The truth is I don't really know what I want.'

Chapter 4

Wednesday 20th March 1996

Eugene stood at the window of Elizabeth's sitting room and inspected the glass of Calvados that she had poured for him. He held it to the sunlight and admired the rich amber colour. 'Smooth it certainly is! You did well to introduce me to this, Elizabeth. "*Tres vieux*" they call it, do they? I wonder if I'll be drinking it in *my* old age.'

'Poor thing, you *are* becoming obsessed with retirement and you've years of work ahead of you.'

'It was *you,* Elizabeth, who raised the subject the other evening. I've a family to think of as well as myself ... Oh yes, I know you have your mother but at any rate she has her husband's pension as well as what you give her. I admit that its not the absence of a pension that's my problem but just what the pension will shrink to. Out here they've got to give us reasonable pay to keep us loyal and effective. Enough of that. Well what did you make of Lewis and his outfit?'

'He's OK and won't be any problem. The business isn't much is it? Once I've got the data processing side sorted out the main difficulty will be in finding enough to do and keeping awake.'

'Perhaps I can find enough orders to keep you busy ... we owe it to him for the assistance that he unwittingly is going to give us in getting into those Swiss laboratories.'

'That's kind of you, I really would appreciate not being bored out of my mind for the duration of this exercise.'

'We'll have to find you something else to do to earn your keep if that turns out to be so. How about joining the local Labour Party in Hampstead ... you could see whether there are friends to be made for the SVR there and it might be worth seeing whether there isn't someone with the right contacts who could be set up by you to be susceptible to a little persuasion to work for us later on.'

'Set them up for blackmail you mean? No I'm not climbing into bed with people that Moscow chooses for me. I had quite enough of that in the USA and Canada. That isn't how I intend to make my living if I can help it. I'm nearly 34 and it's getting time for romance and something permanent ... As for you Eugene, I enjoy your company and your support but I'm not drawn to you emotionally. I know that we've been lovers and that we've had real good times together but there's no future for us in a relationship, it would only be a blind alley going nowhere. If you're looking for a relationship *you* had better join the Hampstead Labour Party ... you could kill two birds with one stone. After all politicians with a future are not all male and it would make quite a change to be able to compromise a female politician in that way!'

'What about setting up as a design consultant - just look at this place, you would never recognise it as the apartment that you took just a few weeks ago. You've got taste and style ... and it hasn't cost the earth. Besides it would give you access to the homes of people that we could bug to our benefit. And what about doing up my apartment for me, I'd like my place to have the same sort of feel as this place. How about it?'

'Set up my Furnishing Services Bureau, you mean? Hardly the sort of thing I could do in my spare time ... though for a friend and colleague I'm always willing to help. OK we do up your place, but you have to do most of the hard work.' She thought for a moment. 'Tomorrow morning you meet me outside Liberty's in Regent Street and we get some ideas there and in other stores of just what you would like. Then I'll sketch what your rooms would look like and you can decide if that appeals to you. But I want a decent lunch as payment ... or at any rate as your deposit, the Café Royal Grill Room will do nicely, the décor is worth seeing I'm told - 'Victorian neo-rococo' the book says - but it will cost you, so you will have to justify it to Moscow or pay out of your own pocket!'

'Done. I look forward to the experience!'

'On your way now and do give some thought to what you would like for your apartment, it will make our task a lot easier tomorrow.'

Eugene would have liked to linger but he knew that any attempt to extend the visit would not be welcome. 'Tomorrow at Liberty's and until then you are at liberty!'

She smiled, 'I'm always at liberty and never more so than now. I like it here in London, I'd love to stay but no doubt we will be on the move again when we've got what we're after from the Swiss.'

'Very likely unless we fall foul of the Swiss authorities - they don't take at all kindly to foreign governments meddling in Swiss affairs, Swiss business secrets are as closely guarded as military ones.'

'10.30 Tomorrow then outside Liberty's Regent Street door, Eugene.'

Elizabeth tidied away the glasses and crockery, rearranged the chairs and their cushions and halted at the door to survey the room. Yes, she felt satisfied with what she had achieved. The work had enabled her to use her creative abilities and she was pleased. Perhaps she could make a go of it professionally, perhaps even stay here in London. Do her own thing, be her own boss, no longer at the beck and call of a remote bureaucracy in Moscow. It was something to think about. But no bugs for clients, she would have none of that!

Later that evening she sat in her sitting room, relaxed as she listened to the music. She had made herself take an hour or so a day to listen, really listen, to music. She had decided to avoid background music when she was by herself. It washed over you and you didn't listen properly. Decent music wasn't written for that and she had decided to sharpen her appreciation rather than blunt it. Tonight as so often recently it was Chopin - she had just got hold of

Rubinstein's recording of the Nocturnes. To her it was poetry reaching deep into her psyche with a calming and cleansing touch. There was so much that satisfied her. But there was also a sense of incompleteness, a wish to share what she had made and the things that pleased her, with another - not an overwhelming feeling but it was definitely there, a slight, wistful sense of longing. At that moment it matched the feel of the music and she sighed and wondered what lay ahead for her. She would keep her thoughts to herself, it was safer that way.

Elizabeth reflected on her visit to Peter Lewis that afternoon. Not much of an outfit but it hadn't been as bad as she had feared. The premises, though somewhat antiquated and in need of a lick of paint, had been comfortable and she had been made to feel welcome. Things weren't in a muddle and she could see how she could take over the secretarial work without too much of an upheaval. The IT system was in need of improvement but she knew what was needed there and Lewis had agreed that changes could be made and that there was money to pay for it. Lucy, the temporary secretary, seemed to have done a useful job in organising both the work and Lewis in the few weeks she had been there.

The shadow of Vera Nash and her death hung over the place - she had felt guilty for the violence inflicted on the woman by her Russian colleagues. The staff had been friendly and welcoming. As for Lewis himself, she thought she would get on well with him. He had enquired about her experience, got her to have a chat with Lucy and, after hearing Lucy's report, offered her the job before remembering to discuss pay. On that she had managed to push up the figure originally offered by around 25%. She had reasoned that she would be able to save Lewis several times that amount by her IT skills and that he would feel that he had achieved something by haggling over the amount. They had agreed that she would come for a trial period of three months and that she would start the following Monday.

How different from her last assignment in Silicon Valley, California! There she had been conscious that the boss had been more interested in her extra-mural potential, in her secretarial skills in the widest sense. She had been subjected there to a very rigorous medical with blood tests, supposedly for the pension scheme, but she thought more likely to ensure that she would be a safe plaything for her boss when they were away together on company business. It had been a pleasure to relieve them of their hi-tech secrets and it had been ridiculously easy. Her contempt for them and their plastic, selfish world had been considerable, it had been hard not to leave a message in the system telling them just what she had achieved but that was not on and she had had to take pleasure from their ignorance of the robbery and from feeding a few bugs into the system.

She had resolved that sex would no longer be one of her official duties in any future assignment. She felt safe about Lewis, that would be no problem in the new job. The problem would come with the next assignment - she knew that she had been recruited in 1986 by the old KGB as much for her looks as for her fluent American English and her IT skills. Still life hadn't been dull and, if the work for Peter Lewis looked as if it would be somewhat pedestrian, there were plenty of things to interest her here in London and who knew what the future would hold? She had been recruited by the communists and now she was employed by a supposedly very different government, although she often wondered just for whom or for what she was really working. Who in Russia used the secrets and know-how that she had ferreted out of Western businesses? It could be the Mafiya for all she knew. Who wanted the secrets from Basel and for what purpose? She knew that she was unlikely to find out. Enjoy life in London and see whether there was some way to stay perhaps? She thought of Eugene and his obsession with his pension: she would have to make her own arrangements for her future, she trusted herself far more than she trusted those back home in an increasingly violent and disrupted Russia. Her thoughts were her own and Moscow couldn't bug them like they might be doing with her conversations in the apartment.

***

Nearby others were also listening in to Chopin, though the sound quality through their earphones was not up to that being enjoyed by Elizabeth. 'She's by herself and relaxing again. By the time we're finished she'll have given me quite a musical education!' His companion looked up and grunted, 'Your music mistress, eh, Sam? Well keep it professional and keep the stress on *music* rather than the other word.'

So Eugene and Elizabeth would both be out shopping the next day. It would allow Sam and his colleagues to visit the apartment, attend to the defective bug and so improve the audio quality.

Chapter 5

Thursday 21st March 1996

He waited in an old Ford Sierra across the street from Elizabeth's apartment. After almost an hour he was wondering whether she would be leaving that morning or not. He gave the impression of reading a newspaper but in reality his attention was held by the front door of the red brick apartment block. Several people had left while he had been waiting but Elizabeth had not been among them. His mobile 'phone rang, the message was terse, 'Sam? It looks like we can do business today, she'll be with you in about five minutes.' So she was about to leave at last!

He locked the car and strolled a little way along the street in the opposite direction from the Underground Station that he was assuming she would use. About one hundred yards from her door he paused and started to read the paper, just as well that it was a fine Spring day, unseasonably warm for the time of year.

Two minutes later he saw her leave the apartment block and walk towards him. She was going in the opposite direction to the one he had expected. She must be going to Finchley Road Station and not West Hampstead as he had assumed. He would have to let her get a good way ahead before he started to follow. She passed him but he did not look up, the last thing he wanted was eye contact with her. He caught the fragrance of her perfume, it was familiar. He gave her half a minute, looked at his watch, folded the paper and set off to follow her. With all the present attention to stalkers and talk of tightening the law he had to keep even more inconspicuous than ever. At the station he would make sure that she was taking a train and that she would be out of the way for long enough for him to attend to the apartment.

She was in no hurry and this made it more difficult for him to stay far enough behind her but he was well versed in the art and kept out of sight. They made their way along the street past old red brick houses, long ago turned into flats, and apartment blocks. Several houses were undergoing interior renovation, evidently to get them ready for the next hundred years of accommodating a cross section of London's cosmopolitan population. They were marked by skips in the roadway and the sound of power saws and drills from their open windows.

As she neared Finchley Road station he speeded up to close the distance between them. He turned into the station entrance and was surprised not to see her. She must be in one of the shops. Sure enough she was in the shoe repairers. That must have been the reason for her choice of station. He studied a railway timetable on the wall and waited. A couple of minutes later she emerged from the shoe repairers, bought a ticket and headed through the ticket barrier. Taking his season ticket from his pocket he followed her down the stairs to the platform which served a couple of lines: he could let her get on a train and leave the station again without attracting any attention. On the stairway he again caught the aroma of her perfume, Chanel No. 5 he recognised it at once this time - years ago a girl friend had used it, no, he couldn't mistake it. He reached the platform, walked towards her stopping about twenty yards short. Looking for the train would let him have a good view of her.

So this was Elizabeth! He had seen her from the distance, now he could study her. He had heard her voice and her activity in the apartment thanks to the bugs they had placed there when she first took the place. He knew something of her views, at any rate so far as she was prepared to make them known to Eugene, and he was being given a musical education by her. Well, she knew how to dress and to carry herself, that was clear. He took in the well tailored coat in an almost midnight blue, her dark tights and smart black patent leather shoes with a medium heel. A small black patent leather handbag completed the ensemble. It was her hair that caught his attention, dark brunette, and with something about its sheen and the way it swung as she moved her head that spoke of health and a very good salon. He remembered the description he had been given a month before, 'She'll interest you, quite civilised for someone in our line of business. About 30, medium height, slim, brunette, busty and full of life.' It seemed that he was looking at the correct woman. What, he wondered, was it that turned a good looking woman into a beauty - a touch of arrogance, perhaps? He found it difficult to categorise her - no, it wasn't arrogance but it was clear that she felt good about herself and about life, confidence was nearer the mark.

The train clattered in, Baker Street next stop. He saw her board it, the doors closed and it pulled out. He looked at his watch, folded his paper and left the station. Just beyond the flower stall at the exit he stopped and put through a call on his mobile 'phone, 'All clear. In you go!' He strolled back the way he had just come, thinking about her. A very attractive woman for sure. He hoped that he wouldn't be called on to do her any harm, but then she was probably well capable of giving a good account of herself in any difficult situation. 'Sam my lad,' he thought to himself, 'don't be fooled by the 'halo effect' - don't let it cloud your judgement, it could cost you your life. You have a score to settle with these people, don't forget that.' Nevertheless he didn't find it very easy to push her out of his mind.

Sam was back at the apartment block within seven or eight minutes. A white van from the 'Swift Lock Service' was parked outside and he went back to the old nondescript Ford Sierra and waited. About five minutes later the telephone rang. The message was short, 'Ready when you are.' He put on his gloves, crossed the street, climbed the steps and pressed the entryphone button for apartment No. 7, the mechanism rasped at him as the lock opened. He took the stairway, having no wish to end up stuck in the lift - unlikely to happen but best avoided and in any case people stood a better chance of remembering you from seeing you in a lift than from passing you on the stairs. Some of the doors had Eastern European name plates, evidently survivors of Hitler's Final Solution. He took in the tidy stairs and landings with potted geraniums and other plants taking advantage of the light and warmth. The place had a clean, cared for feel about it. The door of the apartment opened in response to his light knock and he entered, closing it quietly. Nothing was said as the other two resumed their work on the re-installation of the bugging devices. He smiled to himself at the thought that they were using Russian devices bought cheaply in Moscow from one of a number of companies set up by ex-employees of the KGB - if they found them it would be their own equipment and that might puzzle them into wondering whether they were being spied on by their own lot! His colleagues worked quickly and methodically, careful to leave no tell tale tools or debris behind.

Sam took a look around the apartment. It was not his first visit, he had been there soon after Elizabeth and her colleague first viewed the place. 'Strange,' thought Sam,

'I'm not keen to dignify Eugene with a name and an identity, perhaps it's a niggling sense of jealousy that he has ready access to the apartment. Still he's not her lover though it looks as though he once was.' He found himself agreeing with Eugene's enthusiasm for Elizabeth's skills as a decorator and interior designer. The sitting room was what most impressed him, the matching of duck egg blue upholstery with drapes of the lightest primrose with a neutral oatmeal fitted carpet - that was the only thing he would have changed, he liked Eastern carpets but he admitted to himself that it would have been difficult to make one fit in with the rest of the furnishings. The furniture was well suited to the room, a low sideboard and several occasional tables, all in a medium mahogany, and the duck egg blue sofa and two arm chairs, not too bulky but with a comfortable appearance. It was all reproduction furniture but they were good quality reproductions.

He inspected her bedroom, it was tasteful and not too feminine. He noticed the lingering aroma of her perfume, and immediately he could see her in his mind's eye standing on the platform waiting for the train. He was well trained to use his eyes and memory but it startled him just how vivid his recollection was. 'Well, of course', he rationalised to himself, 'When a number of senses are involved you do remember more clearly.' But he knew that his interest in her was personal as much as professional and he knew that he would have to keep it fully professional. He noticed the photograph of a young man in casual clothing on the dressing table. His careful inspection of the dressing table satisfied him that it had only recently been dusted so he lifted the photograph and looked at the back of the frame but there was nothing to indicate who he was, not that Sam had anticipated finding anything there. He returned the picture carefully to its place. He took a quick look at her wardrobe, making sure that he left the door slightly open, just as he had found it. Not over full, he noted, but the choice of clothes and their fabrics evidenced good taste. A careful look at the labels showed them to have come from Britain and the USA: that was as he would have expected.

He stood there, uncharacteristically irresolute, then he returned somewhat reluctantly to the sitting room to see how work was progressing. One of his colleagues held up a hand with fingers outstretched to indicate five more minutes. Sam stood near the window looking through the vertical blind at the trees in the street, he was grateful for the privacy that the blind afforded them. Strange to think how he and Elizabeth were likely to be on paths that would pass near to one another and possibly never meet. He dismissed her from his thoughts and turned his mind to ensuring that the apartment showed no signs of their visit as the others had completed their task and were ready to leave. They were fortunate, the recent redecoration of the apartment meant that there was no tell tale disturbance of dusty or greasy areas. He made a thorough tour of the areas in which they had been working and satisfied himself that there was no debris. Screwdrivers and other tools were checked, all were back in their places in their canvas bags. He nodded towards the outer door. They paused there, listened for the presence of other residents, heard nothing and left quickly.

Sam remained a couple minutes longer, allowing himself a further look at the bedroom and the photograph on the dressing table - who, he wondered, was the young man? - then he noticed the small flowering cactus on the window sill, a profusion of cream flowers somehow emerging from the spiky and unwelcoming plant. He took a Swiss Army knife from his pocket and very carefully removed one of the blooms, telling himself that she wouldn't notice one less, placing it in a small diary that he took from his pocket. The plant showed no sign of its loss. 'Out you go before anyone comes back!' he told himself. Again a pause at the outer door of the apartment to listen and then down the stairs and through the door onto the street.

He strolled to the Finchley Road and bought a motoring magazine before finding a small cafe which seemed to be run by an Italian family. He was amused at the dado rail dividing the walls into cream coloured upper and tomato coloured lower sections and wondered what décor Elizabeth would have chosen. A practical choice of colour scheme, if he went wild with the ketchup no one would notice as long as he kept the trajectory low! He ordered a coffee and a cheese roll and sat down at a formica topped table.

No signs of anyone following him. He relaxed, not that he had been very tense - it often surprised him just how calm he remained in such situations, when you were pretty sure that the risk of detection was slight there was little to make the adrenaline flow too freely. But of course things could go wrong, people could return home unexpectedly or there might be other people that you didn't know about with keys. He thought about the apartment but found that its occupier was more in his mind. Why, he wondered, had he lingered in the apartment and removed the cactus flower? He took the diary from his pocket and opened it. There the flower lay on that week's page, its petals creamy and lustrous, and there was nothing to indicate the unfriendly, prickly plant from which he had removed it. His imagination was stirred by the idea that she might be like the flower, a pleasant and harmless product of an unfriendly and dangerous organisation. Once again his rational and professional self asserted itself, she was an active agent of the SVR and that concluded the matter. She and her colleagues were the enemy and that was sufficient. He was in London to outsmart them. He knew precisely what the task required and he felt again burning deep down his own personal desire for vengeance. He had carried it around within himself for a long time and now he would have the pleasure of seeing that desire satisfied. And yet ... his rational self often wondered whether there would be real pleasure in vengeance, would his hunger to pay them back be satisfied by what was planned or would it become an insatiable craving, a gnawing cancer, bringing destruction to his own life? Perhaps a desire for justice would be safer and easier to manage. He dismissed these thoughts, closed the diary, replaced it in his pocket and returned his gaze to the magazine. Finishing his coffee he attracted the proprietor's attention and asked for another.

A black construction worker, in blue overalls and carrying a hard hat, joined him at the table. Sam had noticed a building site a little way along the road. He nodded to his companion who lent forward and asked in a conspiratorial voice what Sam thought of the government.

'Not much but then I've no voice in the matter as I'm not a Brit. My problem's whether to vote for Clinton or not. I really don't know what I'll do. How about you?'

'I don't think much of the government here either and like you my ties are elsewhere. My Dad's gone back to South Africa - to Soweto, one of the townships near Johannesburg. Do you know how the place got it's name? Well it's short for south-western townships, artificial name, artificial life or it was in the past. Now there's hope, we've got Mandela but whether we'll ever get prosperity, even enough to make a real difference, I don't know.'

'We've got artificial names for parts of New York: SoHo - South of Houston - and TriBeCa - the triangle below Canal. But I don't think they're anything like your townships. Hope's a wonderful commodity, if it's the real thing and not the moonshine the politicians peddle. Your Mandela does seem to be the genuine article for once. I won't forget the news film of his release - the sight of him walking free after all those years, the sense of injustice bowing to moral stature.' Sam was surprised at his eloquence but he had spoken as he felt, from a heart and mind that had been schooled by his father and which loathed injustice.

'Yes, chum, hope's what we need. I'll probably follow my Dad back to Soweto, that's if the violence doesn't get any worse. White or black, bullies and thieves are equally unwelcome but we've now got the law on our side instead of having it against us.'

Their conversation turned to sport and basket ball in particular. Sam finished his coffee and said his farewells. Outside the cafe the traffic was heavy in both directions, the Capital's road arteries were clogged as usual. There was much more space on Eastern Parkway, Brooklyn. He looked at the faces of the drivers in their stationary vehicles, men in nine to five jobs that had become seven to seven jobs. How much hope did they feel as they looked at life through the windscreen of a car and daily diced with death on the crowded British motorways. Like so many clones of the sales rep in Arthur Miller's *Death of a Salesman*. Sam felt grateful for his job, there was a welcome freedom in being an emissary of hope and working to make sure the other side didn't extinguish that hope for millions in the world. And his mind went back to a young woman standing on the station platform an hour and a half before and seeming to typify freedom and hope. It really was a shame that she was working for the other side!

***

Eugene waited outside Liberty's store for Elizabeth. He had never liked waiting though he had spent much of his working life doing just that: waiting, looking and observing. He was skilled at blending into the background, in not standing out, in being a grey man among grey men or a pied piper among pied pipers. He looked northwards towards Oxford Circus and saw Elizabeth coming towards him, relaxed, elegant and self assured. He was aware just how badly he wanted her, a desire that she now refused to satisfy. Anger welled up in the midst of his desire. To do no more than look or at most hold her hand was for him pleasure mixed with torment. Still, better that than nothing, perhaps she would change her mind again. He greeted her with a smile, 'Your elegant self today, it appears!'

'Flatterer! Well, yes. I've found that you get better attention in shops if you look the part. They like the prospect of a substantial sale and a pretty woman brightens up the day for them - how would you like being on your feet all day and dealing with a mixed bag of customers, many of them difficult and ungrateful? Besides, you know that I like to look good, it's a morale booster.'

He caught a whiff of her perfume. It hit him in the pit of his stomach. 'Well lets get going. What are we going to look at first?'

***

Lewis looked at the month's sales figures that Lucy had just taken from the PC's printer. 'They're good Lucy , don't you think so? Just shows what we can do!'

Lucy nodded, 'Well everyone's put their backs into it and we've got the orders out pretty quickly. You've put in more time than anybody.'

'Thanks to your looking after me in a whole variety of ways.'

She smiled, 'I've enjoyed it Peter, though I wondered what I was letting myself in for when I first came here to help out. I'm glad that I've been able to get to know you - to make a friendship that isn't sexual but where we can just enjoy one another's company.'

'That I have appreciated. Since Ruth and I split up I've needed a touch of feminine charm now and then and you've provided it ... '

'And will be allowed to continue to do so, I hope. I enjoy your company and being appreciated as a person rather than as a source of pleasure. Oh, I know that I still flirt with you a bit, but that's because I feel safe with you.' She touched his hand lightly as she spoke and he smiled in response, he too felt secure in her company, free to be himself.

'Certainly we'll see one another after you've left here and found another post. How about a monthly date for dinner? Get your diary and we'll fix it now.'

'Only another five days and you will be under new management! Your new Canadian secretary arrives next Monday. I liked her, I think. She gives the impression that she knows a good deal about computers and I think that she'll be able to simplify the way you do your paperwork without too much hassle. '

Lewis pulled a face, 'I don't like too much change, you know. I hope that she fits in here as well as you have.'

'I'm sure she will, probably better. Your staff think that I have designs on you and they don't like that. Elizabeth doesn't seem that sort and they'll be relieved!'

'I'm glad that you came to my aid when Mrs Nash was killed. By the way, when am I due to see her husband and their young lad?'

Lucy consulted the diary, 'Two weeks today - four in the afternoon, after the boy has got back from school.'

'Thanks, It's something I have to do but I don't relish the task - their sadness hurts, you know.'

She nodded, 'Would you like me to come with you when you go there?'

'No Lucy, you had better not come or they will be saying that there is something going on between us and, in any case you are going to be busy elsewhere. The offer is much appreciated, you know that.' And he returned the gentle touch on the hand that she had given him earlier.

Chapter 6

Wednesday 10th April 1996

On a cold Moscow afternoon in the offices of the SVR, the External Intelligence Service, successor to the KGB, a small group of men worked their way through a long agenda. What had begun as a lively session that morning, with contributions by most of the members seeking to safeguard the interests of themselves and their Sections, had quietened down as they realised that the meeting would end at an inconveniently late hour unless they kept business on the move.

'... and now Evgeny perhaps you would update us on your London and Basel operation?'

Evgeny took a sip of water, looked around the table and began, 'This, I am afraid, is not going to be the quickest of enterprises but you will remember that what we are after is well worth the effort ...'

'I would be grateful if you could remind us of the reasoning behind that statement.' The speaker was the representative of the Accounts Section - he had been by far the most frequent contributor to the meeting's deliberations.

'Of course, Konstantin, anything to assist your memory,' that pleased the others and had them on Evgeny's side, he could see it on their faces, and he felt that they would continue to give their support - two birds with one stone then, a gentle dig at Konstantin and getting the backing of the others. 'The laboratory in Basel is a small private research organisation which is, we are reliably informed, working on a drug that could be very useful for personality modification. They are near to the completion of the trials but the laboratory is having doubts about selling the drug for commercial use - it's an odd organisation, led by a chemist who is interested in research for its own sake more than in money.' He caught Konstantin's eye and raised an eyebrow before continuing, 'Clearly there would be the certain prospect of a very good return on our expenditure if we could get hold of the drug and also details of its manufacture and trials. It could be very useful in sorting out disturbed personalities, a benefit for both the patients themselves and also for our society. At the same time we could find a world market for our manufacturers. A while back the Serbsky Clinic got wind of rumours of this research - at the time they were the vaguest of rumours - and they got quite excited about it, they saw it as a treatment for dissidents to bring them back into line, a sort of conditioning process that left no physical or mental scars. Of course that isn't how we would use it today.'

Around the table his colleagues nodded assent to Evgeny's implied dismissal of the Serbsky and all the works of the *ancien régime*. Evgeny paused and wondered which of them, like him, really hankered for the old days of a Communist state that kept dissent firmly in its place.

'I can see that there is general agreement that this is a project that is worth time and trouble and so I will not go to lengthy explanations. Suffice to say that we have two of our people in London. One has been placed as the secretary and personal assistant to the director of a company which supplies scientific equipment to the laboratory in Basel. She's started there recently. Then there is our man in Basel working for the laboratory, but security there is tight and *he* has been unable to get at what we need. He has been unable to get near the research that interests us, though he has been able to pick up some information on what is going on. It looks as though the laboratory's trials on the drug will be completed some time in the Autumn, we had hoped it would be earlier but you cannot hurry these things, especially when you have no direct control over them. Security checks on personnel and deliveries are tight but - and this is the reason for the London end of the operation - it is known that Lewis, the director of the company there, is a friend of one of the heads of the laboratory and that when he makes deliveries of equipment to them they do not subject him or his vehicles to scrutiny checks. We intend to use him and his van, as well as exercising a little persuasion on the laboratory head, to get out all we need. But it could take some months and our people in London have some other tasks to keep them fully productive and occupied.'

'Such as setting up in the interior decor business!' Konstantin couldn't resist the jibe.

'They have done the decorating of their own apartments which has saved us cash and they are seeing what can be made of doing the same sort of thing commercially. It would, of course, enable them to build up relations with people who might be useful to us later on and when you are working on a house or apartment the installation of listening devices is simplicity itself. What they could give us might well enable us to twist the odd British Ministerial arm in due course - they have contacts among up and coming Labour Party members as well as the Conservatives, just in case they come to power again at a future election.'

'All agreed that we keep it running?' The Chairman sought to complete their consideration of the matter and push the meeting towards its conclusion. There was no dissent and they moved on to the next item. Evgeny took another sip of water and felt relieved his job was secure - for a few more months at any rate.

***

Sam sat in a comfortable arm chair and took in the opulent decor of the Mayfair apartment. Alan Winters had been called away by his wife to deal with an urgent fax that had just come in and this gave Sam the chance to have a good look at the sitting room. Opulent was really an inadequate word, everything was of the very best, antique furniture - largely Georgian, Alan had told him - dark oil paintings, rich upholstery of a deep plumb colour and matching curtains, oriental carpets and a wealth of vases and other archaeological items in a couple of free standing cases next to the rear wall. He was struck by the lighting - the cases with the vases were gently illuminated and the room itself was lit by large dark shaded table lamps and standard lamps which cast pools of light downwards giving the effect of islands of light in an otherwise darkened room. A lot of thought, care and money had gone into the furnishing of the room and the effect, though not particularly to Sam's taste apart from the oriental carpets, spoke of discernment and culture. Here all was genuine - the presence of reproductions would not have been tolerated. A biography of Bertrand Russell lay open on one of the occasional tables. Sam picked it up and noticed the fine pencilled markings and notes that had been made on most of the pages. Alan clearly enjoyed honing his mind on heavyweight works.

Alan's voice came from behind him, 'I never leave a book unmarked, I fear! I'm unable to read without a 2B pencil to hand!'

'Why should that be a problem?'

'No reason really, so long as they are working books and not collector's items. I've long since given up lending books to people. Not of course due to any lack of generosity on my part but, you know what it is, just when you want to refer to a book you find that it's with a friend or acquaintance and when a book has been away for six months or so you wonder whether the borrower had any genuine interest in it in the first place.'

'It's not the sort of problem that I encounter - when you're on the move most of the time you don't carry a library around with you. Mind you, I get through a lot of varied reading. When you have to watch and wait you need to occupy your time sensibly. I'd like to write but my routine, or rather lack of one, wouldn't help'

'I suppose not. It wouldn't be my sort of life, but then we're all different, though I think we all need roots and to be able to return to them, now and then at any rate.'

Sam nodded, 'I would dread being a wanderer without a base, a perpetual refugee. I need to get back home now and again, to feel that I belong.'

'You'd like a glass of wine I expect. There's a pleasant *Vendange Tardive Gewürtztraminer* from Alsace or a 1988 *Chateau d'Yquem* that have been in the fridge for the last hour waiting for your arrival. Which would you like?'

'The *Gewürtztraminer* will do fine, I suspect the other would be wasted on me! You're always hospitality itself, Alan.'

'I try to run a civilised show. Though the Institute's activities are in one way a sort of sideline I don't treat its people any differently from my wealthier collector customers. Indeed, to tell the truth you are usually more welcome - I don't need any more money from the business, as you can see I'm generally pretty comfortable. But even if, in one sense, my roots are here in another they are where yours are and that makes me secure here. You understand that, I think. ... Ah Judi, thank you for coming to the aid of two thirsty men ... You've met Sam before, come and make his acquaintance again.'

Sam took the hand of Alan's wife and was surprised at the firmness of the grip.

'I'm pleased to see you again Sam. Are you in London for long?'

'And I'm pleased to see you, Mrs Winters. I expect to be here for a few months, so we may see one another from time to time.'

'We may indeed. I hope you won't mind Sam if Alan and I talk antiques for a couple of minutes.'

'Not in the least Mrs Winters.'

'Judi, please'

'Well OK Judi. Is that better?'

She smiled and turned to her husband. They discussed the recent fax and she made a short note of their discussion before taking leave of the two men.

Sam watched them, a pretty dissimilar pair they seemed Alan Winters was heavily built and just under six foot, probably in his mid-sixties. His neatly cut hair, though beginning to recede, was still dark without any trace of grey - that of course might come from a bottle and Sam, detecting a touch of vanity in Alan, thought it probably did. Otherwise his appearance was casual, dark green cords and a beige cardigan that wasn't in its prime, clothes which despite their age still reflected their expensive origins and in which Alan evidently felt comfortable.

Judi's hair was also well looked after, Sam felt glad not to be faced with her hairdresser's bills. She was a little over five foot with a figure that caught and held your gaze, which could be something of an embarrassment Sam concluded. It was in her dress sense that she differed most from her husband. She was wearing a navy suit with white piping to the jacket's lapels and pockets. The skirt came to the knee showing off a pair of extremely attractive legs. Sam had noticed an Yves Saint Lauren carrier bag near the apartment door and even without it he would have known that she shopped well and expensively. She seemed to be in her mid-thirties, a good deal younger than her husband, and she exuded a sense of order and calm. She seemed to be very much part of Alan's collection of expensive and beautiful possessions, that was until you sensed their rapport and, watching their eyes, became aware that they were very much in love with one another. Sam found himself thinking about Elizabeth: they were both striking women but nevertheless very different. He felt a pang of envy for the contentment of Alan and Judi and wondered whether he would ever enjoy anything comparable.

Alan poured the straw coloured wine into two glasses and handed one to Sam. He raised his glass, 'To the success of Operation Basel Formula! Now let's hear how things are going out there on the North-West Frontier in Kilburn.'

Sam took a seat and noticed that the room's lighting was arranged so that Alan could remain in the shadows while most of the other chairs and sofas were more brightly illuminated - clearly he liked to study his visitors while he stayed out of the limelight. It tallied with Alan's role with the Institute; he had the reputation for plenty of excellent work but always in the background. An experienced controller with a sharp insight into people's strengths and weaknesses, he was reputed to have an almost instinctive grasp of the way that people would respond to events. He was said to be able to enter others' minds and share their thinking. The operation was his brainchild. Sam wondered how successful it would be and whether Alan's reputation among his colleagues would be shown to be justified.

'Nothing dramatic to report, Alan, apart from the killing of Lewis' secretary in a hit and run incident that the SVR arranged. Lewis' wife – though they're separated they seem to remain on good terms – found him a temp. It might have been a problem if she'd decided to stay at the business as a permanent fixture, though I suspect they might have then found a way of disposing of her as well. As it is she didn't stay and the SVR have taken the bait and their woman, Elizabeth has been there for a couple of weeks. Her boss, Eugene Preston – that's the name he's going under though his real name is Vladimir – appeared on the scene as a new customer and spun Lewis a yarn about his cousin looking for secretarial work. Not wishing to offend this bringer of new business Lewis agreed to see Elizabeth and, though I won't say she wouldn't have got the job apart from her looks, I'm sure they didn't hinder Lewis' decision. By the way, our two SVR folk are former lovers who have since fallen out, so how that will play out remains to be seen.'

'She's a good looking woman, then?'

'Striking, I'd say, and a cultured one. Into music in a big way, classical music that is. As you know we've bugged her place with Russian bugs. As well as their conversations we've recorded hours of music! We've been back there to replace one of the bugs that was on the blink and it was amazing what a difference she's made to the apartment since we were last there. Then it was austere and forbidding, now it's transformed – light and airy, pastel shades and very comfortable. It seems she did the work herself.'

'Different from this apartment then, Sam?'

'Quite so, we all have different tastes don't we? As you said earlier we're all different. So there it is, this Elizabeth is just about to begin her new career in Kilburn. There's been some talk between her and Eugene about setting up in the interior design business so that they can bug politicians and the like but I don't think the woman's keen and after all she's going to have a full time job at Lewis' place.'

'Thanks, Sam, keep me posted on developments. I have in mind playing this out quite a bit to keep them tied down, we'll have to see. Now there are one or two things I'd like you to attend to for me in Paris. Your number two can take care of things while you're away, it'll give him something to do ... '

Chapter 7

Wednesday 10th April 1996 (continued)

His eye caught hers, blue grey he noted, and he looked away, turning his gaze to the Language School advertisement near the door. Sam was sitting in a crowded Underground train on his way back from Alan's apartment in Grosvenor Square to his own place in West Hampstead. The young woman opposite was quite striking, a dark blonde with good clear skin and high cheekbones. She wore a smart black cocktail dress and had a single string of pearls round her neck. He was struck by the woman's resemblance to Elizabeth and remembered that he had thought the same of a different young woman only the day before. 'Watch out,' he told himself, 'you're moonstruck over that woman. She's the opposition and to be treated as such. You'd better find someone to keep you amused and out of harm.' He analysed his thoughts and noted that he had categorised Elizabeth as 'the opposition' rather than as 'the enemy' - he really would have to take a more professional view of things!

At an off-licence near West Hampstead station he bought some cans of Budweiser before the five minute walk home through the light rain that had been falling since mid-afternoon. Before opening the apartment door he removed his raincoat and shook off the rain then he turned the key and entered - 'Never leave your front door open longer than necessary' was one of his maxims, you didn't know who might be lurking in the vicinity. It was unlikely that anyone would be interested in his activities but you couldn't be sure and simple burglary was a complication that he could do without. He put the beer into the refrigerator and hung his wet coat on the corner of the kitchen door. Sam expected his colleague to be out and a quick inspection of the small apartment confirmed this as well as satisfying him that all was in order. The sound of heavy rain on the window removed any temptation to go out to eat in the Finchley Road or West End Green and he set to in the kitchen to cook a meal. In a few minutes he had prepared a cheese omelette and a side salad and set the table. Taking a can of beer from the refrigerator he looked at the table and, satisfied with the appearance of the meal, felt a sense of regret that he was eating alone. Normally it did not bother him greatly whether he had company or not, he was adaptable, but this operation was moving slowly, boredom had set in and he felt in need of the stimulus of another's company. He had just seen Alan and Judi together and there were his recurring thoughts of Elizabeth. He placed a copy of *The Times* beside his plate and poured the beer into a glass - he had no time for the American habit of drinking from the can, he regarded the practice indoors as uncivilised. He worked his way through the paper, making the meal last for a half hour or so. He never liked rushing a meal, he had the memory from his early childhood of his father telling him that if he had ever had to face starvation he would relish every mouthful of food that came his way. Strange the hold that parents still had on you - even from the grave. He finished the glass of beer as he studied the paper's obituaries, a philosopher, a general and an AIDS stricken actor, 'More words from the grave or its threshold,' he thought. The next few minutes were spent clearing the crockery into the dishwasher, washing the frying pan and tidying the kitchen - he had an aversion to the place being a mess, an aversion that his colleague did not share.

Well, he had a wet evening ahead but with a pile of books waiting to be read that was no hardship. Sam went into the spare bedroom where the receiver for the bugging equipment was kept. He put on the earphones and listened in to what was going on in her apartment a couple of hundred yards away. Precious little it seemed, all he could hear was the sound of music on her hi-fi system and the occasional movement in the sitting room. Without his colleague to tell him what he was hearing he remained for the most part in ignorance as to the composer concerned. Nevertheless he remained listening and in his mind's eye pictured Elizabeth sitting in the room. He ran through the details of the room, its furniture and décor as a memory test. He found himself trying to imagine her there, wondering what she might be wearing - the young woman in the Underground train came to mind, Elizabeth would look good in a simple black cocktail dress he decided. He wondered about the colour of her eyes - perhaps his people had that on file, he would have a look in the next few days.

***

Sam's thoughts were interrupted by the sound of Elizabeth's telephone ringing. She was evidently in no hurry to take the call and let it ring for a full half minute before lifting the receiver. When she did reply all she said was, 'Yes.' That was something that annoyed Sam when he called people, you couldn't be sure if you had the correct number or who was speaking.

'It's me. I'm back home. I'm sorry about what happened earlier, I promise it won't happen again.' Eugene's voice had a plaintive ring about it.

Elizabeth took her time before replying, 'Well you asked for it, didn't you?' She paused, a note of concern creeping into her voice, 'You are all right Eugene, aren't you?'

'Just about. I had to crawl into my apartment and lie on the floor for twenty minutes after the driver helped me in ... he wanted to take me to the hospital, you know. My shoulder and other parts ache but generally I'm in working order. I'm OK now and about to hit the hay ... I just wanted to say sorry before I did so.'

'Thanks for the apology. I hope that there's no permanent damage to your more tender parts. But do remember that if you attempt to rape me again I will defend myself as vigorously as I did tonight. I know that we had a good time together in California, I'll treasure the memories - you know that - but it's in the past. I don't want a relationship that is going nowhere. If I have another relationship I want it to last and to be official. You can't offer that with your wife and kids. That's the end of the matter. Our relationship from now on is purely that of colleagues and ... I hope ... friends.'

Sam noticed the steel that had come into her voice, 'She's a tough cookie,' he muttered to himself. He felt pleased that his earlier assessment of the woman had been on target.

'Good night then.'

'Goodnight, Eugene. And take care in future.'

She put the receiver down and Sam just caught her postscript to the conversation, 'Georgian bastard!'

There was the sound of movement and a door being opened. The sound was now being picked up by the bug in the kitchen. There was the pop of a wine bottle cork being removed and the sound of a glass being filled.

'When under pressure takes to the bottle?' was Sam's

reaction. He found himself hoping that his conclusion was incorrect.

Suddenly she said in a quiet but distinct voice, 'Surely men aren't all like that, perhaps it's just my bad luck to have to experience that sort so often.'

Sam wondered exactly what had gone on earlier in the evening, presumably at least an hour before. He switched on another recorder and began a search on the first to a point about two hours before. After playing it to and fro at high speed he located the encounter between Eugene and Elizabeth, got himself a glass of beer and settled down to listen.

Elizabeth and Eugene seemed to be having a meal together and they were discussing her job in Kilburn.

'Although it really is a bit of a dump it's not as bad as I thought it was going to be. The temporary girl had begun to get things in order and knew what she was doing. He needs a new computer system and seems ready to let me organise getting it set up - even though it's on a small scale it'll be something to keep me interested.'

'It would have been good if you'd had the chance to do that in some of our other assignments - we could have saved a lot of the time and effort spent on extracting information from their systems.'

'Yes, I would have been able to get away from some of those oversexed Americans sooner than I did.'

'That would have suited me as well, I didn't like having them near you ...'

Elizabeth cut him short, 'Enough of that! I've told you before and I'm telling you again, that is in the past. Why do you keep coming back to it?'

'I'm fond of you, you know that, don't you?'

'Fond you may be but you have a wife and kids and you aren't willing to dump them and if you did it wouldn't make any difference - I don't want to have them on my conscience.'

Sam noticed the note of anger in her voice.

She continued to get more angry, 'And why was it necessary to kill my new boss' secretary to get me a job there. There were a number of ways that you could have got her out of the way and you chose to kill her. Did you know that she - her name was Vera, by the way - that she had an invalid husband and a young son? No I don't suppose that you did or that you cared. You must realise that we can't go on with the old methods in work like this.'

Eugene too was becoming animated, 'They didn't plan to kill her, just to get her out of the way for a while - they were a little too effective I'm afraid!'

'Effective you call it! Do you know that I went to her house this afternoon with Peter Lewis – he needed some female help with the visit. Her husband and her kid are still raw with grief and you call it being a little too effective! When you're pensioned off from this I suppose you'll get a job as a diplomat!'

'I wasn't suggesting that it didn't matter ...'

She cut him short, 'What were you suggesting then? You should meet the husband and the kid, they depended on her in every way - she was the breadwinner and ... their emotional support.'

Sam was surprised to hear the break in her voice, he felt admiration for her attitude and the stand that she was taking. He too was convinced that life should not be treated as something cheap. He wanted to cheer her on, to tell her that she was right, that she was showing real humanity, to share in her anger and grief at needless sadness and pain, mental pain that was so intense as to be physical. He knew these emotions very well but so few of his colleagues seemed to know them or, if they did, they failed to appreciate that it mattered that their opponents - yes, that word rather than "enemies" had again formed in his mind - could feel them as much as they did.

'Well one of the pluses about the job is that Peter Lewis does care about people. He took me with him this afternoon to see what he could do to help them ... and his concern is practical, even at the expense of his own pocket. I like him, it's a shame that I seem to meet so few gentlemen in my work!'

'And I suppose that I'm not a gentleman?'

'Do I have to answer that?'

'Your failure will be answer enough!'

There was the sound of liquid being poured.

'Eugene, you've had enough to drink. The last thing you want is to be caught over the limit by the British police. You wouldn't be popular back home ... you'd find yourself back there for good and I somehow think you wouldn't appreciate that!'

'There isn't any pleasure for me in this apartment other than drink and I'm not being lectured by you. One more won't hurt.' His speech was becoming slightly slurred.

'One and no more. Right, now the bottle goes into the kitchen out of your way.'

'Damn, you're getting like my wife ... though she does let me share the bed with her!'

'So she should, if you're sober. But I'm not your wife and besides you're rather less than sober. Enough of this nonsense, it's time you were on your way, I've a number of things to see to this evening including some thinking about Lewis' computer system.'

'OK I'm on my way ... but just let me say goodnight properly.'

There was a pause then Sam heard Elizabeth's raised voice, 'Get your hands off me! Do I have to tell you again that I don't want your attentions? You don't own me ... Oh get off and leave me alone!'

'Just once more, Eliz ...'

There was the sound of them bumping into furniture and then an anguished cry from Eugene, 'What was that for? ... Why did you hit me there? ... You've hurt me.'

Silence followed and Sam wondered what she had done to Eugene and whether she too had been hurt or worse. He hoped that Elizabeth was unscathed and he knew that there was more than one reason for this hope - without her their plan to entrap the Russians could well fail and he was also aware of his personal concern for her safety. He reassured himself that, from the telephone conversation he'd just heard, she seemed to be all right and unharmed. He hoped this concern would never conflict with his duty to the Institute. The silence was broken by sounds of movement in the living room and then the sound of a tap running in the kitchen. Again there was movement in the living room followed by Eugene's angry voice.

'You've thrown a bucket of water over me!'

'Not a bucket, Eugene, just a small glass full. You deserve to be thrown into the Thames to cool down and sober up but it's too far to drag you there.'

'You've hurt me, woman, do you know that?'

'Have I? Well it seems that my basic training in self defence has come in useful. If you ever try to force me again the damage that I do to you will be permanent - that is a final warning and it's non-negotiable. Get that into your thick head and don't you dare to forget it!'

'But you've hurt me, you do realise that don't you? Don't you care?'

'You didn't care when you were trying to rape me a few minutes ago so you surely don't expect me to take your bruises too seriously. But no that's not entirely true, I want to be able to like you as a friend and we've got to be able to work together. I do have good memories of being together with you and I've no wish to harm you. You're good fun when you're sober but not when you've got a belly full of drink - take a leaf out of our one time boss Andropov's book and let the others drink themselves under the table while you stay alert on water.'

'Get me to the bathroom, please!'

'Certainly Eugene, my friend and then I'm getting you a taxi home. Neither you nor I will be driving tonight.'

There was not much more of any significance on the tape apart from the sound of Eugene being sick down the lavatory and a taxi being called about a half an hour later.

'Goodnight Elizabeth.'

'Goodnight Eugene and don't you ever forget!'

Sam heard Elizabeth cleaning the bathroom. Sam just managed to catch her saying quietly to herself, 'A bit of a mess but it's better than the aftermath of rape!' He was grateful for the quality of the Russian bugs his team had installed!

She certainly was a tough one as well as being a good looker. Clearly she was well able to look after herself, so long as any assailant was unarmed. Sam hoped fervently that this would always be the case and that he himself would never have to tangle with her. He stopped the recording and switched in to hear what was now happening. Music, quiet piano music. He recognised it as the slow movement of the Beethoven *Pathétique* Sonata. She had played it before and his colleague had identified it and ventured a guess at the identity of the pianist. He'd also pointed out that the title meant *tragic* and had come up with a quote from a music critic that it was "tragedy as the young feel it". Sam was rather pleased at his feat of recognition but considered the piece as having a calm beauty rather than being tragic. He wondered how Elizabeth regarded it. He sat grasped by the music's inner tranquillity, hoping that Elizabeth was also similarly moved. Strange to be joined in this way while she had no idea that he was listening in or indeed that he existed. 'It's a funny old world,' he thought and he wondered just what Eugene was thinking. Funny indeed, but Sam was beginning to find it frustrating and he wondered whether it wouldn't make good sense to ask to be replaced on the assignment. His personal feelings mustn't be allowed to compromise the project. He would think about it and perhaps speak to Alan once he was sure in his own mind.

Chapter 8

Wednesday 12th June 1996

The early evening sunlight flooded through the window of Peter Lewis' office. It had been unusually hot for the time of year and Lewis sat contentedly, absorbing the sun's warmth. The room was tidier than he had ever seen it. Never, even during Lucy's short tenure as his secretary, had things been so well ordered. The declining sun had reached a vase of flowers in the corner of the room or rather a scientific flask in use as a vase. The idea had been Elizabeth's, she liked flowers and had decided that one of the firm's products would be a suitable receptacle for them. Hitherto his office had had a Spartan appearance as well as being more than a little untidy, it had yielded quickly to Elizabeth's attentions. The pile of old catalogues, which had stood for years in the space now occupied by the flowers, had been thrown out. Out of date volumes in the book case had been replaced by current editions and journals had been found homes in binders. At her suggestion and with his agreement she had taken on board a number of the tasks that he had previously undertaken and she was doing them well. For once he had time to look at the business and think about its development. He appreciated the space that she had given him to plan and not just be hurried along by events. Nonetheless he still felt the loss of Vera: she had stood for continuity and stability, she had been an important part of his daytime family - which was the way in which he regarded his workforce.

The doors of their rooms were open and Lewis could hear music from Elizabeth's room - she had enquired if he minded, telling him that she worked better if she had music playing. There was usually a CD in her computer and it was mostly classical music. 'You won't hear all I like because there's some music that I can work to and some that I can't - you won't hear Beethoven for instance.' So he had begun to renew his acquaintance with music, asking her now and then what was being played. He liked most of what he heard or at any rate it didn't jar with him.

He looked at the calendar: seventeen weeks since Vera's death and eleven since Elizabeth had taken over. A lot had happened in four months! On the domestic front, however, nothing much had happened, papers relating to his divorce from Ruth lay gathering dust on a table in his apartment. He knew that he was still afflicted by a paralysis of the will and, as no one was pressing him to take action, he left the decision to gather dust like the papers. Ruth did not mention the matter when he called to see their son Michael and he had a congenital inclination to let personal matters drift, particularly if they were at all painful. The telephone rang in Elizabeth's room and a moment later she put the call through to him, 'It's my cousin Eugene. He's got a query about the order that we're despatching this week.'

An affable Eugene greeted him, 'Hi, Peter! Just wonder if you could add a few items to this week's order for Canada, that's if you have them in stock.'

'Good to hear from you! If we've got them you can have them. Fire away and then we'll check and come back to you in about ten minutes.' Lewis took down the details and rang off. He stuck his head round the door of Elizabeth's room, 'Elizabeth, could you check whether we've got these in stock, your cousin wants to increase this week's Canadian order.'

She looked at the slip of paper he had given her and keyed the information into the PC. 'OK we've more than enough to meet the order and any other order on hand for those lines.'

'You're sure of that?' He had a distrust of computers.

She looked at him and smiled, 'Oh, ye of little faith. We really are in the computer age not the Stone Age and provided we feed them properly they are more accurate than memories and scraps of paper, you know!'

Lewis shrugged his shoulders, they'd had this conversation or variants of it before. 'I know I'm a sceptic but I just like to be sure.'

'No problem. Just hold and I'll get a printout of our stock position.' They waited while the printer performed. 'Now let me convince you that the new system really does work!' She led the way down the stairs into the deserted warehouse. Here they were in Tom's realm and, old soldier that he was, the place was run with military efficiency and order. Elizabeth was interested that Tom kept her away from the area where he and the men took their tea - when she had checked it out one evening after the warehouse staff had gone home she had found, as she had expected, the younger men's pin-ups on display. She had been amused and also grateful for Tom's concern not to offend her with these ladies of substantial and in some cases unbelievable build - both Tom and Peter were gentlemen, in their different ways, it was something that did not depend on class. She and Peter tallied the stock against the records with agreement until they came to the last item.

'Six cartons short,' said Lewis brightly, glad to have found a weakness in the system.

'This way,' she responded, leading him to the goods inward section of the warehouse. 'These came in this afternoon and I recorded them about an hour ago. Sorry to disappoint you, Peter!'

'I'm happy to have you win. I just find it hard to have confidence in these machines, you know!'

'I don't say that the stock record will never be wrong but you can be satisfied that while I'm here it will be pretty good. You use airlines for travel don't you?' Lewis nodded. 'Well they use computers to get the aircraft safely to its destination and that doesn't worry you does it? Computers make useful servants, you've got to make sure that they're doing what you want, making life easier and not more complicated. After all life is complicated enough without adding to it!' He wondered what lay behind that utterance as they returned up the stair to the office, there were certain mysteries about Elizabeth. At times he wondered why she, with her evident considerable experience of computers, was willing to work in a business like his. Still, she was here and he was glad that Eugene had suggested her for the job. Not only that but he had brought a good deal of new business, with substantial orders going to Canada every week or ten days.

She called Eugene back, confirming that they could meet the order and insisting, to his annoyance, that they should have it formally in writing the next day. Lewis expressed his surprise, 'We don't really need a written order, after all he's your cousin! Surely you can trust your family?'

Elizabeth looked up at him and shook her head, 'Sometimes we get into difficulties when we trust our families. Family and business together can be a recipe for disaster. It's as well to do things properly and, after all, Eugene isn't *your* family.' Lewis was wondering what experiences of family life had caused her to think in this way when she added, 'Eugene was going to accompany me to a concert this evening - a piano recital at the

Wigmore Hall - but he's unable to make it. Perhaps you would like to come instead - that's if you are free and don't mind being asked.'

'Of course I will. I'm grateful for the invitation, Elizabeth.'

She smiled, 'Right lets clear the decks, lock up and leave Kilburn to its own devices for the evening.'

'And call a taxi, we'll travel in comfort to wherever we're going.'

'It's called the Wigmore Hall, Peter!'

'Ah yes, of course!'

'Just give me ten minutes and I'll be ready to go once I've tidied my hair and made myself respectable. There won't be time for us to go via my apartment to let me change.'

Peter wished there had been more time available, he would have liked to see her apartment. Still she was wearing a turquoise high necked blouse and a black knee-length skirt and certainly wouldn't look out of place at the concert. 'You would look fine anywhere just as you are. If you can survive until then we can eat afterwards, perhaps?'

'Why not, that would be nice.'

***

At around 10 o'clock they left the Chopin recital. Peter had enjoyed it and the very English setting of the Wigmore Hall. He'd enjoyed her company, it had been a welcome change from being at home by himself. With her he had felt relaxed and content. Relaxed and yet very alert. He noticed the way in which she had attracted the attention of other concert goers during the interval. He could imagine some of them muttering, 'Lucky dog' as they looked at him in Elizabeth's company. Yes, he was a lucky dog! It was good to have the company of a lively and attractive woman. He had been fascinated by the intensity of Elizabeth's concentration throughout the recital given by a young Armenian pianist and he remarked on this.

'Well Peter, I know the music pretty well. Chopin captures my whole attention so in a way I'm not concentrating so much as being captivated - you might say "hooked" - by his music.'

'And how did you enjoy the last work? You were enthusiastic about the others.'

'Not so good as he should have been. His tempi were too fast and he made too much of the contrast between the themes so that the final resolution didn't come off properly. Still I'm not complaining, he was good, very good, in the rest of the programme and he's only young. I'm glad we went. But what about you, have you enjoyed yourself?'

'Very much. It was good of you to take a musical ignoramus to the concert. I enjoyed the music and ... you know, I enjoyed seeing you enjoy yourself.'

'Thanks Peter! A concert *is* a social event, it's got something that even the best recording hasn't got, a sense that it's happening there and then and that composer, performer and audience are all involved together. You've enjoyed it and that adds to my pleasure too.'

'And now something to eat?'

'I wonder if you would like to have a snack at my apartment instead of eating out? After the recital I would rather eat in tranquillity and not with a crowd ... and I would also like you to hear how that last work should have been played, I've got a good recording of it by Artur Rubinstein. You must hear it!'

'A taxi it is then?'

'Please, Peter. And you won't mind if I'm quiet on the way back and don't converse. I promise you it's not rudeness - I just need to relish what we've heard and come back to earth ... after that I'll be as sociable as can be.'

The taxi took them along Wigmore Street, then northwest up the Edgware Road and Maida Vale, through Kilburn and into West Hampstead. Lewis shared her silence wondering about Elizabeth and her background and the sense of mystery that seemed to surround her. Her quietness did not intimidate him or make for a tense situation where he had to struggle to find something to say. To the exhilaration of the evening was now added the prospect of a visit to her place. He studied her by the light of the street lamps, her head slightly back and her eyes closed. She sat upright, he had noticed that her posture was always excellent, and he appreciated her good legs and striking figure. He was aware of the excitement that she was beginning to generate deep inside him and he was also aware that the enjoyment of the concert was only one ingredient in this.

On their arrival Elizabeth went to open the street door of the apartment block while Lewis paid the fare. 'Everything OK sir?' asked the cabby, nodding in Elizabeth's direction, 'You were both quiet like.'

'Fine thanks. We've been to a concert and we're still enjoying it.'

'Well enjoy the rest of the evening, guv!' and he winked.

At the door of the red brick apartment block Elizabeth greeted Lewis with a smile and a shake of her head that emphasised that her hairdresser knew his job, the light caught the sheen of her hair and its bounce spoke of health and high spirits. 'Come on you must be starving.

We'll be eating in a few minutes. Enough of my silences for now.'

Lewis hung their raincoats by the entrance door of the apartment and looked round, he felt a sense of achievement in being invited here. He was already aware that the place had a welcoming feel about it.

'Sitting room or kitchen, Peter? By which I mean do you want to relax or be part of the workforce.'

'I'll work for my supper if I may.'

'Good, you can open the wine and beat the eggs - will scrambled eggs and smoked salmon suit you? It's a bit late for anything heavier, and there's a selection of cheeses as well as fruit.'

'Fine by me. Where's the wine and the corkscrew?'

'Here's the corkscrew. The wine's in the fridge, the Chablis if that appeals to you, it's a dry white Burgundy.'

'I know, my wife's a wine merchant - I sell empty glass while she sells glass with wine in it! I learnt my wines while we were together. You know that we're separated, don't you.'

'Yes. I'm sorry.'

'Oh, I'm reconciled to it now, somehow we just grew apart. It was our son Michael who made the marriage stay together as long as it did. You have to move on ... and relations between us are cordial, which helps. I see Michael regularly, he means a lot to both of us.'

She looked at him, 'But it hurts at times?'

'Yes ... it hurts ... but I notice it less now.'

'Or you're repressing your feelings perhaps? ... No, let's leave it there, I'm intruding and it's not my business. We're making our supper after rather a good recital and not indulging in analysis. Do open the wine as I'm sure we could both do with a drink! You'll find the glasses in the cupboard over the fridge. Yes, use the Waterford Crystal, it goes well with the silverware and I like it. Do you mind eating here? I think it suits supper better, the dining room's a bit formal for a snack at this time of the evening and it helps to have everything handy.'

'Place, company and menu are all fine by me.' Lewis set the table for two using the light blue place mats that matched the colour scheme of the kitchen units. He still felt the excitement of the evening pulsing through his veins and he urged himself to be cautious. The evening had been something special. He had been impressed by her enjoyment of the music and by her wish to communicate that enjoyment to him, to share it with him, to make him part of it and it part of him. He was aware that her friendship would be an enriching thing for him and he was anxious to do nothing to spoil the evening and that prospect. He was here as her guest and he would respect that. He knew that a lasting friendship with her, even if it did not go beyond that, would be considerably more satisfying than an intense but short-lived relationship.

Supper over, they moved to the sitting room and he could not help contrasting its comfort and taste with his austere and untidy lounge in a similar apartment block not a mile away. 'You did well to find a place like this, Elizabeth.'

'I found the shell. The décor was grim, some old fellow had lived here for forty years and never done anything to the place. It was a challenge!'

'So you had the lot done out before you moved in?'

'No, I moved in and set to at once, spending all my time on it. I can see that you like it, Peter. I do ... but then I'm biased. This is the first time I've been able to do a place up exactly as I want - thanks to some money that came from my mother.'

'I wouldn't like you to see my place. It's nothing like this, though I rate it comfortable enough for a bachelor pad.'

'Well, if you ever want help in decorating it you know where to come!'

'Thanks, Elizabeth.'

'I mean it, you know. Just let me know when to want to have a go at it.'

Lewis glanced at the clock. It was 11.35 and he felt that it was time to be on his way. 'It's been a long and enjoyable day and I ought to be leaving I think.'

'Once you've heard the Rubinstein recording of that last piece you may and not before! Have another glass of wine first and enjoy it with the music. She collected the bottle from the fridge in the kitchen and filled his glass. She searched in the bookcase for a miniature score of the piece, fed the CD into the player and, taking her seat on the sofa next to Lewis, opened the score. 'Just listen to the difference in the way the piece is played. It's pure poetry in his hands or rather at his fingertips - did you know that he said that it wasn't the way you hit the keys that was important but the way you took your fingers off the keys? Well listen and enjoy your wine.'

She started the disc and followed the music in the score. 'Opus 66 (Posthumous)' Lewis read, 'Fantasie-Impromptu'. 'Yes', he said to himself, 'an impromptu evening all right but is this a fantasy?' Who was this woman? He knew very little about her and everything suggested that she was hardly the sort to be working in a backstreet business in Kilburn. But she was genuine, he felt it in his bones. He would just enjoy his good luck and hope that it lasted! The music ended gently and he realised that his glass had remained untouched on the table. He took a sip, letting it roll around his mouth, it was a good vintage.

'All conflicts resolved,' she said.

'Yes, if only life were like that!'

'Well, as you can see from the Opus number, it was published after he died. He would have been in the late stages of consumption, of TB, when he wrote it - so he was hardly above the stresses of life while he was working on it.'

'You would never guess that.'

'No, it's amazing the way people can overcome their circumstances ... transcend them ... isn't it?'

He looked at her and wondered what she was leaving unsaid about her own life and experience. He felt convinced that she would have told him but for some constraint. He couldn't begin to guess at the reason for her reticence. It was the measure of their response to one another that he should nevertheless have felt such confidence in her.

Lewis rose from the sofa, 'Well thank you again for a memorable evening, Elizabeth. You've fed heart and mind as well as providing a most enjoyable supper. I'll look forward to returning your hospitality soon. That's if you would like to accept.'

'Of course I would. I've enjoyed your company immensely. By the way, today was my birthday and I wouldn't have liked to spend it on my own. You've made it special and I'm grateful, Peter.'

'If only I'd known ... '

'Without knowing you made it special ... I couldn't ask for more than that could I?'

She took his arm and led him to the door. 'Goodnight Peter, it's been a special birthday.' She kissed him on the cheek and a slightly dazed Peter Lewis found himself walking away from Elizabeth's apartment wondering about her. He continued to wonder through the small hours of the night and for some considerable time to come.

***

Sam put the earphones down. 'So Lewis has found his way to her place! Well he was bound to sooner or later ... We're both having music lessons from her. How long until she's *his music mistress* I wonder? Lewis should be grateful to his Russian benefactors. They seem to be brightening up his rather dull life!' And he felt a sharp pang of jealousy.

Chapter 9

Tuesday 9th July 1996

"Hail to thee, blithe spirit!
Bird thou never wert,
That from heaven, or near it,
Pourest thy full heart
In profuse strains of unpremeditated art."

"And singing still doest soar, and soaring ever singest."

From Shelley's *Ode to a Skylark*.

Elizabeth looked back from Peak Hill, down over Sidmouth and eastwards along the coast. She saw the transition of the cliffs from the red Devon sandstone to the chalk of Dorset. It was early July and the day, which had started with squally rain, was now pleasantly sunny with a gentle westerly breeze and white cotton wool clouds running before it. She found a bench and re-tied the laces of one of her walking shoes - she was glad that she had come equipped for a proper exploration of the area rather than for hours of sightseeing from behind the wheel of the hire car she had picked up in Salisbury. The wind ruffled her hair and she felt how good it was to be out in the open. The climb had warmed her up and she unzipped her red lightweight waterproof jacket, feeling the heat of the afternoon sun on her back. She had bought the jacket in Exeter the previous day knowing that, if she were going to explore remote areas of the countryside, she should be conspicuous in case of any accident. It was not her nature to be over cautious but her training made her alert to possible dangers and had equipped her to anticipate problems. There was a time to stand out and a time to merge into the background, to be one of the mass of humanity undifferentiated from the others. She usually had to work harder at being inconspicuous than at standing out from the crowd. She could do it if necessary and at times it was a relief not to attract attention, especially from men. She wanted to spend the next few days on her own and not have to fend off the advances of interested males. So she was dressed in a pair of old comfortable jeans, which were a shade too large, certainly not skin tight, and a sloppy and shapeless dark blue sweater that she sometimes wore around her apartment when she was relaxing by herself.

The sea was choppy and a yacht, tacking against the wind, was making its way towards her along the coast. Its crew were having to work hard to make progress but they were succeeding and she envied them, toiling together and harnessing the elements to their purpose. For herself she felt rather blown off course in life: that was the reason for her being away from London. The previous week she had decided that she badly needed a break, she had to get away to find herself. For one thing there was her developing relationship with Peter Lewis, it was not without complications and she would have to move with care if she were to avoid hurting him and others or endangering the assignment. Then for some years she had been used to playing a variety of different rôles, rarely had she had the opportunity to be herself. She continually carried the baggage of a fictitious past and a fictitious present. She acted out scripts written for her by the External Intelligence Service and unlike her stage counterparts she did not have the opportunity to take a bow at the end of the performance and once again resume her real self. She was tired of it all and so for the moment she would let her mind rest. First would come unwinding; after that, in a few days time, she would begin to apply her mind to the situation. You never got anywhere by letting the same thoughts run round and round in your mind - that only made finding solutions harder. Both by nature and training she was able to come to quick and balanced conclusions. In good time she would begin the review and decide on the right course of action. By the end of the week she should know where she was going. In the meantime the walk had sharpened her appetite and she had noticed a pleasant tea-room on her way through the town - tea and cake would be suitably English, she was enjoying being in this country. After that she had plenty of reading that she intended to get through, a pile of English classic novels. Her bedroom in the hotel was comfortable and had a view out to sea and along the coast. She would stay there reading until dinner. The hotel had a conference of tax officials going on and Elizabeth was anxious to avoid their company - she had no wish to be interrogated by these fellow residents and she had a jaundiced view of officialdom at that moment.

A dog scampered up to her and nuzzled its head against her leg. An elderly couple called and it set off back towards them. 'That's how Eugene and the SVR would like me to respond, damn them! Well I won't, I'll be my own woman!' was the thought that came into her mind. The couple with the dog came over to sit on the bench just as she was standing up to go. They passed the time of day and expressed the hope that their dog had not disturbed her. 'Not at all, he's kind of cute. What sort of a dog is he?' she asked the husband.

'*She's* a King Charles Cocker Spaniel', the tweedy woman replied and her less talkative husband nodded.

'Poor man,' Elizabeth thought to herself, 'he's got two bitches to contend with!' However she limited her response to, 'She's certainly a fine dog.'

As she started off down the hill she caught the woman's words to her husband, carried to her by the breeze, 'Did you see how she looked at you? I shouldn't be at all surprised if she wasn't trying to pick you up? *"Kind of cute!"* these Americans murder our language!'

Elizabeth hoped that the suggestion that she had a sexual interest in him would bolster the old fellow's ego, though she somehow thought he was past that sort of thing. 'If animals become like their keepers and keepers like their animals', Elizabeth thought, 'I can understand why Cromwell chopped off King Charles' head.' She laughed out loud with pleasure at her recollection of English history while, at the same time, wondering if the breed of dog took its name from the same king. She resisted the temptation to go back and ask the husband - No, she didn't wish him to spend the night in the dog-house on her account.

Sustained by her visit to the tea-room Elizabeth bought a picture postcard and a First Class postage stamp. She then strolled along the promenade towards the eastern end of the beach. Before her was the English Channel and to one side, drawn up on the beach, were a few small fishing boats. The view pleased her and she sat for a while on the side of a beached rowing boat taking it in, warmed by the sun and soothed by the sound of the waves breaking on the shingle. What should she write on the card? She wished that Peter were with her, she wanted at one level to be able to share the place and the tranquillity with him but at another level that was just what she had come there to avoid: her purpose was to detach herself from things in order to be sure about her emotions and her plans for the future. Better a formal greeting than anything more intimate, time enough for warmer words if that were her decision when the time came.

***

Lewis' Wednesday morning post included the card from Sidmouth:

'Thanks for suggesting this area for a visit. It's lovely and I'm feeling really relaxed. Weather fine and hotel comfortable. A good place to unwind. See you next week. I'm off to Dorset tomorrow.
Elizabeth'

Lewis turned the postcard over and saw the view that she had admired the previous day. He recognised it and remembered, with pleasure and regret, visits there with Ruth and Michael. He turned the card over again and re-read her message. It would be five days before she was back. He was missing her already. A temp was doing the secretarial work - that was no problem - it was Elizabeth that he missed. Her presence had lifted his spirits and pulled him out of the lethargy that had beset him for some months, even before Vera died. He was conscious of this even more acutely now that she was away. But the card had reminded him of the early happy years of his marriage and his emotions once more were mixed. How easy it would be if he and Ruth simply hated one another and there were no child to be taken into account or if their splitting up would be for their child's benefit! But there was Michael and, whatever their deeper feelings for one another had become, Lewis and Ruth were still on cordial terms. He knew that he shied away from decisions that might be hurtful but he was glad that he had seen his Solicitor the previous day in order to make progress with the divorce. Lewis pinned the card to his notice board with a sigh, he was pleased to hear from Elizabeth but he could have done without the reminder of times past.

He made his first telephone call of the day - better to be busy, much better than letting your personal problems and hopes devour you and your time. He later toyed with the idea of calling Lucy for a date that evening - wondering whether he ought to keep up their monthly meetings now that he had begun a friendship with Elizabeth - he felt in need of company in a way that he had not done for a long time. Lucy, he decided, would only complicate matters and he somehow felt that to wine and dine her would be an act of disloyalty, though, such was his confusion, he was not sure to whom he would have been disloyal. Eventually he called an old friend from his university days and arranged to eat with him that evening.

***

12th July 1996

Friday found Elizabeth in Wessex. Peter had lent her some of Hardy's novels and the sight of the Dorset coast from Sidmouth had confirmed her decision to move on to "Hardy Country". She had made her base at the Casterbridge Hotel in Dorchester, more for its name than for anything she knew about the establishment, though she was immediately pleased with her choice. It was a Georgian terraced house in the main street of the town and it felt right, somehow matching her idea of where she wanted to spend the next few days. At the County Museum she had acquired a book on Hardy and after exploring the town had driven around the area, taking plenty of time for walking and getting the feel of the landscape. Places which had evidently changed little over many centuries delighted her. She had the city dweller's romantic view of the countryside, judging it by eye on a fine day, but she was not unaware of the sheer hard work that had gone into keeping it in order and productive, particularly before the arrival of powered farm machinery. She was not oblivious to past struggles against the effects of bad weather and the poverty that crop failure and tight-fisted employers must have brought to many. The tidiness of the countryside was what struck her. How domesticated it seemed! So different from the vast untidy Russian landscape or the huge spaces of the USA and Canada. Here things were on a human scale and she felt comfortable, though not really "at home" in the way that reawakened memories and touched the emotions - she wondered if she would she ever again feel like that anywhere - but she felt in harmony with her surroundings and with life.

The years of subterfuge and nomadic moving from place to place had created a longing for reality and permanence. The one continuing feature of her life had been Eugene and she was now heartily sick of him! Here she was at ease. The week's break had prepared her to face up to the decisions that had to be made. She would weigh up the pros and cons as dispassionately as possible. But, as she considered that agenda, she knew there could never be an analysis wholly devoid of feeling where relationships were concerned. There never could be and there never should be. She was certainly not a desiccated calculating machine: she had a woman's warmth and a woman's compassion. Decisions were far easier when you were the only one involved. But when others might be hurt ... that was a different matter. Still she was pleased to be ready to reach some conclusions about the way forward.

She had a late lunch of salmon with a ginger and lime sauce in Dorchester at "Judge Jeffreys' Lodgings", finding it hard to think of the place inhabited by the crazy and blood thirsty hanging judge referred to in her guidebook. She read the leaflet given her by the waiter in the restaurant, taking in the history of the building which dated back beyond 1398 and gave an account of Jeffreys and the Monmouth Rebellion. The manager seemed to have a proprietorial interest in Jeffreys' reputation, seeking to persuade her that his reputation for harshness was due to illness - "the stone" - and that it had been necessary for him to kill the pain with heavy drinking. Her own country had seen many of that sort in its recent history, Stalin had certainly had no difficulty in finding judges ready and willing to send his innumerable purge victims to their deaths. She had seen Jeffreys' portrait on the stairway and tried to imagine him, three hundred years on as a customer, having to take his turn with her and the generally middle aged customers of the restaurant. She decided that they would probably throw him out as a troublesome oaf. At the next table a tweedy woman, strange how she seemed to be encountering such women on this holiday, was holding forth on the need for corporal punishment of young offenders, at any rate Jefferys would have found in her a kindred spirit!

Afterwards she headed a couple of miles south to Maiden Castle which the guide book told her was an ancient earth fort, the *Mai Dun* or "Hill of Strength" of prehistoric times. From the summit she could see Dorchester to the north with it's spires standing out against the blue sky. For about an hour she walked around the top of the large oval set of earth ramparts, trying to picture the original builders of the fortifications and then their successors including the Roman Legions under Vespasian nineteen hundred years before her. A cynic might say that all their decisions, even if they had then seemed momentous to them, had been of little consequence: time had gone on almost indifferent to them. Yet Elizabeth knew that such arguments did not ring true. She was unsure whether she believed in God or not, on balance she thought that she probably did - her mother's piety had been more persuasive than her school's atheistic teaching - she certainly wanted to believe in a kindly Deity concerned about how his creatures lived. She was satisfied that her decisions did matter for herself and for the others who would be affected to a greater of lesser extent by them. 'Career and Relationships' that was the agenda, or, she wondered, should it be 'Relationships and Career'? Well she would see how they related! She began her analysis calmly reflecting on the varied factors, surprised and pleased at the sense of being able somehow able to stand outside her situation and get an overall view. Elizabeth was grateful for her training in analysis. She took a small red notebook from her pocket and, seated on the grassy bank, began to list headings and make notes. 'Be thorough!' she told herself, 'You may not get such a good chance to think things through for some time and you need to be sure now.' There were two more days of holiday left but she needed to make her decisions now and not find herself with time running out, that would only make things more difficult.

Elizabeth had put away her notebook, her analysis complete for the moment, and was about to leave when the song of a bird caught her attention. She turned and saw it hovering against the backdrop of a cloudless blue sky. It held its place, fluttering against the gentle breeze. She guessed it to be a skylark, though she could not be sure. But its name was unimportant: it was the beauty of the song that held her, song that was answered by other birds from the grass of the hilltop. She lay back on the ground, sheltered from the breeze, smelling the scent of moist warm earth. The heat of the sun was on her face. She concentrated on the birdsong, not that concentration was needed for the song held her attention as surely as it had caught it in the first place. The song ended and she opened her eyes - the bird was dropping to its nest among the long grasses. Silence had descended, the other birds too were quiet. The hill was quiet but not totally silent as the gentle breeze rustled the grasses and sheep were bleating in the distance.

She was possessed by an intense mixture of joy and of longing. The experience had come unsought and she longed for it to continue. But at the same time she knew that this was not to be, she could not hold it nor could she command or engineer its reappearance. It was, for her, the most significant thing that had happened in years. And that was so even though she found it impossible to identify precisely what the experience signified. Reality, perhaps, a reality that defied analysis but which had been almost tangible. She was aware of tears on her cheeks, tears of joy, of profound happiness. At a loss to find a response she whispered, 'Thank You'. She lay back on the grass and was still for a while. Birds sang but the experience did not return. And she was glad that this was so. It had come from outside her without being worked up or sought. It had come as a gift and she had gratefully received it as such. It's preciousness came from its rarity. She remembered Elgar's note on the manuscript of his Second Symphony, "Rarely, rarely, comest thou, Spirit of Delight!" And she counted herself blessed to have been there on that ancient hilltop. She felt cleansed, refreshed, alert and hopeful. It was not just the beauty of the birdsong that had moved her, it was a sense of an underlying reality, a Reality that must be at least personal. The experience had seemed to beckon her on - to what she was unsure.

She would write it up back at the hotel in Dorchester. But long before she put pen to paper she knew that the written record would be a poor thing compared with what she had just experienced. She made her way back down to her car, working through the deep ditches of the defensive earthworks on the side of the hill, slithering down the path in places where the grass had been worn through to the bare white chalk below. For the last two hours she had been alone with nature, apart from meeting a couple of Australians who had passed the time of day with her as she had sat writing on the hilltop. The car was like an oven and she opened both doors for a couple of minutes before driving off with both windows open. In ten minutes she was back at the car park and shortly afterwards she began to record her experience in writing, sitting at the small table in her room at the Casterbridge Hotel. Soon she would turn to the decision she must make before the holiday was over. And she made a note to check the Elgar quotation and find out where he had got it from, presumably from some English poet.

***

Later she had an early dinner at a restaurant near her hotel. She chose the Dover Sole, followed by a selection of sorbets and then cheese, allowing herself a single glass of wine. She then returned to her hotel, oblivious of the eyes of several of her fellow diners following her as she left the restaurant. She got out the cafetière and ground coffee that she had brought with her - the instant coffee that hotels provided in rooms was not to her liking - poured herself a cup and wrapped a hand towel round the cafetière to keep the remainder warm. She chose the upright chair at the table in the corner of the room, took the notebook from her handbag and began to read the notes made at *Mai Dun* a few hours before - the idea of it as a *Hill of Strength* appealed to her. Analysis completed, she would now reach her conclusions or at any rate see whether the way her mind and emotions were tending was right and sensible. But first she paused and reflected on her present mood and feelings. The warm July day in the Dorset countryside had been a good one with a gentle breeze. The glow on her face reminded her of the wind blowing through her hair as she had walked around the hill fort and the weariness in her limbs spoke of her determination to work out of her system the slight sense of unease with which she had begun the day. That was gone, dissipated by her experience on Maiden Castle, which had indeed become her Hill of Strength. Now she was relaxed and at the same time alert. Her experience of overwhelming joy and longing would be the indelible memory of that afternoon. She was happy, happy to an extent that she had not known for many years. Good! She felt glad that the time had come to take bearings and set course. Elizabeth savoured the coffee, was conscious of it sharpening up her concentration and was glad that she had gone easy on the wine at dinner.

The notebook entries ran to several pages and she set about summarising them and drawing up a list of points for consideration. It was not so much a list of points as a list of names and after only half hour she had reduced her thoughts to a single sheet which read:

"**Peter. YES YES YES!** He's a gentleman who cares about people! I haven't met too many of that kind! We get on so well together and seem to understand one another. He needs someone to look after him and **I LOVE HIM !**

Ruth and Michael. Peter has made up his mind to go ahead with the divorce, they separated before I came on the scene. Must ensure that he sees a lot of Michael and not resent it.

Mother. I don't think she will ever leave Moscow. She has a few friends there and wants to be near them. She depends on me for financial help and I can probably do better for her in the West - there is the money I put by in the USA from a variety of sources (get it into the UK).

Eugene. NO NO NO to Eugene! I'll have to keep him at arm's length and beyond.

Assignment. Will continue the assignment but not go home at the end. Peter is unknowingly involved but is in no danger. Won't say anything to him about the assignment though I would like to!

Home. <u>Not Moscow but England.</u> But will I be able to stay there legally? Why not? But will my false papers stand up to scrutiny?

Occupation. Anything to help Peter but interior design if he agrees."

In one sense, but only one, it was a disappointment, she could have written the same answers before she set off on her few days away from London, but she knew that what was different now was the strength of her conviction that this was the best way forward, indeed the *only* way for her. It was something she felt deep down in her inner being. The tranquillity that had followed the experience of the afternoon added to her sense of certainty. She tore the sheet of paper and the pages from the notebook into small pieces and flushed them down the lavatory. Her mind was now made up, there was no more use for the record of her deliberations. She poured herself another coffee and, quitting the chair at the table for the more comfortable armchair, she sat for a while with her head back and eyes closed, wholly at peace with herself. Then she picked up the telephone handset and made the necessary call.

***

Lewis had had a busy week. As was his Friday evening practice he cleared his desk and put into a pile the few items needing attention on Monday morning The temp covering for Elizabeth had performed efficiently but there had been several problems that Elizabeth would have coped with on her own that the girl had had to pass to him. He knew that Elizabeth would probably have sorted them out more quickly than *he* had. How soon she had become indispensable to the business - and not just to the business, he reflected, but to him personally. He was counting down the days until she was due back in the office - it was now three days and he knew that he had to keep himself occupied over the weekend so that he didn't start counting the hours! He had the whole weekend to himself as Ruth had taken Michael with her on a visit to a friend in Oxford.

On the way home he called in at a restaurant in the Kilburn High Road for a pizza, which he ate as he read the evening paper, more to have something to do than from interest or for pleasure. At home he decided on an evening of television with a resort to old videos if, as seemed likely, there were no programmes worth seeing that evening. He remembered that a friend had given him what he had described at the time as "a rather explicit adult video, just the thing to get you excited" and thought he might view it for the lack of anything else to do. Having attended to a few domestic chores, not so much because they needed urgent attention but in order to pass the time, he found the friend's video tape and with a glass of port beside him settled down to "get excited". After a few minutes he turned it off in disgust, feeling soiled by it and consigned the tape to the rubbish chute. He was no prude but this wasn't the sort of thing that appealed to him. He turned through the channels and settled down once more to a programme which appeared to require a certain amount of intelligence on the part of the viewers.

Lewis was roused from his slumbers by the telephone and wondered how long it had been ringing. In his hurry to take the call he knocked over his half empty glass of port. 'Hello, ... Peter Lewis speaking ... '. It was not his best telephone manner but he was out of breath and not fully awake.

'Hello Peter, it's Elizabeth here. Are you all right? You took a long time to answer the 'phone and you're out of breath.'

'Elizabeth! I must have been asleep - the T.V. was so riveting that I dropped off - you can see that I'm having an exciting evening and staying out of mischief! Hold on while I turn it off. Ruth has gone to friends with Michael so I'm having a very ... quiet weekend. Work on Monday will break the boredom ... and it will be good to have you back in the office.'

'Peter darling, I've a better idea. As you're at a loose end, how about joining me for the weekend here in Dorchester? I want to have you with me, it would be fun to do the area together. How about it?'

'You don't have to ask me twice. I would love be with you, Elizabeth my dear. Where are you staying?'

'It's the Casterbridge Hotel. You'll find it in the main street in Dorchester. Have you a piece of paper? Right. The street's called High East Street, the hotel's on the right hand side just past the White Hart. You can leave your car there as you'll be late - you can make your peace with the pub tomorrow if they're unhappy about your parking there. I'll arrange for the night porter to let you in. Oh yes, you take the first Dorchester sign at the roundabout on the A 31 road.'

'Casterbridge is it? We *are* being literary, Elizabeth!'

'I'm just finishing the copy of the "Mayor of Casterbridge" that you lent me, Peter.'

'Right I'm on my way or almost so. I should get there around midnight.'

'Peter, you will promise to drive carefully, the roads down here aren't the best you know.'

'Elizabeth, I promise to take the utmost care. You have already transformed the weekend for me. We'll have a great time together.'

'Don't forget to bring some jeans and solid shoes, we're going to get out into the country or onto the coast and walk and walk and walk, you'll love it! And by the way ... our room has a very comfortable four poster bed.'

'See you soon, Elizabeth, I'm very excited at the prospect, four poster and all.'

'Take care, Peter, please!'

Lewis mopped up the spilt port and put the broken glass in the rubbish bin after wrapping it in newspaper, years of dealing with glass had made him safety conscious. After unplugging the television and the recorder from the mains and unplugging the aerial co-ax from its socket he checked that all was in order in the sitting room, putting out all the lights except the table lamp connected to the timer switch. Then he checked that everything in the kitchen was turned off. In his bedroom he quickly packed an overnight bag. So Elizabeth was inviting him to a literary weekend! Well, there were more ways than one of being a man of letters. In the bathroom be took a packet of condoms from the cabinet and packed them with his toilet gear. He had bought them a couple weeks before just in case they were needed. Yes, a quick shower was in order and he would be on his way before nine. He looked at himself in the bathroom mirror, not bad for the wrong side of forty! He suddenly felt extremely young and lively. What a difference a telephone call could make! 'Elizabeth!' The name was potent music in his ears. He was glad that he had only drunk half a glass of port that evening, he wanted to have his wits about him for the journey. He opened the bathroom window and looked out through the plane trees at the street below, a perfect evening, he would enjoy the drive down to Dorchester. What a joy to be getting out of London and on his way to join Elizabeth! He was grateful to Eugene for suggesting that she should work for him and he was pleased that the divorce proceedings were progressing once again. It was no good being stuck in the past - you had to get on with life, after all!

***

Elizabeth made another pot of coffee and took up her copy of the 'Mayor of Casterbridge', she had started it the previous evening and would have finished it in an hour. She did not expect to have much time for reading over the weekend! After the book she would luxuriate in a bath and then await Peter's arrival She remembered to call reception and arrange for Peter to be let in - it wouldn't do for him to be locked out. She took from the wardrobe a silk negligée that she had bought at a little shop near the Cathedral in Exeter at the beginning of the holiday and held it up in front of herself before the mirror. She smiled with satisfaction and laid it on the bed. Of course she had bought it 'just in case' and not with any particular person in mind! At one and the same time she felt in control of her life and had a pleasant sense of being carried along by the stream of events in the direction she wished to go. Taking up her book again she began her wait for Peter's arrival. The miseries of Michael Henchard were strangely at odds with her mood as she finished the book. However she took in the closing words regarding Elizabeth-Jane, the wretched man's daughter:

"And in being forced to class herself among the fortunate she did not cease to wonder at the persistence of the unforeseen, when the one to whom such unbroken tranquillity had been accorded in the adult stage was she whose youth had seemed to teach that happiness was but the occasional episode in a general drama of pain."

Elizabeth reflected on her own tranquillity. She knew it would not be unbroken but she recognised the experience of the young Elizabeth-Jane as her own in childhood and was grateful that the suffering brought to herself and her mother by a drunken and brutal stepfather had been terminated by the man's demise. Once more her mind turned to her afternoon at Maiden Castle and the song of the skylark, the more to be treasured as it had come to her unbidden. And now Peter should be with her in an hour or so. In prospect was the perfect end to a wonderful day. But he was likely to be tired after his drive from London - well full intimacy could wait until the morning. Better to hold back than to botch things. Tonight they would sleep in one another's arms and tomorrow they would really begin to get to know each other.

Chapter 10

Monday 5th August 1996

' "The scum and glory of the universe", that's what Pascal thought about humanity. ... How do you react to his assessment?' Alan Winters shot the question at Sam as they wandered across Holland Park.

'I'd think that he was about right as long as you allow for most of us having a bit of each in our make up. There are those who are unmixed scum - that's certainly true - however there aren't too many of that type and there may be those who are at the other end of the scale, though I've yet to meet anyone who could be described as the unmixed glory of the universe, present company excepted, of course!'

The weather was warm, with a hot August afternoon in prospect, and they had decided to meet in the park rather than indoors before having lunch at the "Windsor Castle" in Camden Hill Road. Winters had suggested the pub so that when their business was concluded he could look in on an old friend who ran an up-market antiques shop just off Notting Hill Gate. He liked the idea of being able to pull his friend's leg by telling him that he had been to lunch at Windsor Castle. He and Sam had not met for six weeks. Winters had been out of the country visiting Switzerland and Liechtenstein to tend to certain bank accounts and *Anstalten* that housed and generated funds that had to be kept out of sight of various sets of official eyes. Sam had been occupied with other work for the Institute in Paris.

'Not the glory of the universe, that title belongs elsewhere, but I like to think that I display perhaps a little more brightness than many of my fellows. For the most part they have their snouts in the trough and don't see far beyond the daily grind.'

'Maybe that's true Alan, but you do start with certain advantages over the rest of the herd.'

'Advantages like?'

'Like coming from a wealthy family that's been settled here for several generations and not shifting from one country to another in order to survive. And your family has remained intact - your father is 95 isn't he?'

'True but it wasn't without effort that I established myself as an expert in antiques and antiquities. I'm not unused to getting my hands dirty on archaeological digs.'

'I don't doubt that Alan, but there's a difference between getting your hands dirty in pursuit of your hobby and having to get them dirty one long day after another in the struggle to survive.'

Winters nodded, 'Point taken, Sam. But I have worked hard throughout my life and I still do! Take my involvement with the Institute ... it's for free, you know ... in fact I rarely charge my expenses and there are times when it gets in the way of business.'

'How is your father, Alan? You were just about to celebrate his birthday when we last met, weren't you?'

'I'm not sure that celebrate is the right word ... in fact I'm sure that it isn't. He's senile and there's little to celebrate, you know. I almost think that I would prefer to have seen him go in the way that yours did, suddenly and full possession of his faculties. Your memories, though touched with real sadness, are good ones. I look at my father and see myself in thirty years time and it's not nice, I can tell you!'

They were seated on the edge of a raised flower bed facing towards one another and keeping an eye open for anyone eavesdropping on their conversation. There was a feeling of luxury in the warmth. Sam drank in the scent of the flowers and, watching the bees moving from one bloom to another, wondered about their work ethic. What was life like in the bee hive? A friend had remarked that the organisation of the hive was pretty simple, 'One's in charge and all the rest are idiots.' Sam was relieved that he had never worked in such a set up, he had always been made to feel that his opinion was welcome and that he could make a difference to the outcome of whatever task was entrusted to him. He too had been lucky, though not in the super wealthy class like Alan, he had been pretty fortunate in doing work that he liked. The present assignment, though making little progress at the moment, allowed him time for reading, art galleries and cinema going - he was almost addicted to films. It also gave him plenty of time for squash and keeping fit. During his time in the army he had prided himself on his fitness and his men had been in awe of his mental and physical agility, he had always led from the front and they had been hard put to keep up with him. Sam had ensured that he continued to maintain the same standards, knowing that one day his survival might depend on them.

Winters broke the silence, 'Well then, what are your friends doing at the moment and how much longer are you going to have to devote your valuable attention to them?'

'I wouldn't call them "friends". Though, as individuals, they haven't harmed me personally they represent a power which is less than benevolent and has done us a great deal of harm in the past and may do so again in the future. I suppose that I would get on with them if I had any direct dealings with them - though Eugene is somewhat unpleasant, the boozy domineering type, a Georgian who still has a good opinion of Stalin. My guess is that he's on his last outing and that they'll keep him at home when this is all over and he returns to Moscow. The girl's rather different, in fact very different. From their conversations I estimate that they worked together, firstly in Canada and then in the USA, for around five years picking up trade and commercial secrets and know-how. She's quite an expert on computers and was able to get what she wanted out of them and her unsuspecting bosses - she knew how to use her charms on them but I suspect that they got what they hoped for when they took her onto the payroll. She despised them, of course, and now she resents the fact that the SVR encouraged her into her targets' beds. She could have become hardened by the process but it seems that she's turning into a caring young woman. I don't imagine that she'll want to go home at the end of all this. We might be able to turn her or at any rate learn something from her, she's worth some investment on our part. She's a real good looker - stunning in fact.' Sam paused wondering whether he was in danger of giving away too much by his enthusiasm for Elizabeth.

Winters broke in, 'And how does she show this caring quality, she's not another "Queen of Hearts", making night-time visits to London hospitals, I suppose?'

'Nothing like that. She's moved in with Lewis or rather he's moved into her place. At the beginning of July she took off for a week's holiday, we wondered what she was up to of course. It could have been an effort by the SVR to pick up some nuclear secrets from the atom plant in Dorset or something of the sort. You remember the Portland Spy ring that Gordon Lonsdale ran years ago? He had local agents picking up information on the Naval Underwater Research Establishment at Portland in Dorset - I doubt whether there's anything there these days. From Eugene's reaction to her absence it seemed to be a private trip rather than work. She told him that she was pushing off for a week and refused to say why. In fact I can quote her words to him before she left, 'Get stuffed and keep your drunken nose out of my life' - I suspect that he didn't report it to Moscow in those terms! Anyway it seems to have been her way of responding to some sort of personal crisis. We kept an eye on her, of course - she might have been given some task about which Eugene was being kept in the dark. Just as well that it was the holiday season with a good number of visitors around or our people would have been rather conspicuous. We had a bit of luck at the end of the week when she spent an afternoon at some prehistoric site near Dorchester. She was sitting on the top of a great bank of earth immersed in writing and a couple of our people, dressed as hikers were able to approach and film her notebook before she was aware of them. They were lucky, they got a page and a half of her notes, there was no doubt a lot more but it made clear that she was engaged in some sort of personal stocktaking exercise. Here, have a look at the photo they managed to get, the original's more revealing than a transcript, it's more immediate.'

Winters took the print and scrutinised it. 'Not very circumspect, was she? You would think that someone of her experience would take more care wouldn't you?'

A nanny hove in sight with her charge in a perambulator of superior quality. They waited until she was out of earshot - *they* at any rate were being circumspect, in the world in which they operated it was easy to have fantasies about a perambulator full of electronic gear - and then Sam continued.

'A hill fort in the West of England is hardly the front line in international espionage. ... All right she should have been more careful, but she seems to have wound down and been in a relaxed mood - it was the last place that she expected to be under observation.'

'Not very professional. Still it was useful for us. There is one thing that does concern me from our point of view, it's this - *If* she has fallen for the Lewis fellow does it mean that she will spill the beans to him and abort the operation. That's the last thing that we would want isn't it?'

'The thought had occurred to me as well, Alan. On balance I think that she will avoid rocking the boat too much, even though she may have decided to stay here and not return to Moscow at the end. Her mother is there and she wouldn't want them to take any action against her, so I expect Elizabeth to give her masters the minimum of trouble. There's also the apartment in West Hampstead - I know you regard the area as down market but there aren't too many areas that you would regard as desirable addresses, are there?' Sam paused and took in Winters' reaction, a slight sniff and then a hearty laugh.

'OK Sam, I concede that there are people who find the area between the Finchley Road and the Kilburn High Road desirable and I admit that I am not one of them. That's just as well, Mayfair would be a bit crowded otherwise.'

'Not really, Alan, it's not a question of choice but one of money, isn't it?'

'Point conceded, but go on I interrupted you ... No, that's unfair to myself, you were the one who interrupted the flow of the argument weren't you?'

'Point taken, the digression was mine. OK, to continue ... Elizabeth is crazy about the apartment. From my short visit I can see why, she's made it into a very pleasant home on which she has stamped her personality. I expect she has spent years living out of a suitcase ready to disappear at a moment's notice. Anyway, whatever the reason, she's nuts about the place and I don't see her being at all willing to give it up. Lewis has moved in with her, not the other way round, and that I think, is significant.'

'And how is that viewed by her Russian masters? That's the way they have used her in the past, isn't it? Boardroom to bedroom as the quickest route for her to get her hands on the really private particulars? Is this part of the script that they have written for her or is the girl improvising? There seems no need for bedding the boss this time unless they have decided that it's a way of ensuring that she remains in employment as long as they need. From what you have reported previously, she has made herself indispensable to him on the strength of her office skills, so for Moscow's purposes that ought to be enough without her having to become his mistress.'

'Personally, Alan, I've no doubt that she's in love for Lewis. He's very different from the American bosses that she's likely to have had. I suspect that she likes the opportunity to fuss over him, mothering him is putting it too strongly, but she probably needs someone to care for and worry over. She's got her first real home or the first one for some years and she isn't content to be there on her own and the last person she wants to share it with is her Russian colleague, 'that bastard Vladimir,' as you saw from her note just now – she seems to have written down his real name inadvertently. And now she's got a boss who doesn't take advantage of her and treats her with respect - so she falls for him! The problem will be if either of them, for one reason or another, tires of the relationship ... then it might not be possible for her to stay as his secretary and our operation might come to a premature end. Still, my guess is that she will see it through to a proper conclusion and not give us any problems. My only worry is about Lewis, he's the type to be troubled by his conscience, after the initial euphoria of his new relationship he may well start worrying about his wife and child. Oh I know that he's supposed to be getting a divorce but he's the sort who, when it finally comes to it, could well have second thoughts and return to the wife of his youth. I've mentioned her to you? No? Well Ruth Lewis is a pretty successful wine importer and we've kept an eye on her to get an idea of the background. She's a busy woman, energetic and attractive though there's no lover in sight. So she might take him back if he wanted that. They both dote on their son Michael, he's nearly thirteen and at a private school - one of those places that you English call public schools!'

'We'll just have to wait and see what develops Sam. It'll give you enough time to get to know London and to continue your reading or whatever you do to amuse yourself. It seems to me that you could do with some female company of the type that Lewis has found.'

The suggestion was too accurate for Sam's comfort and he pushed it aside quickly. 'I've enough to keep me occupied for the time being, Alan. I've got Mia in Brooklyn to keep me in line. Thanks for your concern, though.' Sam decided that for the time being he would keep to himself his growing interest in Elizabeth and not raise it with Winters. His duty was to see the operation through to a successful conclusion, but if Elizabeth and Lewis split up he knew that it would be hard for him to resist the opportunity that would be presented. He just hoped that, if the chance came, it would do so at the right time.

Winters interrupted his thoughts, 'And about that MP's bank account you were probing for me ... '

***

In Moscow Evgeny stood at the open window of his office in the SVR Headquarters, his jacket hung from a hook on the back of his door and the sweat rolled down his face. Why didn't they have air conditioning that worked properly? It was like everything else he encountered, tired out, below par and obsolete. At the moment he placed himself in the same category. It was difficult to work up enthusiasm for much beyond your personal survival. Not that he *feared* anyone within the SVR, the days of Beria and his successors had long since gone. There was more risk from mindless violence on the streets or from having your identity mistaken by a Mafiya hit man. He re-read Vladimir's report that had reached him earlier in the day:

'... All arrangements in place and we are now biding our time before Lewis' next visit to Basel which is scheduled for November. Unfortunately I have encountered some insubordination from my colleague who, quite unnecessarily, has encouraged Lewis to move into her apartment. She has refused to use her skills as an interior designer to access the homes of politicians whom I have targeted. Recommend that on her return she should be reprimanded and not sent out of Russia for a while.'

Evgeny stared out of the window, he did not enjoy being caged here in Moscow in a constant struggle with his colleagues, and especially the Accounts Section, for funds and their authorisation of his agents' activities but he did not see why Lizaveta should be sentenced to rot here for the remainder of her service. She was a good agent - much better than Vladimir in his view - he was the senior but in Evgeny's opinion it was Lizaveta who delivered the goods and who carried Vladimir. 'Drunken devil,' Evgeny muttered, 'drunken lecherous bastard. She's using Lewis as a shield against Vladimir's advances.'

He returned to his desk and typed a note to Personnel on his PC, reading it through before attaching it to the front of a copy of Vladimir's report:

'Relations between the two have not been good on this assignment, due primarily to Vladimir's drinking and his unrestrained sexual drive. There will be time enough for forays into the homes of the British political elite when Operation Basel is over. We can be grateful to Vladimir for having a good idea though not the right timing. It would be folly for Lizaveta to attempt to take on the full time occupation of interior design consultant while she was working full time for Lewis. The recent deterioration in Vladimir's character will be a further factor for review when the more substantial matter is dealt with on his return.'

The more substantial matter was one that had come to light the previous week. One of the SVR auditors had, by means of a little burglary at a Guernsey accountant's office, discovered that the apartment occupied by Vladimir was owned by a company controlled by him and financed from around $1,000,000 transferred from the USA. Their masters would be less than delighted to find out that the rent they paid was going into the pocket of one of their agents. It was Vladimir who would have a rough homecoming at the end of the assignment. For Evgeny it was an embarrassment he could well do without. It meant that Accounts Section were one up in their running battle with him.

Chapter 11

Monday 9th September 1996

The intense summer heat of Southern France had moderated to a glorious lingering warmth that brought a touch of magic to the September evening and kept the thought of winter far from the mind. Peter Lewis and Jacob Gold were awaiting the return of Elizabeth and Paula Gold from the Ladies Room. They stood at the entrance of the *Oustau de Baumanière* at Les Baux, twenty five kilometres south of Avignon. Jacob had been the host and they had fed well in the luxurious setting of the restaurant. Lewis was glad that Jacob had insisted on paying the bill and that they had a taxi waiting to take them back to Avignon - he felt steady on his feet but knew that it wouldn't have been wise to drive after the wine that they had imbibed, it was not an excessive quantity but it was over the French drink driving limit.

They had skipped the dinner at the conference on scientific equipment and arrived at Les Baux in time to enjoy the sunset from the vantage point of the bare rock spur - a smaller version of Masada, Jacob had remarked. It had been superb, with the sun setting in a blaze of glory over Nîmes to the west. They had stood and watched, silenced by the splendour of the sight until eventually Jacob had said quietly, 'The fool has said in his heart, "There is no God".' And they had nodded an assent which was something deeper than anything they could verbalise and they had felt grateful that no one had trivialised the experience. Subsequently Jacob had remarked, 'That came for free, the rest doesn't - but don't worry the hospitality tonight is on the company!' Lewis' protestations had been met by a firm refusal and Jacob's comment that the Swiss Franc was in its customary good health. Lewis knew that, for once, Jacob was being slightly less than accurate.

'Well Peter, I congratulate you on your catch. She's a fine looking young woman and she has a good mind to match her figure. Above all I like her as a person, she has an openness about her, she is interested in other people and not afraid to let her opinions be known, though not in an aggressive way. Well I like her in every way.'

'Thanks Jacob. She arrived out of the blue, a customer introduced her to me after Vera was killed and she's been a wonderful find although, in a way, there's still a touch of mystery about her.'

'Paula was not at all happy at the beginning of the week about entertaining the pair of you - she is still in touch with Ruth of course - and felt that the two of you should get back together. But once she had met Elizabeth she relented somewhat and you can see how well they have got on this evening. She's noticed that Elizabeth has had a beneficial effect on you. Before she came along you were beginning to look just a little bit, dare I say it, woebegone - sorry perhaps I shouldn't have said that - but now she's put a real spring into your step.'

Lewis smiled, 'Of course you can say so! You're an old friend and you're right in what you've said, Elizabeth *has* put new life into me. She's put new life into the business as well you know. Our sales last month were just over 50% up on August last year - that's because she's taken over quite a lot of the more routine jobs I did and released me to get out and find more business. I'm grateful for that. Also, to tell the truth, she does them rather better than I did'

'Well, Peter, just make sure you do not lose her or it

would be a double blow to your business and your emotions.'

The return of Paula and Elizabeth brought their topic of conversation to a close and the four of them left the restaurant to make the short journey back to Avignon by taxi.

Later that evening Elizabeth and Peter stood at the open window of their hotel bedroom in Avignon. The evening warmth lingered on and enveloped them as they looked down on the waters of the Rhône moving quietly below. They had been silent for some time, simply enjoying being together and remembering a very satisfying evening with the best of food, wine and company. On their way back to the hotel they had lingered by the *Palais des Papes*, watching a display of folk-dancing. With the ancient palace as a backdrop they had enjoyed the sound of drums and flutes. There had been a sense of time standing still while the dancers performed courtly dances from the remote past.

Peter took Elizabeth's hands in his and stood gazing at her. She looked ravishing in the long silk night-dress that he had bought for her in Harrods just before their departure for the conference. He remembered her protest about the price and his reply that a very special person was entitled to something a little out of the ordinary. He was glad that he had bought it, the light pink suited her and she looked wonderful. He drew her to himself, holding her close and feeling the warmth of her body as she eagerly pressed herself against him. Her hair against his face and the aroma of her perfume worked their magic and he felt as though he were treading on air. Elizabeth responded to Peter's gentle firmness. She remembered that he had been somewhat diffident in his relations with her until he had felt sure that she really was willing. From then on he had shown his delight in her and exhibited great gentleness and a concern that she should enjoy their intimacy to the full and that nothing he did should spoil the experience for her. She had never known such concern from a lover, in fact she had been shown very little tenderness by the men that she had slept with, men who had been concerned with maximising their own sensations and pleasure. Their only interest in her response had been to seek reassurance that they were good in bed. She had been part of their ego trip and she had, with few exceptions, despised them. Here she was in the arms of a slightly introverted Englishman and for the first time in her life she was really happy.

To her surprise and Peter's she began to cry. She had tried to hold back the tears and failed. 'Elizabeth, what's wrong? Have I done something to upset you? You're not unwell are you?'

'No, Peter, nothing of that kind at all. ... It's just that ... I'm so happy, happier than I've ever been in the whole of my life. *You've* made me happy, you're so caring, gentle and loving. I'm just being silly but I worry about losing you and all that you've come to mean to me. Tell me that you'll always, ... always love me and want me.' She tried to smile through her tears, 'Sorry! I'm just being a typical woman, I'm afraid, an emotional woman.'

Lewis eased her away from himself so that they could look into one another's faces, 'And I too want to have you always, Elizabeth. Always! I couldn't bear to be without you so don't worry on that score. As for emotion, I'm not afraid of the real thing. Love has to be emotional if it's genuine!' He remembered Jacob's warning, delivered earlier that evening, not to lose Elizabeth, and he pulled her close to himself once again. There they stood without a further word passing between them but each communicating with the depth of the other's being. Time passed, ten minutes or an hour - neither knew - before Peter took Elizabeth by the hand and led her to their bed. Elizabeth turned to find and apply her lipstick and then slipping off her night-dress faced Peter again. The tears had gone and her smile was radiant. 'Peter, I've been longing for this all day. We've only two nights together before you have to collect Michael at Tournon. Our stay here has been the happiest few days of my life. Come to me now I'm longing for you.'

Lewis gazed at her as she stood there in the gentle light of the bedroom's golden silk table lamps. Without embarrassment he looked at her superb body naked before him and relished the sight. Hers was a body that had benefited from regular visits to the gymnasium. She carried no excess weight and her firm breasts and buttocks delighted him. She drank in Peter's delight and stood there a little longer without a trace of wantonness before slipping into bed.

Lewis dimmed the bedroom lights and joined Elizabeth. She wondered whether to tell him that she had stopped taking the pill that month on account of its side effects but felt sure that she was in the safe period of the month. No, why trouble with such artificiality?

'Peter ... '

'Elizabeth my love ... '

They lay alongside one another. In the sexual act they had declared and strengthened their love. Each was experiencing a contentment deeper than they had ever known, feeling gratitude to the other and satisfaction in the delight that had been given and received. Elizabeth reflected on their relationship. Sex was important but she realised with pleasure that it was only one of a number of things that they shared and that had nourished that relationship. There was so much that they enjoyed doing together ... work, books, music, theatre, walking in the countryside or just being together. Neither of them knew it at the time but it would be this diversity of their common interests that would help to ensure that their relationship would survive over the years, though in a considerably different form from the one they had in mind as they lay contentedly together, half awake and half asleep, in Avignon.

***

Eugene waited for a reply from the Paris number that he had rung. His patience, which was never his strong point, was wearing rather thin and he was relieved when he got through and heard a breathless, 'Hello!' at the other end. Another person who didn't know how to answer the telephone was his reaction. 'To whom am I speaking please?' he asked.

'C'est Jean Le Grand à l'appareil,' came the response followed by the telephone number.

'Good, it's Eugene here in London. Have you received your instructions?'

'Oui, it is all in order I will travel to Tournon tomorrow to treat the boy. I will stay until I am satisfied that things are as they should be. Rest assured that I will keep you in the picture at every stage. An early TGV from the *Gare de Lyon* will get me to their hotel in time for lunch. You have no need to worry, the matter is in good hands and I will do all that I have been asked, though I cannot be responsible for the parents' emotional outcome, whether the prediction of the psychological profile people is correct

only time will tell.'

'Thanks, have a good journey.'

'Bon nuit, Eugene.'

Eugene put the telephone down. *'Bon nuit,'* he muttered to himself, 'What sort of a night would it be for him? It was now nearly a year since he had slept with Elizabeth and the more time that passed the more frustrated he became. It wasn't that he couldn't get sex. He had had quite a lot recently and at quite considerable expense. It was Elizabeth he wanted but she didn't want him. She had fallen for this Englishman, how Eugene hated him for it. Well they would see what Pierre could achieve! He picked up his coat and made for the door of his apartment, he would see if he had the same ease in picking up a girl for the night in one of the clubs in West End Lane or in Kilburn. He slammed the door, oblivious of his neighbours, and set off into the London night.

Chapter 12

Tuesday 10th September 1996

The next morning Lewis and Elizabeth rose early, showered and went down to the dining room for an early breakfast before it became too busy. The weather was magnificent and before they ate they stood outside the hotel entrance relishing the cool morning air and the warmth of the sun on their faces. The day was full of promise and life was good, very good indeed. Over orange juice, croissants and coffee they discussed the day's programme.

'Apart from loading the van with our exhibits from the convention stand we have a free day. Would you like to spend it by the sea, Elizabeth?'

She took his hand in hers and smiled. 'What a good idea Peter! I've never seen the Mediterranean and it would be just great to be together for the day. The weather out there is wonderful and we can soak up the sun for a few hours.' She squeezed his hand, 'I love you Peter. Let's go upstairs now, we can have some time by ourselves before we have to go out to clear the equipment - that won't take more than an hour to deal with.'

Lewis squeezed her hand in reply, 'That's the best idea of the day so far! Let's go!'

They had done a considerable amount of work on packing up their equipment late the previous afternoon so the van was quickly loaded. By 10.30 they were on the road to the coast with a CD of Bizet's *L'Arlésienne Suite* in the player - Elizabeth had brought a selection of music that was appropriate to their location.

'Coffee in Tarascon, lunch in Aigues-Mortes - it's an old walled town and the place from which St Louis left for the Crusades - and then La Grande Motte for the afternoon. It so happens that a friend owns a penthouse there and asked me to drop in and see what I thought of it, so if that's OK by you, Elizabeth, we'll have a look.'

'Of course it's OK by me! Whatever you want to do is OK - I just want to be with you.' She reached across and placed her hand on his thigh.

'Have a care Elizabeth! I need to have all my concentration for the road we don't want to end up in the ditch do we?'

She laughed, 'I love you Peter but I will restrain myself for the common good and our survival. Take my mind off what I would like to be doing and tell me about what we're going to see. You know the area from holidays here don't you? ... No don't be embarrassed! Our relationship doesn't mean that you've got to behave as though there were no past, I want to hear about these places.' As she said it she was aware that Peter was going to want to know more of her own background and she wondered when she would ever be able to tell him the whole truth about herself. If only she could come clean now and tell him all about the past, who she really was. That would have to wait until the Basel operation was over and she had severed her links with the SVR. She would have to do all she could to make sure that the operation did not harm Peter or get him into difficulties with the Swiss authorities. It hurt her to have to continue with Peter her life of deceit and lies and for a while it cast a shadow over the day, though his company would gradually dispel it.

'OK we'll start with Tarascon which is our first port of call and which we should reach in the next five minutes.

As you can see it's on the Rhône and ... look there's the château, the castle! The river forms part of its moat. There's a legend about a dragon that came out of the river and devoured children and cattle but was eventually tamed by some obscure lady saint ... they have an annual carnival with a vast model of the dragon. Clearly lady saints are kinder to dragons than St George was! Still I mustn't speak ill of our English patron saint! What do you see yourself as Elizabeth? Canadian or English?'

An interesting question for her to ponder. Just where was she from? To whom or what did she owe allegiance? She wasn't sure, although in reality it was neither of the countries he had named. 'Oh, I feel that I come from all over the place. The world is pretty small these days isn't it.' Her reply had the virtue of honesty and avoided problems. If he pressed her on her past and she had no alternative, then she would have to spin the usual story of deceit but it would be without any enthusiasm and she would come clean with Peter as soon as she possibly could. They arrived in Tarascon, found parking at the Boulevard Gambetta, and set off to have a coffee before taking a quick look at the château.

***

Pierre Le Grand reached the *Hôtel du Roi* in Tournon-sur-Rhône at around 2.30 in the afternoon, having taken the TGV from Paris to Lyon where he had picked up a hire-car. He had eaten lunch on the way, there being little point in hurrying as he was unlikely to encounter Ruth and Michael before the evening. He settled himself into his room, which he had been pleased to discover was conveniently next to that of the 'American woman with the English boy' of whom he had been told when he asked about the Volvo Estate with GB plates next to which he had parked. He was fastidious in his organisation and carefully unpacked his suitcase, hanging up suits, a sports coat and several shirts and ties before stowing underwear and various other items in the drawers of the dressing table. The suitcase was then parked neatly alongside the substantial wardrobe. He viewed the room with satisfaction: all was in order and that pleased him. His methodical and tidy ways, acquired from his years in pharmacies and darkrooms, had spilled over into the rest of his life. His wife found his extreme tidiness rather trying and both of them were glad when the occasional assignment took him out of Paris and gave them a break from one another.

Pierre enjoyed his food and wine, never more so than when the cost was being paid by someone else. He was determined that the assignment should be carried out effectively so that he would continue to get similar work from his Russian friends. He was also determined to enjoy the local cuisine to the full, not that he was a great eater if you went by quantity but he did enjoy quality.

He opened a drawer, taking from it a toilet bag. He unzipped the bag and took out a small phial of clear liquid and a device, rather like a child's joke ring that squirts water. He looked at them carefully and placed them in his jacket pocket. The phial had come from a pathology laboratory where his brother worked, the virus it contained should, if all went according to plan, do no more than seriously incapacitate the child for a few days and produce symptoms which would alarm the parents, while doing no long term harm to the child. He had a number of devices like the ring which he used for administering a variety of substances, these and a *leger de main* that would not have disgraced a professional conjurer were his stock in trade. He liked to be sure of the true identity of what he administered and was unhappy if his Russian friends tried to supply him with the materials to be used. Only once had he killed anybody - that was a long way from France and he had been satisfied that the killing was justified. Now his task was to dose the child and report back on the effect the virus was having on him before leaving Tournon. His contact at the Embassy had told him that the purpose of the action was to bring the child's estranged parents together. He knew that there must be a better reason than that and was sure that the Russians were not in the welfare business - still the fee was good and he was therefore happy to oblige.

He would have liked to have brought his mistress with him but knew that he couldn't have any distraction while he was dealing with Michael. Still, she would be joining him in a few days and they would have a week together on the Riviera. The pharmacy would be in his wife's safe hands: she was not to know how long this assignment, or consultancy as he called it to her, would take. The thought of a whole week with Dominique, a librarian in the next Paris *arrondissement* to his, excited him, 'The sooner this job is complete and out of the way the better - anyway it's got me away from Marguerite for a while so I'm not complaining!' He looked out of the bedroom window and saw with pleasure that the sun was still shining. 'OK a walk by the river, a look at the town and back here in good time to see whether I can encounter the boy before dinner.'

On his return to the *Hôtel du Roi* Pierre found a seat in the bar from which he could see the reception area and settled down with a glass of Pernod and a small bottle of Perrier Water. He opened the sports magazine that he had bought while he was out and began to read a profile of FC Marseille - he had a fantasy about owning the club and taking it to the heights of success in Europe, with enough francs he reckoned *he* could do it without falling foul of the law.

He glanced at his watch, it was just after 6.00 p.m. and through the window he saw a woman getting a motoring atlas from the British registered Volvo Estate. He ordered another Pernod and as he returned to his seat the woman and a boy came into the bar and sat a couple of tables away from him. He caught the woman's eye, nodded and said, *'Bon soir'* to the pair of them. They both smiled but it was the boy who returned the greeting with a rather nasal English accent. Pierre resumed reading the magazine while continuing to observe the pair discretely. They tallied with his briefing, the woman in her late thirties or early forties and the boy around twelve. The woman ordered a Coke and a *Noilly Prat* with lemonade.

'Well Michael, it seems that the train won't be running again after tomorrow until the weekend so you'll have to ask your father to take you on it. He'll be here the day after next and I expect that he'll be happy to delay the journey to Switzerland for a couple of days. If I know him he'll enjoy it as much as you will, so you won't have to work too hard to persuade him.' The woman's accent was American but Pierre noted that the vowels had been toned down, evidently by some years in England.

'I'd like to have both of you with me on the train, Mum. It was good when we did things together.'

'Yes, Michael there were good times but, you know, sometimes the good times don't last and then you've got to move on. Even if Dad and I haven't got one another *you've* got both of us and it will always remain that way for you. You're not by any means the only one in your school class whose parents aren't together are you?'

'No. Most of us are in that boat but that doesn't make it any easier, I wish that the two of you were still together. I don't want Dad with this Elizabeth, why has she taken him from you?'

'Michael, do be careful what you say to your father about Elizabeth. He's very fond of her and I have to admit that she's been a tonic for him - there's more life in him now than there's been for quite a few years, you've remarked about that yourself. No, Elizabeth didn't take him away from me. We somehow both slipped away from one another, perhaps we were just too busy and we had drifted too far by the time we noticed. We're still fond of one another, you know, and we've never rowed have we?'

'Never. I don't understand adults and I'm not sure what I'll be like when I'm one. Teenage will be bad enough, I'd like to hibernate through it, Mum!'

'It won't be an easy time for you but we'll both be around to help.' She put her arm round the boy and gave him a hug.

Pierre folded his magazine and stood up. Now was the time to act, they were the only ones in the bar and the barman was nowhere to be seen. He made his way towards the exit and as he passed their table he dropped a handful of cash on the floor. 'Pardon Madame, perhaps you and your son could assist me, I have a knee which troubles me and I have been rather careless.'

'Sure!' the woman replied, 'Come on Michael, give the gentleman a hand!'

While they went to work Pierre placed his magazine on their table and deftly squirted the viral solution into Michael's glass of Coke. Pierre took the coins from Michael and Ruth thanking them profusely and insisting that Michael should have a 10 franc coin for another drink. Then with a slight limp he made his way out of the bar. He was pleased that the child had been drinking Coke as he reckoned that it would cover the flavour of most things short of carbolic. He was also pleased that he would have done the boy a good turn if his action brought his parents back together. He thought of Dominique, the English could learn a thing or two from the French - having a mistress was a good way of keeping your family together! He was enjoying his trip - business, pleasure and kindness combined, that was pretty good. Now to wait to ensure that the dose did the trick.

***

Late in the afternoon Lewis and Elizabeth neared La Grande Motte on the Mediterranean coast. The pyramid shaped buildings came into view and Elizabeth expressed her surprise, 'Wow it's like something the other side of the Pond isn't it!'

'I believe that the French for it would be *'ultra moderne'*. It's quite a place and to think that not many years ago it was nothing more than a swamp! The French have the style and the confidence to bring it off. We'll have a look around the place and then find my friend's penthouse and check it out. He just wants me to see that everything is OK. Perhaps we could borrow it from him next Spring for a few days, see what you think of it and of the town. Is there anything you would like to do?'

'If we'd brought our swimming things we could have gone in the sea, it seems warm enough.'

'No problem, what the lady wishes she shall have! There'll be boutiques selling swimwear and towels so let's equip ourselves and start with a dip. After that we can find some refreshment and look around generally.'

They parked next to the yacht marina and within a few minutes equipped themselves for the sea. Even though the boutique advertised end of season reductions Elizabeth's bikini was far from cheap but Peter had insisted that he liked the fabric and colour and that it would suit her well. He decided that he would have shorts of the same shade of turquoise and the next boutique had a pretty close match.

'You shouldn't have spent all that Peter, it's only for one dip in the Med after all.'

'If we come back here in the Spring you can get more use out of it, my friend's apartment block has an indoor pool that we could use. So, if we decide to come here again, it will all be in the interests of economy! I do wonder though what the cost of that bikini is per square centimetre.'

They laughed and linking hands set off for the beach where they found a secure deposit for their valuables and then a changing tent. 'And in case it's in your mind Peter, not here, please!'

'That's a shame. Still we've got another twenty four hours together before you take the van and yourself back to Boulogne.'

'I don't look my best with wet hair, I'm afraid.' Elizabeth smiled at Peter across the table as they sat at a pavement cafe.

'You look magnificent my dear. The outdoor life obviously suits you and your vitality shows through whatever you are doing.' He reached forward and ran his hands down her cheeks, 'Elizabeth, I'm so much in love with you!'

'Peter, I feel just the same,' she whispered and held both his hands, kissing them in turn. They didn't feel conspicuous, after all they were in France!

They were silent for a while as they watched the other customers and the passers by. No one hurried - they were all enjoying the autumn warmth and were reluctant to take themselves indoors.

'Peter, do you see that woman over there?' He followed her gaze to where a woman in her seventies was sitting on her own with a coffee and two portions of gateau. She was immaculately turned out, with her blue tinted hair beautifully coiffed. She wore a pale green suit which had evidently come from a Paris fashion house and discrete but expensive jewellery.

'Hungry or greedy, I suppose.'

'No look again Peter! The second helping of gateau is for her poodle ... quick, she's feeding it now!'

Lewis looked and smiled, 'You're right, so it is!'

Elizabeth's face was suddenly very serious, 'God forbid that I should ever get like that,' she whispered. It was as though a cloud had passed over, changing the whole feel of the afternoon.

'You've got to be realistic. Most women end up as widows or on their own. Women live longer than men and, let's be honest, I'm nine years older than you. What's sad about people like that woman is that sometimes they have so little left in the way of human relationships that they have to give their affection to pampered poodles. Now if she had children and grandchildren living near ... '

Elizabeth took his hand and held it firmly, 'I want to give you a child that we can both love and I promise to love Michael as well.' The cloud had passed swiftly and Lewis saw that there was a tranquillity and radiance about her. A gentle smile played round her mouth.

They held hands until the waiter enquired if they wished for anything else and Lewis asked for *l'addition*. He took her hand again and said quietly, 'All in good time Elizabeth, take care for the time being ... but I think that I like your idea as well.'

At the *Syndicat d'Initiative* they obtained a street map and then drove to the block where Lewis' friend's penthouse was situated. Elizabeth washed and dried her hair while they were there and then they stood on the roof garden and looked down over the town with its varied and strangely shaped buildings. In the West another spectacular sunset was reaching a climax. They held one another very gently enjoying the stillness and one another.

Lewis broke the silence, 'We can eat here or back in Avignon. What would you like?'

'My vote is for us to stay here but I don't want you to drink and drive. What about spending the night here and returning to Avignon to have breakfast and clear our things from the hotel room - we can call them and let them know that we won't be back tonight. '

'Fine by me. How about the Vietnamese Restaurant we saw near the marina?'

'So long as the *tête* is not offensive - I mean the *chef* must be inoffensive!'

Elizabeth smiled at his bewilderment, 'Sorry to be so obscure Peter, the Tet Offensive was a successful North

Vietnamese campaign against the Americans in 1968 that led to LBJ not seeking another term in office.' She had smiled, but at the same time she asked herself in puzzlement why she had produced such a contrived joke – was she subconsciously trying to emphasise an American background so as to cloak her Russian origins without actually lying? She would have to be more circumspect in future: in good time she would come clean to Peter about her identity. What a relief that would be!

'Yes ... I do remember it, I would have been sixteen then and into anti-Vietnam War and CND activities. It seems a long way off - in another world even. We expected to change things and where are we now? I'm part of a set-up that I wanted to challenge but which I joined, like most of my friends in fact. The truth is that you easily become very comfortable with what society has to offer, it must be a bit like a drug - maybe fun at first but then addictive. It would be hard to give up all one's comforts even if the very survival of other people depended on it. My business or your apartment for instance. There's not much hope of the next generation breaking out of the mould. I'm sorry for Michael and his contemporaries. They're under more pressure than ever before to perform, to get top exam results at school and then at least a 2.1 at a 'good' university if they stand much hope of a half-way decent job. It's strange, you see me - I expect - as a very well ordered conservative member of society but there are times when I think I would cheer if the whole thing collapsed and we had to start again. Except that I would dread the danger, discomfort and violence. I'm a romantic revolutionary, I like the theory but would run a mile from the reality. Nonetheless it's sad when you know that your fine ideals and hopes have all gone down the drain.' He paused and looked at Elizabeth who had let him talk on without interruption.

She looked thoughtful and took her time to reply, 'Yes youth has hopes, usually unrealistic ones, and they generally don't come to much. There are some people who do break out of the mould and continue to care for the whole of humanity and actually do something worth while. Then there are the rest of us who still care but for a smaller circle of people than we had in mind when we were younger. But don't forget that it's often harder to care for the people we know than for vast numbers with whom we have no real contact. A lot of people think the world of you Peter as a boss, a business colleague and as a father ... ' She paused wondering if her reply had taken a wrong turn.

'And what about me as a husband? No, it's all right, I'm not thinking of myself in relation to Ruth or at any rate not directly. But why should *you* trust me when you come on the scene at the end of my failed marriage?'

'Because I do, Peter. Marriage is like any other relationship - it may or may not succeed - the trouble is that failure is likely to be much more painful than with other relationships. But that doesn't mean that you can't start again and succeed. I trust you, Peter and I love you. Now 'let us turn to more joyful things' - a rough translation from Schiller's 'Ode to Joy', you know, as used by Beethoven - I'll play the Ninth Symphony to you when you get back to London.'

'Thanks, I'm enjoying my musical education. The next time it's being performed in London we'll go to hear it. Now off we go and eat, being in the open air has made me hungry.'

***

At the *Hôtel du Roi* in Tournon Ruth put down her book on the bedside cabinet, 'Michael it's gone eleven and time you were asleep and not reading.'

'Just another quarter of an hour, Mum. Gandalf the Grey is at the siege of Gondor and I must know what happens.'

'OK but we've got a busy day tomorrow and I need your help for visiting the *négociants*, you're my assistant don't forget. These men would make mincemeat of a mere woman but you can keep them in their place Michael.'

Ten minutes later he closed his book making sure that the marker was in place. 'Thanks Mum, Rohan's coming to Gandolf's rescue. It's going to be OK!'

Ruth looked down at him and smiled, 'I envy you all your imagination and excitement. But don't let it spoil your sleep.' She bent down to kiss him, 'God bless and sleep well Michael.' She tidied his bed clothes and returned to her bed. She had enjoyed being on holiday with him and sharing his youthful enthusiasms. In two days time Peter would take over and she would be free to complete her visit to the wine producers and *négociants* along the Rhône. She was surprised to notice that her enthusiasm for business had waned a little in the last few months and that she was not so keen to get out and meet the suppliers as in earlier years. She must be getting a bit stale, perhaps it was time to send her promising younger employees out on some of these visits, there were several with real ability, a discriminating palate and good business sense. And she knew that she would use the extra freedom to spend more time with Michael. She only hoped that Peter would continue to spend time with their son. He gave him plenty attention at the moment but, with Elizabeth sharing so much of his life, would his concern for Michael continue? 'God bless us all,' she said to herself and switched out the light.

***

In the room next door Pierre had made some telephone calls. He had explained to his wife that the work would take him rather longer than anticipated and that he might be away for another ten days. She hadn't sounded concerned and had assured him that she was fully capable of running the pharmacy on her own and that he should give the job all the time it needed. He wondered whether she had found herself a lover and started pondering who it might be. The idea did not please him.

The message to Dominique was different: he hoped to be free by the day after next and he was longing to have her with him. The thought of his mistress was a salve that soothed his concern over his wife. He hoped that the virus would act swiftly so that he could report the next day that Michael was adequately indisposed. Then he would be on his way to the Riviera to join Dominique.

***

La Grande Motte was bathed in moonlight as they looked down from the roof garden of the penthouse and took in the view. The Mediterranean waves reflected the silver of the moon and they could see the lights of boats moving off shore. Elizabeth turned to face him placing her hands on his shoulders, 'Peter have you ever wished that time would stand still and that *now* would last for ever? No I'm not looking for an answer, it's just that it's how I feel at the moment and I've never felt it before ... or at any rate never as intensely as I do now.'

Lewis knew that he would be unable to match the depth of this expression of her feelings. He held her gently, enjoying once again the warm softness of her body and the fragrance of her perfume, 'Elizabeth you've just put into words the way I'm feeling ... '

Chapter 13

Wednesday 11th September 1996

Overnight a blustery wind had arisen and the fine weather of the previous days had fled before it. Rain pattered on the panes of the *Hôtel du Roi's* windows as Ruth awoke from a satisfying sleep. She had not let thoughts about her business or her fears over Peter and Michael disturb her rest. She had always been good at switching off, in her student days she had been calm before examinations while her friends were getting hyped up. It was not something that she had worked on, it was just the nature she had been born with and she was grateful for it.

She looked at the digital clock on the TV - 07.35 - good, she would have a long soak in the bath and get Michael up at around eight. She ran the bath, adding some Blue Grass lotion and hung her beige night-gown on the back of the bathroom door. Before the mirror misted up she looked at the reflection of her body and smiled. She looked pretty good for forty two. She would make sure that she kept herself looking that way.

She was beginning to think about her future after the divorce and, although she was in no hurry, she knew that she would not want to remain on her own. The acquaintance of an old friend from university days, himself recently divorced and working for a publisher, had been renewed. They had met for meals and had allowed one another the occasional kiss and intimacies that didn't go much further, a sort of mutual therapy. She felt pretty sure that there was no long term future in the relationship, it was unlikely to develop beyond friendship but that itself was an undervalued commodity, and she looked forward to their meetings. She must send him a postcard before she left Tournon. It would be far from easy to get Peter out of her memory and, as she was beginning to find, out of her emotions. She loved Michael for himself and also as a link with Peter. 'Well that's life! And I'll just have to see how things turn out. Bitterness isn't a luxury, it's a curse,' she told herself and lay back in the bath enjoying the fragrant foam. She decided to wear her light grey suit with the skirt to the knee and a wine coloured silk blouse. She would look and feel her best for today's meetings with her suppliers, the French responded positively to an elegant woman and she liked that.

A little after eight she returned to the bedroom to find Michael sitting on the side of his bed looking rather unwell. 'Mum, I feel a bit off. Could you get me something to drink, I don't want anything to eat at the moment. I know we've got a busy day ahead, I'll be all right - I want to be there to help you.'

Ruth felt his forehead, he didn't seem to be running a temperature. 'I'll see how you are once I've had breakfast. If we have to postpone our visits it will do no harm. Wash and dress and I'll bring you some fruit juice for breakfast. If I know you, Michael you'll bounce back quickly enough.'

Ruth dressed and went down to the dining room. She nodded to the Frenchman whom she had met in the bar the previous day. He nodded back, half rising from his seat and then returned to reading his paper. He had been there for over half an hour to ensure that he did not miss seeing Ruth. She ordered coffee and bread for herself and a large glass of orange juice to take back to Michael. A few minutes later Pierre Le Grand rose from the table and paused as he passed Ruth, 'Not such good weather today Madame but the summer is almost past. The young man has decided that he prefers his bed to feasting?'

'No, Monsieur, he's feeling a little below par at the moment but I don't think that he'll let it spoil his day.'

'Well give him my best wishes for a good day. Children are very resilient, I am sure that it is nothing serious, Madame.'

***

Pierre returned to his room and telephoned Eugene: all seemed to be going according to plan and he would update him in the evening. He decided to spend the day in the area. The morning could be taken up with a journey southwards down the Rhône to Cornas and St-Péray, he would call at some of the vineyards and sample the wine, then after lunch he would cross the Rhône and head back northwards to Romans on the Isère river. Dominique had given him Le Roy Ladurie's book on the events of February 1580 in that town, during a lull in the Wars of Religion, when the Mardi Gras Carnival had been marked by chaos and bloodshed. The hatred between the nobility and the commoners, who were enraged at the exemption of the aristocracy from the taxes that the lower strata of society found so burdensome, had spilled over into violence and murder. Probably the place was now nothing like it had been four hundred years before, but he liked visiting such towns and re-creating events in his mind. His father had been a small shop keeper and a member of Pierre Poujade's anti-tax party and so he was doubly interested in these events which had been, in their way, a foretaste of the Revolution of 1789.

All this brought Dominique back into his thoughts, not that she was ever far from them: she was his teacher as much as his mistress, keeping his mind fed with a succession of interesting and stimulating books that she had read and which they discussed even during their lovemaking, at any rate during their less energetic moments. He told himself that without her he would be brain dead and emotionally shrivelled. He was grateful for the rainstorm that had led to her accepting the offer of a shared umbrella from the library to the Metro station one Thursday night in November five years before. Was it really that long ago? It didn't seem more than a couple of years since that evening.

***

Ruth found a livelier Michael on her return to the bedroom. He had washed, dressed and made his bed, so she knew that he couldn't be very much off colour.

'You can manage some bread with the orange juice, I hope? You must have some ballast on board or you'll keel over in the breeze! It's a bit draughty and wet out there you know.'

'OK Mum I'm feeling brighter now. My legs ache a bit but, apart from that, I'm fit for our outing to see your *négociants.*'

Ruth smiled, 'That gentleman who dropped the money last night asked how you were and said that he thought you were pretty resilient, it looks as if he's dead right. When you're ready we'll get under way, we haven't far to go, just across the river to Tain l'Hermitage. Wear your sports coat, you're out to impress the people we meet. There are a couple producers of Hermitage and Crozes-Hermitage to visit but first, if the rain stops, we'll climb to the top of the Hermitage Hill - you know the one you can see across the river - I want to see what the grapes there are like at the moment to get an idea of what to expect from this year's vintage. It's 9.30 now. If we hurry up the hill we'll see your steam train getting on its way this side of the river, it's a pity that it doesn't run every day at the end of the season - don't forget to bring the binoculars when we leave the car. We can look out for birds as well.'

'Well Michael it is always a pleasure to see your mother and to do business with her. She is not like the other English dealers that we see which, of course, is because she is American!' the Frenchman laughed heartily, 'Our countries helped each other with our revolutions and so we have things in common. We both removed a King and we both have a President.'

'We've got a Queen and can do without a President. Anyway Mum's a bit of a royalist! And I certainly am!' Michael looked serious but he then smiled and added, 'But as I'm only half English you can take it that I'm only half insulted.' He shook the Frenchman's hand to signify that there was no ill will. He knew that the French were a people of many handshakes and kisses and he fought shy of the kisses, particularly from men.

'A glass of wine before you go, Madame? *Bon* ... and for Michael? Too young? *Jamais*, never! If he is to cultivate a discriminating palate he must start early on. Not a lot of course, and he needn't swallow it, though it's a waste not to do so!'

'When did your son first drink your wine, Alain?'

'He was ... *peut-être* ... eight. And now he has a truly excellent palate, so I was right to start him early. You know of Prince Guy de Polignac, the head of the Pommery Champagne House, Madame? Well, his reply when he was asked about the age to start drinking Champagne was, "It should wet a baby's lips at christening, and one should drink a glass before dying. In between - that is up to you." ' Ruth joined in his laughter, the bargaining over the price for the next delivery had been pretty fierce but both of them were satisfied with the outcome. The badinage was Alain's way of relaxing after a good business session.

'OK if Michael would like a little I've no objection. Would you like to try some, Michael?'

He nodded, 'Please, but tell me what to look for - or rather what to taste for, if that's the right way of putting it - I need to learn if I'm going to help in Mum's business.'

Alain poured wine into three glasses and Michael imitated the actions of Alain and his mother, viewing the colour, smelling the bouquet and swilling the wine around his mouth.

'Bien, Michael what do you think?' The boy was silent. 'No that's not a fair question,' Alain continued, 'I would say that it's a full bodied mellow wine with the taste of red berries that lingers for some while after you have swallowed the liquid. But your English people who write about wine would probably tell you that there was the taste of old bonfires and the like. They often have better imaginations than palates. Do you not agree Madame Lewis?'

'Just so, Alain. But people read them, often people who have no confidence in their own judgement, and that helps to sell wine which is what we both want.'

He nodded, '*D'accord*. You are right about that! But it is better if they enjoy it because they can appreciate it, rather than because someone says they should.'

They bade one another farewell as Alain loaded a case of 1983 Hermitage into the car. 'A gift for a special customer! You will find that there are included two bottles of 1961 Côte-Rôtie from our vineyards further north. I am pleased to mark our ten years of doing good business together. He bowed in a formal manner and kissed Ruth on both cheeks. 'And don't let the young man drink it all before you return to London! Keep the Côte-Rôtie for a special occasion, a real celebration.'

As they drove off Ruth asked, 'Well what did you think of Alain's wine?'

Michael screwed up his nose, 'To be honest Mum, I prefer Coke.'

'Good for you. That's best for the time being! Now back to Tournon.'

Ruth noticed that he was rather quiet and asked how he was feeling.

'Not as good as when we were on the top of the Hermitage Hill. I feel a bit hot and I don't think that it's the wine.'

'OK Michael what I suggest is a light lunch and then you can lie down on your bed for the afternoon while I deal with the paperwork from our visits. After that we will see how you are. You might like to spend the afternoon finding out what Gandalf does after the siege of ... where was it? Ah yes, Gondor ... after he had dealt with who was it?'

'The Black Captain, that's the Lord of the Nazgûl.'

'He sounds nasty Michael ... and what about his troops?'

'Wild men, mountain-trolls and orcs ... '

She laughed, 'Oh Those Awful Orcs! It was the title of a book I think.'

'They're not funny Mum! You wouldn't like to meet an orc! It's a super book, don't laugh at it!'

'No I won't. It's good that you're enjoying it and letting it exercise your imagination. It's better for you by far than endless video games and TV!'

***

Elizabeth and Lewis returned to the hotel in Avignon for breakfast and booked out at around 10.00 a.m. They would have eight hours together before Elizabeth and the van left for Boulogne on the car train. Neither of them welcomed the parting but it would only be for ten days and both of them would be fully occupied, Elizabeth with the day to day running of the business and the aftermath of the Avignon exposition and Peter on holiday with Michael in the Swiss mountains.

'We'll head for Fontaine-de-Vaucluse, you'll like it if the guide book is to be trusted and it's only about half an hour away. You mustn't miss the train this evening.'

Elizabeth groaned, 'Don't remind me of it, Peter. It's been such a wonderful time here.'

They were quiet for a while as Peter navigated them eastwards out of Avignon. Peter broke the silence, 'What about some of your music Elizabeth? Something suited to the occasion.'

'Well, let's see.' She reached for a CD. 'How about this? Its the Bach Concerto for Two Violins, the outer movements are fine and lively and the slow one in the middle has the violins weaving their melody around one another, it's one of the loveliest things I know. I hope that you like it, but say if you don't - you haven't *got* to like it. A few years ago one of the best music critics admitted that he didn't like Bach, he said that Bach was like a blind spot so far as he was concerned. Of course, I think he was a very unlucky critic!'

They listened without talking for the rest of the journey, the music captivating them both. The concerto finished and Elizabeth stopped the player, 'We don't want to start another piece after that. It was so lovely, I could feel that you liked it Peter.'

'Yes it was very moving. Beauty often has a touch of sadness doesn't it, a feel of autumn about it. Who were the violinists? They seemed to play well together, to interact if that's the right expression.'

'David and Igor Oistrakh, father and son.' She paused and added, 'They were Russians and Russians can bring a lot of feeling to their music. It's a country that's suffered a lot for many reasons and it sometimes shows in its artists.' She found it strange to speak of her Motherland as though she were an outsider. It felt even stranger when the comments were addressed to the man she loved more than any other that she had known. Oh to be free of all these constraints and be completely open with him!

They entered the village as the light rain stopped and parked the van.

'Café cognac, Elizabeth?'

'When in France do as the French do! Why not? Lets look for a café or a bar.'

In the Place de la Colonne Lewis struggled with the inscription on the tall stone column and succeeded in establishing that it commemorated the birth of the poet Petrarch in 1304. 'Do you know anything about him Elizabeth because I don't?'

'The name is familiar ... Let me see ... I've come across it somewhere to do with music, not by him of course, but about him I should think. Can we find a guide book in English and see what it has to say?'

'Lets do that first and then find our café.'

They sat at a table inside a small bar as the earlier rain had made the tables and chairs on the outside patio sopping wet. The village had that end of season feel but it was pleasant not to be among crowds. One of the tourist shops had been able to produce a small guide in English. It was a little faded and dog eared and the proprietor had apologised and sold it to them at half price. Peter placed it on the table and both of them read the account of the poet.

'So he was Italian, the Father of Humanism, and was a member of the Pope's court in Avignon.'

'The details that a man would think important! At the age of twenty three he fell in love with Laura but she was married ... '

'And virtuous!' Lewis added.

'And virtuous ... so he worshipped her from afar and she was the inspiration of many of his best poems including sonnets that he wrote to her.'

The waiter brought the two *cafés cognac* to them, 'You have been here before? No? You will like our valley and the Sorgue, our river, I think. You have been to its source? No. *Eh bien*, it is only a walk of a quarter of an hour and it is very beautiful. I see that you are reading about Petrarch. Well I do not appreciate Latin or Italian poetry but I do appreciate the visitors he brings! You are most welcome and if you need to eat later on I will give you a good *dejeuner*, a good ... lunch. The menu is on the blackboard at the end of the bar. You are fortunate to come this week as we close next week until the spring.'

They thanked him and, as he went to attend to another customer, Elizabeth continued.

'Ten years after meeting her he came to this village and when he had been here for eleven years Laura died of the plague in Avignon, then he ended up near Padua where he died at the age of seventy. Those are the facts or so the booklet says. I'm not sure whether to say it's sad and stupid or very romantic and moving. Do you think that she knew and just played him along? No, he wouldn't have loved her for all that time and been inspired by her if she had been like that would he?'

'No, I think you're right. They played it by the rules that they followed and left a moving story and poetry that would be worth reading. We'll have to try to find a translation of Petrarch's Sonnets when we get back to England.'

'I've got it or rather you have given me it! I know where I have heard of him before! Liszt wrote some piano pieces that had as their title something like 'On Hearing a Sonnet of Petrarch.' She smiled with unaffected pleasure, 'I don't like to have something that gets stuck in my memory and can't be retrieved. It's a bit like having information lost in a computer system. The brain's better than any computer though, it's creative and I find it amazing how, when you sit thinking quietly, one idea leads to another in a subtle way. I suppose it's because I'm a woman but I find computers pretty dehumanised, even though they've become essential and I've got no doubts about their usefulness. That's a long way from Petrarch though!'

'I'm glad you're a woman and glad you have some time for computers. Given that combination you fit well into the life and love – not *loves* you'll be relieved to hear - of Peter Lewis! Well if Petrarch was the Father of Humanism you're still on target. The computer might give some sort of translation of his sonnets into English but to write about Laura, that needs someone of flesh and blood and feeling. Lets pay for our drinks and then see the river and its source, the booklet's got something about that too but we can read that later.'

They set off hand in hand upstream along the bank of the river. The water flowed gently by, a light turquoise colour and crystal clear. Higher up the valley sides the wind was moving the trees but down by the river it was almost tranquil. There was the occasional bird call but, apart from that, there was only the sound of water and of the gentle breeze that reached the bottom of the valley. The sun had broken through a couple of minutes after they had left the bar as though it was specially for their enjoyment.

They stopped to read the guide book. 'If we want to see the river at its best we'll have to come in the winter, Elizabeth. It's hard to believe it but the flow then is thirty times greater than it is now. Still we're seeing it in warm sunshine and it's certainly beautiful. I can understand why Petrarch chose to live here for twenty years, or whatever it was, especially if his untouchable beauty was in Avignon!' He drew Elizabeth to him. 'We can share the enjoyment of the valley together. We're very lucky.'

They were quiet together and the gentle sound of the water lapping on the bank soothed the tensions that were beginning to build within them both at the prospect of spending the next ten days apart. Elizabeth opened her eyes and looked over Peter's shoulder at the river as the sun flickered on its surface. Had Laura ever seen this valley she wondered? What did virtuous mean today? Was she, Elizabeth, virtuous? She knew that she wanted to be with Peter for ever. Was he virtuous? His marriage had failed, but that was nothing unusual and he was a good father to Michael. How she wanted a child by him, how she would love it for its own sake and for Peter's. She felt a tear in her eye. She didn't want to be emotional, going their separate ways in the evening would be hard enough without tears, even though they were mainly of happiness.

'OK Peter let's have a look at the source of this thing. After that the castle ruins and then lunch after which ... '

'After which it will be back to Avignon to load onto the car train at four for your six o'clock departure I'm afraid.' He kissed her softly, 'Don't worry it will only be for ten days. We'll both be fully occupied but I'll be speaking to you every day on the telephone. Absence makes the heart grow fonder', they say.

'Mine couldn't be any fonder Peter.'

'Nor could mine for you Elizabeth. Lets be grateful.' Grateful, yes, for Elizabeth without any doubt or any reserve. But how was he to view the events that had brought about their relationship? Two very different women in his life had been replaced by one. He thought of the gradual winding down of his marriage to Ruth, of their eventual separation and their steps towards divorce - that would take a while to get through now with the changed divorce law and its emphasis on children and reconciliation, they ought to have got things under way sooner. Life was full of deadlines unfortunately. Then there was Vera's death or was it murder? - the police had had suspicions but it had never got beyond that. How strange that something as grim as that had paved the way for Elizabeth to come into his life.

'You're quiet Peter, is anything wrong?'

'No. It was just that the thought came that poor Vera's death was what brought us together. I still think of having to identify her body to the police and I sweat at the memory. Then I think of her husband and their son and I could weep for them. If only they had been able to get the yob who did it, drunk or on drugs I expect!'

'Let's hope that they get him!' She had already made clear to Eugene how much she detested him and the others for murdering Vera and it hurt to think that she was part of their set up, it made her feel unclean and far from virtuous.

They set off for the deep pool from which the Sorgue emerges and tried to imagine the vast winter flow gushing up in front of the rock wall and reaching the level of the fig trees growing in the rock above the cave mouth. Then they turned on their tracks and headed back for the castle and for lunch.

***

Ruth looked up from the table where she was attending to her paperwork from the morning's visits to the vineyards. Michael had read for just a few minutes and then said his legs ached a bit and that he would prefer to rest for a while. She had told him that it was the best idea and that he would probably sleep it off. He was now sleeping somewhat fitfully on his bed. Ruth went over and felt his forehead, he might be running a temperature but it was nothing extreme. She went back to her work. Another hour and she had finished and packed all the papers in her briefcase. Tomorrow Peter would collect Michael and she would have another couple of days in the area visiting more producers and *négociants* before returning to London. She was looking forward to a few days in Paris with a cousin who taught American Studies in the University before heading on up the Autoroute to Calais and taking *Le Shuttle* through the Channel Tunnel. The week with Michael had been a good time for them both. He would be a few days late in getting back to school but she had been persuasive with the Head, pointing out that Michael would benefit from using his French skills while on his separate holidays with herself and Peter. The Head, she knew, had recently divorced his wife after years of their living separate lives and Ruth had wondered whether his willingness to accede to her request was due to his interest in her. If so she had not been flattered: she did not like him and regarded him as a dull but efficient pedagogue.

Michael had become more restless and she decided to wake him and see how he felt. He took a while to surface.

'I don't feel at all well Mum. Can you get me some water to drink, please?'

She felt his forehead again. There was no doubt now, he was running a temperature, that was definite. She poured a glass of Perrier Water for him. 'OK Michael, sit up and have a drink - it should help.' She assisted him to sit up and he drank some of the water.

'Can I lie down again Mum it hurts when I try to move my head ... my neck is stiff.'

'It looks as if we're going to need the doctor to make sure that it's nothing serious. I'll go down to reception and have a word with the girl there. You'll be OK by yourself for the next few minutes won't you, Michael?'

'Course I will Mum!'

The receptionist was the proprietor's daughter Paulette, an attractive young woman in her mid-twenties who was pleased to have something positive to do and break the monotony of a quiet afternoon at the end of the tourist season. Ruth explained the situation and enquired about the nearest surgery. She replied that her fiancé Jacques had recently moved from Paris and joined the local surgery. She would call him at once and arrange an appointment. She dialled his number, explained the situation and then passed the receiver to Ruth who repeated the details of Michael's symptoms. 'It will be better if I come to you Madame. I think that we should not disturb your son without the necessity. I will be with you within fifteen minutes, I hope.'

Ruth turned to the receptionist, 'It's very kind of him to come here.'

'He thought it might be serious and that he should not delay.' She saw Ruth's face and added, 'He's always on the careful side and I expect that it's nothing worse than a chill or *la grippe* ... how do you say it? *Ah oui* ... the influenza. But can I get you a drink of some kind, Madame?'

'That's kind. I may be an American but a good cup of tea would go down a treat!'

'You go back to your son ... Michael, I think you said? Good, go back to him and I will have the tea sent up to you as quickly as we can.'

***

Pierre had enjoyed his day by himself. He had eaten well and drunk rather more than half a bottle of a good full bodied 1985 Châteauneuf-du-Pape, as well as sampling some St-Péray earlier in the day. The visit to Romans had been pleasant and he had enjoyed a walk along the bank of the Isère river. Now he would cross back over the Rhône to Tournon and see how the boy was. If the dose had been effective he would be able to report success to that *salaud* in London and then be off to join Dominique later that evening. It must have been while his mind was occupied by thoughts of Dominique that he failed to notice a tractor pulling out of a side road. He skidded on the wet surface and hit the tractor. That was the last that he remembered before he came to in an ambulance taking him southwards, parallel to the Rhône, to the *Centre Hôpitalier de Valence*.

Fractured legs and pelvis meant that he was to spend a couple of months in Valence on traction. He eventually succeeding in getting word to Dominique, who had returned from the Riviera to Paris in a temper, thinking that he had dumped her. She visited him each weekend. Immobilised on a hospital bed - it was for him both a pleasure and a torment to see her. On her first visit his wife encountered the other visitor and informed Pierre that evidently her visits were not needed and thereafter she stayed in Paris.

The magistrate who later heard the drunken driving charge had little sympathy for Pierre, who had hobbled into court on crutches. He took away his driving licence for two years and fined him 5,000 francs. There had also been some difficulty with the police who had collected his belongings from his hotel room in Tournon. They had been interested in the miscellany of equipment for administering drugs in the washbag. Although they could not pin anything on him they kept him under surveillance from then on, hoping to use him as a lead to drug dealers or similar slimy creatures lurking under the stones of urban society.

Eugene was furious that he had heard nothing from Pierre on the night of the accident. It was a couple of days before Elizabeth informed him of Michael's indisposition. He did not tell her of the source of the infection. There had been enough trouble with her over the removal of that woman Vera. Besides, Elizabeth should not be made aware that he was taking steps to get Lewis away from her and back into his wife's arms.

***

The young doctor from the surgery arrived at the *Hôtel du Roi* within twelve minutes according to Ruth's reckoning and this confirmed her suspicion that there might be something seriously wrong with Michael. He introduced himself as Docteur Jacques Blanc greeting her with a formality that suggested the manners of a more gracious era. Yet he had a warmth and humanity about him which, in her experience, were lacking in many of his profession. He carried out a very thorough examination and questioned both Ruth and the boy. After a few moments of thought he had made up his mind. He took Ruth to the other side of the room and spoke quietly to her. 'I cannot be sure at the moment Madame Lewis but there is the possibility that your son may be suffering from ... *la méningite* ... in England you call it? ... Ah yes, meningitis. You must not worry, with speedy treatment it can be cured and there are a variety of forms of the disease, some very much less severe than the others.'

'And some much more severe?' Ruth responded.

'*Ah oui*, but I think that we have caught it early and Madame, we are optimists are we not?. You are to stay with your son and make sure that he is comfortable while I telephone the *clinique* from the office and arrange for your son's admission. You have insurance for this? Good. The *Polyclinique Ambroise Paré* is an excellent establishment and you both will be well cared for there. Now if you will excuse me I will attend to the necessary arrangements. You are not to worry, I believe that we are in good time but we must not waste any of it.'

'What did he say Mum.' Michael's voice sounded sleepy.

'He's not sure what you've got but he is going to have you taken to the local clinic for them to check.'

'Please come with me Mum!'

'Oh Michael, of course I'm coming with you!'

There was a knock on the door and Paulette the receptionist entered. 'A glass of Cognac for you Madame with the compliments of the Hôtel. You may have a long night ahead and it will do you good.'

Ruth nodded her thanks, 'Your kindness is much appreciated. It was very kind of you to get him here so quickly. You have chosen your fiancé well. I liked Jacques and trusted him immediately.' She fought back her tears and took a sip of the Cognac. 'And this isn't any ordinary Cognac is it?'

'It's Courvoisier XO Imperial that we keep for ourselves and our special friends. That is how we regard you, Madame Lewis. You like our area and our traditions and do business here. You have stayed at the *Hôtel du Roi* for how many years now? Ten years, that's some time. I'm sure that your son will be all right. Jacques and his colleagues will do everything that must be done.'

'Thank you Paulette, it's good to be with my friends here in the Ardèche. I need to telephone my husband. He's due here tomorrow to take Michael to Switzerland for the rest of his holiday. He's in Avignon at the moment so, if I can get hold of him, he'll join me at the *clinique*. Oh, we're separated but we're not at one another's throats, we're still quite fond of one another in fact.' She smiled at the younger woman, 'Just look after your fiancé and make sure you don't drift apart! Doctors can become very busy and you have to have time together to make a marriage work properly.'

Paulette left the room and Ruth found the number of the Avignon hotel from her handbag. To her annoyance Peter had booked out that morning and they didn't know where he was. 'Damn, where have he and Elizabeth gone?' she muttered beneath her breath and took another sip of the Cognac. Just when she needed Peter most, and it wasn't often that she needed him that badly, he was nowhere to be found.

She remembered that the van was booked onto the evening car train from Avignon and called Paulette to contact the railway station there for them to put out a message to Peter. A few minutes Paulette called back - the car train had left twenty minutes before and she had persuaded them to put out a message for Peter Lewis on the PA system in French and English but it was unlikely that he was still there.

So Ruth's long night began and she was on her own.

***

Peter left the railway station at Avignon just after the departure of the 6.00 p.m. car train. He booked into a small hotel near the station so that he wouldn't have far to go to catch the train the next morning for his journey to Tain l'Hermitage. Also this hotel was considerably cheaper than the convention hotel and, with only himself to think about, he didn't see the point in wasting money. All he required was a bed for what would be a short night. He would be rising early the next day.

It hadn't been easy sending Elizabeth on her way back to London but they were only going to be apart for ten days and both of them would be busy. They had waited for an hour before loading began and had listened to the Bach Double Concerto again, this time without the distraction of traffic. It had soothed and calmed. He was amazed at Elizabeth's ability to find music to match the mood and on occasion to transform it.

He wandered around the town centre of Avignon and chose a restaurant for dinner. It was only 6.35 p.m. and he decided on a drink before eating. It was still warm, the rain clouds had gone and the sky was clear. There wouldn't be many more days that year when it would be possible to sit out of doors and enjoy it. He parked himself at a table outside a bar in the *Place de l'Horloge* and ordered a *Cardinal*, that seemed appropriate in the City of the Popes! It occurred to him that he ought to call Ruth to confirm the next day's arrangements but then found that his mobile wasn't in his pocket. He must have left it in the van. He thought of finding a public telephone and dismissed the idea, a couple of days before they'd discussed his arrival in Tournon, so there was no real point in repeating what had already been settled. Then he took a paperback history of France from his jacket pocket and looked in the index for references to Jean Jaurès whose name had adorned the road from the railway station. Far more than England, France seemed to be a country awash with history and culture, the street names were testimony to this. He engrossed himself in the book, unaware of the distress of Michael and Ruth. His mind though did turn at times to Elizabeth on her journey northwards by train.

Chapter 14

Wednesday 11th September 1996 (continued)

Ruth put down the telephone, reception had called to tell her that the ambulance had arrived and that the crew were on their way up to the room. She sat on the edge of Michael's bed and looked down on him in his pyjamas and dressing gown. He now seemed rather less disturbed than he had been earlier. She had packed a case with toilet gear for the two of them and a change of clothing for herself as she had no idea when she would be able to return from the clinic. Comfortable clothes were in order and she had changed from her Jaeger suit into a pair of navy blue trousers, a plain red jumper and a navy blazer so that she could keep their valuables in her pockets. She attempted a mental check on the things she had packed, wondering what would be needed that she had omitted.

Her thoughts were interrupted by a loud knock on the door. *'Entrez,'* she called and the ambulance men came in. Their presence somehow underlined the seriousness of Michael's condition. There was a moment's silence and she noticed rain on their uniforms, Michael's raincoat would be needed and she went to get it. However they assembled a stretcher and indicated that the coat would not be required. Gently they lifted Michael onto the stretcher and carried him out of the room and down the stairway. Ruth was glad that it wasn't steep and that they had no difficulty in manoeuvring the stretcher down the stairs. She followed them with the case. At reception Paulette was waiting and Ruth was glad to see her. She accompanied Ruth to the ambulance. The wind had built up again and it was blowing light rain before it.

Paulette gave Ruth a package, 'I expect that they will

feed you at the *Polyclinique* but here is a *picnic* in case you have any problems. If there is *anything* you need, then telephone us, it does not matter whether it is in the day or in the night, and we will see to it right away. Jacques will also make sure that you are properly looked after. As soon as your husband arrives I will bring him to you by car.' She paused, 'God bless you both, Ruth.' Further words stuck in her throat and the two women embraced as the driver indicated that he was ready for Ruth to get into the ambulance. So, in the gathering gloom of an unusually early dusk, they set off for the clinic. If only Peter were with her! If he were aware of what was happening he would be there like a shot. She knew that - but it did not stop her feeling angry at his absence.

Ruth had little recollection of their arrival at the *Polyclinique* beyond showing someone their travel insurance policy, a journey in a lift and being taken to a room on the left hand side of the corridor. The ambulance men carefully transferred Michael to the bed and a nurse removed his dressing gown. She indicated to Ruth that she should make herself comfortable and informed her that Docteur Renaud would be there very soon. Ruth hung her raincoat in the wardrobe and put the suitcase there for the time being, no doubt she would have all the time she needed, and a lot more besides, to unpack it. She moved the chair to the side of the bed and took Michael's hand in hers, 'Well Michael we're at the clinic so that they can check if anything is wrong.' She stopped, there was no point in pretending that he wasn't ill. 'They'll do tests and make you better, Michael.' Dear God what wouldn't she give to be sure that he would get better! Michael replied drowsily, 'I want to be better Mum. Don't leave me alone please ... and get Dad.'

'Of course I won't leave you. Dad's coming tomorrow morning as soon as he knows you're here. I tried to find him but he's changed hotels. He'd be here now if he knew how you were feeling, Michael.'

'I know, Mum, then we'll all be together. That will help. I want us all to be together.' The boy was quiet. Ruth looked at her son, flushed and uncomfortable and obviously very unwell. Oh to be able to show him the strength of her love for him. Oh to be able to give him the strength to fight the meningitis or whatever had afflicted him. Some damned germ she supposed. Some tiny thing that you couldn't see with the naked eye. Some tiny thing and it changes all your plans and turns life upside down. She squeezed his hand, 'Fight it Michael, for yourself, for your Dad and for me!'

Ruth looked around her and took in more of her surroundings. The room was designed to soothe with its light beige walls and pleasant furniture. Good, there was a WC en-suite with a bidet and a washbasin - she wouldn't have to go far from Michael.

A middle aged man came into the room accompanied by a nurse. Ruth rose to meet him. *'Bonsoir Madame Lewis. Je m'appele Docteur Renaud. Et ici votre fils ... Michael, n'est-ce pas? Nous lui donnerons notre meilleurs attentions.'* He commenced a thorough examination of the boy with the assistance of the young female nurse. Ruth sat in the corner of the room and watched. First of all she took Michael's temperature, giving it to the doctor and recording it on paper. After that she took a blood sample. Then they tested his neck movements and noted his considerable discomfort. Next they took to raising each leg in the air with the knee bent and then straightening it. The nurse held Michael's head steady while the doctor peered into his eyes through a telescope-like instrument. Ruth watched their faces and read concern in them. Michael's condition looked serious to Ruth as a mother and their medical response to his symptoms certainly appeared to confirm it.

It was at this point that Docteur Jacques Blanc arrived. He greeted Ruth and then became involved in conversation with the other doctor. They spoke quickly and quietly and Ruth, whose French was adequate for business and for travelling, was unable to follow very fully though she did hear the other doctor say, ' ... *malheureusement c'est probablement la méningite ...* '

Docteur Jacques explained the situation and their proposed action to Ruth. His initial diagnosis appeared to be correct, although they could not be sure until they had taken a sample of fluid and had it tested by the local laboratory. This would be done right away and Ruth's permission was required. It involved a lumbar puncture to remove fluid from the space around the spinal cord and although it would look awful with an eight centimetre needle, it would not be dangerous for the child. While the results were awaited they would proceed on the assumption that it was a form of meningitis and commence injections of a strong antibiotic.

The consent form was sent for and he quickly did his best at translating it to her. She looked at him and he nodded. She signed - what else could she do? She was glad that he had come to the clinic, she trusted him and that helped in what had suddenly become a very foreign country. The men of Babel had a lot to answer for she decided. Events were beginning to assume a nightmarish quality, she just hoped that Jacques and his colleague were in time to treat the illness successfully.

Jacques seemed to read her mind, 'I have every reason to believe that we have got your son here in good time and that we will be completely successful in restoring him to full ... *santé* ... to full health, Madame Lewis.'

The nurse returned to the room with what was evidently the needle for the lumbar puncture. Ruth shuddered when she saw it. They had moved Michael onto his left side with his knees as near to his chin as they could manage and his head down. The doctor gave Michael a local anaesthetic. Ruth saw Michael suddenly move, though the nurse was holding him firmly, and she winced. She flinched as the nurse handed the lunbar puncture needle to Docteur Renaud and she looked away. When she forced herself to return her gaze to Michael's back she saw a clear fluid being collected in a small bottle. She dug her nails into the palms of her hands. The nurse held Michael in his curled up position for what seemed an age but was only about ten minutes, as Ruth found when she looked at her watch. The collection of the fluid complete, the doctor removed the needle and the nurse applied a large patch of elastoplast to Michael's back. She moved Michael onto his back and told him that he had to stay in that position for the next twelve hours to avoid a headache. Drinks would have to be taken through a straw and the lights would need to be kept dim as his eyes were beginning to hurt, she instructed. Ruth wiped her brow and closed her eyes. Thank God that was over but now there would be the wait for the results. She felt that they were in good hands and something was being done about Michael's condition, that was a relief.

Docteur Jacques took the bottle with the spinal fluid and had a word with Ruth. He would deliver the sample to the laboratory who were ready to deal with it immediately. In a couple of hours there would be a provisional result, as they would have done a cell count and checked on protein and sugar, but the definitive result would not be available for 24 to 48 hours. Only then would they know for sure whether Michael had meningococcal meningitis or the less serious viral form. However he reminded her that it would be necessary to proceed with treatment on the assumption that Michael was suffering from the more severe malady. This would require a series of injections of antibiotics - they would do no harm if they weren't in fact necessary and would be vital if it were the severe form.

Ruth looked up at him, 'I'm grateful for your care and concern for us. It's so kind.'

He smiled in reply, 'When I was a child I had my appendix removed in a German hospital while I was on an exchange visit to a German family. I know how it feels to be away from home and in unfamiliar surroundings when things do not go well. Also it is a pleasure to help a friend of Paulette's family. But now I must not stay, the sample must go to the laboratory without delay. I hope to see you again in ... *peut-être* ... an hour and a half. Do try not to worry. Paulette will call later on to see how you are.'

The nurse gave Michael an injection of antibiotics and indicated to Ruth the bell pull if she needed attention. Ruth and Michael were on their own. She sat by the bed and looked at her son. He seemed calm for the moment. She leaned forward and felt his brow, it was still very hot but they were giving him treatment. Again she told herself that he was in good hands. They had shown anxiety but their calm and confident approach reassured her. Docteur Jacques had told her that he believed they were in time, those words were full of hope for her. But then what if he was wrong or if he had only said it to keep her calm? No, she knew that she could trust him and that he wouldn't build up false hopes. He hadn't hidden his diagnosis from her, had he? Waves of alarm and relief swept over her. She must control her emotions or at any rate ensure that they didn't get out of hand. She would keep her mind occupied and that should help.

Ruth went to the wardrobe to get a magazine from her suitcase. She noticed the *picnic* parcel that Paulette had given her when she left the hotel. That would keep her occupied for a while and she suddenly realised that she was ravenously hungry. She moved the adjustable table to the chair and lowered it until the height was correct. She unpacked the meal. They had done her proud - smoked salmon for the starter, followed by a roast beef salad (no *vache folle* she hoped) and a carefully packed *tartelette* of summer fruits. There was a full set of cutlery and two small bottles of wine, one of them Champagne and the other a red Crozes-Hermitage, with two wine glasses to go with them. Two linen napkins had also been packed and a handwipe. The hotel's attention to detail was admirable. She was well provided for and she was grateful to Paulette for her thoughtfulness. Ruth ate with an enjoyment that surprised her.

She felt more comfortable after the food, better prepared for the long night ahead and the wine had lifted her spirits. ' ... wine that maketh glad the heart of man, and oil to make his face shine, and bread which strengtheneth man's heart.' She was pleased at her memory and the aptness of the words of the Psalmist. There was pleasure in the continuity of human experience. What someone had said, perhaps two thousand five hundred years ago, still rang true and that pleased her. Despite everything life went on over the years, over the centuries, indeed over the millennia. How she desired her life to go on in Michael. She knew that she had not wanted further children after the trauma of Michael's birth. Now it was too late, the change had come early for her and now, whether she wanted it or not, child bearing was a thing of the past. She was aware of a sense of vulnerability that had not until now been so strong. Now she was beginning to understand Peter's feelings and his wish for more children. It was typical of him that, once she had convinced him that it was not on, he had left the matter alone and not raised it again. She wondered whether this was one of the causes of the failure of their marriage and whether this might be one of the attractions of Elizabeth for him. Another child would be likely to make him feel more secure and it was more than likely that Elizabeth would want a child by him.

Ruth heard Michael groan and attempt to roll onto his side. She got up and stopped the movement, 'Stay still Michael and lie on your back, that way you'll feel better.' She took his hand, 'Fight it Michael, you're going to pull through!' She was aware of tears in her eyes and fought to keep them away. Her son was quiet again and she resumed her seat, clearing away her dinner. Time to use the en suite facilities, have a wash and redo her make-up. This would help to boost her morale. She took ten minutes to complete her toilette and she sprayed her neck with a light eau de parfume, it didn't seem appropriate to wear a heavy scent in a sick room. The bottle was nearly empty, she would need to get some more when she could, to be without perfume in France was like being badly dressed. The door into Michael's room was open and she heard someone enter. Paulette stood by the bed looking down at the child with concern on her face, 'How is he, Ruth? He seems quiet at the moment I think.'

'Yes he is quiet. I only hope that it's a good sign and not a bad one. Jacques should be back with the result of the tests in about half an hour and I'm beginning to get jumpy. It will only be a preliminary result - the full results will take one day or even two - but the preliminary indications may bring some relief to the anxiety.'

'I'll stay with you if that is OK until Jacques has brought the results and then I will return at midnight to sit with you.'

'No Paulette, there's no need for that. You've got a day's work ahead of you tomorrow. I have nothing else that I can do or would want to do but remain here. Besides tomorrow Peter will be here and that will help a lot.'

'Unless you order me to stay away I will be here for the night. In that way we can be sure that one of us will be awake to look after Michael. And I am having a day off work tomorrow.'

Ruth smiled, 'Of course I won't order you to stay away. I'll be very grateful for your company. Incidentally the *picnic* was most enjoyable and it has done me a lot of good. Tell me how you met Jacques and about your plans for marriage. That word seems to be out of fashion at the moment doesn't it, presumably that's so in France as well as elsewhere?' They rang the nurse for another chair and, keeping Michael under scrutiny, they began to converse as though they had known one another for years.

At five minutes to nine Docteur Jacques returned with the preliminary results that the laboratory had telephoned to his apartment. He showed signs of relief and greeted them both with the good news that the preliminary indications were that Michael had the less serious form of the ailment. This would not be confirmed for possibly two days, but certainly no more than that. Ruth felt her heart sink at the prospect.

'No, Madame Lewis, be encouraged. I am very hopeful. We continue the treatment for the time being just to be safe and there is one more check that we should now make.' He was joined by Docteur Renaud and after some discussion they explained that it would be necessary to discount the remote possibility of TB meningitis and that an X-ray would be necessary. The normal sugar level indicated by the tests made it unlikely but the possibility had to be eliminated.

The nurse was despatched to make arrangements and five minutes later a portable X-ray machine of considerable bulk whirred down the corridor and into the room. The young lady radiographer was wearing a spotless white dress with a blue plastic badge at hip height and a plastic covered lead apron. She was evidently an acquaintance of Paulette and they exchanged greetings. Ruth stood back to watch as she placed an X-ray plate about a foot square under Michael's chest and instructed them all to stand well clear. Then she reversed the machine out of the room and it whirred off down the corridor. Within five minutes she was back with the X-ray in an envelope with a variety of names that had been crossed out on the front. Docteur Reynaud took the plate out of the envelope and went out into the corridor to try to get enough light to view it. He returned muttering, the light was inadequate - would the radiographer bring a viewing box, please. Within a couple of minutes she had returned with the box and plugged it in. The two doctors stood and looked carefully at the plate. Ruth and Paulette waited anxiously, catching the comment ' ... *il n'y a pas une miliaire*.' They turned to the two women and Jacques smiled, 'He is clear on that score. That is certainly good.' The women embraced with relief at the news. 'I'll be back around midnight, in fact I'll bring Paulette with me to keep you company through the night. In the meantime Docteur Renaud will look in from time to time and so will the nurse.' He turned to the nurse and asked her to settle Michael down again. She took his pulse and temperature, noted the chart and told the doctor that they were still high. They took their leave of Ruth and she settled down in the comfort of her chair but not before she had felt Michael's brow and wiped it with his face flannel to remove the sweat.

Ruth opened a copy of *Homes and Gardens* and tried to read but she found that her concentration was not up to the task, she was reading sequences of words without absorbing anything, besides there was little light to read by. For a while she took to leafing through the pages of the magazine looking at the advertisements and the illustrations. How difficult to distract yourself when your mind and emotions are burdened with concern for a loved one! Michael lay there in the dimly lit room and Ruth sat beside him willing him to fight whatever was the cause of the illness and to recover. She tried the television as a distraction, turning down the sound so as not to disturb Michael or other patients. She wanted some image to watch that would hold her attention or at any rate part of that attention. All she found was chat shows and game shows. With a sigh she turned it off, that was no help. It had reminded her of an Alan Sillitoe short story about a family getting their first 'telly' and the kids sitting with the sound off watching - perhaps it was Party Politicians, she couldn't remember - and thinking that they looked like fish in a tank of water. The family in the story had bought the TV from the proceeds of an insurance policy when the father died, she did not wish to dwell on that aspect! Her thoughts were interrupted when a nurse looked in to check that Michael was comfortable. Did Ruth want a drink? She chided Ruth mildly for bringing the *picnic*, did she think that they would fail to look after her at the *Polyclinique*? Ruth explained how she had been given the meal by Paulette and the nurse smiled and apologised. A few minutes later she returned with a hot milk drink and a small packet of biscuits.

Ruth was once again alone with Michael and her thoughts. She looked at her watch, 10.25 p.m. - Paulette would be joining her in an hour and a half, she would be glad of her company. How should she spend the time, reading was out and TV had nothing to offer. Why not draw on her memories not of books but of life, Michael's life. She looked at him, flushed but calm. She was discovering how much he meant to her! Well start at the beginning with courtship and marriage to Peter. She remembered their wedding day with it's excitement and anxiety, despite all the preparation she had only been five minutes late at the church. It came back to her with the vividness of yesterday, the walk down the aisle and the way that Peter's smile as he turned to greet her had taken away all her apprehension. From that point she had been able to relax - free to be herself for the rest of the day - that was the effect that he had had on her in those years. Her mind moved on to their honeymoon on a tiny Greek island, whose name she couldn't remember, but that didn't matter. She could picture the small village *taverna* full of the villagers where they had eaten each evening. That was the place where they had been welcomed on their second evening with a glass of Ouzo which a hungry and thirsty Peter, unaware of its strength, had downed in a couple of gulps and almost ended up on the floor.

She smiled to herself, life had been fun then even though they hadn't been well off. Never poor, she recollected, but having to be careful with their money and grateful for the furniture and curtains that family and friends had given them for their one bedroomed flat in West Hampstead. She took herself on a tour of the flat - now the estate agent would call it an apartment she supposed, strange on coming from the USA she had had to unlearn the word and now twenty years on she had had to relearn it! She felt again the pleasure that she had known at turning it into their home and entertaining friends from university. She pictured herself standing looking proudly at the dinner table set with woven place mats from John Lewis in Oxford Street and candles ready to be lit when they all sat down to eat. The cutlery, she remembered, had come from a newspaper offer and she still had some of it in her kitchen. It had been a stage on their way up in life, away from the frugality and austerity of student days when she had shared a run down house in Paddington with a mixed bunch of fellow students with varied ideas of tidiness and hygiene.

Ruth stood up and looked down on Michael, she felt his brow. It was still very hot. Would he recover? The newspapers regularly reported the occurrence of outbreaks of meningitis and it took its toll of young life. She felt cold despite the warmth of the room. Would Michael get better or be another victim of this illness? Would he recover completely or would he be always beset with some disability as a grim reminder what had overtaken him at the age of thirteen? She sat down and remembered the confidence that Jacques had given her, he was the expert and she would trust his judgement until the outcome was known.

She thought back to her pregnancy knowing that she had tried to avoid this memory. No, she would work her way through Michael's life and her emotions without editing it. She must face up to it and to try to see how her marriage had gradually come apart. She told herself to be honest and to tell it as it was. There had been morning sickness from an early stage of her pregnancy and it had lasted for longer than the doctor had expected. There had been the humiliation of being sick on an Underground Station on the way to work, after that she had always carried a plastic carrier bag with her. Labour had been a nightmare. She had feared that it would be like that and her worse fears had been realised. She had never been so frightened before and that was despite the antenatal course that she and Peter had attended and all the relaxation exercises she had done. She remembered with a painful immediacy her distraction routine of counting down from one hundred. The midwife had told her to shut up and let her take her pulse without all that! The midwives had been rushed off their feet by a sudden influx of women in labour that night and part of the unpleasantness of the experience had been the absence of the reassurance of a medical presence for long periods. True Peter had been with her, and she had no idea what she would have done without him, but he would have had neither the knowledge nor the stomach to deliver a child. The final stages of labour were a dark and painful scar on her mind and there was the memory of having Michael placed in her arms and feeling nothing, absolutely nothing for him. She had been totally washed out and had wanted nothing apart from the opportunity to sleep for a week or more.

Peter had been the proud father and had come the next

evening with a huge bunch of flowers for her and a teddy bear for Michael. She remembered the spring flowers and that they had not lasted long in the heat of the ward. She had shared them with some of the other women, single mothers with no one to visit them or share their experience and encourage them. They had seemed cheerful enough but one had a careworn look on her face and she had discovered that she lived in Bayswater in a tiny damp basement flat and already had two children by different fathers. She had felt sorry for the girl who appeared to be weak rather than bad and who had probably been taken advantage of by the men. She had been glad that she had Peter to care for herself and their child. He had taken them home by taxi to the flat that they had moved into a couple of months before. Their first job on taking it over had been to redecorate the third bedroom, a very small one, as the nursery. She had stood looking at it when they had finished the work, thinking that it would be complete when their child lay in its cot - Peter had said *his* cot and she had said *her* cot, Peter *of course* had been right. Peter had bought a circus mobile to hang above the cot and she had watched Peter stand back when they had placed Michael in the cot for the first time with a rapt expression on his face. For Peter it had been a kind of religious experience, or so it seemed to her - although he had never put it into those words she had been close enough to him to detect his awed response to the birth of their son. Ruth knew that her response to childbirth had been so very different. It was summed up in those two words - never again! She had known that she would have to work hard to love their child and she had felt guilty at her absence of an emotional maternal affection. She had asked herself if she was an unnatural mother and had suspected that she was not alone in feeling as she did and that it was something to which a mother would admit to no one but herself and even then unwillingly.

Two things she knew. Firstly, in those early months she had worked at loving Michael and to a degree she had succeeded. As she had felt his warmth against her breast and his dependence on her she had begun to feel a more emotional response to him, love had grown gradually and slowly but it had never been an overwhelming emotion. She had been able to share something of Peter's delight in their son. However she had had to pretend that her emotions were much stronger than they really were and that had been difficult for her as she and Peter had always been so open with one another. The second thing was that she remained resolved that so far as pregnancy and childbirth were concerned it was most definitely never again. Peter on the other hand had wanted more children or at least another child. She felt sure that this was one of the things that had come between them and eventually cooled their relationship.

Ruth became aware of a hand on her shoulder and opened her eyes to see Paulette who had come to join her for the night's vigil. 'Hello Paulette. I think that I must have dropped off.'

'You needed it and I will see that Michael is all right if you wish to get a little sleep. Jacques is here and he is satisfied that Michael is as well, as he would expect. He asked me to tell you that Michael is doing pretty well. He's coming in at 8 o'clock tomorrow morning and a paediatrician from Valence will visit Michael tomorrow. No, there do not seem to be any problems but Jacques wants to make sure that Michael is given the very best of treatment. Now rest. I will get the nurse to find me a blanket.'

Once Paulette was seated Ruth went to the wash basin and found Michael's face cloth. Once again she wiped his hot brow. She brushed her teeth and made herself comfortable for the night.

'Goodnight Paulette. I value your kindness, I really do.'

The French woman squeezed her hand, 'God bless, Ruth and try not to worry.'

Ruth returned to her journey through her museum of memories and through the long hours of the night. She did not sleep but drowsed, her consciousness was a vague patchwork of her recollections of episodes from Michael's childhood interspersed with her regular checks on his condition. She felt his hot brow and listened to his breathing which seemed faster than normal. She was aware of Paulette watching with her and she was grateful to have someone there who felt for her and her child. A nurse made visits at intervals, checking on Michael's pulse, temperature and progress: this calmed Ruth and reminded her that the clinic was doing everything it could to secure her son's recovery. She thought of Peter and longed for him to arrive and share her anxiety. He was normally very good at ensuring she knew where to contact him - and she remembered that this was more than simply habit, it was because he cared for her even though they had separated and because he cared for Michael. She was no longer angry with Peter for failing to let her know where he was staying for the night: she knew how upset he would be to discover that their son had been ill since the previous day. She knew how strong a bond there had always been between father and son. And she knew just how vulnerable Peter felt on account of the very strength of that bond and the insistent fact of human mortality. She regretted that she had only given him one child, she regretted it for his sake and for now her own. In a few hours Peter would be with her. Apart from Michael's full recovery she wanted nothing else than for Peter to be there.

How strange it was that in a few hours all your priorities could be turned upside down, slimmed down to a very basic minimum. Would it seem the same way next week, next month or next year? She knew that if Michael survived and recovered fully things would not be quite so simple as they had seemed until now but she was determined not to let her business life take over to the extent that it had in recent years. As soon as Michael began his recovery she would begin to put her thoughts on paper and to plan for her business to become less demanding of her time and energy. It would be good for the younger staff to have a chance to make their mark, even to make mistakes, though that would have to be within limits which did not sink the business. She knew that they had ability and that she would not have to be looking over their shoulders and second guessing their decisions - to *pretend* to delegate could mean that you gave yourself more work than you had before, she would avoid that trap. It would give her more time for Michael, but she knew that an adolescent boy needed more than his mother's company. He needed time with his father for proper emotional development. And the good relationship that father and son enjoyed needed to continue. At the moment they certainly had this and with Peter's attachment to his son this ought to remain the case. But she was now more worried about his relationship with Elizabeth, not from her own point of view but from Michael's. It hadn't occurred to her with such force until that evening but, supposing that Elizabeth wanted a child - and it was very likely that she and Peter would want one sooner or later - how would Peter's relationship with Michael be affected? She was wide awake and suddenly felt very cold. Even though the temperature in the room was being kept down it was not as cold as all that! 'Forget it,' she told herself, 'there will be enough time to think about that when Michael is well again.' But it was not easy to do so and the long night continued its weary way towards dawn.

Chapter 15

Thursday 12th September 1996

At around a quarter to six Lewis strolled into Avignon SNCF station. He had set his alarm for five o'clock and had yet to have breakfast - that could wait until he reached his destination. Then he would have time to spare as he was not due at Ruth's hotel to collect Michael until ten o'clock. He was travelling light, with a suitcase and an overnight bag, so the five minute stroll from his hotel had meant no exertion for him. He entered the booking hall and navigated his way between the bodies of students and other young people who were still on vacation and had camped out in their sleeping bags on the floor. No doubt they were 'doing Europe' on Inter-Rail tickets or the like. Not long ago he would have felt nostalgic and have longed for the freedom which they had and which he had enjoyed as a student. Not so now, he knew that their freedom was in most cases an illusion and that they would soon be involved in the frustrating task of starting a career and facing a pretty bleak job market with little encouragement. Job application after job application would be posted off and frequently bring not even an acknowledgement in response. Job-wise his generation had lived in a golden age. He wondered how society would hold together if there was always going to be a residue of youngsters without any prospect of real full time work.

It was not only this sense of social reality that kept him from nostalgia: his relationship with Elizabeth had brought back a youthful sense of elation. He was experiencing emotions that he had not expected to encounter in his forties and it almost seemed as though he had shed twenty years from his age. He knew he was fortunate to have the feelings of youth allied to his maturity. And it would be good to be with Michael and spend time with him in the Swiss Alps. They got on well together though he was aware that Michael did not approve of his relationship with Elizabeth. But then he knew that *he* would not have approved if *his own* father had behaved in the same way, though times and attitudes had of course changed in thirty years.

The train, the 05h55 to Lyon, stopping at all the stations northwards up the Rhône Valley, was alongside the platform and he climbed in and had the choice of any seat in the empty 2nd Class carriage. He never wasted money on frivolities like 1st Class travel if the basic facilities were adequate, especially as you stood marginally less chance of the annoyance of mobile telephones in basic accommodation. No doubt the train would find its quota of passengers as they went north. He stowed his luggage away and made himself comfortable in a window seat. He could dip into his history of France but he would probably spend most of the time enjoying the journey alongside the river. On time and without fuss, at five minutes to six, the train departed. Lewis looked out at an Avignon which was now very much more to him than a name on a map. He wondered when he and Elizabeth would be there again. She must be in Boulogne on the car train at the moment. She had said that she would spend some time there before heading for the Channel Tunnel at Calais. She expected to be home for him to telephone her at 10.00 p.m. Swiss time that evening. He hoped that she had a safe journey in the van without accident or breakdown, he would be relieved to speak to her later. It would probably be best to use a telephone downstairs in their hotel - even if he replaced the missing mobile - as he didn't want to have Michael listening in to their conversation.

The journey along the Rhône was pleasant, with the train running first on one side of the river and then on the other. Lewis watched the sun rising over the mountains to the east and felt the excitement which always took hold of him when he travelled. There were vapour trails in the sky together with wispy cloud. The rock strata showed on the limestone cliffs along sections of the river. A field of cut grass with cypress trees along one side was reminiscent of van Gogh. At Montelimar there were red roses growing on the station platform. Orchards of fruit trees swept past and there was always the river keeping the train company. They pulled out of the old train shed station at Valence at half past seven precisely and within a few minutes Lewis was ready to climb down onto the platform at Tain l'Hermitage. The train heating had been a little too warm and this accentuated the freshness of the morning after the rain of the previous night. Lewis stood there on the platform in the sun looking eastwards to the vineyards on the Hermitage Hill. It was pleasantly foreign but not outlandishly so, it was different and he could cope very well with the place and its language.

Already there was warmth in the sun. It was good to be alive and in no hurry to do anything at all. Nevertheless Lewis looked at his watch, he was not due at Ruth's hotel for at least another two hours. First he would put the cases in the Left Luggage and then have breakfast. A decent cup of French coffee would be welcome. He turned into the *Avenue Jean Jaurès* - so he was commemorated here in Tain, a success rate of two out of two suggested that there must be *avenues, rues, places* and the like with his name throughout France. Jaurès' assassination in 1914 on the eve of mobilisation must have been traumatic. He found the Bar PMU, ordered breakfast and took a seat in the corner from which he could observe the scene. There were six other customers and he was interested at the way in which some of them were beginning the day. One man was drinking a glass of red wine and two women were sitting at the bar drinking tall glasses of some bright green concoction. It was certainly more than he could face at that time of the day. Others were enjoying a more traditional breakfast. The proprietor served Lewis a large black coffee and then slipped out of the bar with a small basket and returned from the *boulangerie* with Lewis' bread and croissants. The radio played French pop music which seemed to him more tolerable than the Anglo Saxon variety. The coffee was good and the bread and croissants were fresh out of the oven. He buttered the bread and spread it with apricot jam. He felt pleased with life. More customers were arriving as he finished the croissants. He called the proprietor over and ordered another coffee so that he could while away another half hour, reading his book and watching life at the bar. It was good not to be in a hurry, to have nothing depending on whether you spent ten minutes or an hour over breakfast. He looked at the clock over the bar – a quarter to nine - he would stay for a few more minutes and then he'd have an hour to spend wandering around Tournon across the river. A few more customers drifted in and ordered a variety of beverages. Lewis carried out another headcount, there were sixteen customers including himself and most of them, like him, did not seem to be in a hurry. The radio was broadcasting a news summary as he paid and left the bar.

***

Ruth surfaced at half past six after being as nearly asleep

as she had been at any time during the night. Once again she felt Michael's brow and found that his temperature had yet to fall. She held his hand and stroked it gently, 'Come on Michael fight it!' Paulette looked up from the chair in which she had spent the night, her face expressed the unspoken question about Michael's condition.

Ruth shook her head, 'I don't know. Perhaps no better but certainly no worse and for that I'm grateful.'

A nurse arrived and took Michael's temperature and pulse. She recorded the details and returned the chart to its place above the bed. She turned to the two women, '*Sa température c'est un peu plus bas. Il fait des progrès.*' She smiled her encouragement willing them to keep their spirits up and they smiled back grateful for the encouragement. '*Merci*. Thank you.'

Michael looked at them, 'Is Dad here yet?'

'He's due in another couple of hours Darling. The nurse says that you are making progress. How do you feel Michael?'

'Hot and weak, Mum. My legs still ache. What time is it?'

'A quarter to seven. We've been here for about twelve hours now. You know Paulette from the hotel, she's been with us all night. Her fiancé is one of the doctors who's looking after you.'

'Hello Michael, I've been keeping your mother company and making sure that you do not run away!'

He detected the humour and responded, 'Dressed like this in my pyjamas I'd look like an escaped convict from the *Château d'If* and I don't think I'm fit enough to swim the Rhône!'

They exchanged glances, pleased that he was alert and able to think clearly and respond.

At seven o'clock the nurse brought them bread, croissants and coffee. For Michael there was a drink to be taken through a straw and Ruth held the bottle while he took it. The nurse returned with a colleague and while they were giving Michael a bed bath Ruth joined Paulette for their breakfast. The coffee was good and strong and sharpened Ruth's slightly fuddled consciousness. After a thorough wash she felt a good deal better. Once she was sure that Michael was really on the mend she would sleep but until then she would try to keep going and watch over him. At one time being a mother had irked her but not now: she had never loved her son with the intensity that she felt at that moment. She kissed his forehead and her tears began to flow. She tried to gulp them back but could not. Michael looked up in reproof, 'Mum don't get upset!'

'I love you Michael!'

'And I love you Mum but please don't cry.'

Ruth knew that he took after his father and never liked people being over emotional. Even when such displays were on television he had found them embarrassing. Now in early adolescence this sensitivity had increased. She hoped that he would not become so buttoned up that he would repress his emotions with all the problems that could follow. Not, please God, an Englishman of no warmth and a stiff upper lip. No doubt it was just a phase but she would have to keep an eye on his emotional development. He was certainly going to need Peter's time and company in the next few years! Her concern revived for the impact on the relationship between father and son that Peter's involvement with Elizabeth might have. She felt cold. But she cheered herself with the thought that Michael was only half English: he shared her American genes - wherever they might have originated - and her family had never been shy of expressing its emotions, though her own slow emotional engagement with Michael was certainly out of line with this. Still she felt sure that she could trust Peter not to neglect the boy, after all he had never shown any signs of doing so. She was well aware that her thoughts kept coming back to the same fears. If only Peter were already with them - still he ought to be in Tournon in less than three hours' time.

Docteur Jacques and the clinic's doctor came into the room. Jacques greeted the two women with a kiss on each cheek. Before the two doctors began their examination of the boy they studied the record chart and conversed quietly. Then they began a thorough physical examination, once more raising each leg into the air with knee bent and then straightening it. They followed this with a thorough examination of the boy's eyes, then once more they conversed quietly, looking again at the previous evening's chest X-ray.

Jacques turned to Ruth and Paulette, 'Michael is no worse and perhaps a little better. I am still hopeful that it is not TB meningitis and, if that is so, we can be thankful. As you know the first indication from the spinal fluid tests was that he has the viral, and therefore less serious, form of the malady but we will have to wait for perhaps another twenty four hours or so to be completely sure about that. We have arranged for a Senior Paediatrician from the hospital at Valence to examine Michael later this morning, he is due at ten o'clock. No don't be concerned, we wish to have a second opinion and he is an expert. We will be here for his arrival.' The doctors left and the women agreed that Paulette should return to the hotel to await Peter and bring him to the *Polyclinique*. Ruth resumed her vigil - at the same time she was both hopeful and fearful, aware of contradictory thoughts and emotions running through her heart and mind.

***

Lewis crossed the wide Rhône from Tain l'Hermitage to Tournon, its twin town, by the old pedestrian suspension bridge. In mid-stream he stopped and looked back to Tain and its vineyards. He was enjoying the warmth of the sun. The hills reminded him that he would soon be in the Alps with Michael. That would be good for both of them. Michael was good company and they enjoyed their outings together. His son had all the curiosity of a bright thirteen year old wanting to know why things were as they were and not accepting that they couldn't or shouldn't be changed for the better. Lewis saw in him his own earlier self and hoped that Michael would, unlike himself, be able to retain his altruism through life and find practical expression for it. He recalled his conversation with Elizabeth on the subject. Yes, he had found affluence addictive. He enjoyed what it could buy but he also experienced occasional pangs of conscience as when he realised what the price of a good meal or a good bottle of wine would do for a family in the Third World. He salved that conscience with considerable generosity to Oxfam and with regular gifts of medical equipment to a South African mission hospital in Alexandra Township, but despite his generosity there remained a residue of guilt. Michael wanted to shake politicians by the scruff of the neck and make them see sense. Perhaps Michael's generation would succeed where others had failed, though Lewis had the realism to doubt it. It was sad that almost everyone grew out of their youthful idealism.

Lewis wandered round Tournon looking in the shops

and killing time. At a quarter to ten he arrived at the *Hôtel du Roi* and asked for Ruth. The grave faced young woman at reception enquired if he were Peter Lewis and then informed him that his son Michael was seriously ill in a local clinic. She introduced herself, called her mother to take over the reception desk and led Lewis to her car to run him to the *Polyclinique*. Gone was the sense of unhurried tranquillity that had marked the day. Lewis' heart was beating fast and he was sweating. What could she tell him about Michael's condition? Paulette did her best to calm and reassure him, 'They think that it is a less serious variety of meningitis and they are hopeful of his recovery.'

Lewis paid more attention to the dread word *meningitis* than to the rest of what Paulette had told him. He had read often enough about the dire effects of this illness, particularly on young people. Newspapers had reported a cluster of cases. Where had it been? He struggled to remember? It was of no practical importance but he wanted to remember. Ah yes, that was it - Stroud in Gloucestershire. For a moment he felt relieved that he had been able to retrieve the information from the depths of his memory. The next moment he was aware of the futility of the exercise. What had the young woman said? Was this real or was it a hoax? This wasn't a bait surely to kidnap him. No, that idea was stupid, no one would wish to kidnap *him* and in any case the woman was obviously a member of the hotel staff and French hotels were not in the kidnapping business. He realised he was frightened, not for himself but for his son and that he was responding irrationally.

'I'm sorry, could you please repeat what you've just told me. It came as a shock.'

She repeated it, adding that Ruth was well and that she

had spent the night at the *clinique* with Ruth and Michael. She was optimistic about Michael's chances of recovery.

Paulette parked the car at the side of the *Polyclinique* and they hurried into the building. A white coated receptionist greeted them with the news that the *Professeur* from Valence was with Michael and that Lewis should wait until he had finished his examination. Yes, of course she would telephone Michael's room to let Mrs Lewis know that he had arrived and to tell the *Professeur* that Lewis wished to speak to him before he left the *clinique*. The seats were arranged in a horseshoe and Lewis sat down. He found himself staring at a mark on the carpet near his feet. He remembered that Paulette was present and apologised for being bad company.

'Do not apologise Monsieur Lewis, you are shocked by the news. I understand. But remain hopeful. I will get you a coffee.' He nodded his agreement, '*Sans lait mais avec sucre, s'il vous plaît*'

Paulette went off to get the coffee and Lewis got up, he did not feel like just sitting there. He found a glass case with a number of cacti, some of them in flower. Strange things to have bright and delicate flowers! He remembered that Elizabeth had several in the apartment. Where would she be now? Boulogne he assumed until the afternoon. He started to count the number of flowers on one of the plants that was covered with a profusion of blooms. It was something to occupy his mind. Paulette touched Lewis' arm to secure his attention. She had placed two cups of coffee on a low table and so they resumed their seats. She took a miniature of Cognac from her handbag, 'You have had a shock Monsieur Lewis. This will benefit you.'

'OK. I mean yes please. I'm very grateful.' He sipped

the fortified coffee. Yes indeed he certainly needed something like this.

'And Ruth? How is she?'

'Like you she is shocked and, like any mother would be, she is frightened. She is willing Michael to recover and she is giving him the will to fight. She will be very glad to see you, she was unable to contact you last night in Avignon.' There was a hint of accusation in her voice.

'I'd mislaid my mobile and I forgot to tell her that I'd be in a different hotel.' He felt guilty and troubled. When would this *Professeur* be finished. All he wanted was to see Michael. And he found that he wanted to see Ruth more than he had done for some time. Since ... when was it? Ah, yes ... the day Vera had been killed in the mews on her way home.

The receptionist called over to them. 'They're ready for us now,' Paulette interpreted for Lewis. He did not need telling twice and was half way across the waiting area before he realised that he did not know the direction he was supposed to be going. Paulette caught up with him, 'This way, follow me.' And they set off upstairs with Paulette matching Lewis' turn of speed, for she too was anxious to hear the prognosis of the paediatrician from Valence.

As they hurried along the corridor of the first floor Lewis noticed that the doors had letters and not numbers, he wondered whether this was to avoid using the number thirteen but did not have time to continue pondering the matter as they were at their destination, He followed Paulette into Room K which appeared crowded. He noticed that the curtains were drawn and that the lights were switched off. Near the door stood three men in their thirties or forties, standing by the window was his wife and in the bed his son. He moved to the bedside and

Ruth joined him, squeezing his hand. He knelt by the bedside and placed his hand on Michael's shoulder, 'How do you feel, old chap?'

Michael opened his eyes and blinked, 'Dad ... you've come at last. We need you with us ... I'm hot, I'm weak, I ache and my eyes hurt. I just want to sleep. But you're here ... Dad's here Mum!'

'Yes Dad's here and we're both mighty glad to see him!' Lewis noted the Americanism, Ruth had Anglicised her vocabulary and usage except when she was excited of under stress. She turned to one of the doctors, 'Docteur Jacques, may I introduce my husband Peter Lewis?' Lewis shook hands with the doctor whom she had addressed and also with the other two who were introduced to him in turn by Jacques who appeared to be the one of the three with the most ability in English and who was evidently acting as their spokesman.

'Monsieur Lewis my colleague, a senior paediatrician from Valence, has examined your son and we have just had a chest X-ray taken. Your son is very ill, we ought not to hide that from you.' Lewis was aware that Ruth had again taken his hand in hers. 'Our hope is that he is reacting badly to viral meningitis and that he will make a full recovery. However there are other possibilities that we cannot discount at this stage, one of these is TB meningitis. The X-ray has not completely resolved our doubts, though we are hopeful for him, and we are therefore continuing to treat him as though it is the more serious form of the malady. This will involve regular injections and capsules. If they prove not to have been necessary no harm will have been done - if it is TB meningitis or the bacterial form then they will be essential to the survival of your son.' The doctor paused, 'Michael and your wife will be better for your presence here

Monsieur Lewis, I will be back later in the day to see how the young man is progressing and my colleague from Valence will examine him at this time tomorrow morning. And of course we are waiting for the results from the pathology laboratory which could be another 24 or 36 hours.'

Lewis nodded, momentarily he was lost for words, then he responded, 'Doctor I am most grateful ... my wife and I are both immensely grateful for all that you are doing for our son Michael.' He was aware of Ruth crying and ignoring the company he held her close and smoothed her hair, running his fingers down the nape of her neck.

The doctors took their leave and Paulette whispered to Ruth that she would be back at mid-day to see whether there was anything that she could do to help.

Ruth and Peter found themselves together with their ailing son. They were silent for a while and he tidied Michael's hair, looking down on his son. So much for all his plans. Lewis turned to Ruth, 'Do you know three hours ago I came through Valence on the train without a care in the world and my mind full of thoughts of Michael and myself in the Alps. Little did I know that my son's life would be in the hands of a paediatrician from that town! And you, Ruth, how are you?'

'Much happier now that you have surfaced, Peter! You weren't replying to your mobile and you'd changed hotel. Paulette tried to get a message to you via the station announcer at Avignon last night but it was a while after the car train had left and we didn't have much hope of contacting you. Paulette's been wonderful, her parents own the *Hôtel du Roi* and she's engaged to Docteur Jacques. She spent the night here with us.'

'She dosed me with coffee and Cognac while we waited

downstairs. I'm glad she did, my nerves were getting pretty strained. I really am sorry about last night, on the one occasion when you didn't have my address this happens and my mobile must still be in the van!'

'You're forgiven Peter. I admit I was angry about it last night but that was unreasonable of me. You're here and that's what matters.'

Lewis looked down at Michael and placed his hand gently on his shoulder. The boy opened his eyes and looked up at him, 'Promise that you'll stay Dad. You'll take us on the train won't you?'

'Don't worry Michael, I won't be leaving you. Mum will tell me about the train and we'll all go on it if we can. Now rest and use your energy to fight the bug, whatever it is!' The child closed his eyes and seemed tranquil.

Lewis and Ruth drew up a pair of arm chairs, alongside one another and facing the bed, so that they could keep their son under observation.

'What's your guess, Ruth, how badly ill is he and how did the doctors react when they examined him?'

'They're professionals, of course, and they don't give much away but what they told you seems to be what they honestly believe.'

'And you Ruth, what do you feel in your heart of hearts. What's your mother's instinct?'

She wondered if she had yet acquired a 'mother's instinct'. 'I don't want to tempt fate - No, I won't put it like that, I don't believe we're in the hands of some malevolent power! - I think he'll pull through but I'm afraid about any lasting ill effects.' She took Lewis' hand, 'You can't guess how relieved I am to have you here with us.' Lewis saw the relief written on her face.

'Once again Ruth, I'm very sorry I forgot to give you the details of last night's hotel. We were busy with the convention and it slipped my mind.' He knew that the explanation sounded hollow and that Ruth knew that he would have had most of the previous day free with Elizabeth before her departure. He flushed slightly. This did not escape Ruth's notice but she did not pursue the point.

'What's this train Michael mentioned?'

'Oh, it runs from here up into the hills. Some sort of old steam train. We've seen it here in Tournon and yesterday – my, how long ago that seems! - we saw it as we looked across the river from the vineyards on the Hermitage Hill. I told him that you could probably be persuaded to delay leaving for Switzerland for a day or two so that you could both go on it. Now it seems that we're all going to make the trip! That's no problem, business can wait. It will be pure joy to see him well and mobile again.' She dropped her voice, 'You asked me just now about my mother's instinct. Well I think that this illness has awakened a real maternal feeling. OK I've always cared for him and loved him in a sort of way but it's never been *deeply* emotional - I never felt the way you did about him, never felt your vulnerability, that is not until now.' She lowered her voice to a whisper, 'The prospect of losing him is more awful than I could ever have imagined. I've never felt such raw physical emotion as I felt last night and feel now.' She paused and looked at Lewis, 'To lose him would be to lose a large part of myself ... and of you, Peter. I understand now how you've always felt. I understand now why you've always wanted more children. It's the danger of having all your eggs in one basket, isn't it? And it's too late to do anything about it, I've no more eggs to give you another, even if you wanted another child by me.' She began to cry softly.

Lewis took her hand in his, 'You're tired Ruth. Don't

upset yourself.' She dried her eyes and they were quiet for a while, watching their stricken son who lay before them. He was flushed but, for the time being, remained tranquil.

'You can't have slept much last night Ruth, would you like to go back to the hotel to get some rest?'

'Thanks for the idea Peter but I'm not leaving here until he's on the mend! But if they can find a bed for me here in the clinic for a few hours that would be welcome.'

Lewis went off to make arrangements for Ruth and a quarter of an hour later he was by himself keeping watch over Michael. There was nothing for him to do but sit and wait. How different things had seemed twenty four hours ago when he and Elizabeth were by the river at Fontaine-de-Vaucluse.

***

Elizabeth had left the car train at Boulogne early that morning, breakfasting at a *hypermarché* where she had done some shopping, with kitchenware particularly in mind. Then she had driven up to the top of the hill, parked outside the old town, *la Ville Haute*, and walked round part of the ramparts. The excitement she had felt during her stay at Avignon with Peter remained with her. She could not remember when she had been so happy, she had had to force herself to concentrate hard on the task of driving, keeping her mind on the road. In the Basilica of Notre-Dame a choir was rehearsing and, although she was unable to follow the words, she was moved by the beauty of the sound. The music and her state of elation distracted her thoughts from her concern at the cracks in the structure which had taken her eye on entering the building. The guidebook informed her that the basilica had been rebuilt in the middle of the nineteenth century after its destruction during the revolution of 1789 - the cracks suggested that the spirit of the revolutionaries lived on! The choir finished their rehearsal and as they were packing up she checked on the work that she had just heard, writing the details on her guide book - she wouldn't lose them if they were written down there.

Now she sat in a restaurant in the old town studying the menu before ordering an early lunch. If she got to the Channel Tunnel by two thirty she ought to be clear of the terminal on the English side by ... two thirty British time, she smiled at the idea of making the journey in no time at all, it seemed an ideal arrangement! With a bit of luck she could be back in West Hampstead somewhere between five and six with time to unpack and eat before Peter telephoned at nine. She missed him already, still she didn't begrudge him time with his son. She would make sure that the time and attention that Peter gave to Michael didn't suffer on her account. She pictured the three of them out together and Michael treating her as an older sister. No that wasn't it, perhaps as an aunt that he got on well with and in whom he would confide. But would he accept her as his father's new partner or would he resent her as having stolen him from his mother? She reminded herself that the pair had separated well before she came on the scene, but would the boy see it that way? And how would he react to a half brother or half sister? Her thoughts were interrupted by the waiter and she ordered the fish soup followed by grilled sole. And to drink? Just a glass of Muscadet - she wanted to have her wits about her for the journey home on the motorways.

She sipped the wine and it sharpened and cleaned her palate. From her handbag she took a pen and a stamped post card with a view of *la Ville Haute*. It wasn't often that she wrote to her mother, and she couldn't recollect sending her a post card before, but in her state of elation she wanted to communicate with her, the woman who had given life to her. Did she love her mother she wondered? Yes, of course she did, neither of them doubted it though neither of them was effusive about their relationship. Her work helped to support her mother whose pension was pitifully small. They saw one another infrequently, in fact it was over two years since they had been together. When would they see one another again? If she went back home when this assignment was over it could be in, perhaps, six months. But would she ever go home to Russia? Almost certainly not. She had to cut clear of the SVR. Perhaps her mother would enjoy a visit to the West. It should not be too difficult to organise but there was still plenty of red tape despite the supposed political colour of her Motherland and if she were *persona non grata* with her masters they could make it very difficult for her mother to leave the country.

She pictured her mother, a woman of short sturdy peasant stock, physically very different from herself. She visualised her sitting in the small living room of her apartment in a drab block. She could see her with her Prayer Book in her hand before a statue of the Holy Virgin in the corner of the room, a statue which her two husbands in their turn had found an embarrassment. Her unyielding devotion to the Orthodox Church had not been something likely to help their careers under the Communist regime but she simply told them that she obeyed a higher authority than husband or Party. And now? She was on the winning side, or so it seemed, the Church had been there to bless Yeltsin's installation on re-election as President. She remembered that her mother had hinted once or twice that Elizabeth's grandmother had been Jewish but she had never been willing to enlarge on the matter and Elizabeth had wondered whether it was fact or her mother's imagination. She had been struck by her mother's excited reaction when Anatoli Sheransky had been released from prison and allowed to leave the USSR for Israel, so perhaps there was something in her hints of their ethnic origins. One day she would ask her about it.

Their apartment was a place of mixed memories for mother and daughter. Elizabeth recollected, with a vividness which startled her, the day when she had come home from school and been told by a waiting neighbour that her mother had been called to the hospital as her husband had been run over by a bus outside his office.

The waiter brought the soup and a plentiful supply of French bread and decent Normandy butter to go with it. A diner at a neighbouring table smiled in her direction. She returned the smile, accompanying it with a slight shake of her head and attended to her soup. It was good to have men take notice of you so long as they didn't make nuisances of themselves!

She had been fourteen when her father died, life until then had been pleasant and uneventful. She remembered him as a short quiet man of great gentleness and culture. The bookshelves in the apartment had carried his collection of the Russian classics by Dostoevsky, Tolstoy, Gogul, Pushkin and the others. Books which he had read and re-read. His job with a State publishing house had meant that he had regularly brought home manuscripts and proofs to read. At times he would wave the manuscript he was reading with contempt and exclaim, 'They're not worthy to tie the strap of Dostoevsky's sandals,' adding for his wife's benefit, 'That's a religious expression from the Gospels, you know!'

Her reply was always the same, 'If you gave the Holy Gospels as much attention as your novels it would do you much more good.' The conversation had never progressed beyond that point. Both husband and wife had been determined in their own views, even stubborn, and both had shied away from conflict of any kind preferring to retreat into their own private worlds. How Elizabeth would have valued her father's help and guidance with her secondary education but there had been three years without a man about the place.

The waiter removed the soup bowl and returned with the sole. With a knife and fork he deftly removed the bones. She asked for another glass of wine, which came with a further supply of bread - with two glasses she hoped she would still be within the French driving limits.

It was what had followed those three years that had so affected her life. At first her step-father had been a welcome addition to the household, he had given her mother a new lease of life. As a widow she had let herself go and dressed in sombre attire. She had become even more assiduous in her church attendance and her prayers at home. Then she had met Igor at a meeting of the tenants of the apartment block. A year before he had divorced his wife, who had left him and returned to the Urals from where her family had originated. He had worked for Security, for the KGB, and had enjoyed access to shops and facilities denied to comrades employed on more mundane work. Their diet had improved enormously in variety and in quality and Elizabeth and her mother had been amazed at the clothes that were now available to them.

They had landed on their feet, or so they thought for the first few months. Then Igor had taken to the bottle, or as they later discovered, returned to it. Life for both of them had become hell. He had begun to beat his wife and, with his inhibitions loosened by drink, Elizabeth had become the object of his sexual advances. She had been able to lock her bedroom door against him and, on the advice of one of her teachers, she had enrolled for a self defence class. After that he had kept his distance from her and she had been able to dissuade him from beating her mother. Elizabeth had never known whether it was her step-father, one of his colleagues or someone at the University who suggested to the KGB that she would make a suitable agent. She had been approached one afternoon at the end of a lecture by a man in his early thirties and had rejected his invitation to a meeting. The next day her step-father had come home and told her that she was to accompany him to his office the following day as a colleague wished to speak with her. This had turned out to be the man who had approached her two days before. He had painted for her a glowing picture of her future with the KGB, the opportunities for foreign travel and the opportunity that she would have to 'do vital work for the Motherland.' He had spoken of her linguistic ability and her computer literacy and he had hinted that her good looks would be no hindrance to her effectiveness as an agent. She had liked the flattery, taken the bait and joined. Her KGB training had begun and life had certainly never been the same again.

One evening, a few months afterwards, her step-father had failed to return home and had been found floating in a canal the next day. They said that he must have fallen in while he was drunk, but she had wondered whether he had been disposed of as a security risk. Unlike the death of her father, the demise of Igor had brought few tears to their home. Both women had been grateful for the removal of a malign influence. Elizabeth had been told that her mother's pension would be larger on account of her agreeing to join the KGB and so it had turned out. Her mother had been able to live comfortably on the pension at first but it had not kept pace with the rampant inflation that had beset the country and ultimately Elizabeth had had to support her mother, something she had been happy to do even though they had never been particularly close.

This was the woman to whom Elizabeth took up her pen to write. The card was complete by the time the waiter brought her blackcurrant sorbet and espresso coffee. She finished the meal and paid in cash adding a substantial tip. She left the table for the ladies room where she read through her message to her mother:

> 'In France with my friend Peter and having a wonderful time together. Business going well here, it's hard work but I am enjoying it. I hope you are keeping well and that you are not short of anything you need. Perhaps I will see you before many more months have passed.
>
> Your Lizaveta'

It dissatisfied her. She felt in her heart of hearts that there was no real communication there. What would it convey to her mother? And she had no wish to visit Moscow in the near future or indeed at any time. It would be nice to get to know her mother better but she could not see how that could ever happen. With a sigh she tore up the card, threw it down the lavatory pan and flushed it away. As she did so she was reminded of doing the same to the notes she had made in Dorchester, the night Peter had come to her to share her bed and her life. She smiled at her reflection in the mirror and looked at her watch, it was

1.25 p.m. Peter and Michael would probably be on the train from Lyon to Geneva. How she would love to be with them. Still, in eight hours Peter would be calling her on the telephone - she would certainly be able to communicate with him, even if she had difficulty in doing so with her mother.

Elizabeth returned to the van and sorted out the papers for the journey back to England. She placed the tickets, Customs papers and her British passport in the door pocket. Then she reached for the box of CDs. She selected several, enough to keep her going until she reached home if there were nothing worth listening to on the radio. The Bach Double Violin Concerto began and she closed her eyes. Yesterday had been lovely, she could picture the sunlight on the clear waters of the Sorgue River. The story of Petrarch and his Laura had added another layer of romance to the setting. *'His Laura'* - in what sense had she been *'his Laura'* she wondered. It seemed so sad, so much unsatisfied longing. Yet it was one of those stories that lived on and still had power to stir the emotions. She resolved to do her research on the sonnets and on the Liszt compositions that they had inspired. She would do it while Peter was away. They could enjoy the poetry and the music when he got back. With that, as well as dealing with the backlog of work that had accumulated during their absence and keeping the office going she would be busy - that was good, it would help to speed the day when Peter got back. She set off down the hill on her way to the Tunnel and home. Yes, she felt that at last she had almost certainly found home and she was determined to stay and not recommence her wanderings.

Chapter 16

Thursday 12th September 1996 (continued)

Ruth and Peter finished a late salad lunch. Neither had been particularly hungry but each had felt that they must make the effort, as much to encourage the other as for any other reason. Ruth had insisted that she should not be allowed to sleep for more than two or at most three hours and had appeared back in Michael's room a few minutes before the limit had been reached. She hadn't been able to enjoy real sleep although she had rested. After washing and drying her hair she declared that she felt better able to face the world with all its problems.

'I don't need to tell you how glad I am that you're here, Peter. It makes all the difference to have your support when things are like this.'

'I'm sorry that you had to face the night alone. I must have missed the station announcement by about twenty minutes. If only the car train had been late in leaving or I'd stayed a little longer at the station, I'd have heard and been here within a couple of hours.'

'That's all water under the bridge. You're here now and that's what matters.'

They put the trays with their empty plates to one side and sat in the darkened room watching their son who stirred now and then. A nurse came into the room, took his temperature and pulse and recorded them. She smiled encouragingly at them and said, *'Le garçon est fort,'* and left them to themselves.

'She said, "He's strong".' Peter nodded and they were quiet again.

Ruth took the record chart to the door to have enough light to read it. Then she returned it to its place and sat down. 'Still high but steady, it's not rising anyway.'

'Ruth. How long do we have to wait until we can be sure?'

'Possibly this time tomorrow or possibly a bit longer. It seems a lifetime already.'

'And yesterday we were all going happily about our business totally oblivious of the threat hanging over Michael!'

'Business for some ... and pleasure for others, I think! Your Avignon *Exposition* ended the previous day didn't it?'

He flushed, 'We couldn't pack up until yesterday morning and then we had to kill time until the car train left in the evening. I didn't want to leave ... Elizabeth there on her own. Well, we did have the day to ourselves and we did some sight seeing at Fontaine-de-Vaucluse. We've never been there have we?'

'We've never been to Fontaine-de-Vaucluse and it's such a long time since the two of us were where you and Elizabeth have been for the last few months.' She paused to control her voice, 'I'm happy for you both, you know that. Things haven't worked out for us and that's a pity. What's necessary is for us to minimise the hurt, especially for ... Michael.' She had difficulty in saying their son's name.

Lewis took his wife's hand, 'If only I could be sure that he would recover ... I would be ready to ... '

Ruth cut him short, 'Come on Peter, no nonsense! We're not plea bargaining with some capricious or malevolent judge! Any decisions that either of us makes will be made rationally and in the cold light of day. It won't do to be swayed by emotion and make rash promises or decisions. That only leads to guilt and upset.'

'Nevertheless I'd give anything to be sure of his recovery. Wouldn't you?'

'Yes, so would I - but it doesn't lie with us does it?. Humanly speaking Michael's in the hands of the doctors and I have a lot of confidence in them. They're very thorough and very caring. Docteur Jacques, the one who speaks good English, was very quick off the mark and got Michael in here very quickly. It was Paulette who put me onto him, they're engaged, you know. ... Oh yes, I've already told you that, things are getting a little confused I'm afraid.'

'That's all right, you haven't really slept. By the way she was here just before you woke up. She said that she'd come again in the early evening and that we're to telephone her at the hotel if there's anything that we need. It's very good of her to be so concerned.'

'She's got a very caring nature. I'm grateful for all she's done. I told her that I approved of her choice of fiancé and that they've got to make sure that they work to keep their relationship in good working order.'

'Advice from hard experience, Ruth?'

'Yes, from experience!' She sighed, 'Life takes surprising turns doesn't it? Though often if you look back they're not really so surprising. I can see how both of us have contributed to getting us where we are now. But let's leave that alone. It's Michael that matters at the moment and we've got to give careful thought to his future. When I saw my solicitor recently he pointed out that we would have to spend time on giving hard thought to the arrangements for his custody and the rest. Oh, I know that's what we would do anyway but it reminded me that we have to make sure that our divorce does as little emotional damage to him as possible. It's easy to think that there are plenty of other boys in his class who are facing the same thing but it's like his illness: there's no real consolation in knowing that many other people are ill

- it's your own pain that you feel.'

She got up and went to Michael's bedside and felt his brow. Then she went to the wash basin and returned with a cold wet face flannel. She wiped his face and then dried it gently. 'I don't know whether it does any good but I feel that I have to do something.' Lewis nodded, he too would have liked to have something to do, some positive contribution to make. He took his son's hand in his and the boy stirred and opening his eyes looked up. 'When can we all go on the train, Dad? Can you get a timetable, please?'

Lewis stroked the hot hand, 'I'll have to go and find out about it for you old chap. How are you feeling?'

'I'm ill, Dad. Is Mum here?'

Ruth moved to the other side of the bed and took his other hand, 'Of course I'm here Michael. We'll both be here until you're well again, either here in your room or just down the corridor getting some sleep. There'll always be one of us here in your room with you and most of the time we'll both be here.'

'Of course we'll both be here together as long as you need us, Michael.' Lewis squeezed the boy's hand.

'I need you both together all the time!'

Lewis found himself sweating, 'Of course Michael.'

'And you'll go and find out about the train Dad - you'll do it now won't you?'

The child returned to a restless sleep.

They sat for a while until Ruth broke the silence, 'I think you had better attend to Michael's errand. The reception desk should be able to tell you where the steam train runs from, if I remember rightly it gets back here around six o'clock. And while you're out I would be grateful for some perfume, I've run out ... the usual ... No make it Blue Grass, Poison's too heavy for wearing in a hospital.'

***

As Lewis left the *Polyclinique* he wondered whether the choice of Blue Grass was for the reason that Ruth had given or whether she was trying to remind him of their early days together. Then she had used nothing but Blue Grass. When, he wondered, had he last bought perfume for his wife?

He rehearsed his question for the receptionist as he went down stairs, *'Quel direction pour le chemin de fer à vapeur, s'il vous plaît?'*

His delivery of the question went tolerably well and the young lady receptionist responded with a smile, *'En français ou en anglais, Monsieur?'* He opted for the English version and noted down the directions on the back of an envelope.

'And your son, Monsieur, how is he?'

Lewis thanked her for the enquiry and said that Michael seemed to be holding his own and that he and Ruth were hopeful.

He left the *Polyclinique* and turned right along the tree-lined street. The weather was fine once again and the warm afternoon sun shining through the leaves created a dappled effect of shadow on the pavement. The traffic was light and not many pedestrians were around, though a few people sat outside the cafés. Across the road on the *quai* by the Rhône some older men were playing *pétanque*. Lewis was alone with his thoughts. Avignon with its successful convention and full order books seemed ages away and pretty insignificant. Even the relationship with Elizabeth seemed clouded. The present and the next couple of days dominated his thoughts to the exclusion of almost everything else. He was preparing himself for the worst on the basis that relief would be welcome: to be too hopeful ran the risk of courting disillusion.

He checked the time, five past five, well first he would get Ruth's perfume in case the shops were closed when he came back from the railway. In the main street he found a perfumery shop and noticed an Elizabeth Arden display in the window. Good he would not have to trek from shop to shop to find Ruth's Blue Grass. He bought the *parfum* and then decided on some *eau de toilette* and bath foam. He asked for *'liquide pour le bain'* and communicated successfully with the elegantly groomed and dressed young woman who served him. She enquired if he wished to have them specially wrapped. He thought for a moment and responded with, *'Bonne idée! Oui s'il vous plaît.'* He was conscious of the inadequacies of his schoolboy French yet pleased that he was succeeding in being understood, particularly on an afternoon like this. Yes, gift-wrapping would be fine, he dearly wanted to encourage Ruth and cheer her up. The assistant wrapped the items, tying each with a bow, and placed them in a classy carrier bag. He paid with his credit card and, with each of them thanking the other, he went on his way.

He looked at his notes. Yes, he was heading in the right direction, he was in the *rue Thiers* - still with the politicians of earlier times evidently. As he passed the *Lycée Gabriel Fauré* he heard the sound of a boy's choir and paused to listen, they were evidently rehearsing as they stopped singing and he heard the conductor speak to them before starting them off again. The music was soothing and he was glad that he'd stopped. Elizabeth would have enjoyed it. How he would love to have her there with him. He suddenly had the idea of getting her to fly back to France, she could come to Lyon and be there by the following morning. As quickly as the idea had come he dismissed it again. No it wouldn't do, having Ruth and Elizabeth together would complicate things and Elizabeth's presence would only upset Michael. This was for Ruth and himself. Still he would be glad to speak to Elizabeth on the telephone that evening and let her know what was happening.

Lewis checked his directions again, he seemed to be almost there, the railway line was ahead of him. He crossed the line by a bridge which led from the *rue de la Solitude* to the *rue de Repos* and made his way down the slope to what was evidently the terminus of the steam railway, alongside the main line station. A freight train raced by on the main line shaking the ground, then all was quiet. He noticed a row of cars parked along the *rue de Repos*, so the train had yet to return from its journey out in the hills. He crossed the track of the steam railway and noticed that it was narrower than usual. A little further on was a small building which appeared to be the ticket office. It was closed but there was a timetable on display. Ruth had been right, the train was due back at 18h00. When the train came in there would no doubt be someone to provide some literature to take back to Michael, he'd got to let him know that he'd done as he asked. It might, he reflected, strengthen the boy's will to recover.

He had half an hour to kill and didn't feel like standing still by the booking office. On the other side of the *rue de Repose* was a cemetery and it exerted a morbid attraction. No doubt it was this that had influenced the name of the road. He returned to the gate out of the railway and a little way along the *rue de Repos* entered the cemetery through one of its two gateways in the high perimeter wall. He stood there and gazed around at the couple of acres before him, surprised at how different it was from an English church yard. No grass, indeed not a blade to be seen. There was gravel on the wide path through the cemetery and gravel on the narrow paths between the graves. He strolled slowly uphill along the main path leading from the entrance. How often must the people of Tournon have driven or walked this way to say *adieu* to the men and women of the town - and, he admitted to himself, to some of their children.

He wished that he had found some other way to occupy himself but seemed unable to tear himself away from the place. The size of the family tombs surprised him, as did the multiplicity of ornaments, plaques with photographs of the dead, plaques from members of their family and plaques from workmates, old soldiers' associations and the like. Some had one or more crucifixes on them and some had medallions recording visits to religious grottoes and prayers for the dead. Almost without exception they were well tended, many having real or artificial flowers to ornament them. They were evidently places of family pilgrimage, the living had not forgotten their dead. Or at any rate there was a sense of a shared mortality from which no one was immune. He wondered whether this emphasis was healthy. Perhaps past generations in England had been more assiduous in caring for the graves of their forebears than was the case today. Perhaps it was due to mobility, most of his acquaintances seemed to live well away from their parents and their home towns, and so the old Sunday afternoon visit to the cemetery - or even the Christmas or anniversary visit - just wasn't on, even if people had wanted to maintain the custom. He recollected that there were more cremations in Britain than in France, odd the bits of newspaper information that littered the memory! That was probably a factor.

He had begun reading the inscriptions on the graves. The word that stuck in his memory was *regretté*. Death brought to the surface a variety of regrets and not just the grief that came directly from the loss of someone you loved or cared for. There were the regrets of broken relationships that hadn't been mended in time. Splits and alienation that either no one had worked to repair or which had resisted all efforts at reconciliation. He was aware of the carrier bag in his hand and reminded of the way in which he and Ruth had drifted apart. How long since he had bought her perfume for a present? He could remember doing so when they had just met and in the early years of their marriage. Occasions when he had paid more than he could afford. He could remember her gratitude as well. They had enjoyed giving one another presents and surprises. But when had he last given her any for a present? Try as he might he couldn't remember. Regret? Yes, he knew the experience, he could and did feel it. But he also felt the excitement that Elizabeth had stirred within him.

Michael was never far from his thoughts. He found himself looking for a memorial to a thirteen year old and stopped himself. He had to keep such morbid ideas at bay. He noticed a tomb where, beside his father and mother, a young man of eighteen was buried: *'Maurice Marion 1926 - 1944 Mort pour la France.'* The father, an *Officier de la Légion d'Honneur,* had survived his son by thirty two years and his mother had lived for a further two. How, he wondered, had they spent that time? How had they adapted to the regrets? Had Maurice been their only child? How had he died? Was it perhaps fighting for the Resistance, killed in the push that took the Germans back out of Vichy France and out of Occupied France? Perhaps executed by the enemy troops? He would have a look at the memorial to the town's resistance heroes to see whether Maurice Marion's name was inscribed there.

Please God he and Ruth wouldn't have to experience heartbreak. Lewis felt fear in the pit of his stomach. Would Michael pull through? Of course he would! Or would he? The next day or so would tell. How different the boy was from his usual lively self. Brought low by something you couldn't see but which could be deadly. He thought of the baby that he had held in his arms - feeling the warmth of the little head, covered with hair that was more like fluff, against his chin. The little boy pulling him by the hand around Hamleys toy shop. The first visit to Chelsea to see football for Michael's eighth birthday. They had reported back to Ruth who, with her American background, hadn't understood a thing, to the amusement of all three of them! So, oh so long ago. Memories suffused with warmth and the glow of recollected happiness.

Lewis was brought back from his reveries by the sound of Michael's watch announcing six o'clock. He had put it into his pocket when Michael had asked him to look after it. He had no idea how the alarm had been set for that time. Somehow he was buoyed up by its sound, he didn't know why. Suddenly the idea of wandering around a cemetery seemed wholly inappropriate - he wouldn't mention it to Ruth. The sound of a locomotive whistle came from the direction of the station and a red locomotive pulled in at the head of a train of old brown coaches. The previously deserted station was suddenly alive with passengers climbing down from the train and making their way out of the station. An untidy milling throng of families, children and adults with carrier bags and picnic baskets, made their way back to their cars or on foot to the town. Lewis walked quickly back down the gravel path out of the cemetery. As he went he contrasted the scene on either side of the boundary wall: on his side the over-tidy geometric pattern of death and memories carved in stone, on the other side life in all its disorder and untidiness, life with its joys, tensions and small sorrows invaded the *rue de Repos*. Life was what he wanted to affirm. The holiday mood of the crowd was infectious. He made his way against the stream onto the station and obtained a leaflet and a booklet with photographs of the trains. The season, he was told, would be over in a couple of weeks' time. Michael would have to get well quickly if he were to travel on the train this year! Lewis somehow felt that he would.

With a sense of hopefulness that he knew might be entirely misplaced and that might desert him as quickly as it had come Lewis set off back to the *Polyclinique*. On the way he stopped at a flower shop to buy a stem of orchids for Ruth and at a newsagents for some magazines for her. With a quick, *'Bon soir,'* he greeted the receptionist at the clinic and hurried up the stairway.

Ruth looked up from her chair beside Michael's bed, 'He's no better, ' she said flatly.

'And no worse?'

'No worse, thank God.'

'We mustn't expect an instant recovery. Even when the infection or whatever it is has gone he's going to be weak and will need time to recover. Still he's young and fit - he's got a lot going for him!'

'I hope so Peter, I really do!

'Some things that I've been able to get for you Ruth.' Lewis gave her the carrier bag from the perfumery and the orchids.

'Oh that was kind!' She paused and looked at the stem of flowers, 'They're lovely.' She took the gift-wrapped packages from the carrier bag. 'Thanks Peter for thinking of me. There are times when a woman's self esteem needs care and attention.' Her voice thickened, 'You've always been a gentleman and you've always cared. Thanks for being here.' She paused again and smiled a tired smile, 'Well tell me about your research on the railway and when Michael next stirs you can give him the information he wants.'

Lewis pulled his chair close to Ruth's, 'Perhaps you would like to use some of the perfume to boost your morale.'

She nodded and unwrapped the packages, 'It seems a waste to throw all this away. Oh Peter, it was kind of you to get all this.' She applied some of the *eau de toilette* to her neck. and smiled, 'Do you know, I feel ... I'm not sure how to put it ... encouraged ... hopeful perhaps.' She put her hand on his, 'Good kind Peter, you haven't changed.'

At one and the same time he was glad at the lift in her spirits and concerned at her reaction to himself. 'I'm not much good as far as our marriage is concerned.'

'No I'm not trying to drag you back but, Peter, promise that you'll always be a friend.'

It was the turn of his voice to thicken, 'Of course, I'll always be your friend and our son's father. Nothing will ever change that.'

They sat quietly until Paulette arrived with Docteur Jacques who, after formal greetings, commenced to examine Michael. He asked the boy how he felt and drew him out so that he was able to extract useful information. As on previous occasions the examination was unhurried and thorough with checks on Michael's eyes and the bending of his knees. He turned to Ruth and Peter, 'I remain hopeful that it is the viral form of the malady and nothing worse. Tomorrow we will have the results of the tests and I am hopeful that the preliminary diagnosis will be confirmed. Until then the treatment with antibiotics will continue. And as for yourselves, is there anything that I can prescribe for either of you, something to help you sleep, perhaps?'

Lewis looked at his wife who shook her head. 'No thank you, Doctor. We'll be taking turns sitting with him through the night and we would both prefer to have our wits about us.' He smiled at Paulette, 'I'm grateful to you Paulette for keeping Ruth and Michael company last night when I was unfortunately absent.'

She smiled in response, 'I was pleased to be able to help. Though you do not want any medical assistance perhaps you would like to use the hotel's facilities to make you feel more comfortable - a bath, a change of clothing and a meal might be a suitable prescription. They will help to boost your morale a little.'

Peter turned to Ruth, 'It would do you good to have a break you know. You've been in this place for twenty four hours and you will feel better if you have a break before we divide the night between us.'

'I don't like the idea of leaving Michael.' She looked at the doctor, 'What do you think Docteur Jacques?'

'I would agree with Paulette's prescription. Nothing dramatic is likely to happen to Michael's condition in the next few hours and anyway you will be at the *Hôtel du Roi* and only five minutes' journey away by car.'

'On doctor's orders I'll comply but I won't be away for very long, an hour or an hour and a half at the most. Keep a good eye on him Peter, I know you will.' She kissed him on the cheek, 'Thanks for the presents they're good morale boosters and so are you.' She kissed her son on the forehead, 'Don't worry Michael, I'll be back very shortly. Dad's here to look after you.' She followed the others out, pausing in the doorway to look back, 'I need you both!' she whispered.

Peter stood by the bed and took his son's hand, 'You've got to work hard at getting well so that we can take the steam train up into the hills.' The boy was much more alert, evidently the doctor's examination had stirred him.

'Tell me about the train Dad. Have you seen it? Do you know when it runs? Does it go every day?'

'You've plenty of questions, Michael, you must be getting better already! How are you feeling?'

'Still weak and achy Dad. Tell me about the train.'

'It was on the other side of town by the cem ... by the SNCF Station. The train came in at six o'clock and it was quite busy with families who'd been out for the day. Let's see what I can remember about the train. The engine ... '

'The locomotive Dad!'

'Sorry old chap, the locomotive was painted red and was pretty shiny. I'm afraid I can't tell you anything technical about it except that the tracks seemed narrower than usual. Ah yes, I bought a booklet about it but it's in French, still your Mum will help with the translation. Here's a photo of what seems to be the eng ... the locomotive. It's red anyway.'

'Show it to me tomorrow Dad, my eyes are still hurting but they're not so bad as they were.'

Lewis made a note to tell the nurse to record this when she next came to take Michael's temperature. 'The carriages were pretty ancient and they were dull brown. Something you would like Michael is that they have a balcony at each end so that you can stand and look out. From the last coach I would think you could look right back down the line and see the way you'd just come.'

'I want to be next to the engine ... now you've got me saying it Dad ... next to the locomotive when we go on the train.'

The child seemed to have used up his supplies of energy for the time being. After a few minutes he asked, 'It will still be running when I'm well enough to go on it?'

'Yes Michael, it runs for a few more weeks.'

Michael was quiet and evidently asleep. Lewis felt his brow, still hot but no worse. His breathing sounded reasonably normal. Nothing to do but sit and wait. He wondered when the test results would be available the next day. Would it be there in the morning or would they have to wait most of the day?

Lewis sat by the bedside in the dimly lit room. He looked at his watch, five to eight. When Ruth came back he would find a telephone and let Elizabeth know the situation. It was earlier than they had agreed but he badly wanted to speak to her. Suddenly he was seized with an irrational fear that Elizabeth might have had an accident on the way back to London. He just hoped that she would be at home when he called. He didn't want further worries that evening!

Ruth would be back within half an hour. Her departing words came to mind, 'I need you both!' Perhaps their divorce would be more complicated than he had anticipated. They all had memories and to a greater or lesser extent they were bound by them. It might be harder to cut oneself clear than he had anticipated. But there were new memories continually being fashioned. His mind went back over the previous few days, the hotel in Avignon, the sunset at Les Baux, the night sky from the penthouse in La Grande Motte and their stroll along the river bank at Fontaine-de-Vaucluse. How he longed for Elizabeth. Yet he had an uneasy feeling that she should not be occupying his thoughts and emotions in his son's sick room.

On Ruth's return Lewis went with Paulette to collect his case from the SNCF Station at Tain and to freshen up and change his clothes at the *Hôtel du Roi*. While there he called Elizabeth on the telephone.

***

Elizabeth's journey back to Kilburn had been uneventful. She had reached the Mews in Kilburn at just after half past six and found Tom waiting to open the doors so that the van could be locked up for the night. He wanted to hear about the convention and the orders that they had taken. What she had to say pleased him greatly, 'It'll keep us busy for some time ahead. You and Mr Lewis have been busy, the lads will be grateful. There should be some overtime between now and Christmas and that will come in handy for all of us.' He had no questions on the more recreational aspects of the visit and Elizabeth did not feel inclined to broach the subject. He insisted on driving her back to her apartment in his old Ford Escort. As she took her cases from the car's boot she teased him, 'Thanks Tom. The neighbours will think that we've been away together for a few nights in Brighton.'

He laughed, 'That will be the day Miss. Still as long as the Missis doesn't know it doesn't matter! What about the cases? I'll give you a hand with them.'

She accepted and when they arrived at the door of the apartment she asked him in for a cup of coffee or tea. He declined politely and took the lift back down to the exit from the block. She had noticed a certain embarrassment on his part and wondered if it was at the prospect of entering a strange woman's apartment or whether it was because he knew that Peter was also living there and was afraid that *she* would be embarrassed by his seeing evidence of it. Whichever way, he was a gentleman.

Elizabeth made herself an espresso coffee, put a CD on the player and sat down on the sofa in the sitting room. She lowered the volume and closed her eyes. It was a good thing that she didn't have to drive round the M25 regularly. She let her eyes wander around the room. It certainly was pleasant, the proportions were right and she was still pleased with her choice of fabrics and wall paper. It had been wonderful to be away with Peter but how satisfying it was to reach home again. It gave her a sense of stability and contentment. She was missing Peter but he would be back with her in less than ten days. She decided to unpack, put her laundry in the washing machine and have a long lazy bath. Then she would eat and wait for Peter to call.

She was finishing her meal when the telephone rang. Her heart leapt with excitement as she gave the number.

'Hello, Elizabeth it's Peter here!'

'And who else might it be? How's Switzerland?'

'I'm still in France, still in Tournon in fact. Michael's in the local clinic with meningitis.'

'Oh Peter, I'm sorry. That's dangerous isn't it?'

He told her all he knew about Michael and the prognosis. She listened in silence as he talked, wondering what to say and feeling for him and for Ruth. There was a pause when he had finished his account, 'And how is Ruth taking it Peter? It must be awful for her, for the both of you.'

It was Lewis' turn to pause, 'Well she is more motherly than I've ever seen her, not that she's ever been anything other than a good mother to Michael, but this has brought out an extra something in her response to him. Fortunately she's had the help and company of Paulette from the hotel,' and he added, 'that's where I'm speaking from at the moment.' Immediately he wished that he hadn't referred to the place and he continued quickly, 'We're going to take turns at sitting with Michael in the clinic tonight. So there's no hotel luxury for me until he's out of danger and then I'll probably stay across the river in Tain until Michael's fit to return home.'

Elizabeth got Lewis to repeat the prognosis and urged him to be inoculated against the illness if he could. Then they discussed the business and agreed that Elizabeth would look after things until Lewis was able to return. She enquired about the fax numbers of the hotel and the clinic and he checked them and gave her the information.

'I feel for you all Peter. Make sure that you and Ruth get inoculated and take care not to catch it, meningitis is dreadful. Peter I love you and I couldn't bear to lose you. Give my love to Michael and ... to Ruth, won't you.'

'And I love you Elizabeth. We had a wonderful time in France, an unforgettable time. I'll telephone at the same time tomorrow.'

'No Peter that isn't good enough! As soon as you hear the results of the tests you will call and let me know what the doctors say and also how Michael is. Do you understand Peter, I'm scared out of my wits for all of you!'

'Of course Elizabeth I'll call as soon as there's news.'

'Promise to call me in the office as soon as you can tomorrow. I'll be there by eight Peter.'

'Of course I will, Elizabeth. I'll 'phone in with the latest news and then let you know the results of the tests as soon as they come in.'

After another ten minutes they said their good nights

and finished the conversation.

Elizabeth found herself in an agitated state. How would this turn out? Would Michael pull through and, if not, how would it affect Peter? What if Peter got the infection? She couldn't bear to lose him. She saw all her newly found happiness disappearing and was badly shaken. She cleared the plates away and tidied the kitchen. Then with a large espresso coffee she made her way to the sitting room and sat reflecting on the situation in Tournon. Just when she seemed happier than she had ever been before, this threatened. She tried to picture them at the hospital, she knew the fear that both Peter and Ruth must be facing. Elizabeth reflected on her own desire for a child by the man she loved. She could feel for Ruth. As she thought about it she recollected something that Peter had just said. What was it? She struggled to recall. Yes, that was it, 'She's more motherly than I've ever seen her ... ' Peter had told her before that, although Ruth was a good and conscientious mother, she herself admitted that motherhood had not involved her emotionally. Elizabeth found this hard to understand, she herself longed for a child with heart and soul. For all their sakes she wanted Michael to recover fully and quickly and if this unlocked the emotional floodgates of Ruth's relationship with Michael it would be a considerable gain for the two of them - so long as Ruth did not go too far in the opposite direction and become emotionally over possessive of her son. Elizabeth vowed again that she would make sure that Peter always gave Michael sufficient of his time and interest.

The thought suddenly struck her, if Ruth was now exhibiting feelings of renewed motherhood how might this affect her relationship with Peter? Would their common plight in the face of their son's life threatening illness reawaken in Ruth feelings for Peter: would she emerge as both a renewed mother and a renewed wife. And, if she did, how would Peter respond? Indeed how was he responding to Ruth and the situation? She went over their telephone conversation in her head: Peter had been worried, that was clear, but she couldn't remember anything that indicated any cooling off in his love for her. She felt better and encouraged. This might change Ruth but Peter had always been emotionally involved with Michael, there wasn't likely to be any sea change in the relationship between father and son. She told herself that it would do no good worrying over what might happen. There was nothing that she could do about it. She was in West Hampstead and Peter and his family were in Tournon. But how she longed to be a part of 'Peter and his family'!

She searched through the CDs for something to calm her and found an anthology of choral music. As she fed it into the player the telephone rang again. She heard the music begin and turned the volume down before answering the telephone. It was Eugene and her voice immediately betrayed her displeasure at his intrusion. She answered his questions in a brusque manner. Yes, she had arrived back that evening and would be looking after Lewis' office while he was absent. No, she did not know when Lewis would be back - his son was very ill and she did not expect Lewis to return until the child was well enough to travel. Michael had been ill for the last two days with suspected meningitis. No, she did not know what variety of the disease it was, hospital tests would not be complete until the next day. No, she certainly had no wish to have a visit from Eugene that evening as she was tired after her journey. She would be busy over the next few days and would telephone him when she had time. She put the telephone down somewhat surprised at herself for the undisguised contempt she had shown for him. They had once got on so well as colleagues and lovers. People changed, she reflected, but please Peter, please don't change. She busied herself with a variety of tasks that evening in an attempt to keep her mind occupied and her concerns at bay.

***

Eugene switched off his mobile and threw it angrily onto the nearest sofa. He walked to the window of the apartment and stood looking down through the trees at the car parked on the forecourt below. Just to relieve his boredom Moscow had sent an auditor to have a look at the expenses of the operation and make a nuisance of himself. He looked down at the visitor's Mercedes, not a bad job for an unimaginative fool. So much easier to earn your living looking at receipts and other scraps of paper, so much easier than facing arrest for espionage.

His visitor spoke, 'You don't seem pleased with Lizaveta. It must be difficult when two of you have to work together and you don't get on. But you have been together for some time now haven't you?'

'The woman's a bitch! A competent bitch but a bitch nevertheless! She likes to goad me whenever she can.' He lowered his voice and continued in a confidential tone, 'You would never think that we were lovers not so very long ago. I don't know what's worse, an estranged wife or an estranged lover that you've still got to work with!'

'Not a problem I face. Audit's a lonely business most of the time - though we do sometimes have time for pleasure ... tonight perhaps we could go out on the town.

Don't worry, you will be my guest so I won't be auditing the expenses!'

'On that basis I accept. We'll have another drink and then go out. Anyway that woman told me that Lewis' kid has gone down with suspected meningitis, so Pierre's potion must have worked. The fellow was supposed to telephone me to confirm that it was working but he didn't. We should stop some of his payment and frighten him into being more efficient in future.'

'I agree that we shouldn't pay for poor service. Another drink would be a good idea. We travel by taxi tonight, neither of us wants to draw attention to ourselves with a drink driving charge do we?' He sat back relishing his drink, he would go sparingly for the rest of the evening. Tonight's entertaining would all be legitimate, he wanted to loosen Eugene's tongue so that he could prise out of him information on the Channel Island companies owning the properties that were costing the SVR so much rent. He had something to add to Eugene's drink that would knock him our for at least four hours, he would probably use that on their return and have a look through his papers while he slumbered in blissful ignorance. Perhaps, as a result of his investigation, Eugene would in future be spared the discomfort of having to work with 'that woman' as he called her: if his enquiries established that Eugene was taking his masters to the cleaners they would either make sure that he didn't get the chance to repeat the scam or they would hold it over his head as an incentive to carry out their more unpleasant and dangerous assignments.

Chapter 17

Friday 13th September 1996

For both parents it had been a restless night. They had taken it in turns to sit for about two hours a time with their son. Neither had slept, though each insisted to the other that they had rested. From five o'clock they had sat together by Michael's bed. The nearer they came to hearing the results of the tests the greater their tension and unease became. They exchanged few words other than the odd sentence of encouragement. Each knew that they would not have wanted to face the day ahead without the company of the other. Neither Ruth nor Peter had remarked to the other that it was Friday 13th, though both were well aware of the fact: they were seeking to keep one another's morale up, not undermine it with nonsense.

Michael too had been restless and was still running a temperature, though it was marginally down. Both told themselves that this was good news, he was evidently holding his own and his condition did not show signs of worsening. Throughout the night nurses had come and gone at intervals, checking the patient's temperature and condition and recording the data.

'Well Peter we should know today for better or for worse. I wonder how much longer we'll have to wait to hear, it's really getting me down.' Neither of them noticed the phrase that came from the marriage service.

'I'm just the same Ruth. It's becoming unbearable.' He got up and, walking over to the window, eased back the curtain to look out. 'It's a fine day out there. I hope it's going to be a fine day in here for all of us.'

He walked round the bed and disappeared into the

lavatory, 'I'll follow your example and freshen up, it might make me feel better.'

Lewis returned to find Ruth holding the bottle for their son to drink through a straw. He waited until the drink was finished, 'Any better today Michael?'

The boy opened his eyes, 'Still weak and aching Dad, but my head doesn't hurt quite so much.'

Ruth forced a smile, 'That's good news Michael. Don't you think so Peter?'

'Good lad, keep on fighting it. We'll have you fit for your train journey. I'm really looking forward to the trip.'

'Thanks Dad, we're all going aren't we?'

Ruth nodded to Lewis, 'We're all going Michael,' he replied.

'Not Elizabeth, I don't like her!'

'Not Elizabeth, Michael, she's back in London working. Getting the business up to date with the orders we took at Avignon.'

The child lay quiet and Lewis and his wife resumed their seats. Lewis wished that Michael hadn't mentioned Elizabeth. If only he could be brought to like her or at any rate not to dislike her! A nurse brought them French bread and strong coffee. Both were grateful for the coffee, needing its stimulus to keep them going. Eating was also something to occupy the difficult silence that filled the room. Lewis looked at his watch, it was only half past seven. How many hours before they knew the best ... or the worst?

'When is Jacques due to see Michael, Ruth?'

'Between eight and nine, I think.'

'Will he have any idea of when the results will be through?'

'I hope to goodness he does. I've never known time

move so slowly. Does it seem that way to you, Peter?'

'Yes, it *has* seemed interminable but we should know today, Ruth ... within the next twelve hours, I hope.'

How utterly different this was from the way time had stood still for him and for Elizabeth, only days before, at Avignon and La Grande Motte.

They resumed their silence. Any embarrassment had gone and their attention was concentrated entirely on their son. He still seemed to be in a drowsy state but he gave the appearance of being more comfortable. From time to time he opened his eyes for a while but he seemed to be conserving his energy and he didn't engage them in conversation.

At a quarter to nine *Docteur* Jacques arrived with a colleague and greeted them, shaking hands formally. The paediatrician from Valence then joined them. Once again the doctors commenced a thorough examination of their patient. After they had discussed their findings Jacques turned to the parents, 'We are very hopeful that your son is making progress and my colleague from Valence concurs with this opinion. It will probably be early afternoon before the laboratory supplies the results of the tests. That will tell us for sure what we are dealing with. For the time being we will continue with the antibiotics. The nurse will give your son a bed bath to make him feel fresher and more comfortable. And how are you both standing up to the stress?'

They looked at one another and Ruth responded, 'Under strain, of course, but grateful to yourselves and the nurses for all you're doing for Michael and for us.'

Lewis nodded his assent, 'That's right, we're very grateful.'

'As soon as I have the results I will be with you. Paulette will be in to see you around ten o'clock. May I suggest that you both get out for some fresh air and exercise. You will feel better for it, sitting in a darkened room is not good. But do take care on crossing the road, you will be preoccupied with your concern for your son and you must keep your wits about you. It will not help him if you are run over. Of course you do not need telling, but our cars do run on the other side of the road and it is easy to forget it when you are distracted!' Jacques and the other doctor shook their hands and were gone.

'By three o'clock, perhaps then Ruth.'

'Maybe another six hours until we know.'

'Somewhere around that Ruth. I'll make a 'phone call to the office to keep them informed and find out if there are any problems.'

'Give my greetings to Elizabeth and all of them.'

***

Lewis found a telephone in a bar near the *Polyclinique* and used a Phonecard to call London. It was just after nine thirty in France, that would be eight thirty in London. He heard Elizabeth's voice and a thrill of excitement ran through him, 'Great to hear your voice, Elizabeth. I was afraid that the line would be engaged. .... Thanks, I'll pass their good wishes on to Michael and Ruth and your greetings as well. .... He seems to be much the same, possibly a little better and certainly no worse. We expect the results of the tests within the next six hours. .... Yes, of course I'll call you as soon as I can and give you the news. And how are you after the journey? .... And I miss *you* badly, Elizabeth. I hope to be back in a couple of weeks but perhaps you could fly out to Lyon next weekend. .... Well I think it would be all right by Ruth, the only thing is Michael. He's a bit anti at

the moment but I'm hoping to bring him round. ....
OK I won't trouble him with it until he's well on the mend. We'll leave the idea of your coming for the moment and talk about it later.'

For the next twenty minutes they discussed a number of business matters. Apart from one or two that needed Lewis' know-how he left the rest for Elizabeth to sort out as she saw fit. He was glad that she was there to keep things on an even keel, he was fortunate indeed on that score.

He decided to spend a few minutes walking along by the river before returning to the clinic. He hoped that Elizabeth hadn't thought that he had tried to dissuade her from coming out to join him at the weekend. No, it was Elizabeth who had decided against the idea. On the other hand he was the one who had raised Michael's antagonism. He put it from his mind, he was tired and didn't want to play mental games trying to work out who thought what. A young woman passed with an infant in a pushchair and Lewis fervently hoped that she would never have to sit by her child's sick bed and wait to know whether he was likely to survive the onset of some frightening infection. He almost stopped her to urge her to have more than one child, his old feeling of vulnerability had taken hold of him with renewed force. He felt raw fear, the results were only six hours away - possibly less - but what would they be? He turned about and headed back to the *Polyclinique* overtaking the young woman with the pushchair. He would remain with Michael until they knew.

***

He returned to Room K, greeted Ruth, hung up his coat and sat down. He mopped his brow and closed his eyes momentarily.

'Are you all right Peter?' Ruth stood by his chair with her hand on his shoulder and a look of concern on her face.

'I'm OK, it's the tension that's getting at me. Nothing to worry about, Ruth. I'm not being struck down by anything.'

'Tension! We've certainly got plenty of it! How is everyone in Kilburn?'

'They all send their love and best wishes. They're quite upset it seems.'

'Your other family, Peter. There's been one casualty this year, they don't want another!'

'Not a good year, first we lose Vera and now this. With Vera it was some yob in all likelihood, with Michael it's just one of those things that happens at random and without reason.' Lewis would never have guessed that there was nothing random about these events: the same malign organization was responsible for both casualties.

Paulette arrived, established that Lewis had been out for a break and persuaded Ruth to come for a short walk. Lewis went to Michael's bed and spoke to him encouragingly. The child looked up at him, 'Thanks Dad.' Lewis resumed his seat. He remembered the woman with the pushchair. Vulnerability, that was it. One child, an only son or an only daughter, and you were well and truly vulnerable. How frail life was, how much at risk from unseen menaces and how little you could do about it. His thoughts turned to Elizabeth. She had told him that she wanted to have his child. That would be a way of lessening the feeling of being constantly at risk. They loved one another and they would love their child. Lewis was growing excited at the idea. Michael stirred, 'Dad,' he muttered and was calm again. But how would *he* take to having a half brother or half sister when he was so antagonistic towards Elizabeth? Tiredness took hold of Lewis again, what was the point of troubling your mind with these thoughts at the moment? All in good time, the immediate matter was Michael and his recovery. He closed his eyes ... he would drowse for a few minutes until Ruth returned, he suddenly felt so very tired. How many hours was it since he was last in a bed?.

He came to with Ruth looking down at him, 'Had a good rest? You obviously needed it as you've slept for a couple of hours!'

'Never!'

'Yes you have Peter. It's nearly noon. You'll feel better for it and it's probably only three hours before we have the results from the laboratory.'

'I'm sorry, you've had an extra night here. You're the one who needs the sleep.'

'I don't doubt that, but women are often tougher than men and I'm learning the emotional side of motherhood. At any rate I'm learning more about it and I'm staying awake for the lesson.'

They were interrupted by an orderly bringing a light lunch but neither seemed to have much interest in eating and they only picked at the food, though they once again welcomed the coffee to keep them going through the next few hours.

At two o'clock Paulette joined them. She embraced Ruth and shook hands with Lewis, 'You will not have to wait long, I think. I am hopeful.' She endeavoured to radiate hope and encourage them. Lewis found an extra chair and the three sat waiting. He picked up a Sunday supplement from *Le Figaro* and tried to occupy his mind but after a few minutes he put it down. There was only one thing in their thoughts. An orderly brought them coffee at three o'clock and they conversed while Ruth once more helped Michael to drink through a straw. Once again the child's temperature was slightly lower, the nurse told them. They felt encouraged but did not dare to put their hope into words. Silence returned to the room. Conversation was a waste of effort in the face of the unknown. Lewis knew that they were in extra time only because they had led themselves to expect word by three - the extra tension was of their own making. He was finding it hard to stand the suspense, 'I must have a break! I've got to get some air and stretch my legs. Perhaps if I turn my back for a few minutes the report will arrive.' He knew that there was no logic in what he had just said but he felt beyond logic.

Ruth gave him a look of total understanding, 'Yes, get some air Peter but don't be too long. I need you here.'

***

At the bar along the road from the *Polyclinique* he found the telephone he had used in the morning and dialled his office. 'Damn the line's engaged,' he muttered to himself. The telephone was at the end of the bar and as he waited he ordered a large Armagnac, he needed something to keep him going. At last he got through and heard Elizabeth reply. 'No news yet Elizabeth. The tension's unbearable. I just had to get some fresh air and hear your voice. .... Thanks, well Michael's temperature is down a little and he seems calmer but it's the result of the tests that will tell us what it is that he's got. .... Yes, of course I'll call as soon as the results come through.

.... It's been a tonic to speak to you. .... I love *you* too, Elizabeth. Bye for now!' He put the telephone down, how he relished her name, just to say it was therapeutic. He knocked back the remaining half of the glass of Armagnac and returned the glass to the barman. 'Thanks, chum.' The barman watched him go, clearly he was a worried man - he saw all sorts in his bar.

***

Lewis looked at his watch as he entered Room K, he had been out for twenty minutes.

'Still waiting, Ruth.'

'Still waiting. Feeling better for the break?'

He nodded and felt Michael's brow. The boy stirred and looked at him, 'Am I getting better, Dad?'

'I'm sure you are Michael. Don't forget we've a train to catch soon.'

'Not today, Dad, I'm too weak!'

'Well in a few days' time.'

He kissed Ruth on her forehead, smelling the familiar, nostalgic scent of Blue Grass while she smelt the spirits on his breath. She had declined some Cognac from Paulette when Peter had been out. She had felt that she wanted to be in full control of her faculties when the report arrived but had told Paulette that if it were bad news then she might want some to sustain her. The three sat once more in silence in the curtained room.

At five minutes to four *Docteur* Jacques and a colleague hurried into the room. There was no need for anyone to ask, his face told all - it was transfigured with pleasure. 'Good news! In fact the best! Your son is suffering from the less serious viral form of the disease. His chances of a complete recovery with no lasting ill effects are very high. He will merely need rest for the next few days until he is up and eating again. It is likely to be a couple of weeks before he is his normal energetic self.'

The women were in tears and Lewis found that he was shaking. He was amazed at the strength of his emotional response to the news and wondered, fleetingly, what his reaction would have been had the news been bad.

Ruth took Michael's hand she whispered to him, 'It's OK Michael, you're going to be feeling better in a day or so. It's good news!'

'Good news,' he responded, 'Thanks, Mum. We'll be able to go on the train.'

'Sure we will.'

'Just so,' Lewis added.

Ruth took Lewis in her arms and held him tightly. 'Thank God the waiting's over. He's going to be all right! He's going to be all right, Peter!' She continued to hold him tightly while her tears ran down her cheeks. 'I'm glad that you've been here with me Peter, I'll never be able to thank you enough for it. Are you all right, Peter, you're shaking!'

'I'm fine, it's the tension and fear coming out Ruth, just give me a few minutes to recover.'

He turned to Jacques, 'My apologies *Docteur*. We haven't thanked you yet. We really are most grateful for all your care and concern.'

Jacques smiled, 'As you can see I'm dealing with Paulette.' She had her head on his shoulder and was wiping her eyes with his handkerchief. The other doctor had disappeared.

'I'll give the clinic instructions on what to do for the next few days and of course I'll look in regularly. You can stay here if you wish and perhaps you will wish to do so tonight but it is not really necessary and you both need to get some proper sleep. I suppose that your son was talking about the *"train à vapeur"*. It is good for a patient to have something to look forward to like that. Paulette, would you like to join our friends on the train once Michael is well enough?' He turned to Lewis and Ruth, 'That's if you would not mind having us with you. It was rather rude of me to invite myself and Paulette.'

'It's a great idea, isn't it Peter? It's so wonderful to be able to look forward again!'

'We'd all like that, it can be our celebration together. No doubt there's a good restaurant at the end of the line.'

Docteur Jacques smiled, 'Quite a number in fact. I would suggest, perhaps the *Hôtel du Midi*, you can watch their chef in action through a glass wall in the entrance hall, he's the star of the show, indeed who else could be in a restaurant *en France*?' He laughed. The tension had gone, for all of them in that room the world had returned to an even keel.

'We will leave you on your own for now but I will come back in about an hour's time to find out where you want to stay until Michael has recovered fully.' Paulette took Jacques by the hand and they were gone.

Ruth looked up from the chair, 'Thank God the suspense is over Peter. I'm completely exhausted but then I've not really slept for two and a half days so I suppose it's not surprising. How about you Peter?'

Lewis was standing by Michael's bedside looking down at the sleeping child. 'He's making up for the sleep we've lost. Me? I've not lost as much sleep as you have but I'm pretty weary. I won't be completely happy until Michael walks out of here but, even at this stage, I'm feeling high emotionally as well as physically shattered.' He walked around the bed to stand beside her. 'You've been wonderful Ruth, you've helped him through and kept his spirits up. You've been with him all the time he's been ill.

I'm sorry that I was late on the scene.'

'No more apologies Peter! It was just one of those unfortunate things and you got here the next day. As for helping people, you've kept me going and Michael as well. Now you must go and telephone your office - Elizabeth and the others will want to know what's happening.'

He flushed slightly. 'I don't like leaving you so soon after we've heard that all's well or at any rate not nearly so bad as it might have been.'

'If the news had been bad I wouldn't have let you go but you owe it to your office family to let them have the good news. It'll be five twenty in London so you ought to hurry.'

'Yes, I must catch them before they finish work.'

***

For the third time that day Lewis found himself in the bar along the road from the clinic. The barman nodded as Lewis passed and read from his face that a burden had been lifted from his shoulders. As Lewis hunted through his pockets for the Phonecard the barman handed him a glass of Armagnac. Lewis passed him a 100 franc note, *'Et pour vous aussi, Monsieur.'* He gave Lewis his change, poured himself a glass and raised it to Lewis, *'Santé.'* Lewis returned the toast, how apt it was and how vital, what a difference health made. You tended to forget about it when you and your loved ones were well but when it was at risk you certainly appreciated it. Lewis decided to attempt to communicate with the barman, *'Mon fils était malade ……. mais maintenant il se rétablit. Ma femme et moi, nous sommes …….. tres heureux.'*

'Et moi aussi, je suis tres heureux avec vous, Monsieur!'
Another customer arrived and Lewis made his

telephone call.

***

The weather in Kilburn was dull and rainy that afternoon and it matched Elizabeth's mood as she kept hard at work, attempting to keep her mind off the situation in Tournon. The telephone had been busy and each time she had expected to hear Lewis only to be disappointed. She was making a cup of coffee - she had lost count of the number she had made during the day - when the telephone rang once again. Surely this must be Peter! And to her relief it was.

'Oh Peter, you at last. What's the news? .... Not life threatening! Oh, that's wonderful, you and Ruth must both be relieved. .... And they expect Michael to be up in a few days time? .... When do you expect to be back here? .... So you'll probably come back by air with Michael in about two weeks time and Ruth will come on her own by car. .... Of course I can look after things, if there are any problems I'll 'phone or fax you. But I'm missing you already.' She looked to make sure that the door of her room was closed, 'Peter I love you *very* much. .... No, it would be better if I didn't fly out for the weekend. You owe it to Michael to give him your undivided attention and this place has been incredibly busy and I need to spend time here on Saturday getting up to date and without any telephone to interrupt. .... OK. I'll make sure that Tom's around, I promise I won't be here by myself in an empty building. .... Where will you be staying? .... Of course I don't mind you staying in the same hotel as Ruth, she is your wife after all. .... No Peter I didn't mean it like that. Ruth is your wife and Michael's mother and you need to make the most straightforward arrangements. .... I'll be by the telephone at ten this evening and we can have a good chat. Now I'll go and tell Tom and the others that Michael's on the mend, it's great news! And Peter, I love you!'

Elizabeth paused for a moment before going down into the warehouse. How strange it was to have Peter explain the need to stay in the *Hôtel du Roi* with Ruth and for him to stress that he would have his own room. As she had told him, Ruth was his wife. What was it about this Englishman who ran a small business here in Kilburn that made her long for the day when she would take Ruth's place in form as well as in substance? She knew that it was in large measure because he cared for people. She just hoped that his caring nature didn't make it too difficult for him to sever his ties with Ruth. She was glad that the marriage had effectively come to an end well before her arrival on the scene and that no one could accuse her of causing its break-up. She was excited at the prospect of married respectability but first she would have the difficult task of telling Peter who she really was and what forces had brought her to his office and his bed. She knew that it would be difficult and that it would raise the question of who had been responsible for Vera's death, but she must be completely honest with him as soon as she possibly could. And she wondered how he would respond to the deception she had perpetrated.

She set off down the stairs, Tom and the others would be glad to hear before they knocked off work that all was well with Michael. Fortunately they would all be still at work as the overtime from the Avignon orders had begun. It was satisfying to be the bearer of good tidings!

***

That evening both Ruth and Peter felt that life was returning to normality. Whether it was due to the psychological effect of the good news or because his body was winning the fight against the virus, Michael began to look and feel better and became quite a chatterbox. Lewis collected his copy of *The Lord of the Rings* from the hotel and was required to read the Siege of Gondor to him and promise to continue reading the next day. Ruth decided to stay at the *Polyclinique* for a further night, sleeping in the room next to Michael's. Lewis was given the room next to Ruth's at the *Hôtel du Roi*, the room that had been occupied by the unfortunate Pierre, the cause of all Michael's troubles.

Lewis felt exhausted but elated as he concluded his telephone call to Elizabeth. It would be a couple of weeks before they were together but Michael was on the way to recovery and they were both happy and relieved. No sooner had his head touched the pillow and he was asleep.

***

Ruth wiped Michael's face with his flannel, not so much to cool him - his temperature was now almost back to normal - but to prepare him for sleep. She was anxious to show him all the motherly care and affection that she could. Paulette had dropped in to see that all was well and had gone off to spend the rest of the evening with Jacques. Ruth was looking forward to a good night's rest but she found that sleep was slow to come. Too much had happened and her mind would not switch off. How she had prayed for Michael's recovery, now she ought to say a 'thank you' - strange it wasn't something that she had mentioned to Peter or Paulette, it was something very personal and she felt better for it. She thought of the months ahead, there would be the toing and froing with solicitors over the divorce, evidently it was more complicated now and majored on children and their care and support and there was talk of conciliation sessions. She only hoped that it would go smoothly and not turn up unexpected problems and strife. No, she felt sure that anything that involved Peter would be fair and civilised. She knew now, with absolute confidence, that he would always be around when she needed any help especially with Michael. Would she find someone to take Peter's place? Only recently she had thought that she would have to do something about it but now she felt in no hurry. Peter would be hard to follow, he cared about people and there weren't too many like him. Still that wasn't an immediate problem. Her mind slowed down and at last she fell asleep.

***

Elizabeth closed her copy of *One Day in the Life of Ivan Denisovitch.* She had decided to read it at one sitting and it was now a little after midnight. The days of the *gulag* for those out of favour had gone, for ever she hoped. She ought to be able to 'retire' from the SVR without the fear of retribution. The only problem was whether the work she was involved in was for Security or for the Mafiya. If the Russian Mafiya were the ultimate paymasters of the operation they might not be willing to let her go so readily.

It was after one in the morning in France and Peter would have probably been asleep for some time. Without him her apartment felt empty, without him her life would be very empty. She wanted the two weeks to pass quickly. She made a milk drink and then luxuriated in a hot bath before heading for bed.

Chapter 18

Friday 27th September 1996

'And how was Brooklyn, Sam?' The technician looked up from his array of recorders and electronic devices.

'It's always good to get back to the place where you grew up and to the people there. It was for an aunt's funeral, not the happiest of occasions, but I met a whole crowd of relations and family friends. I'd have taken several weeks to see them all separately. When you've got more than one place that you call home it's interesting to try to see what's changed when you come back to one of them after a while. Often it's very little, some people look a bit older, someone's got a first child or additions to their family, a shop has changed hands or something like that. Life moves on and, provided there isn't too much that's different, you can handle it. I did my usual trip to the Brooklyn Museum, nothing compared with the Metropolitan Museum of course, but it always reminds me of visits as a kid with my father especially the room with the Rodins. If things are quiet when I'm next in Paris I plan to do the museums and to see the Rodins there.'

'And how was your fiancée, Mia if I remember rightly?'

'Mia was fine, Joe. Her Mom's not too well but apart from that things are fine. We saw quite a bit of each other while I was there – she came with me to the Brooklyn Museum, she always enjoys that.'

'You want to get her over here, Sam, and more than that you ought to put her out of her misery and marry the girl before someone else does!'

'All in good time, Joe, all in good time.' It was time to change the subject, 'And how about our friends whose every move and word you've heard, what's new with them?'

'Not a lot here but things seem to have been happening in Southern France. I know you decided that it wasn't worth keeping an eye on Lewis and the Russian girl at their convention in Avignon, so we have to assume that it went well. From that pair's point of view it seems to have been good, they've been very lovey-dovey on the 'phone since Elizabeth got back ten days ago. The news is that Lewis' kid - Michael his name is – the Lewis kid was taken ill in France with a form of meningitis, not the most serious variety but bad enough to keep him in hospital for ten days or so. He left hospital a couple of days ago and today he's gone on an outing with Lewis and his wife. Then Lewis is bringing the boy back by air the day after tomorrow.'

'So Lewis didn't get to Switzerland with the boy?'

'No chance. He arrived just after the kid was admitted to hospital and he stayed there with his wife.'

'I wonder how they got on. You know they've been separated for a while?'

'Without coming to blows I expect. It's been amusing to hear him assuring the Russian girl that he's had a separate room from his wife. I ask you, assuring the mistress that he's not misbehaving with his wife! Bit topsy-turvy, ain't it?'

'That's the way it is, he's a decent sort of guy. It's a pity that we've got him mixed up in all this, though I expect he'd be very grateful to us for bringing the girl his way ... who wouldn't be?'

'We picked up an interesting bit of information from old Eugene's 'phone calls - the kid's illness wasn't just chance, some pharmacist in Paris was sent off to administer the germs or whatever and make the kid ill. Trying to get Lewis and his wife back together through the kid. Looks as though they're afraid of losing the girl at the end of the operation. You know, they want to make sure that she goes home to Moscow with the goods and doesn't remain in the West. I think you've got it in mind turning her or something.'

'But it isn't working? Their efforts to get Lewis back to his wife, I mean. You said that Lewis and the girl are still very lovey-dovey didn't you?'

'More so - that's how they sound when they're on the 'phone, the tone of their voices and the things they say to each other. I'll run you some of the recordings if you like, we've got transcripts but the recordings themselves will give you a better idea.'

'OK I'll listen to them before I go out. If Lewis is in love with the girl, with Elizabeth, it's hard to imagine him falling out of love with her very easily, I know I wouldn't.' He paused, better say no more on the subject, he didn't want to suggest anything other than a professional interest in her. 'She's the sort of woman most men would find very attractive. Lewis seems to be the SVR's target, or at any rate people connected with him are. First his secretary, to make room for the Russian girl, and now his son, though they only made him ill - I wonder if they would have murdered him as well if it had suited their purposes. Post Cold War or not they're still a pretty nasty crew. I only hope that our people are a bit more civilised.'

'Of course Sam, we only kill in the kindest and most gentlemanly way! Not like the other barbarians.'

'Don't joke, Joe! If we can't rise above that I don't want any part in it. OK play me the recordings ... Yes, I'll have the transcripts, it helps to have both together, sometimes the eye catches something that the ear misses and sometimes it's the other way round. And some decent coffee wouldn't come amiss, don't forget I've been on a 'plane all night ... '

And while Joe got the coffee Sam reflected on himself and Mia. Throughout his visit to Brooklyn he had had to fend off similar suggestions to Joe's. A relationship, that had once seemed so right, was now in jeopardy through the hold Elizabeth had over him. He knew that the logic of the situation was all against him: Elizabeth was clearly deeply in love with Lewis and there was no doubt that Lewis was over the moon about her. Yet he, Sam, was in thrall to Elizabeth, a woman who had no idea of his existence let alone his feelings! *"La Belle Dame sans Merci hath thee in thrall",* it was a quote from some English poet or other. He didn't know about *sans Merci*, though - given who her employers were – that might fit. But there could be no doubt about the emotional grip she had on him. He could not rid his memory of his first clear view of her on Finchley Road Station months before and the shake of her head that had set her hair bobbing and evidenced her confident vitality.

***

The locomotive whistled and the guard called to the passengers to get on board. There had been some debate about whether they should be at the back of the train or as near to the locomotive as possible. It had been left to Michael to decide and he had opted for the last coach, saying that they could probably see the locomotive as they went round the bends of the line as well as look back and enjoy the view. As it had turned out the choice had been made for them.

Michael had recovered rapidly although he still became tired easily. He had been out of the clinic for a couple of days and was happy to retire to bed in the middle of the evening once they had eaten dinner at the *Hôtel du Roi*. Although he had gone to sleep by eight the previous evening, that morning had seen him awake early and wanting to leave for the railway station soon after breakfast. Shortly after nine Lewis drove him there, having arranged for Ruth to follow with Paulette and Jacques. They parked near the station in the *rue de Repos*. As he locked the car Lewis glanced through one of the entrances of the cemetery. 'Thank God,' he murmured and his prayer was for all its shortness real and heartfelt. Michael took his hand, something that he hadn't done for some time, and they went through the gate and crossed the narrow gauge tracks to the booking office which had yet to open.

'Can we go and see them getting the locomotive ready, Dad?'

'Why not Michael, I'd like to have a look myself.'

The carriages for the train were already in the station and they walked along beside them toward the engine shed. A row of plane trees between the SNCF and the steam railway cast their shadow on them, shielding them from a sun that already promised a hot day even though it was early October. A morning mist had dissipated quickly before a light breeze and the heat of the sun's rays. It wasn't just another day, there was a feeling of anticipation about it. Lewis felt in his bones just how good it was to be alive and at the same time he knew how transient that feeling could be. Enjoy it while it's here! He felt Michael's hand in his pulling him forward with impatience and he was so grateful for his recovery. They reached the end of the line of carriages and stopped to take in the scene. The locomotive, the red one that Lewis had seen a couple of weeks before, was being loaded with coal for the day's work.

'Can we go over and have a look Dad.'

'I hope they won't mind, Michael. We'll try anyway.'

They crossed the lines after Lewis had made sure that nothing was on the move. It wouldn't do for Michael to survive meningitis only to be run over by a train! The *ingénieur* looked down from his cab and greeted them, *'Comment t'appele tu mon garçon?'*

The boy furrowed his brow for a moment, *'Je m'appele Michael, Monsieur.'*

'Bon nous avons attendu à ton arrivage. Soi bienvenu!' He opened the door of the cab and extended a hand to help the boy to climb up the steps onto the footplate.

Michael looked at his father, 'Fine, Michael, they seem to have been expecting us. Up you go!' He didn't need any further bidding and almost flew up the steps.

'Come on Dad, I want you to see as well!' Lewis followed at a gentler rate, arriving on the footplate to see Michael shaking hands with the *ingénieur* and the fireman. In turn he shook hands with them and then stood back while they showed Michael how they controlled the locomotive. He was instructed in the art of firing and allowed to shovel some coal into the firebox. Lewis stood at the top of the steps into the cab enjoying the warmth of the sun on his back and the heat from the boiler on his face. He watched his son and the locomotive crew communicating despite their different languages, Michael's face showing his concentration as he sought to take it all in. Footplate instruction over, they climbed down and joined the crew as they oiled the working parts. Michael was put in charge of an oil can and instructed in the task. Lewis looked at his son - blissfully happy and with his hands oily and black with coal. Once he would have told him not to get his clothes dirty, now he didn't care. The boy was well and happy, Lewis wanted nothing more for him, for the time being at any rate. The next task was to fill the locomotive's water tanks and Michael helped to turn the water on. Lewis remembered that he had a camera in his pocket and took a variety of shots of his son with the locomotive - he was pleased that he had avoided calling it an engine which would have incurred Michael's reproof. The *ingénieur* handed Michael a rag which smelled of paraffin to wipe his hands clean.

'Et *maintenant il est nécessaire retourner au quai. Nous allons trouver la voiture salon.*'

Lewis and Michael thanked the crew and returned with care to the trackside that served as a platform. They stood in the shade of a tree near the rear of the train while the red locomotive rolled gently around the yard and eventually came towards them pushing a small blue four wheeled carriage which was attached to the rear of the train. The driver leaned out of his cab, *'C'est une voiture special pour les directeurs du Chemin de Fer du Vivarais.'*

Michael looked disappointed, 'With that in the way we won't be able to look back down the track from our carriage.'

'Perhaps we should travel at the other end near the eng ... locomotive?'

They debated where to travel for a while, turning to see a freight train hauled by an electric locomotive rush through the SNCF station next to them. An elderly gentleman of rather portly build approached them and introduced himself as a *directeur* of the railway. He indicated the blue carriage, *'La voiture salon est pour vous et vos amis. Je crois que c'est un voyage de celebration aujourdhui.'*

Instantly Michael's expression was transformed from disappointment to delight. He shook the *directeur's* hand

and thanked him, *'Mille remerciements, Monsieur!'* He rushed off and climbed the steps to the platform at the end of the carriage, 'Come on Dad, it's super. Just look at the seats and the inside!' Lewis and the *directeur* exchanged smiles, youthful enthusiasm and pleasure were infectious.

'Many, many thanks, Monsieur. *C'est tres belle!* We are all to ride in this ... *voiture?*'

'D'accord, certainement Monsieur Lewis. Please join your son. Look *Docteur* Blanc and two ladies are coming in this direction, your party is complete. It is the *Docteur* who has arranged this for you. *Enjoyez la journée!* '

Formal greetings over, they installed themselves in the saloon carriage. 'They've done us swell don't you think? We've even got curtains and proper armchairs, very civilised!' Ruth was impressed.

'It's *Docteur* Jacques that we've got to thank for our comfort. The *directeur* of the railway told us just now.'

Jacques was almost overwhelmed by their gratitude. 'You've been wonderful already and now this, it's really too kind - Michael, Peter and I are incredibly grateful to you Jacques.'

'C'est rien! Paulette and I wanted you to have an enjoyable celebration of Michael's full return to health. I hope he's enjoying himself.'

'It's wonderful, Dad and I have been on the locomotive, its the red one number 404, I've been shown how to drive it, put coal on the fire and oil it. I'm glad we came here. Thanks for this carriage *Docteur* Jacques, it's super to be your patient and a special passenger. Did you hear the whistle, I think we're going to start!'

Slowly and with much whistling from the locomotive they got under way. Jacques suggested that as the first few kilometres were through a tunnel and along the back of the town they would be better to stay inside the saloon and not ride on the rear balcony. Once they were by the river Doux there would be plenty to see. Despite this Michael spent some time on the balcony "enjoying the steam and smoke" as he put it. Ruth, anxious that he shouldn't get cold, gave him her jacket to wear.

An hour later, after a journey up the river valley and through some high sided gorges, with the line clinging to the cliff side, they came to a halt at Boucieu le Roi. The guard called up to them that they could buy refreshments near by. 'There's no need we've got our own here!' Jacques announced. Paulette produced Champagne and smoked salmon that the hotel had sent along to the railway earlier in the morning, *'C'est une belle journée de celebration!'*

They raised their glasses to Michael, to Jacques, to the impending wedding, to the French President and to the British Queen. 'Can I go and see the locomotive and the *ingénieur* please? I'll finish my Champagne later.' Ruth could see that he was itching to get there and told him to go but to take care. They followed him a little later, finding him on the footplate of the locomotive which was refilling its water tanks. When this was completed he was given the task of sounding the whistle to summon the passengers back to the train to resume their journey to Lamastre. 'Come on Michael, you don't want to be left behind, especially when you've been the one to call the other passengers back,' Ruth put up her hand to help him down to the trackside from the footplate. Unwillingly he climbed down. As they made their way back to the *voiture salon* at the back of the train he chattered to Jacques and Paulette about the railway. Ruth took Lewis' arm and held him back so that they were out of the others' earshot,

'He's sure enjoying himself isn't he. It's such a relief to see him so well and bursting with energy and curiosity.' She paused, 'Though last night he was having nightmares. I had to get him out of bed and wake him with a wet face flannel. He was OK once he was awake and couldn't remember what he was dreaming about. I don't think it's happened before, if it had I think I would have remembered it.'

'He's had a nasty illness so I suppose it isn't surprising. Still, it would be an idea to keep a note of it and to see whether it happens again. If need be, and if it becomes frequent, we could get some advice from the GP.'

'I'll leave my bedroom door open at night when we get home, if he shouts out I should hear. You're probably right that it's the illness that's upset him.'

'You don't think it could be that book of his that he's been reading - *The Lord of the Rings* - it could be too much stimulus for him just before he goes to sleep, maybe he was dreaming that an orc or a Nazgûl was after him!'

'I didn't hear him talk about either of them or anything that seemed to have come from his book.' She didn't say that the one word, clear and distinct, that she had heard was "Elizabeth". No point telling him, if it didn't happen again it would be of no significance - if it became frequent then, and only then, they would have to face the problem together. She was aware that Peter might think that she was trying to undermine his relationship with Elizabeth. For the first time she wondered, just for a moment, whether it wasn't something she might want. Quickly she dismissed the idea from her mind, they were set on divorce and Peter was so very happy in his new relationship. They had reached their carriage and climbed up to find Michael finishing his Champagne.

Lewis raised his eyebrows in mock horror, 'You're giving our son expensive tastes Jacques. I don't think that his pocket money will run to it each week!'

'Each week? No. But for a celebration, always. This is France and it is not a proper celebration if there is no Champagne!'

Michael chipped in and told them what the *Prince de Polignac* had said on the subject of the age to start drinking Champagne, getting it more or less right. His audience laughed. Ruth responded, 'Well that's a relief. Michael was told that on the day when he was taken ill. Your memory's working OK then and that's good news.' She hugged him and hid from them the tears that were forming in her eyes.

Paulette observed the service and the food at the *Hôtel du Midi* with an experienced professional eye and was unable to find fault, not that she wished to, for she, like the others, was wanting the day to be just right in every way. Michael counted the cheeses in the large flat basket with the hooped handle and hinged lid which had been brought to their table. All agreed that they had never seen so large a selection. Jacques quoted Charles de Gaulle about the impossibility of governing a country with 365 cheeses. They all enjoyed the cuisine and the absence of any need to hurry over the meal but at the end Michael was straining at the leash to get back to the railway and talk to the locomotive crew. Paulette took him there with instructions to get him to converse in French. Lewis after a tussle with Jacques managed to intercept *l'addition* and pay on his credit card.

In the early evening they returned to Tournon to be met by the *directeur* who took the men and Michael on a tour of the engine sheds and works. Ruth and Paulette went back to the hotel by themselves on foot, after the wine that had been consumed it was as well that no one had to drive. The men could leave the Volvo at the station and take a taxi if Michael was too tired to walk. The day had been truly celebratory, everything about it had been excellent.

Michael looked at his fingernails as he settled into his bed - there was still some of the grime from the railway that had resisted the bath water, it served as a reminder of the wonderful day they had spent celebrating his recovery.

Monday 30th September 1996

Three days later the family prepared to leave the Hotel du Roi soon after breakfast. Ruth had managed to catch up on her schedule of visits to the wine producers and the *négociants* while Michael was recovering. She would run Michael and Peter to the airport at Lyon to catch a late morning flight to London Heathrow and then drive north up the autoroute to Paris for a couple of days before heading for home. Ruth had wanted to go straight home but Peter had insisted that she should have a break. They had compromised with the arrangement that she would have two full days to see some of the museums and that Peter would look after Michael at Ruth's house until she returned. Now he was worrying about Ruth's safety on the roads, he would be relieved to see her arrive home in three days' time - just as he had been relieved to hear from Elizabeth that she was safely home a couple of weeks earlier. Their departure was attended by Jacques and Paulette who, wreathed in smiles, invited them to their *mariage* which was to take place in Tournon at *Pâques*.

***

' ... and now Evgeny, perhaps you would update us on your London and Basel operation? We are having to exercise considerable patience with it aren't we?' He sat up with a start knowing that he must have drowsed off in the afternoon heat. These meetings at the Moscow Headquarters of the SVR certainly didn't get any more exciting but it didn't do to show your boredom. He had been day dreaming, wondering when he could invite his new young assistant to have dinner with him. She was a welcome addition to his staff and brightened up the place, an attractive and lively little thing who looked as if she could be a lot of fun. He mightn't have another chance like it and he was determined not to let the opportunity slip through his fingers. He dragged himself back from his reveries and into the meeting. He knew that Konstantin from the Accounts Section was not in favour of the Basel operation but that there were enough others to back him provided he presented a reasonable case for continuing. Informal and off the record discussions between Evgeny and several of his colleagues enabled them to come to these meetings confident that their pet projects were safe from premature termination - provided they gave support in return to those colleagues.

'The purpose of the operation is, as you will remember, to obtain a new drug that is being developed in Basel. By its very nature the preparation and testing of a new drug is a slow and expensive business with extended tests on animals, in this case on rats.' He saw a couple of his colleagues shudder, 'Rats I am reliably informed are not in themselves unpleasant creatures. Like people, if they are placed in a decent environment, they themselves generally stay decent.' He wondered to himself why he had commenced this dissertation on rats, still it would do no harm to show that he knew something about the background to the operation. Evgeny continued, 'Our agent within the research laboratory is still unable to get to the project itself due to their very tight security, although he does hear of its progress from time to time. That is enough for our purposes. He has recently reported that they expect to have completed their tests by the end of the year. Until they are complete there would be no point in attempting to acquire the drug, because we need access not just to the drug itself and details of its production but also to the records of the tests that the laboratory has carried out. Through the personnel at the London end we expect to have access to the laboratory and the means of getting everything out through their tight security. At the same time the London personnel have a number of separate information gathering activities, so their time is not being wasted while they wait for the Basel laboratory to complete its research.'

'It's good that there seems to be a reasonably firm timetable for this operation to be brought to completion.' Konstantin from Accounts injected an unusually positive note and surprised Evgeny even more by adding, 'The drug appears to be of considerable commercial value so that the time, manpower and money put into the operation are a good investment. It would be unfortunate if it suffered from any shortage of funds. I think that I could probably persuade the Director to provide additional funds if it became necessary and, of course, if you felt that you could justify the expenditure, Evgeny.'

'Well, thank you Konstantin. It's gratifying that the value of the Basel operation is appreciated.' His colleague's generosity towards the project had come as a shock to Evgeny as it had to most of those present - they were impressed by it. Evgeny must have some really hot goods to deliver if he was being offered extra cash for the project. Experienced in fighting every centimetre of the way for funds, they were suitably awed at Evgeny's achievement.

'It has every prospect of being a most valuable project. So it continues, gentlemen? ... Good. Next item ... ' The chairman moved the meeting on.

Evgeny returned to his fantasies, perhaps she would be free the following evening. He would sound her out when he got back to his office. Then he could prepare the way with his wife, telling her that he might have to toil through the next night to deal with some urgent work that was likely to crop up.

Konstantin looked across the table and saw Evgeny's eyes close. He suspected that he knew what was occupying his mind, he hoped that he was right. He had received the auditor's report on Eugene. His connection with the Channel Island companies owning the London properties occupied by Elizabeth and himself had been established beyond the shadow of a doubt. It wasn't clear whether Elizabeth was also involved, although Konstantin thought it unlikely. As for Evgeny he might well be dishonest and in league with Eugene. No doubt the little girl whom he had recently added to Evgeny's staff would be able to find out. She had been very successful in prising secrets out of other colleagues, all in the gentlest of ways of course. The rough stuff came afterwards.

Chapter 19

Monday 30th September 1996

Elizabeth made sure she reached Heathrow's No. 1 Terminal in good time, the traffic was light and she had no difficulty finding space for Lewis' BMW in the short term car park. She checked the time as she entered the terminal, there was just under an hour in hand before the noon arrival from Lyon. Better to have time to kill than to be racing against the clock. She headed for a newsagent and a while later emerged with *Vogue* and a book on life in Iran. She wasn't quite sure why she had chosen the book, save that she was interested in other cultures and women's place in them, for herself she couldn't imagine being wrapped from head to foot in a *chador*. Neither could she imagine herself surviving in such a male dominated society. She had found her freedom - she would never surrender it and if anyone tried to take it away she would offer fierce resistance.

Over a coffee she browsed through *Vogue* but found that she wasn't concentrating. She was longing to see Peter, the two weeks since they had last been together seemed an age. Life had been busy with a surprising amount to be done, but then she had been doing some of Peter's work as well as her own. Despite this she had found the time dragging. Now he would be with her in less than an hour. She felt like a girl on a first date and was amused at her excitement. Peter would have Michael with him so their greetings would have to be restrained. That didn't matter too much, they would have time together later. The arrivals indicator showed that the flight was ten minutes early. Good, a little less time to wait. She headed for the Ladies' Room to check that she was looking her best and that her lipstick was in order. Yes, she had done it before leaving the car in the car park and it needed little repair work. She looked at herself in the mirror and gave herself a smile. She checked that the jacket of her navy suit was free from any marks and stray hairs. The brooch that Peter had bought her in Avignon was secure. She brushed the biscuit crumbs off her knee-length skirt and pulled her red sweater down at the waist. She was ready to meet Peter. She took another look in the mirror and gave her head a quick shake, watching her hair swing and come back into place. Yes life was good. She was happy with anticipation.

Fifteen minutes later she caught sight of Peter and Michael pushing their luggage trolley out of the Customs Hall. Her feeling was of excitement mixed with relief, they were safely back in England. She saw Michael look at her and felt inhibited. They met at the end of the barrier and Peter gave her a kiss on the cheek which she returned. She and Michael greeted one another with a polite handshake. While waiting for their luggage to come off the carousel Lewis had told his son to be polite to Elizabeth as she was a good friend. The boy had replied that of course he would. He kept his word and conversed politely with Elizabeth, answering her questions about his illness and recovery and telling her about the steam railway. They decided to have coffee before going to the car. When Michael had finished his drink he went off to buy a football weekly leaving them together.

'I've missed you badly, Peter. I was desperately worried for Michael and also for you and Ruth in case either of you caught it as well. It's a relief to have you back and to know that you're all well. You're looking great but a bit weary, I guess.' She kissed him and took his hand.

'And for me too it's a relief it's all over. It was wonderful to see you there when we came through the door from Customs, not that you would know that Customs exist these days their hall seems more like the Marie Celeste, no doubt someone's there out of sight but watching you.'

'Michael seems to have recovered well from his illness doesn't he?'

'He gets tired quite readily but apart from that he seems fine. Ruth tells me that he's had one or two nightmares, but after the stress of the illness I'm not surprised.'

'And what's the programme for the afternoon?'

'First we take Michael home to Ruth's place, he's not going to school until tomorrow but the au pair should be there to keep an eye on him until the evening. After that we can head for Kilburn ... but if you're happy to go via your place that would be more than fine by me!'

She feigned surprise and appeared to be giving the matter thought, 'Well, let me see. I wonder if my boss would mind if I took some time off work to spend a pleasant afternoon with a male friend. What do you think, Peter?'

'It all depends what your boss is like, I suppose. Now if he has your welfare at heart he probably wouldn't mind.'

'And if he has his own welfare at heart?'

'He definitely wouldn't mind! In fact he'd approve wholeheartedly! Especially as he's got to spend the next three nights at his wife's house ensuring during her absence that their son is OK.' Peter kissed Elizabeth and seeing Michael heading their way squeezed her hand before releasing it.

'Got your paper Michael? Anything interesting?'

'There's something on Chelsea, Dad, and I've got to catch up with the results while we were away. Will the papers be at home?'

Elizabeth took her cue, 'They're in the car for you to

look at on the way. I've kept them and sorted them out for you to see.'

'Thanks, that was very kind of you.'

Elizabeth noted that, although his reply was courteous, there was at the same time a lack of warmth in his voice. She stood up and looked for the route to the car park. 'OK lets go shall we? The traffic isn't likely to be too bad so we should get you home by two o'clock, Michael, but I don't expect you'll notice it with the sports pages to read.'

***

The clock chimed four as Lewis stood in the bedroom door drinking a cup of coffee and watching Elizabeth dress. 'The message from your boss, Elizabeth, is that whenever you need time off for extra-mural activities like these you have only to ask.'

'It sounds more like a recipe for bankrupting his business! And perhaps the right label is extra-marital rather than extra-mural! One day, if I become Mrs Lewis, it will only be extra-mural. May I ask about the divorce, Peter? When are you seeing your solicitor again?'

'There's an appointment booked for next week, Thursday afternoon I think. Things should be on the move after that, although I don't know how long it will take under the new law. It shouldn't be too much of a problem - Ruth and I are on good terms and not at each other's throats and there should be no difficulty sorting Michael's interests out.' He held her close and stroked her back, 'I love you Elizabeth, you're so special and I've been longing to be with you ever since the train left Avignon.'

'I love you and I need you, Peter.' She looked up at him and then closed her eyes as he held her and their lips met. The gentleness to their embrace once more generated powerful feelings. For them both time stood still. They were together once again.

***

The staff had welcomed Lewis back, wanting to know about Michael's progress. He had then sorted out one or two small problems with Tom and retired to his office. Back behind his desk Peter felt strange and suddenly weary. He often experienced a sense of let down when he returned from a holiday or a business trip. Back again to the routine and the humdrum. Generally the feeling didn't last long - he enjoyed his work and being with his workforce. This time he felt as though he had been away for an age and a great sense of tiredness swept over him. In France he had experienced the peaks of excitement and the depths of despair and fear. All was well with Michael and his visit to Elizabeth's apartment had renewed the delight of their relationship. Nevertheless he felt worn out and looked forward to an early night. At five thirty he looked into Elizabeth's room, 'Fully dressed this time, more's the pity,' he said quietly.

'Here I'm demure, chaste and pure, or as near to it as I can manage! We don't want to upset your staff, Peter!'

'Quite so, Elizabeth. We owe it to them. I'm ready for a long night's sleep. Do you think that we could push off at six. I'll drop you home and then drive to Ruth's. The au pair should have a meal ready for Michael and myself. Then it will be bed for both of us.'

'You and Michael and not you and the au pair, I hope!'

'With you around Elizabeth no au pair would get a look in! I've only got three nights there and then we'll be together again.'

His attempt at a kiss was rebuffed.

'Not here Peter! There's plenty of opportunity for that elsewhere. I've already said that we mustn't offend your staff, they themselves might behave in certain ways but they somehow don't like the boss doing so. Five minutes and I'll be ready to go, we needn't wait until six. Michael will be glad to see you earlier. By the way, I've done my research on Petrarch - I'll tell you about it and play Liszt's music to you when you move back to my place at the end of the week. Make sure you give Michael plenty of time and attention while you're with him. He was very polite today but he doesn't show any warmth towards me I'm afraid - in time I hope he'll change. I can well understand how he sees me - a threat to the stability he needs.'

'But *you* haven't taken me away from Ruth and he knows that doesn't he?'

'He almost certainly hopes for your return and he must see me as an obstacle to that happening. You must make sure that he has plenty of your time and attention and that he doesn't have cause to think that he's suffering on my account.'

'Michael will get all the attention he needs. He's bound to come round to liking you, Elizabeth.'

'I just hope so, I really do. Keep working on it, Peter! Keep up with Chelsea's progress and take him to as many games as you want, I won't mind in the least. I've been without a father and know how it hurts.' She paused, she couldn't bare her soul any further and it pained her to have to keep so much from Peter. She was in a situation which was completely new to her. On previous assignments she had enjoyed the rôles she had played and had had little sympathy for the power-hungry, money-hungry bosses she had deceived, indeed she had loathed them all to a man. Now it was the play acting and pretence that she hated, if only she could come clean with Peter! But she couldn't - she was afraid about what they might do to her mother or at any rate threaten to do just to keep her in line. 'He died in a road accident, that was bad enough but in a way it must be worse if your father walks out on you - if he abandons you. I know you'd never do that to Michael but he must be afraid of your losing interest in him. You've got to make sure that he realises it won't be like that.'

'I didn't know that your father died when you were young. You'll have to tell me about your childhood and your life, it's odd how little we know about one another.'

If only she could have said to him, *'Look, I'm not who or what you think I am but listen to my story and I believe you will understand'*. But that just wasn't on. It would have put the spotlight on Vera's death and she couldn't see how she could get round it. She hated her masters for their callous disregard of human life, for their contempt for Vera and her family. She would have to be careful to steer Peter away from the subject of her past: it was bad enough to have deceived him as much as she had but to feed him details of a fictitious childhood would be even worse.

'Sometime perhaps, Peter. Leave it alone for the time, it still hurts even now, you know.' That much was true and she hadn't added to the fiction that surrounded her.

'OK and thanks for mentioning it, you clearly feel for Michael and can see things through his eyes. Keep me in line so far as he's concerned if I ever show signs of falling down on my fatherly duties and you ever think it necessary. Promise me that you will, Elizabeth.'

'I promise. And now we should be on our way or I'll be reminding you that you're neglecting your son! And you've got to catch up with your sleep - I want you back in good working order at the end of the week!'

'Wasn't I in good working order earlier this afternoon?'

'I wouldn't dispute that in any way, Peter!'

'What did you say you were doing this evening, Elizabeth?'

'Having dinner with that cousin of mine, Eugene of the many orders. He's a bit of a bore but you know you've got to keep in with relations.'

'Keep him sweet Elizabeth, he's certainly a man of many orders and above all he was responsible for bringing you here to down market Kilburn. I can never be grateful enough to him for that!'

'It's the best thing he ever did for me. I'll be polite to him out of gratitude, Peter, don't worry.'

***

Eugene's choice of restaurants was usually pretty good and his new find in Maida Vale was certainly up to standard. The couple at the next table had been very quiet throughout the meal. Elizabeth had decided that they were on their first date and overawed by the restaurant which seemed to be somewhat beyond their pocket. Fortunately they had not wanted to linger and once they had gone conversation moved on beyond generalities to Avignon and Southern France.

'So Lewis is too tired to see you this evening! He's been with his wife after all so you shouldn't be surprised.' There was more than a hint of sarcasm in Eugene's voice.

'He's had the worry of his son's illness and he's responsible for him until Ruth gets back from France at the end of the week. Michael's close to him. Peter's a father who takes his duties seriously and enjoys being with his son, the two of them get on well together.'

'He's more responsible as a father than as a husband

then! Or don't you think so Elizabeth?'

'You, of course, speak from years of experience as a responsible husband Eugene! Peter and Ruth had grown apart long before I came on the scene. They're on friendly terms and I think that's good - especially for the boy who's at a stage when he needs stability and not conflict in the family. He seems to have got over his illness, though he still gets tired very easily. It was serious, you know, if he'd had one of the other varieties of meningitis it might have killed him.'

Eugene wondered to himself whether Pierre shouldn't have used some infection that would have kept Lewis and his wife on tenterhooks for longer. 'The kid's illness hasn't had much effect on the parents' relationship then?'

There was something about his impatience to know that put Elizabeth on her guard and alerted her to his real interest in the subject. 'You regard it as important do you Eugene? I mean you really seem concerned about their marriage don't you. Are you jealous of Peter or what?' She lowered her voice so as not to be heard by the other diners, 'I've told you at various times and in a variety of ways that the relationship between you and me is over for good. It was fine while it lasted but we've moved on since then, there's no chance of beginning again. There *was* no future in it, there *is* no future in it, you know that! We had good times together but that was in the past I'm afraid, Eugene. Enjoy the memories.' As she said it she knew that she had said something stupid: such memories became painful ones where a relationship was ended by the other partner, there was nothing left to enjoy in them.

'What they ... What I am concerned about is that you shouldn't hurt yourself by an entanglement with Lewis which must come to an end when you return home in a few months time. Have fun with him by all means, you can hardly drop him now, I'm not asking for that - the operation's success depends on your staying in your job until we've got the goods.'

He had given himself away, it was Moscow and not Eugene or rather, more accurately, it was Moscow *and* Eugene who wanted to ensure that she didn't stay in the West once the operation was complete. Her resolve was strengthened: she would *not* go back, *whatever* effort it took she would stay. She would not yield up her freedom! She liked life in the West, she liked London, she liked her apartment and above all she loved Peter. She knew all about the threats and inducements she would face and she knew that despite them all she was not going back. She knew too that she should give them no hint whatsoever of her plans.

'Don't worry on that score, I've had lovers before and I've moved on - sorry Eugene, I'm not trying to twist the knife, honestly I'm not - Peter Lewis is very nice and kind, he's a real English gentleman but you don't think with my past record that I'm hooked by him do you? I like him and enjoy his company and that wasn't the case with my previous bosses. But entangled with him? Not likely!' She saw his face relax a little and she continued, 'Like you I'm a professional and I look forward to new challenges. Life in Kilburn as secretary to a small businessman hardly looks like the consummation of a splendid career, does it now?'

'Well I feel responsible for you and don't want you to make mistakes and get hurt, Elizabeth.' He took her hand for a moment and she didn't resist, knowing that she would have to work to dispel his suspicions so that he could calm any fears that the SVR might have. 'We've worked together successfully and pleasurably for a few years now, Elizabeth. Here's to many more years of creative and harmonious collaboration!'

He raised his glass and she responded with a smile, 'To our future, Elizabeth. Long may we work together creatively.' His face had relaxed. She was relieved, knowing that she had begun to defuse his suspicions. She would have to think carefully about how she could foster this impression and she would have to find ways of avoiding being carried off back to Russia against her will when the operation was over. That wouldn't be easy - her mother was still in Moscow that gave them a hold over her - but she wasn't going to admit defeat. So the agenda for the evening would be to massage Eugene's ego but nothing else. She had expected a boring evening spent on the defensive. Now she was pleased at the prospect of using the time to some purpose and rising to the challenge that their suspicions posed.

'Well Eugene, tell me about what *you've* been doing in the last few weeks. I'm sure that you haven't been sitting at home with nothing to do all day or all evening. How's the interior design business going, you know I'll always be happy to advise. Ah, you've brought some drawings and samples along. OK we can look at them in the bar after the meal and I'll tell you what I think. You can also tell me about your clients and whether they are going to be of use to us in the future.' She winked at him and he smiled.

'Perhaps we could develop it into a going concern that would be useful to our masters and stay on here after the present assignment is complete. What do you think, Elizabeth?'

'If that's what they want, it's OK by me, though the USA was good,' she lowered her voice, 'and it may be that we'll have to make ourselves scarce after the assignment is complete. There might be people here who would like to speak to us, people we would rather not meet. We'll just have to see how the main business goes. What about your social life? You haven't been idle have you, Eugene?'

She smiled a knowing smile and he responded. The wine and her company were having their effect, he felt relaxed and receptive - women did that to him and this woman did so more than the others.

'How's the little girl from the Labour Club, the one who was the mistress of a Labour MP from the West of England?'

'Not from the West of England, Elizabeth, they don't seem to have Labour MPs there. He was from the North West. As for Maureen, she's a useful source of information not only on him but also on several other MPs, she's not been too concerned about the political affiliations of her lovers - though at the moment, with the way the next election is likely to go, it would be better to have dirt on Labour. She has some nice photos of herself and her friends.' He looked around to make sure that no one was near enough to hear, 'I took her away for the weekend to give some of our colleagues the chance to borrow her negatives and make some useful souvenirs.'

'That was very keen of you, working all weekend! I hope that you get recognition for your devotion to duty, Eugene.'

He liked the humour, his inhibitions were slackening and his tongue loosening, 'If they give me a medal I won't know where to wear it on such occasions. You do understand, Elizabeth?'

'I understand very well, Eugene!' She refrained from saying, 'Only too well.' 'So the weekend was a personal success?'

He was finding pleasure in recalling his time with her and he was finding in Elizabeth an appreciative audience,

'How can I put it?' He pretended to be working to find a description, though in truth it had been in his mind for a while. 'It was rather like having lessons with the Kama Sutra as the text book!'

'You surely didn't need lessons, Eugene?'

'Just a refresher course, you understand, Elizabeth.'

'And all in the course of duty! You deserve two medals for all that!'

'All in the course of duty, Comrade! Sorry, I don't know how that slipped out. I'll have to be careful with what I say.'

'Go easy on the wine, the bottle's almost empty so I'll finish it and you can continue with mineral water. Then we will order a cafetière of strong coffee.' She poured what was left of the wine into her glass, she had been going carefully and reckoned that she had only had a couple of glasses. That way she could be sure of being in control of herself, her tongue and her dinner companion. She looked round to catch the waiter's eye. Good, he responded immediately. She had noticed already that the service was attentive - neither fawning nor casual. She would pick up the restaurant's card when they left so that she could bring Peter here when they next had a celebration.

'Peter Lewis sends his greetings by the way. He's grateful to you for the trade that you've brought him, Eugene. Any more orders in the pipeline?'

'As a matter of fact there are a couple of really large orders on the way. I'll be in to see Lewis next week. Do you think that he can cope with the extra business?'

'Don't worry we'll cope all right, we're a team, you know! The lads in the warehouse will be glad to have some more overtime as we get towards Christmas. Bring all the business you can.'

'So you're "part of the team"?'

'What else, Eugene? If I've got to be there in Kilburn I might as well put my back into it.'

'It's not what you do with your *back* that worries me.'

'Eugene behave yourself! You'll have the other diners taking an unhealthy interest in our conversation.'

'Oh yes, talking about *our* team, I had a visit from an auditor from Accounts Division. Must be a nice job wandering round poking your nose into what the real operators are doing, looking for little bits of paper to make sure that we're not wasting money or making off with it!'

'He found nothing to trouble him?'

'Of course not. He went through the motions, of course, and urged economy on me, but there was nothing that he turned up - with everything above board there was nothing for him to find - it gets under my skin when they don't trust you and send people like him around. There was one good thing about his visit, we had a night out on his expense account. We didn't go far away from where you live, pubs and clubs in West End Lane. We met some girls and he was pretty lavish with the hospitality. We must have got back late, I didn't surface until midday and I was surprised to find myself back in my apartment. He must have got me back there, I couldn't have managed it if I had been on my own! Hell of a hangover though. He won't last long if that's how he regularly drinks on his audits.'

'More coffee, Eugene. It'll do you good.' She wondered what the audit visit had really been about. Her stepfather had worked in the Accounts Division in the days of the KGB and he had come home with stories of auditors getting information they wanted by the liberal use of the bottle. She felt concern for Eugene, if the auditors had anything on him he would be heading for a nasty time.

She hoped that she was wrong. Despite everything, at heart she liked Eugene, if only he would avoid his "Georgian bastard" mode and keep his hands off her they would get on well, as they were doing tonight.

'Could you see him to the door please, Driver?' She didn't want the complication of Eugene falling and hurting himself between the taxi and the door of the apartment block. Anaesthetics would be a problem after the drink he'd consumed that evening and in any case there was no saying what he might blurt out under anaesthesia. Once at his door he was on his own, she was not going to venture in there.

The driver returned to his cab, 'He's OK, I took his key and let him in and made sure that he was safe in an armchair. You were wise not to go in with him, lady, a young woman like you can't be too careful. A friend or your boss?'

'My cousin as it happens. Thanks for your concern, a woman needs to take care of herself. Though, to tell you the truth, I do know a thing or two about self defence but it's better to avoid trouble than to have to get out of it.'

Chapter 20

Saturday 26th October 1996

'Well what do you think of your team's performance this afternoon, Michael? Was it worth being out in the cold?' Lewis looked across the table of the cafe in Highbury where they were warming up with hot drinks after the game.

'It's always worthwhile, Dad! I enjoyed the game even if ... ' he lowered his voice in case he was overheard by Arsenal supporters, knowing that he was still deep in enemy territory, 'even if Chelsea didn't win. It's always good coming out with you, it gives me something to look forward to.'

'Well, they picked up one point and you saw six goals – that can't be too bad, can it? And you need something to look forward to Michael? Isn't the whole of life something to anticipate?'

'Yes, of course it is but ... since I was ill I've felt a bit down at times, a bit fed up you know, Dad. Just now and then, you see. It helps to know that you're around and that we're planning to do something together, like today's outing.'

'And I look forward to being with you too, Michael. You must always let me know just how you're feeling. We've got to take good care of you, particularly after that illness. Has the doctor given you anything to take to build up your resistance against other bugs?'

'Mum took me to see him last week, she's probably told you. He wouldn't give me anything special, at any rate not yet, just told me to take plenty of vitamins and keep fit. I told him that we keep very fit at school with games and all that stuff. He wants to see me again in a couple of weeks about my ... about my ... nightmares that I have sometimes.'

'They'll go, I'm sure, Michael. I remember having bad dreams when I was your age. I remember one vividly - or rather what I remember about it is that afterwards, when I was half awake and half asleep, I demanded that my Mum and Dad find me a rubber ball. And do you know what I did with it? Well, I just took it from them and threw it down the stairs. Fortunately it wasn't a cricket ball, that might have done some damage!'

'I wish that Grandma and Grandpa were still alive, it was good doing things with them when I was small. I liked it when you took me to them for the day and when you and Mum went away for a weekend and I stayed with them. They always did something special and Grandma had some special things that she cooked for me. We've still got the bird table that Grandpa and I made together.'

'You have good memories of them, Michael.'

'I want Grandma and Grandpa, not memories. You were lucky Dad, your parents didn't split up did they? You had them together all the time!'

'That's how things were then, generally at any rate.'

'I wish that was how things were now! I guess that over half my class have parents who aren't living with one another. There are even two of them whose parents have swapped partners with one another. If that were me the embarrassment would kill me!'

'Times change, Michael. Things aren't the same as they once were.'

'Why have they changed, Dad? Why is it happening now to me and my friends?'

'Partly because they changed the law. Once a divorce was very difficult to get.'

'I don't think they should have changed the law then.'

'People's attitudes have changed and the law had to change with them.' He was aware that he was arguing in a circle but he pressed on. 'Even the law can't keep couples together, you know. At your age, Michael, you see everything in black and white. You think that you can change the world but I'm afraid that the world isn't keen to be changed. Today's compromising middle aged people like me were once teenage idealists like you. You won't lose all your idealism but you'll become more realistic and flexible. It happens to every generation.'

They were silent for a minute or two and Lewis took the opportunity to change the subject. 'There's some Physics homework for me to have a look at when we get home, isn't there?'

'Some questions on lenses and virtual images, I can't quite sort it out and I'm relying on you to make it come clear.'

'I'll be pleased to try even though I'm pretty rusty, and don't forget that you can always 'phone me of an evening for help or to get me to drop in and have a look.'

'Thanks Dad, but I don't want to talk to Elizabeth. I don't mind talking to her at your office, Dad. That's all right but not at her place, I don't like it.'

'Why not send a text to alert me and I could call back. Would that be OK, Michael?'

'Yes, sounds a good idea Dad.'

'That's sorted then, but I wish you could like Elizabeth, it would help, you know.'

'Please don't ask me Dad, not for the moment anyway.'

'OK but don't forget I still care for you just like I always have, Michael, and that won't change.'

'Thanks Dad.'

'Now about our next holiday together.' Lewis knew it was time to move the conversation on and ease the tension that had built up. 'We didn't get to Switzerland in September, your virus saw to that. How would you like to spend the New Year in the Swiss Alps and improve your skiing? A friend has a chalet there and, as he's going to be in the West Indies for most of the winter, we can use it if we want. How about it, Michael?'

'Great. I'll have that to look forward to. Can I bring a friend? John's parents are in Australia and he's living with an aunt who's rather strict. Don't worry he can pay the fare if we fly. It would be nice to have his company - as well as yours, of course, Dad!'

The excitement showing in his face brought Lewis a sense of relief. He had timed the change of subject well.

'Of course he can come to keep you company. That'll be useful to have him with us - I'm sure my energy won't match yours on the slopes! It's time we were on our way, old chap, with a bit of luck we'll just make the North London Line train.'

They left the cafe deep in discussion of their plans for the trip to Switzerland. The shadow over their afternoon together had been dispelled and both of them were glad that it had gone.

***

At a quarter to eight that evening Lewis turned his key and let himself into Elizabeth's apartment. 'Back again Darling, sorry I wasn't earlier but Michael needed help with his homework and I've had to rack my poor, old, rusty brain on the subject of optics!'

'Your brain isn't poor or old or rusty, Peter. And you know full well that what would annoy me would be your neglecting him. You've got to be a full time father, even if it's sometimes difficult. Did you have a good time together at the game?'

'Great, Elizabeth. It was a draw but I didn't let on to Michael that I was once an Arsenal fan and so we commiserated with one another on Chelsea getting only one point!'

'How was Michael in himself? Is he completely over the illness yet?'

'I'll tell you about our conversations later on but I'd like to change before eating. My nose tells me that you've been busy in the kitchen. It makes me feel guilty, leaving you to slave in the kitchen while I push off to football.'

'No need for any guilt, real or pretended, Peter! I've had a very relaxing time trying out a new recipe and although I've missed you, of course,' she pulled him close and kissed him, 'I love you Peter! Where was I? Oh yes, in the kitchen. Well it was very pleasant to have the time to myself and have a go at a new recipe and to know that you would be back to enjoy it with me. There's not a lot of pleasure in cooking just for one. Food is a social experience. It needs good company, as you're the best of company I'm full of anticipation - even if I am the Chef de Cuisine, or whatever the feminine of Chef might be!' She held him in her arms with her head on his shoulder. How happy and fortunate she felt, deeply at peace with herself and the world. How she loved him! 'You've got a quarter of an hour to get ready and you'll be in trouble if you are late to the table. We've chestnut and bacon soup to start and it's not good if its cold.'

Lewis relished the warmth of her body against his. The fragrance of her perfume worked it's usual magic on him. 'Hold it Elizabeth! Go easy if you want to be at the dinner table in fifteen minutes, you're increasing my pulse rate by the second!' He held her away from himself and looked at her. She wore a midnight blue silk blouse and matching evening trousers. 'In that gear you don't look like the Chef. You are every inch the accomplished hostess. Svelte and lovely. You're stunning, absolutely stunning, Elizabeth. I'm the luckiest of men!'

'And next jugged hare. You've got to disbelieve your nose with this Peter but I can assure you that the effort's worth while! You can pour the Châteauneuf-du-Pape while I serve up, it's had plenty of time to breathe. We bought a dozen bottles of it on our way back from Fontaine-de-Vaucluse to Avignon, remember? Of course you do! It was something special wasn't it? I'll never forget our time in France together, Peter! Never! By the way I collected the book of Petrarch's Sonnets from a book shop in West End Lane this afternoon, they were very helpful there - nothing was too much trouble - different from some of the so called book shops in the West End itself. And I've been able to get the CDs of the music, so it's really going to be a multi media evening! But food first and then when we've eaten and cleared up we can attend to Petrarch and his Laura over coffee.'

'Fine. You've returned to your English roots with tonight's meal, Elizabeth. Well done, I haven't had hare for years! I'm glad that I've brought home a hefty appetite to do justice to your efforts.'

'There's some dessert wine in the fridge, Peter, to accompany the summer pudding. It's a half bottle of Muscat de Baumes-de-Venise, I've stayed loyal to the Rhône vineyards like Ruth does in the case of her business. And mentioning Ruth, you were going to tell me how Michael was weren't you? Has he got over his illness completely yet?'

'Physically he's fine, he can walk the legs off me - as I

found getting to the ground this afternoon. He says he's a bit down at times, ever so slightly depressed you know, as a result of the illness. But I'm sure that it will go, he responds well to events and people, even though Chelsea only drew the game he enjoyed it. By the way I've told him about the skiing trip to Switzerland for the New Year. It was good of you to say that you didn't mind my going with him, Elizabeth. I'd rather not leave you out but, as things are at present, there is really no alternative.'

'He's showing no sign of softening in his attitude to me then, Peter?'

'Not yet, but stay tuned, he's bound to change in time.'

'You know I want him to. I can't be his mother but I'd like him to treat me as an aunt or something like that. Did he say anything about me?'

'He's against divorce, so he said. No he didn't say anything specifically about you except that while he's happy to speak to you on the 'phone at the office he not keen to 'phone here in case you answer the call.'

'He accepts me as secretary but not as mistress. Well that's somewhere between 25% and 33% of my time, so perhaps I'm making progress with him! No, I'm not upset Peter. I understand how he must feel about you and me. He's at a difficult age when he desperately needs stability and in addition he's been very unwell. I'll be patient and hope that he'll come round to at least accepting me.'

'I've suggested that he should text me so that I can call him back, you know to advise on homework and that sort of thing. I don't really like the idea but it seems a way of keeping communications open and being available to him.'

'I don't mind how you keep your communications open as long as you give Michael all the time and care he needs, Peter.'

'Thanks for being so concerned about him, Elizabeth, it's a great help.' Lewis went off to the kitchen in search of the dessert wine to accompany the sharp red fruits of the summer pudding.

'That was splendid, Elizabeth. A meal to remember.' He looked up at her as she poured the coffee. She had been quick to realise that though he liked espresso coffee he did not like it in tiny cups. Since then she had served it in decent sized cups.

'Statesman-like as usual?'

'As usual, my Dear!' Early on in their acquaintance she had asked him how he liked his coffee and he had responded with a quote from a French statesman of the past, which one it was eluded his memory, "Hot as hell, black as night and sweet as love." From then on she had used the description "statesman-like" for his coffee. It was little things like this that cemented relationships, and at times she wondered what special expressions he and Ruth had used in the good days of their marriage.

'And so to Petrarch and his sonnets as interpreted by Liszt. If you're comfortable, Peter, I'll tell you what I've found out and then play the music.'

'Go ahead and further my education, I can picture his river valley and our visit. What was the river called? Was it the Source?'

'Not quite, the Sorgue, I think it was. First of all then, Liszt set the words of three of the sonnets in the Italian of Petrarch's time to piano accompaniment and he also wrote solo piano pieces based on the three - I assume that the songs came before the solo piano versions, but that's a guess - he also revised both sets of pieces so there are at least two versions of each. I've got the earlier version in each case. Sorry if this sounds like a talk on Radio Three! I think that there must have been something in Liszt's own experience of life and love that matched Petrarch's and made the sonnets significant for him. It's interesting how one thing leads to another, I've got the book shop looking for a readable biography of Franz Liszt. OK, we'll have the songs first and then the piano pieces. After that we'll look at the words together - you can follow them in the songs from the leaflet with the CD, the translation's a bit different from my book - but which is better is anyone's guess if you don't know Mediaeval Italian! You're having a real day of culture, Peter, first the *prima donnas* of the pitch at Highbury and now this! I hope that it isn't all too much. A little Cognac to go with the coffee and then I'll put the CDs on.'

'Thanks, a *digestif* will do very nicely after the rich fare you've served tonight. You've obviously enjoyed your research on Petrarch and Liszt and I'm looking forward to benefiting from your efforts.'

'A tortured soul, our Petrarch. Is that how you see him, Elizabeth?'

'I've been thinking about that since this afternoon. Certainly in the first of the three sonnets he's hurt, confused and experiencing contradictory emotions and physical symptoms to go with them, feeling hot and cold, being a captive in a prison without locks, hating himself and loving another and that sort of thing - a suitable case for treatment, ripe for the shrink! The music catches something of the turmoil. But the second one is different. He's moved on and he blesses the day he met Laura. He accepts and even enjoys the bondage to which her "two beautiful eyes" have brought him. He's still got "sighs, tears and desire" but he regards his earlier anguish as his "first sweet suffering" and he's definitely obsessed with her, "my thought that is only of her, no other has any part". And he speaks of being "in love joined," whatever that may mean in their situation!'

'Do you think it's healthier to suffer your pain and to see it as hurt or to welcome it as "sweet suffering", Elizabeth?'

'I think it's progress if it enabled him to cope. He's happy that he met and fell for her. Why do you think he makes so much of her eyes, Peter? It's the only physical aspect he refers to.'

'Perhaps it's got something to do with the conventions of the day. She was another man's wife after all and he probably had to be careful about what he said. He seems to have published his sonnets about her, what does he say? Ah yes, here it is, "blessed be all the writings where I fame for them" - that's his tears and his desire for her - "where I fame for them obtained." I wonder if she was really called Laura or whether he invented the name to spare her and her husband embarrassment. More research for you, Elizabeth. That's once you've sorted out Franz Liszt!'

'It all makes you want to know a lot more about them and the world in which they lived. I bet a lot of guesses have been made, just like ours, Peter.

'It's the last one that intrigues me. *Her* "beautiful eyes" are weeping. *She* sighs. "Love, wisdom, virtue, compassion and pain" make a harmony with her tears and it ends with intense harmony and sweetness filling the air.

'You wonder if she was in love with him but was held back from any physical expression by her very virtue which he celebrates. So for her, love plus virtue equals pain. Or the weeping might have been due to the plague that killed her, I just don't know. The more you read the more you want to know about them.'

'Well Elizabeth, he's made them both live on. If theirs had been a happy, fulfilled love then, I suppose, we would never have heard of them and we'd be discussing something else tonight!'

'Just so and ours is a very different world. On the other hand even though Petrarch was a member of the Papal court that wouldn't necessarily have made *him* virtuous - the Popes themselves didn't set a very good example at times did they?'

'I was telling Michael this afternoon that times and attitudes change.' He paused wondering whether he should have taken up the point but found he had to go on and explain, 'He was lamenting the prevalence of parents splitting up - it seems most of his friends' parents have done so and that Ruth and I are in the majority so far as Michael's statistical sample is concerned. When I said that the divorce laws had changed he said that they shouldn't and I explained that attitudes had changed so that changing the laws had followed.'

'It's not at all surprising that he's upset at the prospect of your divorce. It'll hurt him, you know. He's very sensitive at the moment after his illness and don't forget he's at a difficult stage of his development. There probably couldn't be a worse time for you and Ruth to divorce so far as Michael is concerned.'

'And so you don't think that we should divorce?'

'I didn't say that Peter. I love you and I want to be your wife as soon as possible. I've never loved anyone as I love you. You've made me happy, almost impossibly happy, and I want to be yours always. But you must be very careful not to hurt Michael, it won't be easy but you must take his feelings into account.'

'Thanks for your concern Elizabeth. I haven't forgotten

that you lost your father when you were young - I know you don't want to discuss it and I respect that, pain can be very deep and long lasting.'

'He died in an accident - as I think I've told you Peter - but in many ways it must be worse if a father just takes himself off and abandons his kids - I'm sure I've also said that to you before. Then they haven't just lost a father, they've been abandoned by a parent who's gone off to amuse himself - that's most unnatural and very hurtful to any child. I want to marry you Peter more than anything but I'll wait, if necessary, so that Michael won't be hurt in the process. Now how about a little more Cognac, then we'll listen to the songs again and after that head for the bedroom and bring the evening to a fitting conclusion. That's if the idea appeals to you, Peter!'

'Try as I might, Elizabeth, I'm unable to beat that as the best idea imaginable for the remainder of the evening. You have my vote in favour, so you can take the motion as having been carried.'

***

Sam was on his own, he had sent Joe off to enjoy a Saturday evening in the pub or wherever he fancied. The bugs in Elizabeth's apartment had brought little of note to his attention so far as the operation was concerned. She and Lewis had eaten late and appeared to be in the sitting room listening to music by someone called List, so far as he could make out. She had played piano music and some songs in a language Sam couldn't penetrate, though it sounded like Italian. He listened in to their conversation. It had something to do with their time together in southern France and it seemed to be about someone called Patrick, though that didn't sound like an

Italian name. He'd written poems about a woman called Laura - Sam thought he'd caught that accurately - who'd captivated him but he'd only been able to admire her from afar. He'd admired her, written his poems and then she'd died of plague. Somehow Patrick had kept going even though he'd had no fulfilment of his love for Laura. Two of the phrases from their conversation stuck in Sam's mind – Patrick had been "a captive in a prison without locks" and Lewis had referred to him as "a tortured soul". It seemed that the son, Michael, was being affected by the impending divorce. Might this impact on Lewis' relationship with Elizabeth? Who could tell?

Sam went to the kitchen to make himself a coffee. While the kettle was heating up he pondered their discussion and his own situation. *He* was captivated by Elizabeth. Had *he* created a prison without bars for himself and was he in danger of becoming a tortured soul? He thought again of speaking to Winters and being assigned to another job but immediately rejected the idea, aware that this decision testified to the strength of the infatuation. While there was the slightest chance of finding fulfilment he would continue his thraldom. He would have to be careful to keep busy and occupied in the weeks ahead. To redirect his thoughts he turned to the word "soul" and retrieved from his memory what he had once taught his students on the subject, better for the moment to turn his thoughts away from the attractive Elizabeth Fielder! Another comment of Lewis' came to mind: he had said of Patrick, 'He's definitely obsessed with her.' Sam wondered whether things were as bad as that with himself.

***

Lewis was sleeping soundly. As Elizabeth lay beside him the phrase that kept running through her mind was from the last of the sonnets, *"tanta dolcessa - so much sweetness."* How lovely the river had been at Fontaine-de-Vaucluse with its crystal clear water. The gentle breeze had blown in their faces as they had stood on the bank drinking in the scene and enjoying one another's company. She pictured Petrarch there with his love, pain and desire turned to sweetness. How sweet life was here in London with the man she loved. How fortunate she was to have him. The spectres that might threaten the sweetness and joy of her love for Peter seemed far away for the moment and almost forgotten. Not entirely out of mind but safely distant and under control. How she would fight anything that threatened their love for one another! No fighting now though, she put her arms around him and enjoyed the reassuring warmth. Theirs was *"armonia sì intento - a harmony so intense."* For another hour the music ran through her mind, then she too slept calmly and deeply, to awaken in the morning refreshed but still excited at their ability to share and enjoy life together.

***

Ruth mopped Michael's brow with his face flannel. A few weeks before she had been doing this to cool his fever while he lay ill in the clinic, now she was waking him up after another of his nightmares. He hadn't had one for a week and she had hoped that they wouldn't recur, but tonight's had been one of the worst. She looked at the clock, nearly one o'clock, she had been in bed for an hour before his voice in the next room had woken her. It was like listening to one side of an argument on the telephone. Since their return from France Ruth had slept with their bedroom doors open. The au pair had her own flat and Ruth did not want to involve her in Michael's problems, that was a parent's rôle.

'It's all right Michael, I'm here and nothing will hurt you.'

'Sorry Mum, I didn't wake you on purpose but the dream frightened me. Don't remember what it was all about but there was a rock and I was on it - on my own, I think, stuck there without you or Dad.' He lay quiet. 'Thanks for coming in to be with me, Mum.'

'That's what Mums are for. Why don't you go to the bathroom now that you are properly awake and I will get you something to drink. I could do with something myself, how about a hot chocolate, that's what I fancy. OK I'll get it once you've been to the bathroom.' She made sure that he was steady and not in danger of falling over. While he was out of the room it she checked his bed. Good he hadn't wet it - that was a problem she could do without! She shook his pillow and tidied the bed which looked as though it had been hit by a tornado. Michael returned and climbed back into bed.

'It's OK Mum, you needn't stay up, I'm OK.'

'No problem, Michael, I need a drink and I expect you could really do with one yourself.'

She went off to the kitchen and sat on a stool waiting for the milk to heat up in the microwave and looking at the holiday postcards stuck on the wall next to the breakfast bar. Her friends certainly roved the world! She made the hot chocolate in a couple of mugs, having recovered one of Michael's Chelsea Football Club mugs from the dishwasher.

'Here we are for a loyal Chelsea fan. Sorry about today's result but they can't always win can they. That wasn't what upset you was it, Michael?'

'No, I don't think so. I enjoyed being there with Dad. ... I just wish he was here now and that he hadn't gone away. You don't think he'll come back do you, Mum?'

'It's a bit late at night for all that Michael, but I would be deceiving you if I said "Yes" to your question. But don't worry, your Dad won't neglect you and neither will I. We both love you and we'll keep loving you.'

'I wish you loved each other as well Mum.'

'We did but we've both changed, I suppose.'

'You and Dad won't change with me will you, Mum?'

'We won't change, I promise that.'

'Didn't Dad and you promise that to each other?'

'But that's different Michael. A man and woman can fall out of love. A parent's love for their child is different.'

'James at school hasn't seen his father for two years and he never hears from him.'

'That's unusual, Michael. Don't forget your Dad's been gone from here for eighteen months and he hasn't neglected you has he?'

'He hasn't had that Elizabeth for eighteen months has he, Mum? I'm afraid that she'll take him away from me. What if she has a baby? Will he still be interested in me?'

'Did James' father take much interest in him before he left James' mother?'

'I don't think he did, Mum.'

'That's your answer, Michael. Both your Dad and I have always loved you and cared for you and that won't stop when we get divorced. I've met Elizabeth as you have and I'm sure she wouldn't stop your Dad from spending time with you, Michael. You're no threat to her after all and she's a caring person. So don't worry. Now I must get back to bed myself. If you want to do something before you go to sleep then read one of your football papers, nothing that gets your lively imagination going, please!'

She kissed him and took the empty mugs to the kitchen.

Back in her bedroom she unlocked her bureau and took out a small red notebook. She thought for a while - so Michael too had realised that Elizabeth and his father might want to have a child of their own. She knew that it was very likely that they would. How would Michael respond if it did happen? She took up her pen and wrote down what Michael had said. She hoped his problems would go away, but if they had to get help it would be important to have a record. The clock said twenty to two. It was a good thing that it was Sunday morning and that she and Michael were visiting friends near Oxford for lunch. They could both sleep on and if they left by eleven thirty they would be there in good time.

For a while she lay wondering how long Michael's problems would continue. He had never been like this before - no doubt it was just a passing phase made worse by his recent illness and it would go. Or perhaps it wouldn't! She remembered the psychiatric problems that her own brother had had and which still persisted. When Michael had recovered from his illness she had been so thankful. Now there were more problems. Michael was right - it would be far easier if Peter hadn't left her, indeed that seemed to be part or most of the trouble so far as Michael was concerned. Until recent weeks she had taken the idea of their divorce in her stride, in the early hours of that morning the doubts that had recently begun to gather in her mind became stronger. It would be so much easier if Peter were there. And not just that, she had come to realise to her surprise that she was beginning to miss Peter's companionship as well as his support. When he had moved out she had been busy with her business and she had responded by becoming even busier. Her resolve, in response to Michael's illness, to ease back and delegate work to others was having the unexpected result of making her *feel* Peter's absence. Being an adequate parent was hard work on your own - even when the absent father was as attentive and responsible as Peter.

Chapter 21

Monday 18th November 1996

Lewis and Ruth sat self consciously with Michael in the waiting room of the Child Guidance Clinic. Their appointment was the last one of the afternoon and they were glad when the previous family were called, leaving them on their own. In the corner of the room was a Christmas tree with tinsel and glass balls decorating it. Christmas in that place evidently began some time before the end of November. The room itself had decorations that came out of a box each year and were put up by the secretaries in an effort to bring a touch of cheer and perhaps to bring the year to a close as speedily as possible. The premises were in need of a coat of paint and the carpet was overdue for replacement.

Conversation had been exhausted, but with the room to themselves, they were more comfortable. They had the feeling at the back of their minds that they ought not to be there and that their presence in that place was somehow demeaning. Other families might have difficulties but they had not themselves expected to have problems of this kind! Ruth picked up a women's magazine from the pile on the table. She noted without enthusiasm that it was six months old and one of the more down market magazines with lurid subject matter. 'Probably the sort of experiences that most of the clients of this place have had or are going to have,' was the thought that ran through her mind as she scanned its pages. But here *she* was with Peter and Michael, sent there by their GP! How often were they going to have to come to this place or places like it? Michael sat reading a football paper, seemingly totally absorbed and oblivious to parents and place. Peter Lewis gazed out the window letting a variety of unconnected thoughts run through his mind.

At length their turn came and an elderly secretary showed them into the psychiatrist's room. It was a relief that the session was about to get under way. They were greeted by the child psychiatrist, a wiry young man, probably in his early thirties, wearing a tweed sports coat that seemed older than himself and green corduroy trousers. His metal spectacles seemed to be part of his identity. He rose from his desk to greet them and to show them to easy chairs where he took his seat with them at the other end of the room, 'Good to see you, I'm Jim Parker. You'd better introduce yourselves to me and tell me how you want to be addressed.'

'I'm Michael Lewis the cause of us all being here. Please call me Michael.' He looked up, meeting and holding Parker's gaze. This man was a challenge that he intended to meet.

The thought that went through the minds of both Lewis and his wife was the same, 'What will he read into the order of our introductions and how we wish to be addressed?' They knew that they, as much as Michael were under scrutiny in that place.

'Peter Lewis, call me whatever comes easiest to you.' He pushed the initiative back.

'Peter, then if you don't object.'

'And I'm Ruth Lewis - Ruth will do OK'

'Ruth it is then. Do I detect an American accent?'

'You do. It surfaces when I'm under stress.'

'You're under stress? I mean at the moment?'

'At the moment, yes, I am. But then I expect that most of your clients are under stress when they come to you, aren't they?'

'Yes, they usually are but the first task is to try to

remove the stress and encourage them to be open, relaxed and honest. Building up a good working relationship is important if we're going to succeed. What part of the States are you from, Ruth?'

'California, the Napa Valley - my family have vineyards there but I've been in England for some years.'

'My sister works in LA, she's in the same line as I am - no lack of business out there! She's a very busy woman.'

'And a wealthy one?'

'She doesn't do too badly. But you, Peter are from these parts aren't you?'

'Quite right, I'm a Londoner. Ruth and I met at University and she stayed on rather than going back to the USA.'

'Now we ought to get started, I'm running about fifteen minutes late but don't let that worry you. Incidentally, apologies for the delay, but it isn't always possible to keep precisely to a timetable and I had a client in earlier who needed more time and so, of course, I had to attend to them.' There was something about the word 'client' that held for Lewis and his wife a touch of clinical menace, though they would have been hard pressed to say precisely why this was so or what alternative description he might have used.

'Now Michael, I've heard about your problems from Dr Wilson, your GP. You'll tell me about them in a moment, I hope, but first of all I'd like you to tell me what you think I'm going to be able to do for you.'

'I hope that you're going to make me better and sort out what's upsetting me.'

'First of all you have to realise that I'm not able to 'make you better'. I'm not in the magic wand business! What I can do is to help *you* Michael, with your Mum and Dad, to sort things out and deal with them. Together we've got to get at the causes of what's upsetting you. Then I hope to be able to show you how to deal with them. Does that disappoint you?'

'It does a bit. I'd hoped that you could do something quick. But you say that I've got to do it myself?'

'You're willing to do all you can to deal with things? You want things sorted out?'

'Oh, yes!'

'Good, because you won't get a list of instructions from me. It won't be a case of do this and everything in the garden will be lovely! But I can help you to see the way forward and how to deal with your problems. And that goes for your Mum and Dad as well because it may be a family problem and not just your problem, Michael.' He turned to Ruth and Peter, 'You understand that it is more than likely that you will all have to work together to get things right for Michael. There may not be a perfect solution but there may be ways of reducing the effect of your problems on Michael - Dr Wilson has told me that you're separated. I'm not, of course, going to ask you things in front of Michael that will embarrass you but if he is willing to say, in front of you, how he sees things are you willing to have him do that?'

Both nodded their assent and Lewis added, 'Of course, that's if you're willing, Ruth.'

She nodded again, 'OK by me.'

'And Michael, if there are things that you only want to mention to me and not to your parents then you can speak about them when they're out of the room. Right, let's get going. Michael, tell me about your recent illness, about what has happened since and any things that are worrying you. I don't expect that I need to tell you that the years from 12 to 16 are probably the most difficult of a person's life.'

Michael broke in, 'There I told you Mum, I wanted to hibernate through them!'

'You sure did Michael! That I do remember.' She was glad he wasn't tongue-tied in this setting.

'But that's not an option we can offer you, Michael, hard as these years are going to be – they're all part of reaching maturity, coming to understand the meaning of your life. It all takes time and it won't necessarily be easy. First of all the illness itself ... '

'And I don't believe that Michael reading imaginative books by authors like Tolkien will do him any harm at all. The imagination needs to be fed so that children are able to cope with their emotions.' He turned to Lewis and Ruth, 'If either of you have the time you might like to read Bruno Bettelheim's *'The Uses of Enchantment'*, it's about fairy stories and what they can do to help children cope with their emotions and fears. Believe me kids could do with a helping of stories of that kind, it would be better for them than most of their TV and video diet. By the way Bettelheim was imprisoned by the Nazis in Dachau and Buchenwald so he wasn't someone who wrote from an ivory academic tower or even the Lady of Shalott's gray tower. He really knew what evil was at first hand.

'The next appointment I can manage will be around the middle of December and I'd like you all to be present. After that I would be able to see Michael at monthly intervals. May I suggest 16 December at half past four?'

'Before we came here,' Lewis looked at Ruth, 'we discussed whether it might not be better if Michael had private appointments, weekly if that would speed the effectiveness of the treatment. Could that be arranged Dr Parker and would more frequent sessions be beneficial? It would help if Michael could attend in the early evening after school so that he didn't have to take time off.'

'I'll see what I can arrange. Would it be convenient for me to telephone either of you tomorrow morning?'

'Call me. I'll be in the office all day.' Lewis took a business card from his wallet and passed it to the psychiatrist.

After the usual courtesies they left Parker's room and found their way out of the building. Darkness had fallen while they had been with Parker and nightfall had intensified the rawness of the damp. They were glad to get into Ruth's Volvo Estate - there they were back on familiar territory.

'Let's leave the post mortem on that until we've had a little time to take it in. How about a chat after supper? You said your au pair would have some supper ready around six, may I invite myself, Ruth?'

'You know you're always welcome Peter, of course you can. What you suggest sounds a good approach. What do you think Michael, leave talking about what Jim Parker had to say until later?'

'Fine by me Mum!'

***

Their discussion of the afternoon's session was over and they had been pleased at Michael's favourable reaction to Parker. Michael had retired to his bedroom to do some homework and Lewis and Ruth sat facing one another across the kitchen table.

'He seems to have taken it very calmly and in his stride, don't you think Ruth?'

'He gives that impression, I agree. It's mainly at night when he's asleep and not repressing his thoughts that the distress shows through, a sort of safety valve I suppose for him. His nightmares are very vivid, you know.'

'I wish that he'd had one while I was here waiting for you to get back from France in October. If you haven't experienced a person's distress it's hard to be able to deal with it properly. You said that it had to do with me, Ruth?'

'I didn't elaborate earlier as I was hoping that it would go away of its own accord. It hasn't and so, I suppose, we've got to face it. After all that's what this afternoon's session was about.' She paused and looked at Lewis, 'He's badly scared of losing you, that's my assessment of what seems to be disturbing him. That might account for him not being disturbed while you were here. By his reckoning you were where you ought to be and he felt safe. It's just my guess, like you I'm not trained in these things. You feel hopeless don't you, in the hands of the professionals. And you wonder whether they really know anything about it or whether it's all a game that keeps them employed in the priesthood of a Freudian or Jungian cult or something like that!'

'We don't seem to have much alternative though do we? What else can we do for Michael?'

'There's nowhere else that I know of, Peter. I don't like it any more than you do. It isn't comfortable having to open up to a stranger is it? And we're all going to have to do that if he's going to get anywhere with Michael. But if it will get him right it's a price we've got to pay.'

'*If* it works. Don't worry, Ruth, I'm fully committed to giving Parker a proper chance to see what he can do for Michael, even if it's painful for myself. You've told me something about Michael's nightmares - you obviously think that they give the clue to what is disturbing him - I want you to be completely open with me ... just what do they seem to be about? What has he said to you?'

'You are sure, really sure, that you want to know?'

'I want him better as much as you do.' There was a touch of anger in his voice.

'OK Peter, I know that. We're united on that point.' She found her handbag and took from it the small red notebook. 'I've been keeping a diary on Michael so that I wouldn't have to rely on my memory. I'll be able to give Parker accurate information if he wants to hear from me, which I assume he will.'

'Subject to Michael's approval, I suppose!'

'I expect so. Well, you want to know what he says?'

'I've already said so Ruth, haven't I?'

'Sorry, Peter, it isn't easy. OK here goes. This was 30th October when he woke at 1.30 in the morning - it's pretty typical, "Dad don't go! Stay with us! I don't want to lose you!" He addresses you in each nightmare, I'm afraid.'

'And anything else, Ruth?'

She paused trying to make up her mind. Lewis observed her reticence, leant across the coffee table and took the notebook. He looked at the open page in Ruth's familiar tidy handwriting. Elizabeth's name was there as well as his own. *"I hate that Elizabeth, she's taken Dad away from us. ... I want her to die then Dad will come back home again ... "* He leafed through the notebook and saw her name on most pages. He closed the book and handed it to Ruth. She tried to avoid his gaze. Her embarrassment and his agitation had brought a sharp increase of tension between them. There was a prolonged silence which was eventually broken by Ruth.

'I'm sorry Peter, I would rather that you hadn't known. It's not a fair accusation. She hasn't taken you away from Michael, you give him plenty of time - though of course you're not here when he comes home at night wanting to talk about the day. But then plenty of fathers are out at work until late or away on business for days or weeks on end and their children don't see them every night. And she didn't take you away from me, we'd already drifted apart by the time she came on the scene. When you first took up with her I was glad in a funny sort of way because I knew that you needed a woman's influence to keep you organised and a woman's company to prevent you from becoming a crusty old bachelor! Elizabeth's been good for you, very good. Since you moved into her apartment you've been more relaxed than I've seen you for a very long time.'

They were silent again.

Once more Ruth broke the silence, 'I'm sure that Michael *knows* that you won't abandon him and that Elizabeth didn't take you from me. It's just that he *feels* differently. That's what Jim Parker's got to sort out for him, or rather with him, isn't it?'

'I guess so, Ruth.' Lewis was numb and churned up inside.

'I'll get you another coffee before you go, Peter.'

'Please, I could do with it Ruth. And while you're making it I'll go to the bathroom.' Both noticed that he didn't say lavatory, at home he always followed Ruth's American usage. Despite everything this place was, in some sense, still 'home' - the grip of their shared memories still had a strong hold on him.

***

Lewis' stomach still felt churned up as he drove back to Elizabeth's apartment. He was very edgy throughout the journey and was relieved to park the car safely in the street near the entrance to the block.

'You've had a rough time with the shrink by the way you look, Peter! Just relax and I'll get you a drink - Scotch Whisky, Irish Whiskey, Port or something hot?'

'A toddy as a night-cap, I think. I've had enough coffee for the moment - I do want to be able to sleep tonight.'

'Good, make yourself comfortable while I do the necessary. Then I want to hear how you got on and how Michael and Ruth have taken it.'

Lewis headed for the lavatory. Was he getting old, or was it the stress or merely the quantity of coffee he'd imbibed during the day? He felt ill at ease with himself and with the world in general. Back in the sitting room he slumped into the sofa and relaxed a little. The gentle lighting and the music from the hi-fi soothed him. He was beginning to wonder what he should tell Elizabeth, when she came into the room with two steaming tumblers on a small silver tray.'

'Sorry that we can't afford a butler, Peter. You'll just have to make do with me, I'm afraid.' She placed the tray on the sofa table before removing the tumblers to coasters at different ends of the table and taking her seat at the other end of the sofa. 'Well how do you reckon that it went this afternoon?'

'Reasonably well, I think. Michael seems to feel that he'll be able to unburden himself to the psychiatrist and that he's a person he can get on with. So that's a start. We found him OK as well. I must admit I was afraid that Ruth and I would come under fire and be accused of causing all the trouble, in fact that we and Michael would be grilled to make sure that he wasn't a victim of child abuse! That didn't seem to be the line, though you can never be sure that they won't follow that trail if it appeals to them later on. We've nothing to hide, but I can do without the distress of being suspected of that sort of thing. There are enough cases, here and in the USA, of "memories" being planted in children's minds by these people and distraught parents being falsely accused, to make you a bit wary when you get involved with shrinks and their ilk!' He sipped the toddy, 'It's good to come home to you here Elizabeth and to begin to unwind a little.' He took her hand and smiled, 'You're the best therapist a man could have. You personally and your music, Chopin, isn't it? With Rubinstein as the pianist at a guess.'

'I'm more than happy to provide effective therapy and you're right, it's Rubinstein's recording of the Chopin Nocturnes. Nocturnes and night-cap go together well don't you think?'

'Perfectly, Elizabeth. I can feel the stresses falling away under your influence.' He kissed her hand. 'Your talk of butlers has made me quite old fashioned, m'dear!' They sat quietly for a few minutes listening to the music.

Elizabeth took a sip from her glass, 'And do you think that the shrink will be able to sort things out for Michael? Is there any suggestion of what's at the root of his distress, Peter?'

Lewis thought for a moment, 'His illness in France, of course, made him feel low and he's taken a while to really get well after that, a sort of mildly depressed condition. But it seems the main thing is ... him worrying about losing me. He's got to both *know* and *feel* that I'll always be around for him. I hope that Parker, the shrink, will be able to deal with those worries.'

'I can promise you Peter that I'll always make sure that you give him all the time he needs. In fact I'll chase you into doing so if you ever fall down on your duties.'

'You've already made very clear that my responsibilities to Michael are not to be skimped and I'm grateful to you for that, Elizabeth.'

'I like him very much, Peter, you know that. Perhaps I'll be able to convince him of it in time.'

'Of course you will!'

'I just hope so, I really do!'

'No problems with the business this afternoon?'

'No problems. Eugene 'phoned in another order for despatch to Canada in early January. This one's worth £195,000 so it will be a useful start to the year.'

'He certainly has brought in the business since he came on the scene. In fact the two of you have fairly revolutionised things since you discovered Kilburn. It's been quite a year, hasn't it?'

'A year I'll never forget, Peter!' She moved alongside him and kissed him on the lips, 'You've changed my life, Peter, and I'm so grateful ... so grateful!'

'And you've transformed things for me. I can picture me by myself in my apartment near here at the beginning of the year. On my own most evenings and bringing work home and getting pretty jaded. Then you came along and ... wow, what a change! Vera's death was awful though, if only you could have come my way without that! We mustn't forget her family at Christmas, perhaps you wouldn't mind going round there with me next week, taking some things and seeing how they are. It must be three months since I last saw them.'

'No problem, of course I'll come. I'd already got it in your office diary, for the week after next I think, so I'll change it tomorrow and you can give me some idea of what you want to take them.' Once again anger welled up within her at the way her SVR colleagues had been willing to dispose of her predecessor as Peter's secretary to make way for her to take over. She felt a sense of guilt and shame whenever she thought of Vera and her family and she still didn't know how she would ever be able to tell Peter the truth about Vera's death. This knowledge was a burden she carried within and from which she could see no prospect of release, a secret canker that might well harm their relationship. Of course she would go there with Peter but she knew that the visit would renew her feeling of being soiled by the ruthlessness of her colleagues. The sooner she was rid of them the better. She longed to spared the play-acting. If only she could be herself! If only she could be completely open and honest with Peter, what a relief that would be! But first she would have to break clear of the SVR and she wondered whether her mother would be used by them as a pawn in the game.

The music finished and after a couple of minutes Lewis raised his tumbler to make sure that it was empty. 'Some more, Peter?'

'No thanks. Nocturnes and night-cap have done their trick. I'm much more relaxed than when I got home. If you're ready for the next phase of the therapy then I am.'

'The next phase?'

'Bed and my personal therapist, Elizabeth. I welcome the prospect of total relaxation!'

'Therapy, yes! Therapist, no! That's too clinical! I love you, Peter, that's what matters!'

***

The clock in the hall struck one o'clock. Elizabeth tried to be still so as not to disturb Peter as he lay sleeping somewhat restlessly alongside her. Lovemaking over, she had asked him what Michael had said about her. He had replied that Michael wasn't reconciled to their relationship and had added that he hoped it would only be a matter of time before he changed. She had known instinctively that Peter was holding back. She suspected that Michael had been much more forthright than that: she was well aware of his coldness to her. She hoped and prayed that this would not become another canker eating away at her relationship with Peter, the only real relationship she had had with a man since her father died. Sleep did not come for several hours and she awoke feeling unrefreshed and apprehensive.

Chapter 22

Friday 20th December 1996

'... the loving relationship between husband and wife is clear - just observe the way his eyes are fixed on her face - what the painting does not tell you is anything of the relationship between Lavoisier, his wife and the portrait's painter Jacques-Louis David. As I have said, Mme Lavoisier was a pupil of David, you can see her portfolio of paintings on the chair behind the couple, the painting *does* draw attention to that. A while after the portrait was painted Lavoisier was tried by a revolutionary tribunal for being a senior tax collector - the French Revolutionaries seem to have felt the same about their tax authorities as our G. Gordon Liddy about the Internal Revenue.' The group laughed and the guide continued, 'David was a member of the Tribunal that condemned Lavoisier to be guillotined on May 8th, 1794 and shortly afterwards he attempted to get the widow, his former pupil you will remember, *to marry him*! So as you look at the tranquil portrait of this couple you are made to wonder about the thoughts and feelings that they and the artist had as it was being painted. There's also a contrast between the calm and elegance of the couple and the chaos of the Revolution beyond their walls that destroyed their life together. It's a fine portrait and David deals wonderfully with the scientific glassware on the table and below it - look at the reflections of the window which is out of sight to the left of the picture - but there are hidden tensions there. Now we must move on to the next work.'

'Sam, can we stop here, please. I don't want to finish the tour, we've seen a lot here in the Metropolitan Museum and I need to talk.'

'OK by me, Mia. I've enjoyed what she's told us. Like having an extra pair of eyes, and well trained ones at that, isn't it. How about a drink? Not the cafeteria, that's always crowded when I'm here, there's a place near Rodin's sculpture "The Burghers of Calais" that's more peaceful, how about trying to find that?'

'Yes, I don't want to be in a crowd. I want to be able to chat with you for a while, Sam. I want to know what's bugging you. You're not yourself, something's wrong isn't it? Things aren't the same between us are they? I must know why, Sam.'

'OK I've been meaning to talk to you but it hasn't been easy. Thanks for the opportunity, Mia. We'll see if we can find the place for a drink. OK, here's the plan of the Museum. Let's see which way round I've got to hold it. Yes, the entrance is that way and we're here. So we head in that direction ... '

They sat facing one another over a marble topped table, Sam with a lager and Mia with a glass of orange juice. In five minutes they had said little to one another, each respecting the other and knowing that the conversation was not going to be easy.

'I've seen those "Burghers of Calais" all over the place, Mia. Old Rodin must have had a production line churning the things out. As you know there's even one of the figures from the group back in the Brooklyn Museum. I remember seeing it as a child, never guessing that I'd see the rest of the group in Calais and in Paris - you should see the Rodin Museum there, in a château almost next to Napoleon's tomb, full of Rodin's works. That one of course, then there's "The Gates of Hell", "The Thinker" and "The Kiss".'

'You forget I've never been out of New York State, Sam.

And perhaps I never will!' She pushed a strand of her dark hair back under her head scarf and looked him in the eye, catching and holding his gaze. 'There's something wrong between us, isn't there Sam? When the guide said that the Revolution had destroyed the Lavoisiers' life together I wanted to cry. Something is wrong isn't it?' Tears were forming in her eyes. 'Is there someone that *you* kiss in Paris, Sam?'

He took her hand, 'This isn't easy, Mia, it isn't at all easy. No, there aren't any stolen kisses in Paris, in London or anywhere else! It's much more vague and indefinite and for that reason it's harder to talk about and deal with. I'm glad that you've made me speak about it - it's got to be faced and I've got to be honest with you.'

He was used to tough situations and dealing with all manner of people but nothing in his experience had prepared him for this explanation to his fiancée. He wanted to get it right and, although he had rehearsed it in his mind any number of times, he was having difficulty in getting his act together. He wanted to get it right but he didn't want her to feel that he was serving up some kind of prepared statement of self justification, delivered like lines in a play. He was still very fond of her and that made it more difficult, much more difficult.

'This isn't easy, Mia, but I'm going to be honest with you and hide nothing. I am in love with a woman in London but there's nothing going on between us.' He read the pain in her face but continued, he had to get this over as soon as he could. 'She's a woman I see on business and I first set eyes on her in March. Since then she's gradually taken hold of my affections until now I can't get her out of my mind. I'm so sorry to hurt you like this, Mia. I'm still very fond of you. We've known one another for so long, our families have been just like one family, doing things together at holiday time, sharing our Thanksgiving Dinners. This hasn't made me happy, Mia, and even worse it hurts you. I wish I'd never seen her and that's the truth!' And he wondered to himself whether he would end up like Petrarch, always admiring from afar – for he had followed up the subject of Lewis and Elizabeth's discussions after Avignon.

'What does she say about it, Sam?' Mia had wiped her eyes and was watching him intently. 'You're on friendly terms with her presumably?'

'I haven't ever spoken to her.'

'You haven't spoken to her about how you feel!'

'It's stranger than that, Mia, I've never spoken to her! Period!'

'You mystify me, Sam. I don't understand it.'

'You know that I can't talk about my work. You've been very good about that, Mia. You've never quizzed me about it and I'm very grateful. All I can tell you is that this is a woman I see because of my work but to whom I have never spoken. And I'm in love with her. And I'm very sorry, Mia. I've never wanted to hurt you and I should have told you before now.'

'You can tell me her name, Sam?'

'Elizabeth.'

'She lives in Paris?' Although she was listening intently she wasn't retaining everything that he said.

'No, she's in London.'

'A Brit?'

'I'm not sure I can answer that question. I'm sorry.'

'I'll guess then. She's Russian.'

He lowered his voice, 'OK you're right but how did you guess?'

'Look Sam, although you've never told me about your work there are enough clues to give me a good idea. I know that you have been involved with Russians and Algerians in the past and, as Elizabeth doesn't sound like an Arab name, I opted for Russia and I was right!' Despite her hurt she smiled with pleasure at having guessed correctly. 'And I guess that your work prevents you from talking to her. You see her and *hear* her,' she caught and held his eye. 'No, I not wanting you to confirm or deny that, Sam. Is she a happily married woman, then?'

'She's living very happily with a Brit who is in the process of divorcing his wife.' She saw the sadness in his face.

' *"La Belle Dame sans Merci hath thee enthralled"*, Sam!'

'It's "in thrall" not "enthralled" unfortunately. A spectator can be enthralled and then go his way, it's different for a prisoner!' His voice dropped so that the end of the sentence was barely audible.

'Poor Sam! It's that bad?'

'It's that bad, yes. And the worst thing is that she doesn't know, Mia. She doesn't know I exist, let alone that I'm pining for her!'

'She is la Belle Dame? I mean she's lovely?'

'Yes, she's lovely. But I don't want to have to describe her - don't ask me why. I honestly haven't compared her with you and then found you wanting in any way. Do you believe me, Mia.' How vivid the memory was of his first sight of Elizabeth at close quarters on Finchley Road Station and the slight movement of her head that had made her hair swing and bounce back into its immaculate place. That gesture, that bubbling up of life and exuberance, had been the beginning of his captivation.

'I do believe you Sam. Promise me that you won't let this endanger your life, that your infatuation won't drive you into doing anything stupid. No, don't say anything about your work but I know it's dangerous. I still love you and if you were killed I would consider myself your widow. ... Yes, I would Sam! I can't ever imagine loving anyone but you. Sorry, I'm making it worse for both of us but it's the truth. I love you Sam. I don't want you to break our engagement. Can we leave things as they are for the time being? If you can bear to do so, leave it alone for now. If nothing comes of this infatuation then I want you as my husband.' She paused and took his hand, 'And if it does come to something, if you make contact and get a response, then I want you to come here and tell me. Then *I* will break the engagement. Yes, *I* will do it.'

'Why, Mia? To save face?'

'To save face for you Sam. You know how they will respond if *you* drop *me.* Well I don't want that to happen, I want you to always be a welcome guest of my family and friends, not someone whose name is avoided because they think that you have slighted me.' The tears ran down her face and Sam was relieved that she was facing into the corner and did not have an audience. He squeezed her hand gently and they sat in silence. An attendant hovered nearby wanting to clear their table, finish his shift and go home. Sam beckoned to him to take their glasses and gave him a smile but got no response, the youngster seemed lost in his own thoughts. They were the last ones there and the bar had ceased serving customers.

'Mia, you're so good and kind, I don't know what to say. I don't deserve anything like your concern for my welfare. I'm sorry for the hurt I'm causing you.'

'You're hurt Sam, that's clear. There's no one to blame, is there? No, I'm not being sarcastic. You're not to blame, Elizabeth's definitely not to blame - she doesn't know you exist - it's like something from a Greek myth! A suitable subject for Poussin or the like. It ought to be hung on the wall here. Instead it's us who find ourselves acting out the tragedy - no that word won't do but I don't know a better one. Sam, I think we ought to go ... but before we do you *must* tell me whether you still consider yourself my fiancé. I need to know!'

'Yes, Mia ... Yes I do ... as long as it doesn't cause you more hurt. As that's what you wish I'll willingly do what you want. Well, where now? What would you like to do next? Where would you like to go?'

He saw the look of determination in her face as her will took charge of her emotions. She would not let their last couple of days together in New York before his return to Europe be spoiled even by what he had now admitted to her. 'We'll stroll down 5th Avenue to see the Xmas windows and after that you'll treat me to an English tea somewhere that I choose. Then over tea we'll think how to spend the rest of the evening. Perhaps we could go up the Empire State Building and look down on all this, I love seeing New York spread out down below. I love being with you this side of the East River. Do you remember when you first brought me here to the Museum? Thanks for all the things you've introduced me to, all the things that we've done together. This time tomorrow you'll be at JFK waiting for your flight back to London and I'll miss you, Sam.' She smiled, saying his name was pleasure for her. 'Sam, we'll always be friends won't we, whatever happens?'

'Yes, Mia, always friends, never less than that, I promise.' There were tears in his eyes. He sniffed them back, 'OK let's go and see the town. There's nowhere like New York and no time of year like now.' He put his arm round her and they set off for the exit of the Metropolitan Museum and outside the crisp evening air and the bustling traffic.

***

Elizabeth and Peter emerged from the church of St Martin-in-the-Fields. They stood next to the Crib and looked out over Trafalgar Square. In the dark the Christmas tree lights shone out. Above the noise of the traffic the sound of carol singing reached them.

'It's magic, Peter! It really is. Our first Christmas together. It's a lovely time of year and it's been fun getting presents for you.'

'You're right, Elizabeth, magic is the word. Despite all the commercialism there's something extraordinary about this time of year. It almost seems true doesn't it? - the Christmas story, I mean.'

'Perhaps it is, Peter. That would be shattering for most of us wouldn't it?'

'Wouldn't it just, but I suspect it's what people would *like* to believe, wishful thinking really.'

'Maybe Peter, but just because people would like to believe it doesn't make it untrue. You're looking forward to presents? No, don't pretend you're not! That's not wishful thinking as I'll prove to you when the time comes.' She smiled at her logic and kissed him. 'Can we hear the carol singers before we eat, just for a few minutes, please? Once we're in the warm you can tell me all about your latest visit to the shrink. You were lucky to make the beginning of the concert.'

'Only by the skin of my teeth, I only just caught the Tube Train at Baker Street - the doors had to be reopened and I pushed in. It's not a civilised way to travel at this time of year, we'll take a taxi back home after we've eaten.'

They stood at the back of the crowd listening to the

carols, arms around one another and with their coat collars pulled up against the cold.

'OK let's go in search of food, Peter, but first we'll put something in the collecting box.'

Lewis discovered that he had no change and put a Five Pound note into the box only to find that Elizabeth had also produced a note from her handbag and put it in.

'They've done well from us, Elizabeth!'

'And what will we have spent on ourselves this evening, Peter? It's Christmas and there are people with very little!'

'Sorry, I didn't mean to play Scrooge, my dear. Anyhow we ought to be on our way, it's cold here. We can go along the Strand and then cut up into Covent Garden, there should be a pub or restaurant there where we can get a meal and warm up.'

They crossed back over the road to the East side of the Square and passed the South African Embassy before setting off along the Strand.

'Well some things do move on and improve, Elizabeth, there's no need for vigils and demonstrations outside here any more, perhaps there is such a thing as hope.'

'And forgiveness, some of those people had a lot to forgive and they've done so. I just hope it doesn't go wrong. Look at Ireland, another false hope and we're worrying again about exploding packages and trash bins. That car over there might be full of explosives or that bus might have some madman with a briefcase of Semtex. We're certainly paying for the sins of the fathers.' She remembered the KGB course on Britain and the Irish problem and wondered how accurate it had been. 'What do you know about Ireland and its history, Peter, have you any idea why there's been all this trouble for centuries?'

'Sorry, to be completely honest I know very little about it. I suppose I should find out because it's one of those problems that won't go away. I suppose that 99% of us have no idea about what really lies behind it and don't bother about it until we read of the next bombing or, worse still, find ourselves in the middle of one. Here we are, left into Southampton Street and we won't have far to go to warmth and food.'

'Good and I'll find you a book on Ireland for your Christmas stocking and then borrow it to read myself.'

A minute or two later they fought their way into a crowded pub and found an empty table in the corner.

'You hold the fort here and I'll get something to drink and find what food they've got on offer.' He put his coat on the chair and made his way to the bar, returning with two glasses of mulled wine.

'Try this as an antidote to the cold, I think you'll like it.'

'Yes it's good. What do they put in the stuff? There's cinnamon, I recognise that from the States - I used to have cinnamon bagels there and have you ever tried the Cinnabons they sell at the JFK departure lounge in New York? No? I'll take you there sometime just to try one! They're gorgeous, you see them rolling the dough and baking them and you have them fresh from the oven.'

'When you've finished enthusing about American buns, Elizabeth, I'll tell you what's likely to be in your glass! Red wine of course, watered down and with sugar, cinnamon - you were quick to spot it - cloves, and orange and lemon slices which stay in the bowl and don't reach the glass. You heat it up and it's a very economical and seasonable drink. Ready for another already? I'll finish mine and order, you've seen the menu? What do you fancy, you'll look in vain for subtle cooking in a place like this. It's basic English fare, steak and kidney pie and the like. With BSE and the experts' confusion it might be safer to go for a fish pie, though. How would that suit you? OK, I'll order two and recharge our glasses.'

He returned and they sat waiting for their pies, enjoying the warmth and the buzz of the pub and its customers who thronged the bar. At the far end of the room were a group of women on a night out who had had too much to drink and were becoming noisy. He was glad to be away from them and seated next to a table of Japanese businessmen who were taking in the scene, eating haggis and chips and offending no one.

'Did you see those young people in the doorway back there in the Strand, Peter?'

'Yes, it's a shame that they live like that.'

'But however do they manage to end up there? Can you imagine it? Your belongings in a bag and your home a cardboard box in a draughty doorway! And what do they do by day, apart from wandering round in the cold looking for shelter and help where they can find it? It must be dangerous and unhealthy. Why is it happening, Peter, why?'

'I suppose there are always those who opt out, kids who run away from home, people on drugs. Then there was a policy called "Care in the Community" that the Government thought up, the idea was that patients in psychiatric hospitals were sent back into the community where they would be cared for. The trouble is that for many of them there is no community and little care. You've probably just seen some of the victims of their enlightened policy.' He winced at the thought of Michael's problems. The world of psychiatric medicine was one that he had avoided until now and he was not happy at having to make its acquaintance.

'Poor souls, they've nothing to hope for, nothing at all. Just think of the cold, the wet, the danger and the lack of privacy. No one wants them and they're hardly safe on the streets! Think of it, Peter, you're feeling a bit weary after a bad day at work, so you go home. It's warm, dry and friendly. You close the door on a hostile world and you're safe and secure, without anyone threatening you or snooping on you. It's like returning to the womb, you feel safe and protected at home. I know that you think I've a thing about my apartment but, after years of moving from place to place, wherever work took me, it's lovely to have somewhere that I've been able to do out in the way I like and make it my own. It's one thing I would never give up. And, Peter, it's even better to have you with me to enjoy it - to share it together! But to see those people in doorways, and particularly at this time of year when everyone else is enjoying themselves and spending, spending, spending, it's ... disgusting ... and it hurts. It makes me feel guilty.'

'You shouldn't feel guilty. At any rate not personally, it's society that's caused their difficulties or rather failed to deal with them properly - and the Government as well.'

'But Peter, what's society if it isn't us? It's no good passing the buck that way, if we do then nothing will ever get done. They would still be sending children up chimneys if they could get away with it but someone kicked up and wouldn't let go ... '

'Shaftesbury, Earl of, you mean?'

'Yes, Shaftesbury. He got working on their consciences and things changed.' How strange she felt to be talking about English history as though it were her history and as though this were her country! At least her training had been thorough and she was glad that she had a very retentive memory. A year before she had been busy preparing for her assignment to England and now here she was, sitting in a London pub with an Englishman she hoped to marry, discussing English social history. Momentarily panic took hold of her, how was she ever going to manage to tell him of her real identity, the longer the pretence went on the more problems there would be and how would he respond to her disclosures? She changed the subject to one which Lewis knew he would have to talk about but which he would have been happy to avoid.

'How did you get on with the shrink this afternoon, James Parker isn't it?'

'James Parker it is. Well we told him about our meeting with Michael's year tutor at school and about what he'd been up to there. He said we shouldn't be surprised, it was attention seeking, that sort of thing. It's funny but you come out of a meeting like this afternoon's wondering what went on ... it's a bit traumatic, you know. Ruth took notes, she's always been good at that, and she'll let me have a copy tomorrow, she'll fax it to the office. Then I'll be able to recollect in tranquillity.'

'It can't be easy when it involves someone you love.'

'Nor when you feel personally responsible for what's upsetting the lad! And I still feel worried about someone deciding that Michael must be a victim of abuse and accusing us. Nothing like that ever took place, believe me, Elizabeth, but you know what can happen.'

'I know what sort of man you are Peter. I know that you would never abuse your son. I can also understand how you are worrying - but you shouldn't, it's the sort of mistake that shrinks have made in the past but they are much more careful now, they're not too keen to be sued you know!'

'Yes, that's true. Anyway the fact is that Parker thinks the causes are very straightforward. Michael's always been very dependent emotionally on people close to him.

His ties with us have been very strong and that has made him vulnerable. For instance, when my parents died within a few months of one another, he was very upset but he wouldn't let it show. I don't know why but he wouldn't and then one day it all came out. He howled for an hour or more, quite frightening for us but cathartic for him. That took some of the sting out of it but you could see that even then he was still hurting. He got on well with them, a sort of special relationship across the generations. It was good to see them together.' He paused to collect his thoughts.

'And did you grieve for them, Peter? How about you?'

'I don't suppose I did, really, now that I think about it. I know that I should have.'

'So it's not surprising that Michael had problems with it?'

'No it's not surprising. I remember that their funerals weren't much help either. Soulless ceremonies in a drab North London crematorium with paint peeling from the walls, a sort of efficient disposal of the remains of Homo sapiens. And then we all went home for sandwiches and cakes and got on with life, but with the spectre of mortality to keep you company for a while.'

'And more vivid for a child.'

'Yes. Well that's the past. The report on the present is that Michael's illness has given his nervous system a nasty jarring and that he's worried about the divorce ... despite everything I've done to persuade him otherwise, he's worried about me abandoning him. He knows he's got no reason to think I ever would but it's what he feels deep down that's disturbing him. So we've got to keep working at making him feel secure and convinced deep down that I'll always be around for him.'

'You've got all my encouragement there, Peter.'

'Christmas is a problem. Michael wants me there for the

day and I can hardly refuse him. And I so wanted to spend the day with you. In the back of my mind I knew it was going to be a problem but I left it there and didn't disturb it. Now I'm letting you down.'

'No you're not. It's been obvious all along that you've got to spend the day at Ruth's. Haven't I told you that you've got to be a full time father to him? Well I mean it! You must spend the day there and any other days of the holiday that he needs you.'

'But I'm going to be away with him skiing over the New Year as well!'

'So, you're going to be away then. I'll miss you but I'll survive. I'll be busy, I won't rust!'

'Busy at what?'

'I've just decided as it happens. Funny how things suddenly come to you isn't it! I suddenly realised that there must be charities that look after the homeless at Christmas and I've made up my mind to give a hand. It will make the time go quickly and it will do something to salve my conscience.'

'I admire your concern, Elizabeth. Honestly I do. Some of these people are not very attractive and could do with a wash. They might even be dangerous … '

'Don't demonise them Peter, most are ordinary people for whom it's all gone wrong and who respond to a little bit of human kindness.'

' But *our* Christmas that I hoped to have together?'

'We'll celebrate the Russian Christmas instead! It should be just after you get back on 7th January.' She wondered what on earth had possessed her to say it but she pressed on. 'We'll have out own special Christmas and drink a toast to Boris Yeltsin. You can be Father Frost and I'll be the Snow Maiden, I think they're the characters who bring Russian children their presents.'

Lewis laughed, 'I don't mind being Father Frost but you're no Snow Maiden, Elizabeth! Flesh and blood, that's what you're made of - Robert Browning, I think. How about another glass before we go, some antifreeze so we don't suffer from hypothermia on the way home.'
He left her still wondering why she had introduced the Russian Christmas to his calendar. It was probably coming out of the cold into the heat of the pub and having the mulled wine that had made her light headed. And yes, there were things deep down in the psyche striving to come to the surface. She was finding it more and more difficult to continue hiding her true identity and deceiving Peter. Once they had been to Basel and she had finished with the SVR she would be free to come clean. That shouldn't be long now. The thought came as a relief but it brought with it renewed concern about his reaction once he knew of her deceit.

The Japanese businessmen had gone their way, probably back to the Strand Palace Hotel, and the group of women at the other end of the bar had quietened down and now looked rather sad and tired, the evening out had evidently been something of a disappointment for them.

She lifted her glass, 'To Father Frost!'

'To the Snow Maiden who, under her disguise, is all warmth and concern!'

His words were too accurate for comfort but Elizabeth smiled her response.

***

Waiting for Elizabeth on their return to the apartment was a message from Eugene on the Answerphone. She was to call back as soon as possible.

'Eugene can wait Peter, I feel like a drink before

anything else. How about you, do you fancy a coffee or a hot chocolate? ... OK chocolate then, I'll call him while the milk is heating up. Put the TV on and we'll see the news or choose some music, whichever you prefer.'

She took the cordless 'phone into the kitchen and called Eugene. 'Elizabeth here. Something urgent? Not a cancelled order is it?'

'Nothing to trouble your lover's crummy business. Our man at the Basel lab has gone missing. Just taken off and gone. Left no message. Nothing. There's already enough delay. It's going to be difficult to know when the goods will be ready for collection. Nothing you or I can do now, but we'll need to meet this week once I've been told more about it and HQ have decided what to do.'

'OK Eugene I'll wait to hear from you. Don't lose too much sleep over it!'

'Don't take it too lightly, Elizabeth. Like you I'm in no hurry for the operation to finish. I can put up with life here very happily for quite a while longer. But we might have to go in before the product is ready or they might call the whole thing off. As you know the last word we had was that their tests on the drug would be completed at the very beginning of January.'

'Sleep well, Eugene.'

She had hoped the operation would have been over in November, a month before, but there had been delays with the drug tests in Basel and it was now likely to be early January before the product was ready for collection. Peter's next visit to Basel was now scheduled for February and she would be going with him. Within two months' she hoped to become an honest woman and leave behind the world of play acting and deceit. She made the mugs of chocolate and returned to the sitting room.

'How's Eugene?'

'He's OK. An aunt of ours in Canada isn't too well. She had a fall, nothing serious. She lives with one of her daughters so there's no problem looking after her. You've chosen music, Peter. You've had enough of the harsh outside world for tonight then?' She hated having to lie to him.

'The homeless in the Strand? You're still keen on spending your Christmas Day with them? I don't want any harm coming to you, you know!'

'There you go again demonising them, Peter! They're a sorry enough crew without that! If any of them are dangerous I won't be on my own and anyway I do know a thing or two about self defence. Besides I'd rather be doing that than sitting here on my own. No, I'm not complaining about you being at Ruth's for the day. You know that's where I think your duty lies and where *I* want you to be. ... Now the music ... a Mozart piano concerto it is. Which one? No let me guess! Is it No. 27?'

'No. 27 it is and you weren't guessing, Elizabeth'

'You're accusing me of cheating?'

'Never! I'm accusing you of knowing! Music seems to be in your bloodstream! Do you play an instrument? It's odd but I've never asked you before!'

'The piano, passably but not brilliantly. I enjoy playing but I haven't played for a couple of years though, I haven't had access to one. And you Peter?'

'I played the clarinet in the school orchestra. Perhaps I should have kept it up.'

They sat listening until the music had ended. She collected the mugs and took them to the kitchen. Lewis switched off the hi-fi, took a look round the room and headed for the bathroom. It had been a stimulating day. Worries about Michael surfaced once again. The causes of his distress might be straightforward: nevertheless getting him right wasn't going to be easy for any of them.

Chapter 23

Monday 6th January 1997 (Russian Christmas Eve)

Lewis looked down from the window of the apartment through the leafless branches of the plane trees to the road below. The police cones were still there keeping a parking space for the delivery lorry. He was restless and excited. They were half an hour late and he had already been edgy when he arrived back from the West End at two o'clock that afternoon. He felt like a glass of something alcoholic but was determined to resist the urge, he tried not to drink during the working day. He had switched on the radio but turned it off five minutes later as it was simply irritating him. The day's edition of *The Times* lay open on the lamp table: that hadn't interested him either. 'Better do something and then they'll come. I could do with a cup of tea and I expect they will as well,' he told himself and went through to the kitchen. He looked around, it was tidy as always but yet it wasn't clinical: a place that was used and lived in but nevertheless kept in good order. Elizabeth's insistence on sweeping the floor to clear up any crumbs before they left for work each day amused him. His comment, 'You're depriving the mice of a meal!' always drew her response, 'It saves having to chase them with a carving knife!' This was one of their rituals, enacted most mornings of the working week.

He switched on the electric kettle and looked at the calendar next to it, tomorrow would be 7th January, Russian Christmas Day. Just like her to find another day for their celebration once she knew that he would have to spend 25th December with Michael at Ruth's. He recalled returning that evening at nearly eleven to find her relaxed and happy, 'I missed you, Peter, of course I did, but it was worthwhile spending the day as I did. They weren't all rogues and villains, you know, most of them were like us but everything seemed to have gone wrong for them. You remember Hardy's "The Mayor of Casterbridge" that you read after I had my trip to Dorchester and how everything went wrong for him, Michael Henshard wasn't it? They're a bit like him, they've had breakdowns, lost their jobs and families and things like that.' She had added, 'And some of them their self respect with it, which is even worse.'

He had learned quickly that her interests and enthusiasms had to be treated seriously, 'How many were you and how many homeless were there?'

'A dozen of us looking after nearly a hundred of them. I was in charge of the potatoes and the pudding.'

'And alcohol free brandy to go with it?'

'You should know that alcohol free brandy, if it existed, wouldn't burn! No they had proper brandy which I begged from the four star hotel down the road together with some other things, it's interesting what an appeal to conscience can do at Christmas. Even the most hardened and cynical find it difficult to resist an appeal to their better instincts. Wow, I'm suddenly feeling quite drained. I think I could do with a drop of Cognac myself!'

He had poured it for her, put some seasonal music on the hi-fi and made her a coffee. She might be tired but she was aglow with enthusiasm.

'And what about your day, Peter? How were Michael and Ruth? Did they like their presents?'

'Easy now Elizabeth! You're too high, ease back or you won't be able to sleep. I'll take one question at a time. I've a thick head - indoors for too long and a little too much to drink. Ruth was anxious to find out what I thought of some of her new wine growers' products, she has a theory that most wines need to be accompanied by food if they're to be rated properly one against another.' He smiled and added, 'At the meal table you can't spit them out like at a tasting!'

'Where I've been, Peter, it wouldn't occur to anyone to spit the stuff out! Sorry, I interrupted you, go on.'

'We played a lot of board games and that was hard work after the wine I can tell you! Michael enjoyed his presents especially the one from you.' He had exaggerated, Michael had shown little inclination to open the parcel once he had seen the writing on the card that Elizabeth had attached to it but, on Ruth's insistence, he had done so. In fact she had pressured him into writing his thank you letter to her as soon as Lewis had left that evening, striking while the iron was hot and not wishing to be involved in a long battle to coerce an unwilling child to write. Ruth had old fashioned standards of politeness and etiquette and insisted that the rest of the family comply with them. 'Ruth was rather tired and went off for a rest once we had seen the Queen on TV. Michael and I cleared up and Ruth surfaced an hour later looking better. She's had several disturbed nights in a row, Michael's nightmares have been more frequent lately, maybe it's been the excitement of Christmas and he'll improve. I'll find out in two or three days time when we get to Zermatt for the skiing.' And there had been no problems in Zermatt.

Lewis looked at the kettle, it had evidently boiled without him noticing. He switched it on again to bring it back to the boil and took the larger tea pot from the cupboard, if the lorry turned up there would probably be several men with it. He poured some of the boiling water into the pot and swilled it round before pouring it into the sink. Three scoops of tea should do, no make it four, you needed rather more Ceylon tea to give it a reasonable strength. He was stirring the pot when the door bell rang. He put the lid on and the cosy over the pot and then replied over the entry-phone.

'Sorry Guv, we had a puncture on the way but it won't take long to get it in.'

"Hold on and I'll be down.' He wanted to make sure that nothing went wrong. He made sure he had a key in his pocket, went down three floors to the entrance and greeted the men, 'You're psychic it seems. I was just stirring the teapot when you arrived.' They showed pleasure at the prospect. 'Now the bad news, you won't be able to get it into the lift and the apartment is three floors up - but you know that already don't you?'

The men's leader nodded, 'I expect we'll manage, Guv. We'll be as careful as we can.' Somehow the message that a little encouragement and reward would not come amiss was implicit in his look and reply.

'Make a good job and you won't be disappointed.' What was another twenty Pounds compared with the cost of the thing? Though the need to tip them rankled a little, perhaps more this afternoon than would have been the case with a more relaxed Lewis.

'For yer Missus, is it Guv?' Lewis nodded. 'Lucky woman ain't she! Hope the neighbours don't mind the noise.'

'We're the top flat, it's going into the corner of the building and the old lady in the flat below us is deaf, so she won't be disturbed.' He had checked with her before ordering it.

Half an hour later, after sending them on their way with their tip and refreshed by tea and biscuits, Lewis stood in the sitting room admiring the grand piano. The room looked as if it had been designed to take it. He saw to his relief that it didn't look too crowded. Indeed the room, which he had previously thought of as perfect in its furnishings and proportions, looked even better than before. The beige Draylon upholstery of the stool toned in perfectly, he'd wondered whether it would. He remembered an entry under "colour words" on the first use of "beige" in "The New Fowler's". She had given it to him for a present at the "real" Christmas. He took the book from the shelf. Good, he hadn't imagined it, there it was, "beige (first recorded as a colour word in 1879)". He smiled to himself and his frayed nerves calmed a little. He was pleased with himself. In the hall he picked up a paper bag. He had made a visit to Soho that morning and bought some piano music scores from a music publisher there. He took one and, after checking with a note he had made on a slip of paper, opened it to the right piece and placed it on the piano. The bell rang. Good this must be the piano tuner, it must be just right for her to play this evening!

***

'Christmas Eve, Russian calendar, Elizabeth and you must do just as I tell you and keep out of the lounge until I say so.' He had collected her from Kilburn and brought her home.

'So there's a present in there? OK, I'll do as you say. It must be big, a painting perhaps?'

He feigned disappointment, 'You could be right about that but first a light supper from Marks and Spencers. I dropped into their Marble Arch store and raided the delicatessen this morning. You have half an hour to get yourself ready. The turquoise evening gown would do admirably, if I may be so bold as to make a suggestion. You look stunning in it, Darling.' He was aware that he was completely relaxed for the first time that day. Happiness flooded in. 'A drink first. Clairette de Die? - it's light, sparkling and with the aroma of roses. Good, it's in the fridge. "Come and get it" as they used to say on the movies.' Care had flown and he was excited.

'Happy Christmas Elizabeth and Happy Christmas to Boris!'

'And a Happy Christmas to you Peter and health to Boris Nikolayevitch, he certainly needs it.' She saw the puzzled look on his face and immediately regretted her mistake. It was a formula that she and Eugene had used when they had been lovers with things going well between them. 'It's his patronymic, it comes from his father's name. I picked it up from Tolstoy, I think, and some report in *The Times.* I'm a Kremlin Watcher you know! We'll have to see whether we can break into the Russian market!'

'It's a long way to send our glassware and we really would have language difficulties ... unless, of course, Kremlin Watchers are proficient in Russian!'

'Half an hour it is but you *will* wear your dinner suit, won't you? You will? Good! It's fun having a special Christmas all of our own, Peter.' She couldn't readily admit to proficiency in Russian!

'Can we have coffee later, Peter. I just can't wait to have a look in the sitting room, I'm all curiosity. I like having surprises!'

'Of course we can go through and have a look. I'll make coffee later on.'

He got up and stood by Elizabeth's chair, ready to move it as she rose from table. She looked up at him, 'I like having a gentleman about the place, Peter. Women's Lib is all very well, and I think women should have the same rights as men, but it is really nice to be treated as a woman. Stay with your old fashioned courtesy, I like it and I love you!' She folded her serviette and put it into its silver ring, blew out the candle in the middle of the table and rose to face Lewis. 'Let me guess. It's a print of a Monet, water lilies or something like that. Am I right, Peter? I saw your disappointment when I guessed that it was a print.' She kissed him. They were both relaxed and delighting in one another.

'You'll just have to come and see won't you. I hope you'll think that it goes with the decor.'

He took her hand and led her to the door of the sitting room. 'Right then, open up and see for yourself, Elizabeth!'

She tried to open the door and couldn't. 'It's locked Peter, I need the key.'

He handed it to her, 'I didn't trust you not to have a look while I was getting ready, so I played safe.'

She feigned outrage, 'So you didn't trust me, Peter. I'm almost ready to call off our alternative Christmas but ... on further consideration I won't, I'm too curious about what's in there.' Elizabeth unlocked the door and opened it. She stood unmoving, staring into the sitting room, 'Peter you shouldn't. What an absolutely amazing present. It's incredible.' She threw her arms around his neck and kissed him before bursting into tears. 'You're so kind, so kind, and I'm so happy.' He felt her warm body pressing against his, her hair against his face. The subtle fragrance of her perfume worked its magic. He too felt close to tears. How strange that both joy and sorrow, such contrary emotions, were accompanied by tears.

'Perhaps you would like to check that it's not a

cardboard cut-out replica, Elizabeth, you never know with these alternative Christmas presents.'

She needed no further invitation from him. She turned back to the door and walked to the end of the room. He had expected her to rush in but she didn't. Instead she went slowly, like a sleepwalker, she seemed unable to believe that it was true and that the present was a full sized grand piano. She stood and looked at the keyboard. 'But it's a Steinway, Peter.'

'Isn't it any good then?' She had feigned outrage, now he feigned surprise.

'You know full well that it is and you must have a huge bill to prove it!'

'I admit it's given me quite a few Air Miles on the Credit Card. We can have a free flight to Paris on the strength of it. We'll see the genuine Monets I couldn't afford to give you!'

She pulled out the stool and sat down. 'Wait a moment how does it work?' She inspected it and adjusted the height. 'And what's this?' She looked at the music. 'Oh, Peter, the Chopin Nocturnes. It won't be like Rubinstein you know - if that's what you're expecting you'll be disappointed! And I haven't played for over a year.'

'You'll never disappoint me, Elizabeth. Just find your way and get back into form. I haven't booked you to perform at the Wigmore Hall yet, so there's no pressure! This is for your enjoyment, Darling.'

'You've got the score open. Is this what you would like me to play, Opus 9 No. 2? Well I'll try but don't forget I'm rusty and my fingers will have to go back into training. Computer keyboards don't call for the same technique!'

Lewis seated himself at the far end of the sofa and watched her readjust the stool. She wanted to get the height just right. For a while she looked at the score. He saw the intensity of her gaze as she absorbed the music. There was recognition in that look - the music was not unknown to her but familiar from the past. He wondered when and where she had last played it. He was conscious of the mystery that surrounded her, a mystery that was only gradually yielding to him.

'Just let me get the feel of the instrument.' She played a few bars, 'The piano's marvellous, Peter, but I'm a bit rusty.' She repeated the bars, 'Now, that's rather better.' She turned the page and played a few more bars and again repeated them. 'OK, here goes but you'll excuse me if I go wrong, won't you?' She rubbed her hands together and flexed her fingers. A moment later the music was transformed from the printed page to sounds that delighted the ear. No, it wasn't Rubinstein, he thought, but it was good, very good. He was so glad that he had bought the Steinway and not a lesser make, so happy to see her there, young, elegant, intelligent and lovely - absorbed, totally absorbed in the music. He blinked back his tears, Michael's problems and the stress they created seemed so far away and he persuaded himself that they would be sorted out somehow. He felt younger than he had ever felt before, life seemed to be pouring back into him. A year ago he had felt tired and jaded. Tonight he was more alive than he had ever known himself. And yet he was conscious of violent mood swings, only yesterday Michael's problems had been dragging him down emotionally. But now, like something effervescent, joy was bubbling up inside him. What a difference this woman had made to his life. 'Elizabeth, Elizabeth, Elizabeth!' he murmured to himself. The music was all around them. It was as near to ecstasy that he had ever been and he was grateful that it was no more intense, for he was not sure that he could have coped with greater joy. His experience, he knew, was inward, even though it had been brought about by Elizabeth and the music she was playing, but there was something about it that went beyond the personal, that seemed to come from beyond himself, from something at once "out there" but so near that you could touch it. If he had had to describe it he would have called it a spiritual experience. To his surprise there seemed little sexual content to his joy, there was a purity about it which, however, was not sex-denying. He loved her for what she was, not for anything that she could do to or for him.

'Peter, are you all right?'

He detected the concern in her voice and was aware that the music had ceased and that she was sitting beside him on the sofa. Tears were streaming down his face and he fumbled for a handkerchief to wipe them away.

'Wrong, Elizabeth? No nothing's wrong. It's just that everything's right, ever so right. I can't find the words for it. It's ... joy, happiness, contentment and ... love. I love you and I'm so happy, Elizabeth. I don't know how to talk about it but you've just given me an experience that is ... that is nothing like anything I've ever had before.'

She had not intended to tell him that evening but she couldn't stop herself, 'Peter, I'm pregnant. We're going to have a child!'

He paused and looked at her radiant face, 'You've completed the celebration, Elizabeth, tonight's one that we will never forget.' Tears of joy ran down both their faces.

On later reflection Lewis was to realise that he had felt such a deep, overpowering emotion once before. That had been in response to Michael's birth over thirteen years ago, when he had stood with Ruth gazing down on the baby, newly installed in his cot. But for the time being

Michael's problems were forgotten, though they would soon be back to haunt him. In Zermatt there had been no nightmares but then, by Ruth's reckoning, that was only to be expected.

***

Sam put down the earphones and looked at his colleague. 'He's a generous guy that Lewis. He's just given her a Steinway as a present.'

'What's that, some kind of jewellery?'

'Come on, you know what a Steinway is, don't you?' His colleague looked at him blankly. 'It's a grand piano. I just hope their floor is strong enough to take the thing. How would you like to live below them and have a grand piano fall on your head one day?'

'I'd feel a real schmuck if that happened!'

'If you had time to feel anything! Once it was on the move it would take you all the way to the basement.' He paused and reflected, 'They're getting on real swell don't you think? He was a fortunate man when she walked through his door, very fortunate. And it's not one sided, she seems as smitten as he is.'

'A grand piano's a bit big for her to take home to Moscow when this is all over, Sam!'

'I don't think that home in Moscow features in her plans. Home in West Hampstead perhaps, but Moscow? No! If they want to get her back there they'll have to drag her screaming or under sedation more likely! Her buddy Eugene's had his nose put out of joint because he's no longer her lover and he's concerned that she won't want to go back. I've heard their conversations and what Eugene has said to his boss as well. They'll put the screws on to get her back. She's got an elderly mother there in Moscow, that will let them apply their powers of persuasion.' He sighed. 'I wonder if it would be worth our trouble to pick her up at the end, once they've got what they're after from the Lab, and whisk her off to safety.' The idea had formed in his mind some time before, it was now time to start flying a kite. The best plan was always to sow seeds and let others, the people who planned operations, think that it was their idea. That meant that your masters were committed to seeing the action through and you had the pleasure of them urging you on instead of getting in your way! He would feed the idea to Alan Winters when he saw him the next day and see whether he took the bait. Nothing too specific, just the odd comment on the woman's apparent disenchantment with her masters and the information she could give them on the SVR and its activities. Of course he would argue against any suggestion by Winters that they should take action, but he wouldn't do so very persuasively!

'And how's Mia, Sam. Have you heard from her lately? You saw her last month didn't you when you were back home?'

'She's OK. Well to be honest, things are a just bit strained between us at the moment. We don't see one another as often as she ... as we would like. She's decided to take some holiday from the hospital and come over for a visit. She'll be here next Monday to stay with an uncle. Big adventure, she's never been outside New York State before let alone flown the Pond! I'll be taking her out to see the sights of London and its museums.'

'Don't let your woman distract you from your work chum!'

'I'll try not to let her.' It wasn't just Mia who was distracting him - it was reasonable that *she* should - more and more it was *the Russian* - and he knew that the infatuation was unreasonable. He hated himself for the disloyalty to Mia. Not just that, he would have to be careful not to compromise the operation. Elizabeth was not just another woman, she was an agent of the SVR, the organisation he was there to undermine. He would not let the infatuation threaten the operation itself but if he could get authorisation for snatching her at the end, to give her the choice of freedom and to find out what she could tell them of the SVR and its organisation, he would take it with determination and commitment.

His colleague watched him, 'Oh to be young and in love! She's a nice girl, Sam. You shouldn't have a care in the world. Look after her though.'

'Which one, Mia or Elizabeth?' Sam asked himself.

'Don't worry, I will. Oh, one other small thing, the Russian woman's pregnant.'

'That'll be the end of their quiet musical evenings, once the kid's arrived, Sam'.

'You're probably right there, Joe'. He yawned, 'I'll be turning in now. You can leave the recorder running and sign off yourself if you like. Nothing of interest on the 'phone since they lost their man inside the Basel Lab? Wonder where he's gone? Took off with the Lab chief's wife apparently, so the Russians and ourselves aren't the only ones looking for him. People at the banks are falling over one another hoping that they'll get a fix on them when they next use their credit cards!'

***

Sam lay awake. He couldn't get the sound of her playing out of his head. He pictured the sitting room in his mind and wondered where the piano had been placed. Lewis must be doing all right in business as well as in his personal life. Eugene's orders were evidently pushing up the profits. The Englishman was a lucky dog, there was no doubt about that. And Elizabeth was pregnant - how would that complicate things? Sam felt pangs of jealousy, her pregnancy didn't mean an end to the infatuation. She still held him in thrall. Sleep would not come and he got up and made a cup of coffee. Then, sitting at a table in his dressing gown, he began to sketch out the programme for Mia's visit.

***

Elizabeth relished the warmth of the bed as she lay, lovemaking over, half awake and half asleep, next to Peter. She thought of the evening and her present. How like him to think of such an incredible gift and keep it a secret from her. How she would love to have her mother meet him and see their apartment. Compared with hers in Moscow it was a palace. She was surprised at the warmth of her feelings for her mother. She had always respected her but emotional feelings towards her were new. Perhaps it was the overflowing of the delight and happiness that Peter had brought to her. Then she thought of the child being formed within her and she knew that her mother *must* one day see her grandchild and hold it in her arms. Her roots *were* important to her, she knew she did not want to sever them totally. She fell asleep wondering how she could ever bring them all together: herself, Peter, their child and her mother. Not easy, not at all easy, she knew that, but she felt with confidence that somehow it could be done. Michael and his problems were for the moment pushed to the back of her mind.

***

Eugene had returned late from a night out with one of his contacts, a lobbyist on the fringes of the Conservative Party. The man had a fund of salacious and juicy stories about politicians and businessmen and Eugene knew that if only half of them were true he had rich material to pass on to Moscow for future use. He wondered how Elizabeth had got on with her celebrations that evening. Of all the stupidest things, celebrating Russian Christmas! He was determined to ruffle Lewis' feathers and as he didn't feel tired he found a writing pad and began an anonymous letter. In it he suggested to Lewis' Tax Office that they should have a good look into his affairs and hinted that there were offshore bank accounts hidden from them. He concluded the note, "Takes his son and friends skiing at Zermatt and maintains a mistress on his payroll." At one and the same time he liked and hated the sentence - it should bait the hook for the Inspector, the suggestion of sex on the business should get under his skin - but it also brought back powerful memories of a relationship that was over. He signed it "Taxpayer" and put it into an envelope. He would have to check where to send it tomorrow, probably somewhere in the Kilburn High Road.

Sleep would not come. So he poured himself a glass of vodka and commenced committing the evening's conversation to paper, checking his memory by playing back the recording he had made on his pocket machine. He was glad to be usefully employed for his country, perhaps they would let him stay on in London after the action in Basel was over. A head office job in Moscow and life with his family did not appeal to him at all.

Chapter 24

Friday 14th February 1997

Lewis and Elizabeth were on the road in northern France an hour out of Lille. They had pulled onto the hard shoulder of the *autoroute* to clean the windscreen as the washers had frozen up. 'Stay in the van and I'll use some de-icer to clean the screen. Why they don't fit heaters to the screen washers I don't know. Anyhow stay where you are Elizabeth, it's not the safest of places on the edge of a motorway.'

'Don't forget to give the wing mirrors a wipe while you're out there, Peter.'

She watched him cleaning the screen. The sun was in his eyes but she knew that he was stressed and unhappy. She had watched him over breakfast at the motel by the *autoroute* at Lille and known that he was preoccupied with Michael and his problems. To her enquiries he had responded, 'It just won't go away, will it Elizabeth? He seems to get worse, to be more distressed rather than less. Ruth wondered about psychoanalysis for him but, knowing the mess that it got one of her friends into, she just doesn't know and neither do I.'

She had left the matter until they were back in their room and quietly reminded him that the cause of Michael's troubles was, in part at any rate, the break up of his parents marriage. She had added, 'If it would help you all, I could disappear from the scene.'

He had taken her in his arms. 'So easy if I didn't love you Elizabeth, so easy. But I love you and you mustn't do that. I must be poor company for you at the moment, I'm afraid, Elizabeth, but I need you badly and you're going to have *our* child. Promise me that you won't go, you're my rock and stability!'

She had looked into his tired eyes, 'I promise! You didn't sleep much last night did you, Peter? You look worn out. There's a long drive ahead to Basel and I want us to get there safely, so I'll do most of the driving today. No, don't object, I'm determined and that's that. We don't want any accidents. I may be pregnant but I can still drive!'

She was aware of her own inner tensions, partly from her reaction to his condition and partly from the uncertainty of her own future. And now she was pregnant. Would she be able to avoid being taken back to Russia by Eugene. Would they be willing to accept her "retirement" from the SVR? She had fantasised over the idea of a visit from one of the high-ups, being presented with a gold watch and thanked for her work for the Motherland. He would wish her a happy retirement and ask for her bank account details so that her pension could reach her on the first of each month! And if she ever wished to return to their employment in the future she had just to contact their London representative and they would have a post waiting for her! Pure fantasy, of course. They would do their damnedest to make sure she came safely home to base. They would certainly not want her talking to British security about what she had been doing there and before that in North America. Again she wondered who her real employer really was. Was it the Russian government who were after the drug in Basel or was it the Mafiya? Maybe it was some oligarch. Whoever it was they would want everyone back afterwards. As an insurance against being snatched back in Basel, once they had the drug, she had become more involved in Eugene's interior décor activities. Better to have some unfinished work in London. Then they would want her to go back there, or so she hoped. And, in case they tried to put pressure on her in Basel, she had brought with her the small handgun that the SVR had issued to her. It came apart and, mingled with the contents of her camera bag, it was unlikely to be spotted by Customs, even if they bothered to look in the bag. Once in Basel she would keep it in her handbag, always available to warn off any assailant.

'I'm sorry that I've got to stay with Jacob and Paula and that you'll be on your own in Basel for much of the time, Elizabeth.'

'There was no choice, Peter, I know that. Once Ruth and Michael were coming, Paula was clearly not going to ask me to join the party. Jacob accepts our relationship but Paula still has her doubts and, in any case, you want to calm Michael not stir things up with my presence. I'll have a lot to do in the city and I might even take a trip to the mountains one day. You said that there would be a carnival while we were there, didn't you? I'll miss having you to share the enjoyment but we'll be on our way back before the end of next week. It's Friday today and we return next Thursday.'

'Jacob has wanted the family to come for the carnival for some years. He says it's quite an event, a sort of *Mardi Gras* affair but a few days too late for it to be called that. I'll miss out on having you with me all the time, but perhaps I might visit you in your hotel?'

'And give me a bad reputation as a woman who entertains strange men in my room? Really a young woman has to take care of the position she occupies!'

This brought a smile to his face. 'It's funny is it, Peter?' She had been glad to see that smile but pretended to be affronted.

'As we'll be apart for most of the coming week it occurred to me that I know precisely the position you should occupy for the next few minutes.' He had guided her towards the bed. 'You don't change despite your problems, Peter! And I'm glad you don't!'

An hour later they had checked the van's contents and satisfied themselves that all was secure before setting off for Basel. For a while some of the tension they were both experiencing had been dissipated.

'You said you had somewhere in mind for lunch, Peter. Beyond Reims wasn't it?'

'About 50 miles past Reims, on beyond Épernay and the Champagne vineyards and towards Verdun. We'll have a break near Reims for a coffee to keep us both alert and to give you a rest. You really shouldn't be doing all this driving. I should be driving or at least taking my turn.'

'The male rôle model, Peter. Got to be driving unless there's a chauffeur - male of course! You'll have to put up with me at the wheel. It's a long journey but don't forget that I've driven across the States a couple of times. Relax! If you're up to it after our coffee break you can take us for the fifty miles before we stop for lunch. What's the name of the place?'

'Sainte-Menehould, you won't have heard of it but I've been there before - it's a convenient place to stop for lunch in either direction between Basel and the Channel Ports. They've got certain local specialities which you might like to try. No, you'll find out when we get there, Elizabeth! Time for music? Shall I put another disc in the player? The box you put them in is handy.'

'See if you can find the one with the Mozart piano concertos, it's got Nos. 21 and 27 - 27's the one you played the other day back in the apartment.'

'I remember you guessed that it was No. 27!'

'*Knew*, I didn't guess, Peter! I knew which one it was or so *you* told me! It's one of my favourites, especially the slow movement, the tears are only just below the surface. It's certainly not pattern music! There's real feeling there. I'm glad you like it. It means so much, sharing what's important to one another. You've introduced me to a lot of things and it's good to know that you like a lot of my music collection. I'm not asking you to like it all, of course.' She smiled and touched his arm. 'Don't worry, I'm keeping my eyes on the road. I'll keep the kiss until our coffee break - I almost said our Champagne break - at Reims.'

'No Champagne today! Clear minds and sharp eyes for the road! Do you want to stop for another windscreen cleaning session, we're coated in salt from the road?'

'I'll try the washers and see whether they are still frozen.'

'OK but be ready to pull over and stop if the water freezes. Ease back on the speed. Now have a go. Good they're working. That's better, less eye strain for you now.'

They were quiet, keeping a sharp eye on the road ahead as they continued through the flat landscape, and enjoying the music. Each let Mozart work his spell on their restless minds and emotions. The slow movement began and Lewis recollected her description of the "tears only just below the surface" - she was right, for all its beauty there was sorrow there, all the more moving because of the control and restraint. He was aware that Elizabeth was also listening with rapt attention. She didn't take her eyes off the road but he knew that deep down in her being the music was evoking a powerful response. She was right, it wasn't "pattern music". For Lewis tears had come much nearer to the surface of late. Were they the sort of tears the Mozart had known? Life was a strange mixture of events, relationships and emotions. If only Michael were better! Then life could go on without the stresses that were now affecting all of them, Michael, Ruth, Elizabeth and himself. He thought of Elizabeth's arrival at his office in March and of their growing delight in one another. They had been together since she had been away for those few days in the Westcountry. He remembered with a vividness that surprised him exactly what he'd been doing when she had telephoned to ask him to join him in Dorchester – sleeping! He never ceased to marvel at the good fortune that had brought her to him. The spectre of Vera's death remained. He mustn't forget to call on her husband and son before the end of the month, the first anniversary would be hard for them both.

***

Lewis drove away from the toll on the Sainte-Menehould exit from the *autoroute*, he made his way cautiously down the hill into the town, it was important to adapt to ordinary roads after the *autoroute*. Good, it was as he remembered it. He parked across the road from the *Hôtel de Ville*. He set the alarm on the van and they got out.

'Just down the road on the right, *Le Cheval Rouge*. There it is. In we go. The restaurant is at the back, we'll go there - there's a *brasserie* at the front but we'll eat in style.'

'I'll join you in a moment, Peter, I've just seen the sign for the Ladies Room.'

He made his way into the restaurant and asked for a table near the fire but not too close to it. The dining room, with stone pillars and a stone chimney breast and its wood panelling and ceiling beams, had a comfortable and civilised look. A haven of peace after pounding the *autoroute*. He ordered a couple of fruit juices and a jug of water. They would have a half-bottle of wine with the meal. They really shouldn't have anything with the driving that still lay before them but you could hardly call it a meal in France if you had no wine. Elizabeth came into the room and he rose to pull the chair out from the table, just beating the waiter in doing so. In five minutes she had freshened up and done her hair. He was aware of her perfume, not overdone but distinct nevertheless.

'You're looking great Elizabeth. You turn a meal into an occasion.'

'Flattery Peter! What are you after? My mother warned me against men like you. I'll have to be careful!'

She threw back her head and laughed. Lewis saw other diners looking in their direction. Their looks weren't of disapproval, far from it. The French valued an elegant woman and he could read in the eyes of his fellow diners a touch of envy.

'You have the approval of a number of the others here, Elizabeth. Being with you is good for morale.'

'You are the only one, Peter, whose approval I care for. You know that. Still, if the French approve, who am I to object! But we are here to eat and you've something in mind, their speciality I assume.'

'Yes, its *"pieds de cochon à la Sainte-Menehould"*. They can be excellent and they excel in them here at the *Cheval Rouge*.'

'In English that is?'

'It sounds a bit pedestrian but it's pig's feet.'

She smiled at him, 'By definition feet are pedestrian, Peter, but those on offer have ceased walking I hope.' It amazed her how quickly the tensions had slipped away and they had returned to an easy intimacy.

'You'll try them?'

'I'll throw caution to the winds and proceed with *cochon*! I trust your recommendation, Peter. What do you suggest as a starter?'

'The local *pâté* is usually good, otherwise the *soupe à l'oignon* is worth trying.'

'OK *pâté* it is. And not too much wine to go with it - we've still got a long way to drive.'

'We think alike, Elizabeth! The *pamplemousse* - grapefruit - juice is evidence of my sense of responsibility. I had in mind a half bottle of a light red wine. The wine list has an Alsatian Pinot Noir - it's quite light and won't send us to sleep at the wheel. Does that appeal to you? Further South in warmer areas it gives a heavier wine but not in Alsace. Have you ever been to Alsace? No? We'll drive through this afternoon and we can have a look at the area when we return next week if you like, perhaps spend a night there and sample the wines and the cuisine, both are outstanding, you know.'

'Thanks for the wine and travel lecture, Peter? Ruth's pupil? No, I'm not being nasty. Ruth obviously knows the subject well, otherwise she wouldn't have been as successful as she has in the wine trade, would she? Don't feel that you can't talk about Ruth with me, you've spent a substantial part of your life with her and there's no reason why we should ignore it. It may seem strange to you, Peter but I would really like to get to know Ruth better. From what I've seen of her, on the few occasions we've met that is, I've liked her. She's a capable and caring person isn't she?'

Lewis ordered and asked for the wine to be served *frais*. He mentioned that they had a long drive ahead but stressed that they didn't want to rush the meal. If they could be finished in an hour and a quarter ... The waiter appreciated that a satisfied customer was more likely to be a generous customer and responded, *'D'accord, Monsieur.'*

'Don't worry, Elizabeth, I'm not displaying ignorance, it's how they serve it in Alsace, the way they treat a light red. It's just a bit darker than a *rosé*. ... Yes that's a fair assessment of Ruth. And she would like you, only ... '

'Only she's your estranged wife, or perhaps it's the other way round with you as her estranged husband - tell me Peter can one be estranged without the other being estranged? - and I'm your mistress.'

'Don't say that word *maîtresse* too loudly or our French fellow diners will be highly jealous of me - though I expect they're already active enough in the direction of *l'amour* anyway. I remember a newspaper report on the election of *Monsieur le Maire* in a French town. The previous day he had been driving through the place with his mistress when his wife had fired at the car with a pistol. The reporter had asked how much harm it would do to his campaign for re-election and been told by the *Maire*, "None at all, that shot was worth a thousand extra votes!" Interesting people the French!'

'Yes, aren't they just. I expect they find things as odd on the English side of the Channel or whatever they call it.'

'La Manche ...'

'A few miles of water and it has divided the Normans into two very different cultures.'

'We're not just Normans, you know! Saxon, Dane, Celt, probably some Roman and Jewish blood. A good old mix and for years it kept us energetic, building an Empire and that sort of thing. Now others have taken over and we're just a little bit too tired. We tend to live in the past and we don't trust our fellow Europeans. We're a sad lot really.'

'Don't be so dismissive of yourselves - of ourselves - we're not finished yet!'

'I tend to forget your English roots, Elizabeth. Think of you as American or Canadian.'

'When you've moved around so much you sometimes wonder where you really belong. Since I began to work for you I've had no doubts, my roots are deep in West Hampstead, you've made sure of that!'

The *pâté* plates were removed and the *pieds de cochon* arrived. *'Notre spécialité Monsieur et Madame, bon appétit.'* They smiled their thanks.

'This is better than eating at a service area on the *autoroute*, Peter, much better. I'm having these on your say-so. Tell me about them, what do I have to do?'

'Eat the lot, bones and all.'

'Bones and all!'

'That's right. The first time I had them here I ate some of the bones and wondered whether I should. Then we left the restaurant and there across the road was another restaurant advertising the same thing and saying "the bones are so soft that you can eat them." See what you think, they cook them for 36 hours.'

'Mm, I wouldn't have believed it - that's if you hadn't recommended them, of course - they're delicious and you're right about the bones.'

'I once had them somewhere else and the bones weren't like this. I ended up with something that looked like a miniature version of a skeleton dinosaur's foot from a museum on my plate. Not an appetising sight, I can assure you. If I hadn't known what it should have been like I wouldn't ever have wanted another one!'

'Must have thought that you were at the Jurassic Diner, Peter! And that's harking back to Dorset again. That's where it all began for us.' She placed her hand on his and smiled.

They finished with a lemon soufflé and coffee, declining

liqueurs. The meal had occupied sixty five minutes, Lewis complimented the waiter and tipped him appropriately. The other diners were still enjoying a leisurely lunch, evidently under no pressure to be back on the road for a two hundred mile drive to Basel. They watched them leave the restaurant. That English woman - or was she an American? - had definitely got something about her. *'Cet homme est un chien fortuné!'* or so Lewis imagined the French as saying.

***

They agreed to take the driving in turns as Peter had revived with the meal and their conversation. The worries of the night were still there, though they had receded somewhat into the background. The way in which the other customers in the restaurant had paid attention to Elizabeth hadn't escaped Lewis' notice and he was pleased. Half an hour later Lewis, who was taking the first spell at the wheel, pointed out a road which went under the *autoroute*. 'That's *la Voie Sacrée*, the road from Bar-le-Duc to Verdun. They came to think of Verdun as a sort of Calvary, a place of sacrifice. Verdun's a little to the north east of us. We'll soon cross the River Meuse. It's World War One territory, a battlefield where the French and the Germans slogged it out with vast loss of life and dreadful injuries. I once took Michael there when he had the idea that there was something splendid about war. The cemetery at Verdun was worth a whole book of anti-war arguments, it did the trick ... the number of graves and the ages on the stones. Frightening really. Did you know that there were French villages that for years after that war had almost no male inhabitants - they had all been killed in places like Verdun?'

'It's horrible. Why were they willing to go? I don't think that women would have gone.'

'If you didn't go you'd be shot by your own people and then there was all the patriotic fervour generated by having a ruthless enemy at your throat. There were mutinies here but they were put down. When some of the troops were moved up the road from Bar-le-Duc to Verdun, along *that* road, *la Voie Sacrée*, they began to bleat like sheep being taken to be slaughtered. It was their protest at the futility and horror of the thing. The French and German dead totalled over 400,000 and twice as many were gassed or wounded - and that was on a fifteen mile front.'

'That's horrible Peter. You did say fifteen miles? So many casualties in so small an area, it's beyond imagining. The conditions were awful weren't they?'

'If you can imagine summer and winter out in the elements, mud and more mud, great shell holes in the ground full of water where soldiers drowned. Then think of bullets, shells, poison gas and the like. Then add poor food and primitive medical care! You're right, it was horrible. So as we go through Strasbourg we'll give three cheers for the European Union and give a hefty kick in the teeth to our faint-hearts who don't like the EU!'

'My word, you *are* becoming political, Peter! You said that with feeling didn't you?'

'Yes, it's something I do feel strongly about. It makes sense for us to be what we are, Europeans. As I said at lunch, we Brits are a real mix of races and all the better for that, even if we've lost confidence in ourselves for the time being. Do you know what I thought was the most hopeful photo of political leaders I've seen? Well it was Mitterand and Kohl standing hand in hand at a commemoration at Verdun. I don't expect many Brits gave it a second thought but it moved me.'

'Significance is in the eye of the beholder?'

'Perhaps. But I think many French and Germans would have found it moving as well. By the way, you said that women wouldn't have gone to war like the men. There are countries where they do, you know equal opportunity and all that, China, Israel and other places and even the Royal Navy now have women on warships.'

'Change isn't always progress is it? How about some music? There are some Mozart and Haydn Symphonies to choose from, something lively to keep us going - Haydn's No.100, *"The Military"*, might be appropriate. When do you think we'll get to Basel?'

'At a guess we should reach the French/Swiss border at Basel some time after six. Then it depends on how long we take to get cleared by the Customs. Once we've got the van to Jacob's place we'll probably have a drink and then I'll take you to the hotel by taxi - and that's the down side of this visit, I'm afraid, Elizabeth.'

'Absence makes the heart grow fonder, they say.'

'We'll see one another during the week and we'll be on our way back in less than a week's time.'

In the previous year's newspapers she had read of the significance of Battle of the Somme for the British. Verdun was evidently as traumatic for the French, perhaps even more so. For her people it was Stalingrad in 1942 and 1943 that was an indelible memory. She vividly recalled an old newsreel film of the fighting going from street to street before the eventual repulse of the German assault and the encirclement of their armies. She felt pride at the heroism shown by her people. It had been a genuine success and not mere propaganda. Eugene was right, to call the place Volgagrad was wrong, whatever Stalin's errors. It was the name Stalingrad that excited her and made her nerves tingle. It had stood for all that was vital for her people in the struggle against Fascism - and at incredible cost they had won. Though she had never been there she felt she somehow knew the place. She was surprised at the strength of her feelings. She was determined to stay in England and not go back to Mother Russia. But that didn't mean she no longer belonged to her people - you couldn't cut your roots and emotions just like that. Once again she felt the hurt of not being able to share her thoughts and feelings with Peter. Soon the operation would be over and she could try to open up to him and have done with the pretence. She wiped her brow, she was sweating. The emotional effect of her memories was showing. She lowered the van's heating, telling Lewis that it was a little warm. The Haydn symphony was well under way and she concentrated on the music as well as on the road ahead, although she wasn't driving two pairs of eyes were useful on a long journey like this.

***

Eugene had arrived at Basel/Mulhouse Airport on a British Airways flight from London at the beginning of the week. He had used his Canadian passport and, after recovering his luggage from the carousel, he had taken the Swiss exit. He had been fortunate to find a decent Calvados at the Duty Free shop at Heathrow and this, his briefcase and one suitcase with a decent suit were all he had brought. He preferred to travel light if he could. He wasn't going to the moon and if he were short of anything he could always buy it in Basel. The Customs and Immigration officials hadn't been very interested in him. There had been nothing to hide from them anyway. It would be the same when he left Switzerland. The drug and the paperwork were to go out of the country in the diplomatic bag. That would be simple and trouble free. He had taken a taxi into Basel from the airport, travelling at first along the corridor of road through French territory to the border proper, though there were no Customs formalities there as that was dealt with at the airport. He had decided to spend his time in the city in comfort and had booked into the *Hotel Euler* near the *Bahnhof SBB*, the main station of the Swiss Federal Railways. The hotel had a good reputation for comfort and food and it was conveniently located.

The beginning of the week had been taken up with getting his team organised and ensuring that everyone knew exactly what was required of them. He had checked out the premises and the equipment they were to use. Grigor, who was in charge of the vehicles, hadn't known when they had last been serviced, so he had been sent off to see to it and to ensure that their tyres were all within the legal limits. Eugene wanted no breakdowns or problems with the Swiss Police. Mobile 'phones were checked and everyone made to carry two in case one went dead or was out of range. Once he was satisfied that all was in order he had told them to have a couple of days off and to report back to base on the Friday at ten o'clock, there was no point in starting too early. Eugene intended to enjoy the facilities at the *Euler* and have a leisurely breakfast. He had ideas of finding a pretty girl to spend time with, if he were successful it would be a shame to have to hurry off in the morning. With a show of concern for his team, he changed the time for Friday's meeting to ten thirty. He needn't have bothered as there turned out to be a dearth of attractive and available women in Basel, or any rate in Eugene's vicinity.

Friday morning arrived and, with no one to distract him, Eugene decided to get there early. He took a tram and then walked the last half mile to the premises, a disused light engineering warehouse, not far from the city centre and a block away from the Rhein, which they had rented as "storage space for textiles". Once the gate was closed outsiders couldn't see in and, in any case, even when the gates were open the offices and their entrance were out of sight around a corner. He let himself into the yard and made his way to the office. There was water in the kettle and he switched it on. A coffee would be welcome and he could read through his notes and make sure that there were no loose ends. He had done that often enough lately, but you never knew, sometimes the most obvious things escaped your attention. He couldn't afford to have anything go wrong: the Swiss took a severe line on industrial espionage and you would find yourself spending a long time in jail if they caught you. While, if he botched the operation, but got out of the country his masters would take their revenge. Nothing to trouble a professional, he told himself, and put his notes in his pocket. Still only a quarter to ten. He closed his eyes and commenced an erotic reverie. Perhaps he would find a passable woman that evening, he was tempted to wander round the city and see what he could find. If only Elizabeth were still as amenable as she had been in the past!

***

Eugene was not the only one who had Elizabeth on his mind. She was also occupying the thoughts of Sam who was not a quarter of a mile away listening in to events at the warehouse. Eugene had been very helpful in that respect. In the middle the previous year he had involved himself in choosing the premises and it hadn't been difficult to follow him there and to other buildings in the area. They had then discovered which one he favoured and bugged it in anticipation. They had not been disappointed when one of Eugene's associates had taken a short lease of the old warehouse, paying the rent in advance. It had been easy to get access and install the bugs as well as to look at the premises and photograph them. The letting agent had been able to supply plans in the period while Eugene was still making up his mind, so Sam had a precise idea of the place and its layout. He also knew the details of how Eugene and his team intended to act. The final briefing was to be that morning and Sam would make sure that there were no changes that would throw him and his own team.

He could hear that someone was in the offices, the Russian bugs that they had installed were pretty sharp and they hadn't cost that much. The KGB had been skilled at listening in to their own people and he was glad that their excellent technology was now so readily available to others. As always the thought of the Russians' own equipment being used against them pleased Sam greatly. He closed his eyes and tried to think of Mia but the face that came to mind was that of Elizabeth, it was no good he couldn't get her out of his thoughts. He had been relieved to find that she had not got a major part in the operation, she had been planted to find out about Lewis' arrangements for the long delayed visit to Basel and, despite being in the city, she would not have a front line rôle in Basel. He knew that Lewis' wife and their son were due in by air the next day and Sam wondered how Elizabeth would be spending her time in Basel. Lewis was bringing his son to see the Fasnacht

Carnival, that and the kid's psychiatric problems were the reason for Michael being there. Lewis would have to spend most of the time with his wife and kid, so Elizabeth would be at a loose end. Despite his better judgement he had booked into the hotel where Elizabeth would be staying. Once he knew her room number he would have the place bugged. At the very least he would be able to observe her from the distance. He knew it was a risk he shouldn't take. He knew it was disloyalty to Mia. He knew but he couldn't help himself. He took the book of war poems from his pocket, it was beginning to fall apart. No, he didn't want a replacement, the book had been with him on many operations, it was like an old friend. War was like this, waiting for something to happen and hoping against hope that when it did you wouldn't be the victim and that, despite the efforts of the enemy, your plans would succeed! Yes those lines of Edward Thomas were his experience:

"Often footsore, never

Yet of the road I weary,

Though long and steep and dreary,

As it winds on for ever."

Life went on like an endless road along which he was still driven by his determination to avenge his father. Memories of him were still vivid. Working first on his taxis and later on a variety of vehicles and machinery, adept at finding the fault almost by instinct and making a reluctant engine perform. The father who had always had time for his kids, doing things with them, telling them marvellous stories. Then in an instant wiped out. Sam gritted his teeth. There was a lot of waiting with this work but it did nothing to lessen his determination to press on with it. They might not call themselves the KGB any longer but many of its former agents were now in the SVR. His masters were expecting someone who had worked at the Serbsky Institute to be with the SVR team. The dossier on the Serbsky's abuse of psychiatry over the years to silence and punish dissidents on behalf of the KGB had horrified and angered Sam. Alan Winters had told him, 'If you can put a bullet through his brain, after telling him why, you should do so - only don't let it compromise the rest of the operation.' He had said it in jest but Sam had known that Winters would have liked it to have been a genuine order. The Serbsky man was for Winters the icing on the cake.

There were the sounds of people arriving at the warehouse. Sam checked that the recorder was running and put on the earphones, someone was making drinks for them. The meeting began with Eugene once more going over the plans. The meeting was over in half an hour and the bug picked up a number of inconsequential conversations.

Sam turned to his companion. 'We'll have a listen to that later. It was good of them to spell it all out so clearly for us. I reckon that there are eight of them including the man from the Serbsky Institute. They will be ready for action at the *Moorgestraich*, the beginning of the carnival at four o'clock on Monday morning but they don't expect to make the snatch until the afternoon procession, that's at two o'clock. It all turns on the plans that Paula Gold and Lewis' wife and kid have for seeing the carnival. There's another meeting on Saturday at five in the afternoon. I'll be here with you then, leave the recorders on just in case anything happens earlier. And you think you can pick up their mobiles?'

'When they tried them out the equipment scanned through various frequencies and picked up a number - so we should be able to listen in if we need to, Sam. The digital 'phone companies think that the encryption keys are secure, would you believe it?'

'OK, there's not much to do until tomorrow afternoon. Check the recorders this evening at around five and tomorrow morning at eleven. Apart from that the time's yours, Jon. You know how to contact me at the *International* in an emergency.'

'And what do you recommend as a way of passing the time here?'

'Wander round the city and see the sights. There's the *Rathaus* with its painted walls, the Cathedral - they call it the *Münster* - and the University. Then you've got the bridges over the Rhein, cafes and restaurants and the rest. Plenty to keep you amused for a day or two. Pity that we're going to be busy during the carnival, they say it's worth seeing! Still we're not here for a vacation but for work! Oh yes, there's the *Historisches Museum* at the *Barfüsserplatz*, they've got a painting called, "*Totentanz*", that's "The Basel Dance of Death". It's worth seeing.'

'No thanks, Sam, that's a bit too close to work for comfort. A while in the fresh air will do me good. It'll be a change from sitting for hours over these things and straining my ears.'

Sam made his way back to the *Marktplatz* opposite the *Rathaus*, which stood with its red/brown walls like a backdrop to a stage ballet set. He wandered round the market stalls with their fruit, vegetables and flowers. It took him back once more to his father. Sam had been surprised how quickly he had adapted to the rural life of the *kibbutz* once he had sold the taxi business and left Brooklyn. Involvement in agriculture had proved a stimulus for him and brought a new lease of life. Sam pictured him in the workshop, gazing out at the fields with a look of fulfilment and delight on his face. He had enjoyed having a part in growing things and getting them to market. He had been all set for a golden old age, part of an extended family and appreciated for his wisdom and experience when it had been abruptly brought to an end by mindless violence. And it had been the Soviets who had equipped the killers. Again the bitterness welled up, since then it had been the driving force of much of his life. Yet it was not so powerful as when he had vowed vengeance at his father's graveside, there in the countryside he had come to love - so different from Crown Heights in Brooklyn. No, it was not so powerful now, but it was still there - though at times he had wondered what would have been his father's response to his motivation. The old man had been open to all, singularly oblivious to distinctions of race, colour, nationality, religion and wealth. Sam looked at the red peppers and tomatoes on a stall and felt a longing for the simplicity of the soil. Perhaps, one day ... but for now he was committed and had a task to complete. He looked for a café and decided on the *Mövenpick* restaurant facing the *Rathaus*. He would have an early lunch and burn up excess energy with a long walk around the city. He wondered where Elizabeth and Lewis might be on the road from Calais, they must have crossed by ferry as the Tunnel was probably closed or running well below capacity since the fire. He knew that Mia would be busy in her hospital, she had told him, when they had spoken a couple days before, that she was beginning a week of night duty. She would be helping to ease the entry of more babies into a hostile world.

***

At nearly seven thirty that evening Lewis brought the van

to a halt outside Jacob and Paula Gold's house in the Basel suburb of Allschwil. The afternoon's journey had been tedious, with driving rain at times and he was glad to be safely at his destination. They had spent longer at the Customs on the border than he could remember in the past and that had added to his displeasure. Throughout the afternoon Michael's problems had again been troubling him. He sensed a growing resentment towards the boy: if only he hadn't chosen to act like this just when all was going so well with Elizabeth! But, of course, he knew that Michael had in no way chosen to be unwell. One might as well accuse him of having chosen to have meningitis. That illness was one of the causes and the other was the child's fear of being dumped by his father. Lewis knew that he would never do that. He would never abandon a child of his. Beside him was Elizabeth, carrying his child. It was coming home to him that once Michael knew that he had a half brother or half sister he was likely to become even more disturbed and insecure. Hell, the timing of everything was wrong. If he had met Elizabeth a year earlier then, though Michael might still have had psychiatric problems, choices would already have been made, the divorce would have been obtained and he would have been married to Elizabeth. Then they would have dealt with things as best they could. Now to divorce Ruth and marry Elizabeth would most likely increase Michael's insecurity and make him even more disturbed. As for Elizabeth's baby, he viewed her pregnancy with a mixture of anticipation and anxiety.

Elizabeth had felt his darkening mood and chosen music to counter it. She would talk to him later about Michael but strange roads in the rain and eventually the dark were not the place for difficult conversations. So she had sought to get him to talk about Alsace and about

Basel and the carnival. This had lifted his spirits a little, though even then his underlying unease remained there in the background.

Jacob had been keeping an eye open for their arrival and was soon on the drive shaking Lewis by the hand and giving Elizabeth a kiss on the cheek. 'Drive it into the garage and take your luggage out. The van will be safer locked up for the night. Yes, set the anti-theft alarm. You must be weary after all that driving. You ate on the way? At Sainte-Menehould? Oh yes, on this side of Reims. No, I would not have been free to choose the *"pied de cochon"* so if you have both developed a taste for them you will not find them here - Paula wouldn't let them into her kitchen! But I think you will enjoy what she has got ready for dinner. Come on, she is waiting for you. We will eat as soon as you have had a drink and freshened up. Or the other way round if you prefer. It would have been nice if you could have made it for the lighting of the *Shabbat* candles but the important thing is that you've reached us safely.' He smiled at Elizabeth, 'Don't worry, you will not find our *Yiddishkeit*, our Jewishness, oppressive. When we observe these customs it is with gratitude for our survival as a people, despite all that our enemies have done to try to blot us out. If others share with us in them it increases my pleasure. We are not in competition with the rest of humanity, we are very much part of it.'

He closed the garage door with a touch of a switch and led them through a door at the back of the garage into the house. Elizabeth could tell immediately that she was in a continental home, though she wondered what it was that made it so different from what she had encountered in North America and England. Perhaps it was the dark timber that marked it out as different. It had a welcoming feel, she thought, particularly after hours on the road.

Paula Gold emerged from the kitchen to welcome them, 'Two travellers from a distant land!'

'It's "from an antique land", Paula.'

'What is?'

The quotation. It should be, "I met a traveller from an antique land", Paula.'

'What a lot of nonsense, Peter! I simply made a statement of fact and quoted nothing and you set about correcting me! Really I think I should send you straight back to your "antique land" but for Elizabeth's sake I won't.' She laughed heartily and the others joined her. 'Do you want to freshen up first or would you like a drink? Freshen up? Both of you? Fine. Jacob, if you will take Peter up to his room I'll show Elizabeth where the cloakroom is.'

Jacob took one of Lewis' cases and led the way up the stairs. 'Here you are, this one is yours. You have slept in it before, I think. Ruth and Michael have the rooms beyond yours along the corridor.' He lowered his voice, 'I was relieved that you arranged for Elizabeth to stay in town at the *International*. I would have been happy with you being together but Paula is concerned about the effect on Michael.'

Lewis nodded wearily, 'We're all concerned, Jacob. It's not getting any easier. Perhaps the *Fasnacht* Carnival will cheer us all up. I know that Michael's looking forward to it.'

***

At eleven thirty Lewis left the *Hotel International* in the centre of Basel and made his way to the stop for the Allschwil tram. He had taken Elizabeth into the city by taxi and seen her settled in at the hotel. After a long goodnight he had left her there. He would 'phone her the next morning and collect her after breakfast. They would have a day in the city - Ruth and Michael were being met by Jacob and Paula at the Airport in the early afternoon and he wouldn't have to be back with them until later in the day. He wanted to make sure that Elizabeth was happy in the hotel as she was going to have a lot of time on her own in the next few days. He sat on the tram reflecting that, despite the tensions, it had been a good day. They had had a safe journey and Jacob and Paula's welcome had been very warm. It was a shame that Elizabeth would be on her own for their stay in Basel and that she would not be enjoying more of their hospitality.

***

Facing the conclusion of the Basel operation, Elizabeth experienced a mixture of frustration and relief at being on her own. Things were coming to a head and she felt the tension growing inside herself. It was difficult having to deal with Peter's stresses as well as her own. There was also their child to consider and care for. How strange it would be to have a son, she felt sure it would be a boy, with a British Birth Certificate. At any rate his roots would be there in that "antique land" or so she hoped.

Chapter 25

Saturday 15th February 1997

For the participants in the coming drama it was a day of waiting and of trying to relax so far as they could. Sam and Eugene and their teams were aware that they were killing time, waiting for Monday to arrive and for the action to get under way. Eugene had decided to keep Elizabeth in ignorance of the planned kidnapping, saying only that they would be picking up the drug and papers during the carnival when the Laboratory's security would be relaxed.

***

Jacob and Paula Gold were attending the *barmitzvah* of a friend's son at the Basel Synagogue. They were to go directly from there to the Airport to collect Ruth and Michael on their arrival from London. It was Sabbath so Paula would do the driving. Jacob sat in the synagogue, his ears and mind filled with the Hebrew tongue. He thought of the history of his people over the millennia and of the transitory nature of the individual life. It was here that he had celebrated his own *barmitzvah*, which had also been a celebration of survival, both personal and national. As a three year old he had been brought from Berlin to Basel late in 1938 by parents apprehensive of events in Germany. It had been the events of *Kristallnacht*, the night of 9th November, with the destruction, led by the SS, of hundreds of synagogues as well as numerous shops and homes, that had made them act. Thousands of Jews had been carried off to concentration camps at that time. He had been put in the care of an aunt, his father's sister, and had become one of their family. From his arrival in Basel until the middle of 1939 he had seen his parents a couple of times, when they had come to Basel for the holidays, but they had returned to Germany each time. His father had believed that things would improve for the Jews once the German people had come to their senses and seen through Hitler - after all, the German Jews had assimilated themselves and they had made an immense contribution to German culture and science. Jacob's grandfather had won the Iron Cross at the Somme in 1917 fighting for his country, that was the measure of the family's commitment to Germany. How wrong his father had been! It wasn't good to be too optimistic in a world such as this. They had all perished, none of Jacob's family who had stayed in Germany had survived. It was only his father about whose fate he had any information. As a chemist he had been useful to the Nazis and had been sent to work in the artificial rubber factory at Auschwitz and allocated to the *Chemical Kommando* until, with his health broken by the life of the camp, he had been discarded as surplus to requirements and had gone the way of the gas chamber and the crematorium. As for the others they too had vanished into the unspeakable horror that was the Holocaust.

His eye moved to the balcony of the synagogue, Paula would be there. They had not been able to have children of their own but they had a fine adopted son who was a regular officer in the Israeli Army. Jacob had seen to it that he had a strong feel for his common humanity as well as for his Jewishness. The Palestinian *intifada* had been a very trying time for him with its conflicting claims on his loyalties but he had come through it without a stain on his record, though he carried, as a reminder of being hit by a piece of rock, a scar on the side of the head. That phase was over but Paula often said that she would welcome the day when the IDF would be able to leave southern Lebanon as well. Whenever there were IDF casualties there she became apprehensive about Yehuda's safety. Perhaps they should have adopted another child as well. He looked at the *barmitzvah* boy, the son of a colleague, about to read the Torah portion assigned to him for the day. He remembered the work that he himself had put into his own preparation all those years ago. He remembered his shaking knees at having to read in this language before the congregation, the strangers were no problem - it was the host of relations and friends that your family brought along. If you got it wrong they would know and they were the ones you would meet time and time again!

His cultural roots were firmly European and yet somehow it was here, as a language older than any European language poured over and immersed him, that he felt at one with his Creator and with humanity. Paula looked down to where he sat, hat on head and prayer shawl around his shoulders, the garment in which he would one day be buried. She sensed the strength of his emotion and knew that a variety of memories would be thrusting themselves into his consciousness. The emotion itself would be short lived. She knew that there would come a mellow gentleness that was often followed by his best work as a scientist and as a poet. It was a gentleness that had touched and shaped their married life together. She looked down at him and was glad from the depth of her heart that she had been given him by the Almighty as her husband.

***

Jacob's colleague Bernhardt Sussmeyer was at work that morning. He was well aware that his laboratory was being used as the bait in a trap set by one intelligence service for another and had been happy to be paid for the assistance given. His paymasters' instructions were that there should be no mock heroics on the part of himself and his colleagues: the Russians were to be given whatever they wanted concerning the new drug.

He had, however, been less than pleased when eight weeks before his wife Trudi had disappeared with Heinrich Nussbaum, the man planted by the Russians in his laboratory. There had been a number of meetings and receptions since then and he had resented her absence, she had always added a touch of colour to the proceedings. Friends and colleagues had noticed her absence and he had told them that she was having a short break in the USA with a friend. The short break had now become a long one and there was still no sign of her. Apart from a note she had left in their bedroom the day she had departed and another posted from Bern he had heard nothing from her. He had told the Swiss Police that he could not be sure that Trudi had gone voluntarily and they were looking for her, but without success. He had not told them of Heinrich's background, that would only have complicated matters, and he couldn't very well tell them how he knew. She had gone with substantial amounts of cash from their bank account and it was unlikely therefore that she or that fellow Heinrich (the name almost caused him to spit, though of course he would never have done anything as unhygienic as that!) would draw attention to themselves by using their credit cards in a hurry. He was angry at her ingratitude towards him, he had seen to it that she always had anything she wanted so far as her wardrobe was concerned - it had been important for his business that she should look the part of the wife of a wealthy and successful man.

***

At a little after ten in the morning Lewis collected Elizabeth from the *Hotel International*. She saw immediately that he hadn't had a good night. His mood swings were becoming more difficult for both of them to cope with. In his own words he was riding an emotional roller coaster. More and more he was feeling Michael's distress and blaming himself for it. She knew that he wished that they had met a year earlier and that divorce and remarriage had been out of the way before the onset of Michael's problems. She wished so too. If only this Basel operation were over. It was hard trying to calm him when she herself was becoming stressed at the uncertainty over her own future.

They spent the day in the city sightseeing, wandering around looking at the shops and getting the feel of the city. There was a sense of anticipation, the solid citizens of Basel seemed impatient for the carnival to get under way and give them the chance to let their hair down. Confectioners' windows had cakes and sweets in the form of carnival characters and department stores had souvenirs. From cellars in small alleyways came the sound of drummers practising.

'It's exciting looking forward to something like this, Peter. From what Jacob was telling us it's quite an occasion. Michael's bound to enjoy himself, I bet he's up ahead of any of you on Monday morning. Did Jacob really say that you had to be at the Allschwil tram stop at 3 a.m.? That seems an incredible time of the morning.'

' 'Fraid so, the carnival kicks off, they call it the

Morgenstraich, at 4 a.m. - and you've got to give yourself time to find a good place to see what's going on. As for Michael, you're right, he's sure to enjoy it. He'll have plenty to talk about when he gets back to school.'

They had reached the *Stadttheatre* and were looking at the pond with Tinguely's fantastic fountains, metal sculptures that see-sawed, rotated or moved in a variety of other ways. Or they would have done so had they not been thickly coated in ice, assuming the appearance of ice sculptures on metal frames.

'Iced up and unable to move. A bit like my emotions before I met you, Elizabeth.' He smiled and put his arm round her. 'You've done me a world of good.'

She turned to face him, 'I sometimes wonder, Peter. When we first met you didn't have such a careworn appearance as this.'

'That's not your doing, Elizabeth, you know that! Michael will be on the mend soon, I'm sure of it. Then I'll look as I should under your gentle influence.' He pulled her close, ran a hand through her hair and kissed her. She saw his face relax and was glad that he had brightened up a little. He was good and stimulating company but she was beginning to worry over whether he was near to a breakdown. He suffered the anxieties of the over scrupulous. How often those with less conscience seemed to have an easier life, unaffected by guilt and self doubt.

Back at the *Hotel International* they had a coffee and a pastry before going up to Elizabeth's room. 'When do you have to be back at Jacob and Paula's for dinner?'

'In a couple of hours time, around six thirty - dinner's at seven.'

'And how would you like to spend the time remaining to us, Peter?' She affected a look of complete innocence.

'I suppose I could go down to the kiosk in the foyer and buy a pack of cards - you know the place where I bought the little *Fasnacht* badge for your jacket. Here let me fix it to your lapel.' He took the envelope from his pocket, removed the badge, pushed the pin through the fabric and attached the little disc behind the lapel. 'It's a little drummer, I think. We've heard plenty of them busy practising this afternoon.' He slipped his hand under her jacket, feeling the lace beneath her dark blue silk blouse. 'Though I can think of something better than playing cards for the next hour or so.'

She pulled him close, 'Do you know, Peter, so can I!'

A while later Lewis sat on the tram back to Allschwil. Around him were Baslers returning from an afternoon of shopping and visiting friends. A variety of separate lives meeting up for a few minutes in a tram but not communicating with one another or wanting to. Lewis felt so bound up in Elizabeth's life and the life of their child, his oneness with them persisted even though the tram was taking him further and further from the *Hotel International*. He prepared himself for his return to his other family, his original one, and to his friends. He hoped the carnival would keep Michael's mind off the things that were so troubling him.

***

Sam checked in with Jon that morning to make sure that there was nothing of significance on the recorders and was assured that nothing at all had been picked up. He went for a long walk around the city, returning to the apartment where the team were based in the early afternoon following lunch at *Mövenpick* in the *Marktplatz*.

There was no need to return to the *Hotel International*, Elizabeth would be out with Lewis and a colleague was looking after the recorders there. Also Jon had 'phoned in to report that Eugene had cancelled the five o'clock meeting. Evidently there were to be no changes to the Russians' plans. Sam returned to their base, showered and then spent the afternoon reading a pile of international newspapers that he had bought earlier in the city. At five thirty Anna arrived. She was to be the evening's diversion, not for Sam but for Eugene.

'You're early Anna, can't you wait to get at him?'

'That's not very flattering Sam. The truth is it's good to see you again and I thought that a few extra minutes here would be some compensation for the evening ahead. No, I won't have a drink, I'll need to have my wits about me if I'm to emerge intact from the encounter you've arranged with Eugene!'

'You had no problem meeting up with him at lunchtime?'

'None at all, apart from having to keep other males at bay until he arrived on the scene. What's wrong with this place? There seems to be an excess of lusty males and a distinct lack of willing women.'

'I'm not surprised you attracted interest, you're looking a million!'

'Flatterer! I've got to admit that I've been busy getting myself ready for your scrutiny, oh yes and for your friend Vladimir as well, although he calls himself Eugene Preston as you know. This morning I used my fresh-air-girl look. Tonight it's the sophisticated lady touch that you're seeing.'

'I like what I see, Anna.' He looked at her, a petite blonde with a good figure and a lively face and personality. She wore a dark turquoise shot silk cocktail dress that came to just above the knee. Her fur coat, a musquash he thought, lay alongside her on the tired looking sofa - he had not gone for luxury in the accommodation he had chosen for their base, it wasn't necessary. 'When did we last work together? A couple of years ago was it?'

'That's right, Sam. When we picked up the Libyan bomber in Paris. That was one that went like clockwork. And this one, going to plan?' Being a blonde she was a highly effective bait with Arabs.

'Going to plan, with a few extras like yourself, but I've got to admit there's something about it that to my mind doesn't quite add up. No, I don't think the Russians have an inkling of our involvement. There's something about the whole thing that I can't fully understand, not that it's necessary for me to do so - sometimes, of course, it's right to keep it in little compartments on a need-to-know basis so that the operation isn't compromised if something goes wrong.'

'And how is Mia?'

'Well, very well and working hard in that hospital in Brooklyn. She came over to London for a few days last month and we did the galleries and the sights. The first time she had been out of New York State, you know.'

'If I were your fiancée, Sam, you wouldn't keep me in New York State - I can assure you of that! You're not free after I've done time with Eugene by any chance?'

'Free to debrief you after your time with him, debrief in the less pleasurable sense that is, I'm afraid!'

'You had me excited for a moment, Sam. You ought to marry that fiancée of yours. It would put you properly out of bounds.'

'And stop you from having designs on me?'

'Probably not, Sam, but it might be some restraint, you never know. And what about Mia, you ought to make sure she doesn't get fed up and look elsewhere - she's a very attractive woman.'

'OK, OK I'll give it serious thought. Now to your evening out.'

'In the call of duty not of pleasure, I can assure you!'

'OK then, your evening of duty. Run through the timetable, I don't want you having any problems.'

'I've arranged to meet him in the bar at the *Hotel Euler* at a quarter to eight but I don't want to be there until eight, it'll keep him on edge. Dinner should take about an hour and a half, I'll take my time with the food and he's talkative - I found that out at lunchtime - so I'll lead him on and let him think he's impressing me - and, if his tongue's loosened enough there's the chance that he'll let slip something useful. So that makes it nine thirty for our stroll up to his bedroom. I'll have told him that my ancient banker husband will be arriving at the airport at eleven forty five but that he's off to New York at midday tomorrow. Must give Eugene something to look forward to, mustn't I?'

'Indeed you must, Anna. Keep him ever hopeful, that's the name of the game. How long do you need before your ancient banker husband calls you on your mobile to say he's got in early and wants you to collect him from the airport at once because he's got a splitting headache and he'd tired out?'

'I want to be safe, Sam. Eugene's not my choice for a lover but with the prospect of another less hurried encounter the next day he's likely to keep his ardour in check, so lets say half an hour no more - remember he's already spent the previous hour and a half chatting me up and being led on.'

'Right. Tom will be in the bar from a quarter to nine with one of the other folk - you know him don't you? Good. As you leave the dining room you'll see him there and that will be some reassurance. He'll give you twenty five minutes with Eugene then he'll go outside and call your mobile using his own. Do make sure it's switched on, I won't be responsible for you if it isn't! If you don't appear in five minutes Tom's buddy will go up to the room, No. 214 isn't it, and set off the fire alarm in the corridor - that should get him out if it's difficult for you to disentangle from him.'

'Thanks for your concern for my safety, Sam. If I ever have to bait a trap with you I shall be just as careful. I wouldn't like to have you perish in the arms of some Amazon and neither would Mia!' The woman who came at once to Sam's mind was no Amazon even though she was Eugene's colleague.

***

Eugene paced his room. Damn woman. Damn Swiss bankers with their early 'planes and splitting headaches. It was catching, his head was aching as well. It wasn't simply the drink, though he hadn't done badly on the expense account that evening, it was the sense of frustration. He'd had to wait all that time from two fifteen to eight to see her again. An excellent dinner, with her looking absolutely splendid, gift-wrapped so to speak, and then just when he was about to remove the wrappings her damn 'phone goes off and some old fellow summons her to the airport! Eugene opened his wardrobe and took out a bottle of John Jameson whiskey. He poured himself a couple of centimetres or so in a tumbler. He sat down and raised the tumbler to let the light from the table lamp shine through the golden liquid. A nice drink and one in the eye to those superior Brits as it came from south of the border in Ireland. He hoped the Irish would never give the Brits peace until they got what they wanted and, preferably, not even then. He raised the glass, 'To the festering of old wounds! So long as no one blows *me* up in the process.' He relished the whiskey. You needed something to keep you going when you were on active service for the Motherland. His plans for the evening were in ruins but she would be free of her old banker tomorrow. She was worth waiting for. He would just have to be patient until she 'phoned him around midday on Sunday.

***

Sam's evening was very different from Eugene's, as he certainly did not end up with intense frustration and a hurt ego. On his return from briefing Anna he went straight to the *Hotel International* and into the restaurant to find it crowded and without a free table. He was asked to wait until a table became vacant and said he would do so once he had got a drink from the bar. On returning he found that, in the meantime, Elizabeth had arrived and been given a table that had been vacated while he was at the bar. When the waiter proffered his apologies Sam looked in the direction of the table and Elizabeth, sensing that there was a problem, looked up. For the first time the two made eye contact. To Sam's surprise she didn't look away but calmly and steadily held his gaze. To his amazement he heard himself ask the waiter, 'I wonder if you would mind asking the lady whether I might have the pleasure of her company and share the table with her.' It brought from the waiter a slight shrug of his shoulders and a look suggesting that he thought Sam was wasting his time, this wasn't the sort of woman who would let herself be picked up in his restaurant.

The waiter returned, 'The lady would be pleased to have your company, Sir. So if you'll follow me ... ' He led a startled Sam to her table. What, he asked himself, did he think he was doing? In no way was this part of the plan. Anna's dinner with Eugene was a calculated addition to the plan, this was uncalculated. He had no further time for reflection as they had reached her table.

'It was very kind of you to say that I might join you, but I feel that it's something of an intrusion and if you would rather remain on your own ... '

'Not at all, you're welcome. I would enjoy some intelligent conversation, I've just spent an hour watching the Saturday night television and it numbs the mind, it really does.' Once again she held his gaze. He had the feeling that she was looking deep within him not just into his eyes. And now he knew the colour of *her* eyes – hazel – *that* hadn't been on her file.

'Sam Charles from Brooklyn, pleased to meet you.'

'Elizabeth Fielder from London, though I know I don't sound as if that's where I hail from.'

They shook hands and Sam took his seat facing her, 'This OK?'

'That's fine. We can interrogate one another. The geometry of confrontation or something of that sort.'

She was relaxed and going to be good company, he knew that he would have to take care, find out about her and keep her talking. At any rate he had given her a false surname that tallied with his papers. But he remained Sam, that kept things straightforward in emergencies as you didn't have to wonder who they were shouting for.

Elizabeth was also surprised that she had agreed to let this stranger keep her company. Her plan had been to have a quick meal and an early night before taking the train to the Alps early on the Sunday morning to spend a day among the mountains in the snow.

They conversed about places they knew, finding that there was much of the USA that they had both visited. She told him about her job with Lewis, adding that her boss was in town but staying at a friend's house with his wife and son who had arrived that afternoon. She found herself explaining that she lived with Lewis, whose son had problems, so that he had to be where the boy was staying and not with her. She was surprised at her openness with this stranger but there was something about him that spoke of understanding and trustworthiness and she was glad to be able to talk to someone. She told him of the piano she had been given by Lewis and Sam got from her its location in the sitting room, something he had wondered about since he had first heard her play it. Sam told her of the Brooklyn of his childhood but kept much about himself under wraps. He was, he told her reporting on Switzerland and Germany for a number of US papers which catered for Swiss and German communities.

The meal was over and they were about to leave the table. Sam had insisted on paying. 'I'm an intruder who's disturbed your quiet evening, Elizabeth.' He relished the opportunity to call her by her name but made sure that he didn't give the impression of being excited by their encounter.

'Not an intruder at all, Sam. You've been good company and I'm grateful.' She paused, 'I wonder if you are doing anything tomorrow ... I'm planning to take the train to the Alps, to Luzern and its lake. Would you like to come as well? You could write about it for your Swiss Americans back home.'

He paused, there would have to be some changes to his schedule but it could be managed, 'I'd like that. It would be a pleasure to spend the day with you.'

'We'll meet in the lobby after breakfast tomorrow, say eight o'clock.'

'Fine, see you then, Elizabeth.'

Back in her room she looked at herself in the mirror. She was surprised at herself. Why on earth had she invited him to spend the day with her? He had impressed her with his respect for her relationship with Peter and the absence of any sexual advances, though she sensed that he was not a celibate. Would Peter mind? She somehow felt he wouldn't, though she wasn't entirely sure. 'I'll just have to take care,' she thought as she closed her eyes and wondered about the day ahead with snow, mountains and, she hoped, sunshine.

***

Sam took a taxi to their HQ in the apartment and waited for Anna's return. He made a note of the tasks to be entrusted to his deputy while he was in Luzern. He picked up a book and began to read. It was a strange world and he certainly had a strange job, but it was never dull! He looked forward to the next day's visit to the Alps but he knew that he would have some explaining to do to his bosses.

***

'Good night Dad. Thanks for bringing us here, Jacob and Paula are very kind and I like them. It's a shame we're not going skiing tomorrow. We had a great time here at the

New Year and I'd like to have another go.'

'I want you fit and well to see the carnival, not in hospital with a broken leg, Michael! Jacob's got a couple of sleds and we're taking them with us tomorrow, so you'll have your fun in the snow but in a gentler fashion. We'll have a good time I can assure you. Now time for sleep, we're up early tomorrow to make the most of the sunshine - they're forecasting a sunny day in the Alps.' Lewis tucked him in and ruffled his hair. 'Sweet dreams and a quiet night.' He fervently hoped that his wish would be granted.

'Night Dad. I'll race you down the hill on the sled!'

Chapter 26

Sunday 16th February 1997

It was a day of clear skies and sunshine in Basel and in the Alps. For some of the participants it was to have a significance far beyond anything they could possibly have imagined. And for all of them it started quietly enough.

A telephone call late the previous evening had informed Eugene that Svyatoslav Gordeyev had arrived in Basel by train from Berlin. He was to meet him for a briefing at nine o'clock the next morning, Grigor would bring Gordeyev to the warehouse. Eugene had wondered about meeting him at his hotel, but the arrangements had now been made and it would be easier to keep the meeting brief in the relative discomfort of the warehouse office. He would then be back in good time for Anna's telephone call to let him know that her damned banker husband was on his way to New York and that she was heading for the *Hotel Euler*.

He decided to get up early and walk to the warehouse. He hadn't slept particularly well, the exercise would do him good and get some of the agitation out of his system. He hadn't felt like this before, but then he hadn't had to gather information in this sort of way. It had always been quietly and without anyone knowing, either while the extraction was taking place or afterwards. And it had always been just himself and Elizabeth, not the whole team of people that this operation involved. Too big for his liking and with too much chance of his making a fool of himself, but he'd had no choice in the matter. At any rate the months in London had, apart for Elizabeth falling for the Englishman, been satisfying and he was looking forward to returning there and getting on with gathering dirt for future use against unwitting politicians. An occasional attack of morals by the Brits was very useful to his masters.

He showered and did some press ups and sit ups, you needed to keep fit - especially when you were eating and drinking as well as he was doing at the moment. After shaving he dressed with a black high necked sweater and a tweed sportscoat. A coffee would do for breakfast, as he had eaten well the night before. He took his gray overcoat from behind the bedroom door and made for the lift. The morning air was fresh, not cold, but he needed to pull on his coat when he reached the pavement.

He was enjoying the walk through the city. Why not have a look at the river on the way? He consulted his map, out of *Aeschenplatz* into *Dufourstrasse* and then, beyond the *Kunstmuseum*, turn left into *Rittergasse* which would bring him to the *Münster* - the cathedral - from there he should be able to see the river. The walk had calmed him and he was enjoying the exercise. In the *Münsterplatz* there was activity in a tree-fringed part of the square to the side of the *Münster* as workmen assembled tents and stalls, evidently something to do with the carnival. He wondered whether he would have a chance to see anything of it or whether the operation would take all his time, it probably would - their instructions were to get well clear of the place once they had the goods. He just hoped that the carnival wouldn't make things too difficult by holding up the traffic and blocking streets. According to their plans it should be all right.

The river lay beyond the *Münster* and he strolled along the side of the building to a viewing point at the rear from which he looked down on the river. Below him the Rhein sped by at a considerable rate and a ferry, seemingly attached to a cable by a pulley, used the flow to edge itself to the other bank. Further down river a green tram crossed one of the bridges from *Grossbasel* into *Kleinbasel*. Downstream on the West bank of the river were the chemical and pharmaceutical factories and near them the laboratory that was their target. That was the direction he was heading - he should reach the warehouse in another twenty minutes, a few minutes ahead of this fellow they'd sent from Moscow. If Heinrich hadn't chosen to take off with the boss' wife it wouldn't have been necessary to send Gordeyev but they couldn't do without an expert and he would have to be briefed on the operation.

Eugene made his way down the hill from the *Münster* past some of the University faculties until he reached the road that led to the *Mittlere Brücke* on which he had seen the tram. Yes there it was, something he'd been looking for, up on the corner of a building and facing the bridge, the carving of a king with his tongue extended in the direction of *Kleinbasel* across the bridge. Not very Swiss, he thought as he crossed the road and passed the *Hotel Drei Könige*. He remembered some UEFA meeting there, something about keeping the Brits out of European football competitions after their thuggish supporters had caused mayhem somewhere or other. The Brits who thought themselves so superior! The *Drei Könige* looked properly Swiss, prestigious and expensive, perhaps he could bring Anna here for lunch, it would make a change from the *Euler*. The thought of the little blonde put a sense of purpose into his stride, get the briefing over and he would be free for the rest of the day.

The office at the warehouse had a chilly feel, he would have preferred the warmth of his hotel. Never mind, with its discomfort no one would want to linger here. He switched on the kettle and cast his eye over the office. Good, nothing to identify who was using the premises. He had told his people to leave nothing of theirs behind. The tins of food, in case they needed to hold their hostages for any length of time, were in boxes in the corner. A first aid kit was on a table nearby, just in case anyone needed treatment - not that anyone was going to get hurt. He hoped it would be a low key affair, all over within a few hours. The door of the office opened and Grigor arrived with an elderly man in tow. They greeted one another, each curious about the other.

'Welcome to Basel Mr Gordeyev! You've brought the sunshine with you.'

'You're Eugene, as I believe you're known for this operation? Good. And yes, I've brought the sunshine - though they would have been better to send a younger delivery man. It's *Dr* Svyatoslav Gordeyev. I've been sent because I'm a pharmaceutical chemist and have considerable expertise in the sort of goods you are to collect.'

Eugene scrutinised the older man. He was in his mid sixties, neatly dressed in a dark business suit and maroon tie but evidently not well. There was a greyness about his face and he was sweating.

'You're all right, I hope. You look a bit under the weather. Take a seat, don't stand around.' Eugene sought to inject a note of concern into his voice.

Gordeyev took a seat but then got up to put on the overcoat he had been carrying, 'I will be honest with you. I'm not well. A recurrence of prostate cancer I'm afraid. I should never have been sent here but they decided that I had the skills they needed and the money will be useful to the family if not to me. I'm not here as a sightseer. The sooner you get this business over and I'm on my way home so much the better.'

'They've told you what it's all about.'

'Yes, they weren't so stupid as to send me here in *total* ignorance. Shall I summarise what I know and say why I've been pulled out of retirement and in my present state to come here? Good, I won't keep you long - I want to get back to my room and lie down and, by the way, I shall probably want one of your people to help me get back to Moscow afterwards, I might not make it on my own. Here's a note they gave me to pass to you.' He searched in his pocket and produced an envelope that was slightly crumpled at the corners and addressed to "Mr E Preston, Basel." Eugene's curiosity was roused and he opened it. He sat reading it and re-reading it. The note was on plain paper and read:

> "We wish you well with your negotiations. Your newly arrived colleague is fully conversant with the technical aspects and you and your London colleague are to return to us with him by the route he will give you. There is to be no delay and you are to give him every assistance."

The note carried the necessary authentication code so he had no doubt that it was genuine. The blood drained from Eugene's face. His pleasant existence in London was at an end. It was back to Moscow for him. Probably back to a desk job there. Back to that wife of his and the kids. It had been good while it lasted but now it was over. The one consolation was that Elizabeth was going back as well. It would serve her right and perhaps, away from Lewis, she would be more responsive to his advances - that would be some consolation. But he knew that he couldn't risk a divorce and incur the wrath of his wife's family until his father-in-law had retired from the SVR and could no longer damage his career.

He looked up from the note, screwed it into a ball and put it into a jacket pocket. 'You'll be in good company Dr Gordeyev, I'll be taking you back to Moscow and Elizabeth who assists me will be coming with us. Shall I take the details of our route from you.'

'I have the details in my head and will give them to you when we need them.'

The old man was asserting himself, trying to preserve some dignity and authority in a situation which did not entirely please him, he didn't like the company into which he had now been thrust. Grigor had listened to them as he made coffee at the end of the room. He was quietly amused at Eugene's instructions, knowing that he was in no hurry to leave what had become a sinecure in London.

The three men sat around the table with their mugs of coffee and Dr Gordeyev began, 'The laboratory here is an independent development and testing laboratory. It is run by Sussmeyer and Gold, a couple of Swiss who have a very good track record in the discovery and development of drugs. They are both strong individualists who didn't fit into the structure of the local drugs companies' research and development departments. They set up on their own and have been able to work together because they each regard the other as a lesser evil than the large corporations and because they have strict lines of demarcation between their individual responsibilities in the laboratory and in dealing with its clients. I have seen the reports that the vanished Heinrich made while he was working there. He is still vanished? I blame him for bringing me here, once I would have enjoyed the visit, but in my present condition. ...... No, it is not good to travel in my state. To return to the laboratory, the report somehow got to the ears of our masters that they were well advanced with the development of a new drug which could have significant uses for psychiatry. You have heard of I. P. Pavlova - Pavlov to Westerners - of course you have. His conditioning experiments are, of course, well known, even to children in school. Well this drug, the Basel Formula let us call it, is believed to make such conditioning a simple and a gentle process. Now both those factors would make it very useful in treating people with certain psychotic disorders and in helping them to conform with the way the rest of the community think and behave.'

He paused and looked at Eugene and Grigor, 'Do you remember the trouble that we had back in the 1970's and 1980's over our use of psychiatry to deal with dissidents who were making a nuisance of themselves? I was working at the Serbsky Central Research Institute of Forensic Medicine in Moscow at the time, testing out new drugs on the disturbed dissidents who were brought there for their own good. We were able to drug them up to the eyeballs but it didn't achieve much and we had the International Congress of Psychiatrists to contend with. They slandered us, accusing us of using psycho-pharmacological treatment to punish and "re-educate" dissenters when we were only trying to protect those disturbed people from the consequences of their delusions. There are always people whose mental derangement, paranoia and other psychological symptoms can lead them to anti-social actions which are illegal - they disturb public order, slander people in authority and behave aggressively. People like that can be cunning and to the layman they can appear sane. That was our problem and we and our country were accused unfairly, by dissenters at home and enemies abroad, when we were trying to save patients from the consequences of their illnesses.'

He had become excited and now he mopped his brow. Grigor brought him a glass of water and he began again, 'So you can imagine how useful we would have found a drug like the Basel Formula to deal gently with these people - they would probably not even have known that it was being administered to them. Circumstances of course have changed, we are no longer under attack and we have had an interesting reduction in the incidence of mental illness of this type, but if circumstances were to change for whatever reason and this became a problem once again it would be necessary to avoid bringing international wrath, however unjustified, on our country and our people. That is one reason why we are all here in Basel. The other reason is a commercial one: the drug is one that could be exploited commercially and the Russian economy would benefit greatly from its exploitation. We are not sure whether the laboratory here will register the patent of their drug, Sussmeyer and Gold are an odd pair, sometimes more interested in an idea for its own sake than in turning it into money and they may have doubts about the ethics of its clinical use. So what we must send back to Moscow is not only a sample of the drug but also the details of how it is produced and the fullest details of the testing they have done. It's not the sort of material you can get by climbing in through a window. They have to be made to give it all to us. That is your area, I think, gentlemen.' Again he mopped his brow and drank some more water. Grigor went to refill the glass.

Eugene began, 'It was good of you to come here Dr Gordeyev despite your health. I hope that your task will not be too strenuous for you. We will do all we can to help you and to get you back home in as much comfort as possible.' The sick man nodded his thanks. 'What you have just told us has increased our resolve to ensure that the operation is a complete success. We appreciate the importance of obtaining not just the drug but all the reports and paperwork.

'Now as to our part in the operation. The laboratory operates a very high degree of security and commercial vehicles leaving the premises are very carefully searched, as are its personnel - except those at the very top of the organisation, Sussmeyer and Gold. They are the only ones who ever take papers out of the laboratory, apart from the post of course. Private cars are parked opposite the premises, that's outside the entrance to the site, so you can't use a car to take things out. But, and this is important, there is an Englishman, a fellow called Peter Lewis who is a friend of Jacob Gold, he supplies them with glassware and brings it from London in his van. I don't know why he doesn't send it for delivery in the normal way but, whatever the reason is and perhaps it's simply that he likes a visit to his old friend Gold, he brings the goods himself. Now because he's Gold's friend his van goes in and, more importantly, it comes *out* without being checked by the security staff. So, Dr Gordeyev, that's our delivery vehicle because Lewis has a delivery to make - he's combined business with the carnival which starts tomorrow and which will give us cover for our action.

'The other thing is to persuade them to hand over the goods to us without too much debate. In other words we have to present them, Sussmeyer and Gold, with a persuasive argument for giving the goods to us. Although Heinrich Nussbaum has seen fit to deprive us of his services, and in doing so inconvenience you Dr

Gordeyev, he was able to establish that Gold in particular would be susceptible to pressure. Gold is a Jew who came to Switzerland as a child from Berlin in 1938 when his parents were worried about the actions of Hitler and the Nazis. He was brought up by an aunt in the safety of Switzerland but all his family in Germany – including his parents - perished in the Holocaust. He is a happily married man and they have an adopted son who is a soldier in Israel. Our psychological assessment is that Gold would yield to our requests for the drug and the papers if the life of his wife Paula were at stake. So we snatch her and deliver our request. In addition Lewis' wife and son are likely to be with her so, if we pick them up as well, he is likely to feel that the obligations of friendship, hospitality and all that sort of thing are further irresistible arguments.' Eugene smiled, pleased with the logic of the plan.

'So we pick up Paula Gold and probably Lewis' wife and kid, deliver our request for the goods and then attend at the laboratory to collect them. You come on the visit to the lab to make sure we're not short-changed. We depart with the goods, return the ladies and the kid once most of us are well beyond Swiss borders and after the goods are in the diplomatic bag making a safe journey to Moscow.'

Gordeyev looked at him quizzically, 'As simple as that?'

'So we hope.'

'So do I. I have no wish to be shot in the process or to spend my last days in a Swiss prison.'

'No one is going to get shot. It will all be very low key and even gentlemanly. Sussmeyer and Gold have a product that they might or might not turn to good account. We come along intent on the good of humanity and worried about the sort of disturbed people you have been talking about, Dr Gordeyev, and we take the project over and put the drug into production. It sounds very reasonable don't you think?'

Gordeyev mopped his brow, managed a tired smile and drank the remainder of the glass of water, pushing it in Grigor's direction for a refill. 'As humanitarians we can work together for the common good.'

'Now the timetable. Grigor, perhaps you would like to tell us quickly so that Dr Gordeyev knows when we're likely to need him.'

'Eugene is in overall charge of the operation and my task is to look after the practical side of things, picking up the women and the kid, holding them here so that they don't give any trouble and returning them as payment for the goods. We will move when they are separate from the men-folk. Tomorrow is the first day of the *Fasnacht* carnival. It starts at 04h00 on the Monday morning and goes on with precious little respite, I understand, for three days. At some stage, and I hope it is tomorrow, though it's unlikely to be at four o'clock, we expect to find the women on their own or with the kid and bring them here. If we could do it tomorrow afternoon during the main carnival parade at 14h00 that would be best - the laboratory will be on holiday and there will only be a security man on the gate, so the collection of the goods would be without an audience. Otherwise it's going to have to be one evening after work at the laboratory has finished. So take it easy, rest at your hotel and we'll probably bring you over here after lunch tomorrow. Is that OK?'

'It will do. Now I just want to be back in the hotel and lie down, that is after I have been to the lavatory.'

Eugene and Grigor looked at one another. Was he going to last out or would he expire before he'd done his part in the operation?

He saw and read their faces, 'Don't worry, I've got

another two months left, it could even be three. You won't have to bury me here. But I would appreciate the comfort of my hotel room, please.'

Somehow this disconcerted Eugene more than if Gordeyev had slumped dead over the table. He shook the old man's hand, 'They'll decorate you, I hope. Until tomorrow then. And you Grigor, I'll 'phone you later. We can meet late this evening at the *Hotel Euler*.'

Grigor removed the cups and the glass to a table at the end of the room, they could be washed the next day while they were waiting for the action to develop. No, he changed his mind and rinsed them. They would take them when they went, better not to leave signs of their presence and finger prints. 'Back to your hotel then, Dr Gordeyev.' He nodded to Eugene and they were gone. Eugene sat at the table for a few minutes. He had been uncomfortable looking into the face of death. Gordeyev said that he had been pressured into the job but there was something about his manner and the fervour of the way he had spoken of the problems with dissident mental patients in the 1970's and 1980's that had suggested a personal commitment of some kind that was driving him. Without any effort on Eugene's part Anna came to mind, petite and vivacious. Alive, very much alive! The very epitome of life and fun - fun that had been denied him the previous evening but which he looked forward to that afternoon. And then he thought of the screwed up piece of paper in his pocket, the message from Moscow bidding him to return. It was bad news but Elizabeth would be coming as well. Telling her would be some pleasure at any rate. He would have a word with Grigor if she showed signs of wanting to ignore the order. That fellow Lewis could drive his wretched van back to London on his own once they had used it at the laboratory. Lewis could take piano lessons - Elizabeth wouldn't be around to play her expensive present. And he could go back to his wife for the kid's sake. Eugene stood up, 'Let's play while we can!' he said and made his way out of the warehouse and into the road. The sun was shining and Anna would be on the telephone in a couple of hours. A romp in the hay while the sun shone would suit him fine. Though the setting at the *Hotel Euler* would be less bucolic than that - a pleasant afternoon and evening were in prospect. An enjoyable farewell to the West, for the time at any rate.

***

Ruth Lewis gave her husband a kiss on the forehead. 'It's been a good day Peter. All that sunshine, fresh air and snow! I could see you brighten up as soon as we got to the snow. You really felt alive there didn't you? It was great to see you and Michael enjoying yourselves on the toboggans, like a couple of kids together! No, that's good, the way it should be - letting your hair down together. You were a bit uptight earlier, you know, but you soon relaxed. Elizabeth's certainly changed you that way, you've lost a lot of your inhibitions and you can let yourself go - which is good. When are you due to see her?'

'Tomorrow evening if that fits in. I hope she wasn't too bored being on her own today. Still, she was talking about a train ride to the mountains and doing some sightseeing there. I hope the weather was as good for her as it was for us. She's due to 'phone in at ten to say how she's got on.

'Tomorrow afternoon, while you and Michael go with Paula to see the carnival procession, Jacob and I will take the van to the laboratory and unload it. There won't be any staff on duty and we'll have to empty it ourselves but it'll get the job done and then the rest of the visit will be all relaxation.'

'Right Peter, early to bed! Don't sit chin-wagging with Jacob! You've got to be up at a half past two to catch the tram at three. Michael was out like a light as soon as his head touched the pillow. Tomorrow's going to be a long day for us all but it should be quite an experience. Paula says we won't forget it in a hurry.'

***

Elizabeth was aware of her mixed emotions as she sat in her hotel room. She had telephoned Lewis and told him where she had spent the day - she would tell him about Sam when they were together the next evening, he would see that she had nothing to hide about the matter. She found a concert of light classical music on a local radio station which suited her relaxed and thoughtful mood. The day with Sam had been perfection itself. The sun, snow, fresh air and the view from the summit of the Rigi, southwards across the *Vierwaldstättersee* – Lake Luzern – towards the lofty peaks which appeared in the distance with unusual clarity, crowded her memory. There had been an empathy between them, a sense of communicating even in the silences in their conversation. Indeed the silences were something she remembered with their sense of sharing the enjoyment of the spectacular scenery and one another's company. You could share silence with a friend and it didn't become an embarrassment. It was when you were ill at ease that you chattered and soon ran out of topics of conversation.

Sam had been the perfect escort. He hadn't tried to push their relationship beyond friendship and that had been a large part of the enjoyment. They had responded as people who respected each other and took pleasure in one another's company. For both there had been self disclosure and areas of life that had been kept firmly under wraps. Each had sensed the reserve in the other and accepted it, knowing somehow that it was not without good reason. They had exchanged addresses through which they could be contacted and there was no reason why they should not meet again. At one and the same time she both regretted and welcomed his departure on the night train to Hamburg that one of his editors had requested. She regarded him as a friend, the sort of person you could share things with. Certainly no rival to her affection for Peter, she was carrying his child and she and he loved one another. She had felt no qualms at telling Sam about Peter and admitting - no that wasn't the right word, it suggested guilt and she felt none - that she was pregnant by him. She had told him of Peter's problems with Michael and the effect that the planned divorce was likely to have on the boy. He had listened with a sympathy she could feel but had offered no solution to their dilemma, there was no easy answer and he had not tried to pretend otherwise.

She put her hand on her stomach and tried to imagine the foetus developing within. So commonplace yet so incredible. There was a sense of wonder about life.

Would she meet Sam again? She had his uncle's address in Brooklyn, so she could get a message to him if she wanted. She wondered why she should want to do so. If she had been unattached ... But friends were important, men didn't all have to be potential lovers, to regard them in that way robbed women of a lot of companionship she felt.

Her reverie was interrupted by a knock on the door. She

checked that it was Eugene and let him in. He stood and looked at her without a word. His face reflected his inner struggle to control his feelings. Apart from her formal 'Well, good evening Eugene,' Elizabeth matched his silence with her own. She was anxious that nothing should spoil the day in her memory and she hoped she could keep her tongue in check.

Eugene had been trained to observe quickly and accurately. There was no evidence of anyone other than Elizabeth having been in the room. That pleased him. She was wearing a loose-fitting cream-coloured sweater and a black pleated skirt. As ever her dark brunette hair was immaculately ordered. There was a freshness about her face that spoke of a day in the open air. She looked calm and relaxed and that got under his skin. She had clearly been enjoying herself while Anna had strung him along with one delaying 'phone call after another. At five forty five she had called saying she was on her way to the *Euler* but he had heard nothing more and she had not turned up at the hotel. Elizabeth waved him to a chair on the far side of the bed from where she was standing and sat down. The bed formed a barrier between them. He looked around the room taking in the décor, 'Pleasant enough but not up to the quality of your work,' he said, indicating the room in general with a wave of his hand.

'Standard sort of thing for an international hotel', she responded, glad that he had the sense to start off on a positive note. 'The workmanship is good but the choice of fabrics and paper lacks imagination, I feel.' He nodded. She continued, 'I'm pleased that you agree - too much gold in evidence, I think'. She smiled at him, 'Like a drink?'

'You haven't a Calvados, I suppose?'

'As a matter of fact I do,' she responded and, opening a

drawer, she produced a miniature, 'I brought some with me knowing that you liked it.'

Despite himself, Eugene smiled, 'Well done Elizabeth, you do know how to look after a fellow ... in some ways,' he added and immediately wished he hadn't - he needed to keep her calm and amenable this evening. 'You are always very thoughtful,' he continued in order to defuse the atmosphere. She brought the miniature and a glass round to Eugene's side of the bed and left him to pour out the Calvados while she returned to her chair.

'Thanks, can I get you something?' It was Eugene's turn for a show of hospitality.

'An orange juice would do fine, please.'

He opened the refrigerated drinks cabinet and found a bottle of juice, 'Cool like her, at any rate so far as I'm concerned,' was his unspoken thought. He stood with his back to her, found a glass and before pouring in the juice added a tablet which he had carefully removed from his pocket. His friend Grigor, who had supplied him, had nodded knowingly when he had asked and told him to enjoy himself but to be careful, he had remarked that the substance was made by one of the pharmaceutical companies in Basel but was no longer on sale, having acquired notoriety in the USA as the 'date rape drug'. Eugene handed her the glass and returned to his side of the room.

He had better deal with her unauthorised absence and get the matter out of the way. 'Where have you been all day?' he asked just managing to keep the note of anger from his voice.

'I might ask the same question of you about yesterday evening and this morning, but I won't,' she responded quietly. She hoped that the soft answer would turn away the wrath she knew to be simmering just below the surface, but she didn't known of the hours of frustration that he had been suffering.

His control failed him, 'You might, but you bloody well won't. I'm in charge and I *would* like to know where you have been all day.'

'That's easy,' she responded, 'I met Sam Charles, a rather personable American newspaper reporter at dinner last night and we spent today in the Alps. We came back to this hotel, changed in our own rooms, had dinner at the *Drei Könige* and said goodnight in the bar here, at which point we went to our respective rooms. It was all very chaste and, for that reason, very pleasant. He's gone to Hamburg on the night sleeper and that's that.' She did not refer to their swapping addresses. 'And as for not letting you know that I was going out for the day, the fact is that I couldn't make contact with you before I went out after breakfast, no more than I was able to find you last night - when you were probably amusing yourself.'

Eugene's face now showed his anger and frustration even more clearly as he struggled to keep his feelings under control. He had intended to take Anna to the *Drei Könige* but instead he had had nothing but hours of frustration. And this woman had been there tonight dining with some American she had picked up the previous evening! Elizabeth saw the veins beginning to stand out on his neck.

'Don't be so dammed impertinent. This morning I was meeting another member of our team, a technical expert, and for the rest of the time I was following up a lead.'

'Not chasing a bitch in heat?' she replied and knew at once that she had unwittingly landed a jibe right on target. She regretted at once that she had allowed herself to needle him.

'A bitch in heat is better than a frigid bitch!' was

Eugene's response, which he in his turn immediately regretted. 'Sorry that was uncalled for ... but unlike you I've had a very difficult day, but I won't bore you with all the details.' There was a lull in the conversation and Elizabeth succeeded in pouring a little of her orange juice over her skirt as an excuse for a visit to the bathroom, away from Eugene and to give him a chance to take full control of his emotions.

Elizabeth returned to the room, picked up the glass and drank the rest of its contents sitting silently, looking away from Eugene. During the lull in their conversation she refilled the glass from the refrigerated cabinet and went back to her seat. Both of them were ill at ease, the impending end of the operation and Eugene's stressful day were having their effect and making it difficult for them to avoid antagonising one another. Elizabeth's absence with Sam on their day out in the mountains continued to grate with Eugene and like a dog with a bone he wouldn't let it go, 'Just what do you think you were doing by going off for the day without a word, you might have been involved in an accident and anyway who was the fellow who picked you up?'

She took strong exception to this, 'Picked me up? I don't like the expression, I'm not a tart looking for customers. Let me tell you again what happened! At dinner last night I met an American to whom I took an immediate liking, no nothing sexual, he was clearly good company and when he offered to go with me to the Alps, by train I would stress - not in his car - I was pleased to accept. I had no wish to spend the day here just waiting for the action to begin tomorrow - whatever it might be that you've planned. As it turned out I was right in my assessment of him ... we had a splendid day out and the weather was simply glorious ... and he made no attempt to get me into bed with him. He was attractive and at the same time a complete gentleman, someone who respects women and doesn't take them for playthings!' Her eyes met Eugene's and she was aware of his pent up anger.

'He might have been from Swiss Security or the CIA!'

'And pigs might fly - he wasn't one of *your* sort, I've told you that he was a *gentleman*!' came her cutting retort. Eugene met this with silence but his face spoke clearly enough.

'You *are* sure that you know what to do tomorrow?' he asked, finding himself stumbling to find a topic of conversation and keep himself in her room until the spiked drink had worked. Immediately he wondered why he had raised the subject, she wasn't directly involved and because of her relationship with Lewis he had kept her ignorant of the details of the operation.

'*Really*, Eugene I'm not a novice and neither am I stupid. We've been through it all often enough. I'm to be available if needed but otherwise keep out of the way. I'll have the mobile 'phones in my purse so I'll always be in touch if you need me. You've chosen to keep me out of your plans and I am very happy with that. Ask once more and I'll take the first 'plane to London and leave you to your own devices!' She took a sip of the fruit juice and began to relax thinking the storm was past. 'How old are your children, Eugene?'

He was glad at the change of subject. 'Evgeny is twelve and Sera ten.' He paused and then produced some photographs from his wallet, 'These are some recent shots of them.'

She looked at the photographs, 'They're fine kids ... you should be proud of them ... and you're not keen to go back home, I don't understand it.'

'The kids are fine, it's my wife who's the problem, you should know that, I've told you often enough! We just don't get on together any more and the kids, fine as they are, take her side. Besides, it isn't fair on them to make them take my side – they're on her side already and I'm not wanting to bring conflict into their lives.'

'They need a father!'

'I'm fully aware of that but I would bring more problems than benefits you know!'

There was a silence during which Elizabeth wondered if his story were at all true or whether it was the lure of the West and it's pleasures that shaped his attitude to home. Eugene was another man who had problems with his offspring. She was also well aware of his inability to shake off the grip of the memories of their time together in the USA.

The tension was getting at him. He felt the need for a visit to the lavatory. 'I'll just make a visit to your bathroom,' he muttered. While he was there he flushed the wrappings from the tablet down the lavatory and washed his hands. He returned to his chair and looked at her glass, she had finished the spiked juice a while ago. A feeling of anger took hold of him. He had already spent a day of sexual frustration in Basel! He wanted her. He wanted her badly and was becoming increasingly irritated at the delay. She had been happy to have him as her lover on and off for six years while they were in the USA, those had been good years, why wouldn't she continue the relationship. He'd had to put up with her falling for Peter Lewis and now she'd had the audacity to disappear for the day with some American that she'd chanced to meet.

Elizabeth noticed his change of mood and grew wary. She noticed that his hands were trembling slightly and that he was beginning to sweat. She took another drink from the glass.

Eugene broke the silence, 'Besides I'd rather be away from Moscow and life in the West is to my taste, especially when I can feel that I'm exploiting it for the benefit of our Motherland. It's the only job for which I've been trained. It's good to feel that you can enjoy life and at the same time be of service to your country.'

'You'll have to go back home for good one day!'

His patience snapped, 'I was given instructions today that we are *both* to return to Moscow immediately this operation is completed.' It had been needling him all day, now he would see how *she* liked the summons.

Elizabeth was silent and he marvelled at her control. He had controlled himself when Gordeyev had handed him the note, but there he had been with two colleagues who would readily have reported any strong reactions he might have shown.

Elizabeth knew it was now that she must break free of the SVR. She would not let them force her to go back to Moscow. She had a number of plans to frustrate them if they tried to coerce her. Tomorrow she would be moving out of this hotel and they wouldn't find her easily, certainly not in Basel.

'I don't know what they'll have for me to do next. What about you? Will they have another .... job in the West that's to your liking or will they have .... a desk job waiting in Moscow?' She didn't betray any agitation but she was puzzled at her voice.

She saw him shudder and at the same time she became aware that she wasn't feeling quite right and that her speech was becoming slurred. She suddenly knew, with absolute certainty, that he had tampered with her drink. She knew it and fury took hold of her. He was not going to have her as his plaything! Nor was he going to drag her back in a drugged state to Russia! She had an instinctive fear for the safety of her unborn child, what might be the consequences for it of the drug that she had been given and, now that Eugene had become so promiscuous, had he some deadly infection that would harm both herself and the child? There were only a few seconds in which she could act: she had no doubt about how to respond.

Eugene was now on her side of the bed. 'Please, Elizabeth, I want you in bed ... I want you now, remember the good times we had', his voice was loud, he was having difficulty in controlling it, and he attempted to kiss her. She felt his shaking hand on her shoulder and was offended by his aroma of sweat. 'Just a moment ....' she was struggling to put words together, ' .... I must get my lipstick.' He moved aside to let her get to her handbag. She began to rummage in it and then to his surprise and horror he found himself looking down the barrel of a small but menacing pistol. 'You're not having me! You've doped my drink! You want to rape me! You want to abduct me!'

'No, Elizabeth don't!'

She was on him like a Fury - threatened by rape, abduction and harm to her unborn child she would give him no opportunity whatsoever. He tried to push the pistol away and, failed. He turned towards the door which in his panic he failed to open. She pulled the trigger and as her vision and consciousness faded she saw blood spurt from a wound in the back of his head.

'Oh, Vladimir why?'

Elizabeth staggered back and collapsed to the ground. Striking her head heavily on the bedside cabinet, she passed into unconsciousness.

Apart from a Strauss waltz playing quietly on the radio, the room was silent.

***

Earlier that evening Grigor had spent a while wandering around the city seeing the preparations for the carnival and reviewing the plans for the next day. The citizens had seemed hardly able to wait until 4.00 a.m. to get started. He had seen several "lanterns", some of them up to ten feet high, in evidence. None had been illuminated and all but one had been draped with sheeting to keep their designs secret. He had stopped to look at the one that wasn't covered. It had sat on a trolley with its top about twelve feet above the ground. He had made out a name on the side, "*Barbara Alte Garde*", presumably the name of the group to parade with the thing. An elaborate design on the front and back seemed to have the Basel sign but the significance of the rest was hard to grasp - classical columns, a man with a military hat and a glass of red wine, angels and a host of other things. He had shaken his head and wandered on, 'An odd bunch these Swiss!' In the next street he had passed a group of people in ordinary clothes pulling a smaller lantern which was under wraps. A few children of just about school age had joined themselves to the couple at the front who were pulling the lantern and some of the adults walking behind were playing piccolos. It seemed a strange way to spend a Sunday evening but he could tell that they were excited at the prospect of the next day's festivities.

Now Grigor was concerned. He had been unable to get a reply from Eugene's hotel room or from the hotel 'phone. Neither of his mobiles nor Elizabeth's had brought any response. At eleven thirty his knock on Elizabeth's door had brought no reply. He asked himself what had become of them, wondering whether they had gone on the run or defected to Swiss Intelligence to avoid returning to Moscow. The SVR would surely be on their tail very quickly if they were on the run. Elizabeth's English lover might be motive enough for her. But what of Eugene? Then he remembered rumours about Audit having something on him – perhaps that was it.

In Eugene's absence it would be for him, Grigor, to take over. But first he would have to clear it with their controller. He called a Bern number explained the situation in deliberately vague terms and was told to await a reply. It came at a half past midnight: Grigor was to take command, but the team were to proceed with care in case Swiss Intelligence had been tipped off. He asked himself how else any professional in their line of work would ever think of proceeding, certainly not by shouting, 'We're the SVR from Russia, come to steal your secrets!' Although it then occurred to him that at carnival time here in Basel people might think it was some kind of joke!

Chapter 27

Monday 17th February 1997, the first day of *Fasnacht*.

A long day for Baslers, an even longer one for all of our protagonists.

12.05 a.m.

An agitated colleague woke Sam with the news that something disastrous had happened at Elizabeth's hotel. 'So far as we can make out someone has been shot in her room. No don't ask me who! It's all very confused, Jon at the *Hotel International* is re-running the recording.'

'I'll be with you immediately.' Sam struggled out of bed and pulled on a navy blue towelling dressing gown. He was filled with an anxiety that caused his stomach to churn. How alive and vibrant she had been as they had sat that afternoon having lunch on the balcony of the restaurant at the top of the Rigi with the high Alps as a backdrop! How relaxed and intimate had been their dinner at *Die Drei Könige*! Could it be that within just a few hours she was dead? A feeling of horror and guilt took hold of him - was this the result of their day out, had someone suspected that she was being turned and liquidated her? Had their meeting, a selfish moment of indiscipline on his part, compromised her and cost her life? Sam was aware of a sense of mental paralysis, he felt numb deep inside. This was difficult, he knew that he should have declared an emotional interest in Elizabeth long ago and excluded himself from the operation - but he had not done so and, now that things were not going to plan, he wondered whether he would be in a fit state to make sensible judgements.

Kurt, one of the electronic eavesdroppers, was taking a telephone call from Jon, located in a room on the same floor as Elizabeth's at the *Hotel International*. He switched the telephone's loudspeaker in so that they could all hear Jon.

Pallor crept into Sam's face as blood drained from it. 'If it's my fault I'll never forgive myself,' he muttered under his breath.

Kurt looked up again, 'Are you OK Sam, you don't look too good?'

They heard Jon again, 'Hold it, I think it's becoming clearer ... '

Sam's thoughts kept coming back to Elizabeth. Whatever had gone on in the few hours since they had parted in the hotel bar?

'I think I know why she shot him, Sam.'

'OK let's hear what you've found.' It didn't sound then as if Elizabeth was the victim of the shooting.

'It's not very clear but I think he was trying to rape her and she put up a robust defence. Listen to this bit of the recording. Before this they've been rowing, I can play it for you if you like but first listen to this.'

Sam and his colleagues all gathered round to hear.

There was movement in the room at the *International* mixed with an electronic hiss before the volume was turned down again:

First the man's voice, 'Please Elizabeth, I want you in bed ... I want you now, remember the good times we had.'

'Just a moment .... I must get my lipstick .... You're not having me! You've doped my drink! You want to rape me! You want to abduct me!'

'No, Elizabeth don't!'

The sound of a gunshot.

'Oh, Vladimir why?'

There was silence among Sam and his colleagues. Then Sam spoke, once more in full command of his emotions, 'Sounds like you're right Jon. He tried to rape her and wished - for the few moments that remained - that he hadn't! Do me a transcript of the whole conversation as soon as possible and I'll send someone over to collect it from you. Then I'll see whether there's anything that changes our plans. How it will affect theirs we can't tell, of course. We'll just have to see whether they tail the Gold and Lewis families in a few hours time.'

He took the 'phone, 'Jon, see if you can hear anything outside her door but don't make yourself obvious. You'll have to keep a watching brief over the hotel, find out what happens next. For the moment keep listening-in to her room and try to make contact if she gets on the move, we may have to try to lift her. If she wants help then give it and contact me immediately.' There was nothing Sam could do personally. He was known at the *International* and any appearance there would most certainly compromise the entire operation. He could only pray.

Sam turned to his colleagues, 'OK we go ahead, but keep our eyes open for any warning signs. Tom and Martin you'd better push off in ten minutes - you've got to get to Allschwil and park on the far side of the Gold's house. You ought to be there by two thirty, though the Golds and their visitors probably won't be on the move until nearer three. Wrap up, it's colder out there than you think and, by the way, don't forget to date stamp your tram tickets.'

'Look boss, they're shooting one another and you're worried about tram tickets! As if we don't know what to do with them, we're not in the kindergarten class.'

'Point taken but when you're trying not to be noticed it's

little things like that which can be forgotten and then you're suddenly the centre of attention and that's the last thing you want. Just keep an eye on the Swiss and their British friends and see whether they're followed. It'll be a sure indication that it's business as usual for the SVR despite the demise of their leader. All the signs are that the real action won't be until this afternoon. Anything unusual, then call in on the mobiles. Good luck and enjoy *Fasnacht*!'

***

The Golds and their visitors left home at 2.55 a.m. and took five minutes to reach the tram stop. Michael was the liveliest member of the party, the adults showing signs of suffering from Jacob's lavish hospitality the previous evening when he had demonstrated conclusively to Ruth that, with his discriminating palate and eye for a bargain, he would have done well in her trade. Among the trickle of people following them to the tram were a Russian man and woman and Sam's people, Tom and Martin. These all lost themselves among the crowd waiting for the 3.05 a.m. tram.

'We *will* be able to get on, won't we Uncle Jacob?'

'No problem, Michael, we are at the *Endstation*, the terminus. The trams arrive here empty and we will all cram in, it is all part of the fun. There will be a party atmosphere, wait and see. They run three cars, or whatever you call them, coupled together so there's space for quite a few passengers.'

The tram passed them on the other side of the low platform, rolled round the loop beyond the stop and then came to a halt facing them. Passengers pushed the buttons to open the doors and they all squeezed in. The women took seats but the men stood. There were carnival participants among the passengers, dressed in costume and carrying great *papier maché* heads - some of them encumbered with military drums but others having nothing larger than their piccolo cases to carry. Jacob pointed out different costumes to Michael, 'They're *Alte Dante* - old aunts - *Harlequins* and *Glauns* - clowns.' He lowered his voice, 'When the Swiss let their hair down they take care to do it under a *papier maché* head!'

Paula looked up, 'Any more of that Jacob and they'll have you deported as an undesirable. We are above criticism - don't you forget it!' There was a twinkle in her eye.

'Above or beyond, I doubt whether it matters. It's been a safe haven for me for all these years and I certainly won't grumble about the country that's made me welcome.'

The tram rolled on, becoming more and more packed at each stop, and eventually came to a halt at the *Theater*. Jacob led the way, 'Out we all get, it goes no further. We walk from here to the *Barfüsserplatz*, we should get a good view from there. There will be a couple hundred thousand people but they will be spread around the city centre so it will not be uncomfortable for us.'

The morning air was crisp and without a hint of a breeze. They set off at a comfortable pace for the *Barfüsserplatz*. At a distance came their Russian followers and further behind were Tom and Martin. They had studied photographs of the callers at the warehouse and there had been no difficulty in identifying Eugene's, or rather Grigor's, people. Martin dropped back and called Sam, 'We're in town and our competitors are still in business.' He rejoined Tom and watched the two groups in front looking for a suitable vantage point. Jacob and his group had settled at the back of a fountain on the corner of the square. On the other side of the fountain a couple of children with fur hats and padded jackets were balancing to Ruth's concern, though as it happened they refrained from falling into the bitter water despite their excitement. Sam's men remained a short distance behind the others and let them sort themselves out, it would be time enough to move forward later on when the crowd began to pack together. Once they were nearer they would be able to hear what was said and watch reactions.

At precisely 4.00 a.m. the clocks around the city began to chime and the street lights went out. Lewis nudged Michael, *'Morgenstraich - reveille.'*

Jacob intervened, 'Almost right Peter but not quite, it is "*Morgestraich*" without a letter "n" but in the *Basler Deutsch* it is different again, there it is "*Moorgestraich*". We must make sure that Michael's record of the proceedings is completely accurate!'

Lewis had the video camera but wondered how successful he was going to be in the dark. Michael had a separate tape recorder to record a commentary to go with the video. Both were managing to balance on the edge of the fountain and attend to the events in front of them. From several different directions came the beat of drums and the shrill sound of piccolos and then lanterns came into sight with carnival characters pulling or carrying them. Most of the big lanterns were on wheels though some were carried on poles. The *cliques* - Jacob had told Michael that that was what the groups were called - came in different directions along the two sides of the square fronted by roads, an organised chaos of *cliques* going on their own routes rather than forming a procession - that would be for the afternoon.

From where they stood it wasn't possible to identify many the themes of the various lanterns. A succession of tantalising images passed before them, teddy bears, pink pigs, the Statue of Liberty, the "Phantom of the Opera" - Paula pointed out that it had played to Basel audiences recently - and protests at French nuclear tests. Lewis liked its slogan, *"Le mort, c'est moi!"* and remarked to Jacob that it was a pity that they couldn't work out the themes.

'You should not worry about that. You will see them again several times. If you like we can see them in the *Münsterplatz* tomorrow during the daylight or by night when they will be illuminated or on both occasions.'

'Both please, Uncle Jacob!' Michael was insistent, 'We can take the video camera and have a good look at them, can't we?'

'Once your father and I have unloaded the glassware from the van this afternoon there will be all the time in the world for us to see all that goes on for the rest of the carnival, young man.'

'Won't you be with us this afternoon then?'

'First things first. Peter and I will be at the laboratory but you will be looking after the ladies at the *Cortège* - the procession - and you can take them out to tea afterwards before you come home on the tram.'

Sam's men noticed the Russian couple respond to this and caught a muttered, *'Ja, sehr gut.'* The programme for the afternoon evidently fitted in well with their plans and expectations.

Jacob turned to Lewis, 'You should have seen them last year. Quite a few were celebrating - that is not the right word but it will have to do - the downfall of the Bishop of Basel who had a child by his housekeeper. There were candles in condoms, a naked cleric chasing a buxom woman round the cloisters and storks with mitres - the man's name was Vogel, bird in English! Celibacy is not natural, we men need our women.' He remembered that Ruth was next to Lewis and changed the direction of his comments, 'You will find that the lanterns are beautifully painted and attractive by day and by night.'

The carnival activity had slowed down and one of the *cliques* was taking a break in the square behind the crowd, their *papier maché* heads stacked in a pile on the paving as though the French Revolution had been imported late to Basel. Jacob led the way from their vantage point. 'It is rather colder than when we came here. It must be the breeze that is blowing. It is time for an early and unusual breakfast. We need to find a restaurant, though they will all be busy and we may have to wait.' They made their way across the *Barfüsserplatz* and stopped to look at the parked lantern and the pile of heads. The lantern was only partly painted and carried a caption which Jacob translated as, "We have no money and no time, therefore the *Sujet* - the theme - did not get done!" 'They might get inspiration as the carnival progresses, we will have to keep a sharp lookout for this one as the week goes on.'

'You know something don't you Jacob?' Paula had her suspicions, 'I know that you have an instinctive feel for chemistry but I don't think that it extends to the workings of *Fasnacht Cliques*, Jacob!'

He laughed and called over to someone among the clique members who were taking their break, 'Carl can a young Englishman try your head for size?' A fair haired man in his late twenties came over and, after everyone had shaken hands, located his head and lifted it out of the pile. He handed it to Michael, a white face with long yellow hair and a flat black hat. He tried it on to the amusement of them all while Lewis filmed him on the video. More thanks and handshaking and they set off on their way to the restaurant.

Whether they hoped to obtain more information on the timetable for the afternoon or whether their instructions were to stay with Jacob and his group, the Russian couple followed them at a discrete distance. Sam's men continued to tail them, it was just as well to make sure that the Russians didn't move in prematurely.

After a few minutes wait Jacob found a table for his party in the busy restaurant. In the entrance lobby carnival heads, drums and the other impedimenta of one of the *cliques* were piled neatly in a corner. The *clique* itself was having a lively time over its breakfast at the far end of the dining room. Sitting with them were a number of friends and supporters, the remaining breakfasters were sightseers like themselves.

Ruth sighed with relief, 'We haven't been standing for long but it's good to sit down and peel off some layers of clothing. We seem to have overdressed, it's quite warm out there when you're not in the breeze and in here you'd cook in your outdoor things.'

'It's not always as warm as this at *Fasnacht*, I can assure you. There's the menu, what would you like to set you up properly for the busy day ahead?' Jacob passed the menu cards around. 'It's traditional to have *Määlsuppe* - meal soup - and then either *Kääswaaie* or *Ziibelewaaie*, that's a sort of cheese or onion quiche - not a *Quiche Lorraine* that's French and you will see this afternoon how the Baslers poke fun at the French, certainly they do at the Alsatians. You will see a lot of characters with farmers' smocks, big red noses and long yellow hair, they are called *Waggis*, and are supposed to be farmers from the Voges mountains.' He turned to his wife with a smile, 'When the Germans laugh at the Swiss, and the speakers of Swiss German laugh at the execrable accent of the Baslers, then the Baslers have to look over the border to find others at whom they can poke fun!'

She pretended to be offended, 'Jacob! I'm afraid you will never make a real Basler - a *Beppi*. After all you've only been here for, how long is it now ... only for fifty eight years. It's going to take a little longer to make a *Beppi* of you.' She laughed and the others joined her.

The waitress, a Chinese girl, took their orders and disappeared towards the kitchen. This was the busiest day of the year for the Basel restaurants and it was the longest for them as well. She was feeling weary already as some of the cliques had been there for refreshments at 3.00 a.m. You needed to wet your lips with something before an hour on the piccolo and white wine did the job rather well!

Lewis broke into the conversation, 'I've enjoyed the start of the carnival and it's solved something I never understood at school. We had a German reading book, I can't remember the name of the thing, but there was a story about a man who was arrested by the police somewhere and it was important, don't ask me why, for him to prove that he came from Basel. Well he asked them for a drum and played it. That was proof enough, the police said, "Only a man from Basel could play the drum like that!" and they let him go. When I heard the drumming start up at, what do you call it ... Ah yes, *Moorgestraich*, well when the drumming started I discovered what that story from all those years back was about. There you are Jacob, if you want to be a real Basler - a *Beppi* is it? - you'll have to join a *clique* and play the drum!'

'Never! Don't encourage him to do that Peter, he would drive me crazy. I couldn't stand that all year!'

'All year, Paula? You call yourself a Basler and you don't know that the drummers practise for eleven months of the year on a *Drummelbegli* - a drum pad - rather than a drum. That's how our citizens remain sane and are still around enjoying three days of carnival to lift our spirits at this time of the year.'

'They don't just play Swiss tunes - one group, sorry *clique*, was playing the British Grenadier!' Michael joined the conversation.

Ruth followed him, 'And there was one from the Appalachian Mountains in the States, we call it "A Gift to be Simple."'

'You should know that we Swiss are good at turning anything to our advantage, we do not mind where it comes from, and we pay only if it is necessary. However I suspect that those tunes are conveniently out of copyright!'

'And how long has all this been going on, Uncle Jacob?'

'The historians say from 1376, if not earlier. It's a very venerable event though, to tell the truth, it has only been in its present form since 1945, a year that is well worth remembering as a scourge on mankind was wiped out then!'

'Where's my drink gone?' Lewis looked puzzled and Michael looked guilty.

'I just thought I'd try it and I liked it, sorry Dad.'

'What were you drinking, Peter?' Ruth couldn't remember what he had ordered.

'*Kaffi Lutz*, some sort of potent brew isn't it Jacob. We could have taken some to your lab for analysis, that's if he'd left any!'

'Coffee with a liberal helping of *schnapps*, Peter. You

are introducing the young man to bad habits early in life. He will sleep well when we get home but he's got to be back on the tram for 1.00 p.m. to see the *Cortège* this afternoon.'

On a nearby table the Russian couple paid the waitress and got up to go. In the entrance lobby, now clear of the *clique's* belongings as they had just marched off down the road, the man was speaking on his mobile 'phone, he then called to the woman who was looking at excursion leaflets and they left. Like the other tourists and Baslers they had a day's activity ahead.

Sam's men had paid a while before and they too made their way out of the restaurant, having satisfied themselves that the Russians had genuinely signed off for the time being. They called Sam to let him know that they had a busy afternoon in prospect.

***

Once Grigor's men were back at base he set off on his own for the *Hotel International*, he would find a place in the restaurant for an early breakfast – late by *Fasnacht* standards – and keep an eye on things in case Elizabeth returned. He had given a colleague a similar rôle at the *Hotel Euler* in case Eugene should return. Whatever were they up to?

Chapter 28

Monday 17th February 1997, 7.00 a.m.

Frau Brunner had begun her cleaning duties at the *Hotel International* early. She had come in straight from breakfast in a café with her daughter's *clique* after they had paraded at *Moorgestraich*. She was keen to finish in good time so she could see them again in the two o'clock *Cortège*. The previous day she had met Elizabeth leaving for the mountains and she was hoping that once again her room would be available early for cleaning. She knocked, and getting no reply, used her key to open the door. Confronted with a scene resembling a battlefield she screamed and fled.

Within a few minutes a group of guests and staff was crowding the doorway, wary of going in but knowing that help was needed. One of the staff with first aid qualifications told the others to remain in the corridor and went cautiously into the room. Eugene's head-wounds and the absence of breathing made clear his decease. He turned to the bystanders with a terse, 'He's dead', and turned his attention to Elizabeth. Thank God, she was breathing and seemingly coming to. He saw heavy bruising on her forehead. He moved her to the recovery position and was pondering what to do next when the paramedics arrived. With considerable relief he surrendered his patient to the experts.

Within a further couple of minutes the Basel Police had also arrived. Declaring the room to be a crime scene they sent the bystanders away and placed a colleague on the door, which they closed using a plastic glove on the door handle. They questioned the first aider on Elizabeth's position before he had moved her and marked it on the carpet with white chalk. The position of the pistol was also marked, as well as that of Eugene's corpse. Clearly Elizabeth needed medical attention and the paramedics were instructed to prepare to take her to the *Universitätsspital* as a matter of urgency. She began to stir as her pulse and temperature were checked and they lifted her carefully onto the wheeled stretcher they had brought with them. Accompanied by two women police officers who had just arrived they headed for the ambulance waiting outside the *Hotel International*.

Meanwhile Frau Brunner sat in the hotel kitchen drinking a second cup of strong black coffee waiting to be interviewed by the police, the morning's happenings had put a damper on her first day of *Fasnacht*. These were supposed to be the three most magnificent days of the year!

Grigor was aware of considerable activity outside the hotel. Several Police cars were parked on the roadway and there were two ambulances. Their flashing lights produced an oddly disconcerting effect. A number of people were standing at the entrance and others were standing across the road trying to see what was going on, they seemed to have appeared from nowhere and in no time. He was surprised that so many people were around at that hour of a Monday morning but, although they had been up early for *Moorgestraich*, some Baslers evidently didn't believe in sleep at carnival! Someone in the crowd said he had been told that there had been a shooting. Was this the reason for Eugene's absence?

Grigor was glad he was posing as a German journalist. He produced his press card and made his way back into the lobby, pushing through the crowd. Inside, others stood around waiting for someone to tell them what was going on. He knew better than to ask one of the managers for information - Swiss hotels did not welcome notoriety - although they could hardly stop the story from reaching the papers, they wouldn't wish to assist the press. Their customers were entitled to be kept out of the spotlight of press publicity and a hotel like this offered order and discretion as part of the package, as did a variety of other Swiss institutions. Grigor knew where to turn however. A night porter stood at one side of the foyer keeping an eye on things but otherwise inactive. There was a look of weariness and discontent on his face. Grigor was pretty sure that here was his source of information.

'What's going on at this time of the morning? Half the City seems to be here.

'We've been told to say nothing. The Manager will no doubt issue a statement later ... or the police will.'

Grigor smiled and produced his press card, 'I'm a newspaper reporter and of course I don't expect to get my information without payment. Come over here a moment.' He indicated by a nod of his head an area to the side of the bar that was out of the public gaze. The man's expression changed to one of anticipation and he followed Grigor.

'I want to know what's happened so that my paper can carry the story tomorrow and carry it accurately.' He produced a 100 Swiss Franc note from his wallet and was pleased to see the night porters eyes fasten onto it. 'This is yours for all you know.'

'Well sir it's always a pleasure to help if I can!' He took the note and slipped it into the breast pocket of his uniform jacket. 'Hotel work doesn't pay us a princely wage and anything extra always helps. I'll tell you what I know and I may be able to find out some more if it's worth your having.' His hand went to his pocket and he touched the note.

'OK, all you know and if it's good you get another payment of the same amount.'

'We've had a shooting on the fourth floor, in one of the rooms. A man has had his brains blown out and a woman is unconscious - they say she's had a bash on her head.'

'What can you tell me about them? Appearance, ages, names, nationality - that sort of thing.'

'I don't know about the man but I would think the woman was in her late twenties or early thirties. She had a North American accent. She was - I suppose she still is - a nice bit of stuff, a real good looker if you know what I mean. Brunette hair, dark brunette, and quite a figure, she was more than just pretty, she'd got something special about her. But she wasn't a snob like a lot of them. It just happens that she was speaking to me this evening, telling me that she had been out ... ' he fingered the note.

'If what you tell me is useful and not an invention I'll pay you fairly for the information.' The porter looked disappointed but he continued with his story.

'She had been out on the Rigi - that's a mountain near Luzern - with a young American gentleman for the day and they'd had dinner out at *Die Drei Könige*, that's an expensive place you know! She stopped for a chat after she'd had a drink with him back here in the bar. I got the impression that she was in good spirits and wanted someone to share it with. That's why she spoke to me.'

'You think that it's the young American gentleman that's dead?'

'No, he's not the corpse, that's some other fellow. The American checked out before all this happened and took a taxi to the SBB Station - I took his cases out - he was generous with his tip, I'd be generous if I'd had a day out with the likes of her!'

'And what about the woman, is she Canadian or American?'

'Canadian.'

'OK their names if you have them.'

'That I don't know, sir.'

'Find them and let me know what's happening and another 200 Francs is yours.'

'I'll do all that I can,' and he was off, first to the office and then to the fourth floor.

A quarter of an hour later he returned to a restless Grigor with their names. Elizabeth Fielder was suspected of being involved in the murder and was about to be removed to the *Universitätsspital* under police guard. The dead man was also a Canadian and he thought his name was Eugene Preston but this might not be accurate as the man didn't seem to be staying at the hotel. Grigor paid his informant and planted the idea that the killing was the result of a lover's jealousy or that it might be the work of the Mafia - such disinformation could help to throw the police off the scent. He knew that the porter would be likely to pass it on to others in the hotel and to any genuine reporters that he met. A few minutes later he saw Elizabeth being carried to the ambulance. She lay on the stretcher with closed eyes and a bad bruise on her face. So now he, Grigor really was in charge of the operation! He would have to proceed with extreme care. How would the night's events impact on their plans? What would the police make of Elizabeth and what would she tell them? Above all was she Eugene's killer and, if so, why? There wasn't too much time for reviewing the situation and for making changes to their plans if that were necessary

Jon had been in the crowd around the door of Elizabeth's room and had gone down to the foyer when the police had closed it to inquisitive eyes. Down at reception he hadn't been far from Grigor when Elizabeth was taken to the ambulance. Having passed word to Sam he hurriedly cleared his equipment into its suitcases and checked out of the *Hotel International* rather earlier than planned. If they found the bugs in Elizabeth's room they might well come looking!

Chapter 29

Monday 17th February 1997, 1.05 p.m.

At a little after 1.00 p.m. Paula Gold emerged from her house in Allschwil with Ruth and Michael Lewis and headed for the tram stop. The Russian couple got out of a car two hundred yards along the road and set off in the same direction. Sam's men, Tom and Martin, had decided to wait near the tram stop rather than run the risk of drawing attention to themselves. At 4.00 a.m. it had been dark and the streets had been busier. They were whiling away the time, looking in the shop windows, as the women and boy came into sight. A tram approached from the Basel direction ran round the loop and returned to stop at the platform. Paula and her visitors boarded without having to rush but the Russian couple only just made it. After a few stops there was only standing room available. A ticket inspector boarded the tram at the *Morgartenring* stop. He worked his way through the passengers and reached the Russians. The man produced the tickets from his overcoat pocket and held out his hand for their return. The inspector said something and the man coloured and pointed to the tickets. In his turn the inspector pointed to a notice above the window opposite the Russians and the man fumbled for his wallet and withdrew some bank notes. Martin translated the notice quietly to Tom, ' "For not having a valid ticket (including a card not date and time stamped) SF 50 with an extra SF 10 if payment is not made immediately." That's about $90's penalty down the drain for them. Still I bet the penalty would have been worse if they had stamped their tickets but lost their quarry.'

'Sam's good on detail isn't he? We laughed when he

told us to make sure about our tickets this morning. Was it really this morning? It seems one hell of a long day! They're pretty conspicuous now, they've given the locals some amusement and a subsidy to their trams.'

Paula got up and the others followed her towards the exit. Most of the passengers were getting out and heading into the city centre for the *Cortège*. Another procession was on its way led by Michael, who despite his breakfast dose of *schnapps* was well in the lead and exhorting the women to hurry up; Tom and Martin brought up the rear and the Russians, though they didn't know it, were in the middle.

'Hell, I feel cold, Tom! It isn't the weather though!'

'It's the impending action. It's always like this. *We've* got nothing to do apart from observing and letting Sam know when they start the action. Those guys in front are probably sweating. They're the ones who have to do a clean job and lift the women and the kid. Look he's calling up someone on his mobile, probable Grigor now that he's been promoted in Eugene's unavoidable and regrettable absence. That shindig fair shook up Sam didn't it? But look at the way he bounced back, the fellow's a real professional, a great guy to work with!'

As they neared the centre they passed *cliques* formed up and ready to move when the procession started at two o'clock. As well as the drum and piccolo *cliques* they had seen that morning there were *Gugge cliques* with an assortment of brass instruments. Unable to wait until the official start they were blasting away with brash, joyful, noisy jazz and popular tunes.

'Did you catch that one, Martin? "It's a long way to Tipperary" doesn't sound very Swiss, does it? Seems we're going to have quite an afternoon of it!'

'Some others are going to have even more of an afternoon of it if all goes according to plan - their plan and ours!'

'You've got your carnival badge on? Good, Sam said that unpleasant things happen to sightseers without one - you get confetti stuffed down your neck and that sort of thing. He's done his homework for us! Did you see whether those dummies in front had badges, I rather think they didn't!'

The women and the boy had reached the *Stadttheater* and taken up their position on the north west corner of the square at the junction of *Steinenberg* and *Theaterstrasse*. In front of them in the middle of the intersection was a vintage tram which was the base for the carnival officials and judges.

'When will the action begin Tom? $100 on twenty past two!'

'They'll wait a bit longer than that. The bet's on, I'm for two forty. That gives them almost three quarters of an hour to let the crowd become immersed in the carnival. We don't need to be in their pockets, as long as we can see what's happening and let Sam know that'll be good enough.'

'There's a third of them now, that guy to the left of them. He said something to the man who nodded. Then he moved near the women and the kid.'

'Yep, I noticed him as well. Part of their team by the look of things.'

The procession was under way with *cliques* moving north along the *Theaterstrasse* as well as others moving in both directions along *Steinenberg*. There was noise, colour and action as sprigs of mimosa, sweets, oranges and other fruit were thrown from tractor-drawn trailers to the crowd by a variety of oddly dressed characters riding on them. Some had compressed air canons powering clouds of confetti over the crowd.

'Look, Mum, those are the *Waggis* that Uncle Jacob told us about this morning.'

'At breakfast when you were becoming a hardened drinker? It's as well that you've had time to sleep it off. You haven't got a hangover, have you?'

'No chance of that Mum. Catch that orange Mum! Well done, we've got five now. If we run out of pockets we'll have to eat them.'

'And then find somewhere for the peel, the tidy Swiss won't like it being left around. They hate litter.'

'Except at *Fasnacht*. That goes for confetti at any rate. By the time we're finished we'll be ankle deep in the stuff. Mind you they will sweep it up quickly enough. By the way, Ruth, when you get home you'll have to shake the confetti out of your knickers, it gets everywhere!'

'Look at them Mum. A Scottish pipe band in Highland uniform. Do you have Scots living here Aunty Paula?'

'You have Swiss rolls in England and they aren't Swiss! That's the *Schotte Clique*, look it's written on the drum, get it on your video, they're all Swiss, I think, Michael'

'They're super! How tall do you think they are, Aunty. I'd say seven feet.'

'I don't know what feet are but at a guess a little over two metres, say 2.2 metres. They're tall men and when you add those *papier maché* heads and hats - what do you call them?'

'Bearskins, I think,' Ruth chipped in.

'With bearskins it adds a lot to their height.'

'Did you see that Martin? Someone heaved a cauliflower into the crowd and it caught our friends' chum a hell of a blow on the side of the head. I hope he's not out of commission, he's probably got some significant part in the action.'

'Some pitcher to heave the thing with that force! And talking of real sport, look what's coming, a jazz band in American football gear. They sound pretty good. They should've been up to the minute and appeared as the Packers! They've probably never heard of them here though.'

'You saw the Super Bowl on the box? Yes? What about Des Howard's run? Hold it something's happening over there! What's the time? Two twenty-five? Looks as if you've won the bet! Call Sam, tell him to stand by and that we'll confirm action as soon as possible.'

The new member of the Russian team had bumped against Paula Gold as he reached out to catch an orange thrown from a carnival float and had immediately apologised to her. A moment later he looked at his watch, muttered something and pushed his way out of the crowd before strolling off towards the *Theater* behind them. Shortly afterwards Paula began to have difficulty with her vision and took Ruth's arm. 'Ruth I'm not feeling too well, do you think that we ...' She didn't finished but crumpled up and it was only Ruth's grasp on her and the crowd packed in around them that prevented her from reaching the ground.

'Michael help me, quick! Paula's just passed out.'

He put the video camera back into its bag and helped to support Paula.

'We've got to get her out of the crowd, Michael.' She turned to look for assistance and this was immediately forthcoming.

'Can I help at all, Madam? Your friend is unwell? I'm a doctor and if I can be of assistance I will be only too pleased.'

'Thank you, that's a relief. Can we get her out of the crowd first? She's probably just fainted.'

The man and his woman companion helped to carry Paula out of the crowd and laid her on the ground with the woman's coat under her and the man's raincoat as a pillow. He knelt on the ground and examined her as Ruth and Michael looked down. They were both frightened, it had been such a sudden transition from being immersed in the carnival one moment, to having Paula taken ill and to be standing there so helplessly. For the second time in a few months Ruth was faced with the problem of what to do in a foreign country when someone was ill. Once again generous strangers had come to her aid. She was grateful for their assistance.

The doctor looked up, 'I don't think it's dangerous but she should have attention at the hospital to ensure that it really is nothing serious and that, if unfortunately it is, she can be treated without delay. I will telephone for an ambulance.' He made a call on his mobile, returned it to his pocket and smiled at Ruth, 'Don't worry, they are on their way. They will be here in five minutes, there are always ambulances near at hand for the *Fasnacht* carnival.'

Tom and Martin had also moved back from the crowd and from a distance were watching the group clustered round Paula Gold. She lay on the ground and Ruth had spread her own coat over her to keep her warm, while the Russian woman's coat was under her.

'They don't spare any expense for your comfort once you've attracted their attention do they?'

'OK Martin. The ambulance crew are here, let Sam know.'

'Ten years ago communication wouldn't have been this easy would it?' He moved out of sight of the group and put through his short message, 'Pick up now commencing.' Sam and his boys would be on full alert now. He returned to his companion. 'We're nearly finished, what then?'

'Stay here and enjoy the carnival. If Sam needs us he'll call. We can see some more and then get back to HQ and wait for his return. Hell I bet he's sweating at the moment!'

The ambulance men and the others were making their way across the square to the ambulance. They saw them get in and the doors close. 'Hey Sam, it's 2.37 and the limo's on its way. Best of luck to you all!' Now to collect a few more oranges and wait to hear how things had gone.

***

Sam stood in a workman's hut two hundred yards along the road from the warehouse. He'd had a few metal barriers and some sand delivered to the site late on Saturday and it looked all set for road works to commence after the carnival. The JCB digger appeared entirely at home parked by the kerb next to the sand. It was there in case they didn't time the action right and the gate was locked after the arrival of the ambulance. Sam had spent a day getting used to driving the thing and was proficient in moving it in the right direction. He adjusted the straps on his blue workman's overalls and looked along the road. All was quiet. The properties were commercial ones, it was a holiday and no one and nothing was moving. There was an unnatural silence about the scene, the strong sunshine adding to the strange effect. It was five minutes since he had opened the hut window as a signal to the others that the ambulance was on its way. He breathed deeply, keeping the tension at bay yet knowing that it was the adrenaline flow that counted when the difference between failure and success depended on split second decisions and actions.

Eight minutes since they had left. Perhaps they were caught up in the carnival somewhere. No! Here it was! The ambulance came into view at the end of the road, seemingly in no hurry to reach its destination. He looked the other way and saw the doors to the warehouse yard being opened to let the ambulance enter. He picked up his mobile, the line was open and he checked that he was being received, 'Ready?'

'Always ready!'

'Ten seconds. ... Five ... Now go!'

'Message received!'

The ambulance had slowed and was going through the gates. The lorry that had been parked in front of Sam's hut suddenly moved off, swung across the road and went through the gates before they could be closed. At the same time a lorry further along the road, draped in carnival trappings and with large loudspeakers on its roof suddenly began to broadcast a *Guggemuusig* version of "The Stars and Stripes Forever". It was, Sam said afterwards, a surreal touch and one which, like most of the action, had been his brainchild. In the distance he could just hear dull explosions, that would be the gas and the stun grenades. No sound of gunfire, thank the Almighty! It sounded as if they were succeeding in sweeping up Grigor's team.

***

The journey in the ambulance had been a fairly silent

affair. Ruth sat beside Paula, the doctor checked on her condition at intervals and the woman helped him. Michael gave up on conversation when he found that he was getting no response from his mother who was clearly worried about Paula's condition. He removed the video camera from its bag and took some pictures through the ambulance window. Everyone else was taken up with Paula and took no notice of him. He saw that they were in a rather grubby area of Basel. The ambulance turned into the hospital entrance. He was disappointed to see that it looked as tired as some of the London hospitals. A moment or two later he began to wonder whether he had come to the Royal Tournament. They had stopped in a yard and swarming over the wall at the end was a group of half a dozen soldiers in black trousers and sweaters and with balaclavas over their faces. Fascinated he continued to film the scene as they rushed the office at the side of the yard. He heard small explosions from inside. There was now pandemonium around the ambulance as the front and rear doors were pulled open and more soldiers dressed like the others stood there with sub-machine guns pointing at the driver and his passengers. He put the camera on the seat beside him and watched his mother, wondering how to react.

The order was given by one of the soldiers, 'Out!' His instructions were explicit enough, the weapons added their own persuasion and the ambulance crew with the couple who had helped climbed down. Michael looked at Ruth who was frozen to the spot, 'What's this about, Mum. Something to do with the carnival?' Events had become too extraordinary to be real.

'Goodness alone knows, Michael, but this doesn't look like a hospital, more like a military training ground.' She looked enquiringly at one of the soldiers.

'Stay there we'll do you no harm, Mam.' She detected the American accent.

'Is this serious?'

'Yep, Mam, it's serious but none of you are in any danger. We're getting a doctor for your friend.'

'A doctor? That's what the last one said he was!'

The four from the ambulance had been made to stand facing the yard wall and one of the soldiers was talking to the doctor who had got them into their present situation. The soldier came round to the back of the ambulance, 'Your friend will be out for maybe another half hour but she's in no danger, they gave her a knock-out jab but it will do her no lasting harm. We'll tell you what's going on shortly but I repeat you're in no danger from us and you can see that the reception committee that was awaiting your arrival is otherwise engaged.' He began a thorough examination of Paula.

'Are you a real doctor, the last one said he was.'

'I expect he is a real doctor, just as I am, but you can use doctoring for different purposes.'

'I want the rest room, my bladder's had enough of this.'

'Don't know about a rest room but there's a lavatory here if that will do!'

'You call a spade a spade! It will do me fine! What about you Michael?'

'I'm OK Mum.'

'Right, Mam, this way, we have a woman who will look after you.'

'That will be convenient! Who's in charge of this show, the US Marine Corps or the Mafia?'

'Could be either Mam, or a joint force. Always pleased to be of service.'

'Michael?'

'I'm OK Mum. I'll keep an eye on Aunty Paula.'

Ruth was led into the offices where a bitter smell of gas lingered and four men lay face down on the floor with their hands and feet shackled together. The woman accompanying her waited outside the lavatory and would not allow her to lock the door. She rejoined Michael and Paula to find a man in workman's overalls and, like the others, with a balaclava talking to her son.

'Mrs Lewis? I can't tell you who we are but I'm sorry that you've had to get mixed up in all this.' He sounded genuinely sorry and he too had an American accent. 'As soon as Frau Doktor Gold regains consciousness we will make sure that she is taken to the *Universitätsspital* for a check up.'

They sat and waited. At last Paula began to surface, eventually opening her eyes and enquiring where she was.

Ruth was to the point, 'Sorry Paula, I don't know and if I were to tell you what has happened you wouldn't believe me!'

Two large vans were driven into the yard and the civilians were taken to them by the soldiers, some of whom stayed in the back of the vans. The others moved to the cabs and drove the vans to the exit, removing their balaclavas and replacing them with carnival masks. Michael noticed that the vans' registration plates were obscured with mud. The yard was empty except for Paula, Ruth, Michael and the man in overalls. He had seen the vans out and locked the gates after them.

'Well ladies and young man I don't suppose you'll ever know what this was all about but on dark winter evenings you can try to think of explanations.'

'I could bloody well do with one now.' Ruth was angry and Sam noted that, American though her origins might be, her oaths were English.

'Sorry that's not possible, but again I apologise to you all, especially for any shock you have suffered.' He knew the kid was susceptible and hoped that it hadn't done him any harm. 'I'll be with you in a moment, please wait.'

'We haven't a choice have we?'

'No Mam.'

A couple of minutes later he was back dressed in a Harlequin outfit and a carnival mask. 'Right, back into the ambulance. We're on our way to the *Universitätsspital*.' He drove to the exit, unlocked the gates, drove out, stopped the ambulance to lock the gates again and then they were on their way back along the road past factories and warehouses. Once again nothing moved in the road except the ambulance. Michael looked out of the window, it was as though he had imagined the events of the last hour! In five minutes they drew up at the *Universitätsspital*. The Harlequin looked back at his passengers, 'Go in and explain what's happened to Frau Doktor Gold and insist that they give her a thorough check up. And ... have a nice day!' He climbed from the cab and was gone, a carnival figure carrying a briefcase.

'Damned Yankees!' Ruth was less than pleased. 'At least we're all still in one piece. How do you feel Paula? A thick head? I'm not surprised. Let's go and look for some more doctors if we dare!'

***

The telephone call that Jacob and Lewis received at four o'clock that afternoon was not the one that Grigor had intended. The plan he had inherited from his late colleague involved a call to the laboratory to tell Jacob that he held the women and the boy and that their safe return would be assured if the drug and the paperwork were handed over. Instead it was Ruth who made the call to tell them to come at once to the *Universitätsspital* where Paula was being given a check-up. Nothing serious she assured Jacob, but he and Peter should be there immediately. And by the way, would they make sure that the van hadn't been tampered with in any way, just a quick look underneath to make sure nothing had been attached. She didn't mention the possibility of a bomb but her imagination was running riot following their experience earlier that afternoon and she was becoming paranoid.

The van had been unloaded and the two men enjoying coffee when Jacob had taken the call. Within a quarter of an hour they were at the *Universitätsspital* to be met in the entrance by Ruth and Michael.

'Jacob, you're not to worry. Paula's having a thorough check-up and I will take you through to her in a moment. You won't believe the story but we were kidnapped this afternoon right there by the *Stadttheater* with the *Cortège* going by! Then we were rescued and now we're here. Don't ask me who did the kidnapping and don't ask me who rescued us. They were Americans, the lot who rescued us, but they wouldn't tell me who they were.'

'It was exciting, Dad. Like World War Three had started!'

'I sincerely hope it hasn't, Michael, or if it has I hope you saw it being won by our side!'

'OK Jacob, you come with me and see Paula. She'll be glad you're here. The police have been called and you'll be able to help us with their questions. Oh yes, I hadn't told you but they knocked Paula out with a jab of some kind. Peter and Michael can stay here, though the police will probably want to speak to Michael.' She took the bemused Jacob by the arm and led him off in the direction of the casualty department.

'It was really exciting Dad! We got to the hospital - it wasn't a hospital but I'll call it that - and there were all these men in black swarming over the wall. Look, I'll show you!' He got the video camera out of its bag and rewound the tape. 'Look I'll play it for you.'

Lewis watched it, first with a sense of disappointment and then with utter amazement. First rather shaky views of the Basel streets and then commandos coming over the wall as Michael had said, ambulance doors being thrown open by more commandos and people being made to get out of the ambulance. After that the tape ran out. 'And you survived World War Three? Yes you clearly did! And you got it all on film, the police will want to see it. It will tell them where you were taken. Didn't anyone try to stop you from filming?'

'They were all too busy to notice and the camera's a small one. I just kept it beside me and let it run after we reached the hospital or whatever it was.'

'You could do with a drink, Michael?'

'A Coke Dad, it's made me quite thirsty. When Aunty Paula's ready can we go and see some more of the carnival - this has been a great holiday!'

'Not today! I expect that Paula will want nothing more than to get back home after this. You seem to have enjoyed the experience more than the ladies.'

'I want to be a commando one day!'

Lewis knew that his efforts to demilitarise the boy's thinking had, for the time being, come to nought.

***

The Basel Police were more than interested in Michael's

video recording of the afternoon's events. At first they needed convincing that they were not being set up as some sort of carnival joke. The status of Jacob and Paula Gold in the community persuaded them otherwise and they then knew that they had serious crimes to deal with including, one of them said, the invasion of Switzerland by a foreign army. This seemed to trouble them more than the knock-out jab that Paula had received.

***

At 6.45 p.m. the Golds and their guests arrived home in Allschwil. Paula went to her bedroom to lie down and Jacob assisted by Ruth set to and began to prepare a light dinner. They would have a quick meal and then an early night. It had been a long and ultimately disturbing day for the adults. For Michael it had been a long and interesting one, he would have a lot to tell them when he got back to school next week. He was displeased that the Basel Police had taken his video recorder and tape. They seemed to think that he should be happy with the receipt they had given him!

Chapter 30

Monday 17th February 1997, 7.45 p.m.

The others were to have an early night but Lewis had arranged to see Elizabeth that evening. He wondered how she had enjoyed the *Fasnacht* and wished that he'd been able to spend some of the day with her. She'd be amazed at what had happened to Michael and the women.

He telephoned the *Hotel International* and asked for Elizabeth Fielder. His request was met with a moment's silence and then the girl on reception asked him to wait a moment. She returned to say that she would need to find her and then call back. What was the number she should call and for whom should she ask? Lewis told her. Elizabeth must be in the restaurant or somewhere other than her room. It was 7.45 p.m., they wouldn't have long but it would be good to be together.

The telephone rang, it was a man's voice, 'Herr Lewis?'

'Speaking.'

'This is Inspector Paul Burkharter of the Basel Police. I would like to speak with you.'

'Your people have already seen my wife Ruth and our friend Paula Gold as well as our son Michael about the kidnapping. I wasn't with them when it happened so I don't see how I can help you.'

'Kidnapping, Herr Lewis? I do not know about a kidnapping. My enquiries are about a murder at the *Hotel International* yesterday evening.'

Fear took hold of Lewis and he began to shake, 'Not Elizabeth ... Elizabeth Fielder?'

'Not as victim, Herr Lewis. We are holding her on suspicion of the murder of a man known as Eugene

Preston, though we are not sure whether that it is his real name.'

Lewis had sat down on a chair next to the telephone. He was having difficulty in speaking and his teeth were beginning to chatter, 'I know them both, they are related. Elizabeth is my secretary in London and Preston is a customer. When can I see Miss Fielder.'

'I am unable to tell you whether you can see her but I will have to ask *you* some questions about them and about your relations with the two. Where are you staying?'

Lewis gave him details of the Golds' address.

'Thank you Herr Lewis. One of my officers will collect you in about twenty minutes. You have eaten? Good, it may take us a considerable time to deal with all the matters before us. Incidentally you spoke of a kidnapping, who was kidnapped and when was it reported, please?'

Lewis supplied the details and put the telephone down. He sat staring at the painting on the opposite wall. He forced himself to get up and went into the sitting room. Only Jacob Gold remained as the others were all upstairs. There was a glass of Cognac on the table beside his chair, 'Like a drop before bed, Peter?' He looked up and saw Lewis' face, 'What's wrong, you look dreadful!'

Lewis stood there and after an effort managed a reply, 'That was the police on the 'phone. Elizabeth is being held by them on a murder charge and they want to question me? She's supposed to have killed her cousin, one of our best customers.' Once again he slumped into a chair. To Jacob Gold he looked like a toy that had lost most of its stuffing. His shoulders were hunched and he held his head in his hands.

'I am coming with you to the Police Station, Peter, and I

will stay there with you. You and Elizabeth will need lawyers, better to have different ones so there is no conflict of interest. I will call the law firm that acts for the laboratory and make arrangements for criminal lawyers to be present. But first you need something to counter the shock.' He poured a generous measure of Cognac into another glass and gave it to Lewis. 'Here this will help. It's a good thing we have not been indulging in our wine this evening. I will telephone the lawyers and then tell Ruth.'

He left Lewis alone with his thoughts and the Cognac. Lewis' world was turning upside down. He didn't know what might happen next. He felt very lonely and yet grateful that he was staying with friends and that Ruth was there.

'Peter!' Ruth was sitting next to him on the sofa, 'What on earth has happened? Jacob's just told me that Elizabeth has been charged with murder. Did I get it right?'

'That's what the Police Inspector said on the 'phone just now. I only hope I've imagined it!'

She could see from his face that it was real and not imagined. 'My poor Peter! This was supposed to be the first day of the carnival revelry and we've had a kidnapping followed by goodness knows what with a commando unit and now there's murder! Poor Peter! Poor Elizabeth! There must be some explanation. Jacob's going with you and he's told me that he's 'phoning his lawyers.' She put her arm round him and felt him begin to shake once again. 'You're not leaving here until you're feeling better and I will tell them that. They've given you a dreadful shock.'

Jacob had returned. 'The lawyers are on their way to the Central Police Station in Basel. You had better get ready to go when the police car comes. I am ready to go with you. Ruth, please explain to Paula what has happened and where we have gone.'

'And Ruth, don't tell Michael for the moment. We may be able to sort it all out without any trouble. I'm sure it's all a mistake.'

***

At just before eight thirty Lewis found himself sitting in an interview room in the Central Police Station. Behind him sat Jacob and a lawyer who had been introduced to him and whose name he had immediately forgotten. Across the table sat Inspector Burkharter and a colleague. Both wore sports coats, they were evidently detectives. The room had plain cream walls and the lighting was too bright for Lewis' comfort. He felt like a rabbit caught in the headlights of an oncoming car. He felt confused, vulnerable and lost, completely out of his depth and in alien surroundings. This would have been bad enough in Kilburn but add the complication of another country and another language and it was far worse. He closed his eyes and then opened them.

'OK you can get started, I'm ready. I'm tired and want it over and I want to see my partner, Elizabeth Fielder whom you are holding. In this building?' He was surprised at the loudness of his voice.

'No, not in this building Herr Lewis. She is still at the *Universitätsspital* where she was taken this morning. They seem to have been busy today, Herr Lewis, looking after people connected with you. This morning Miss Fielder was found in her room at the *Hotel International* suffering from severe concussion and she is still being treated and assessed at the *Universitätsspital*. In Switzerland we always proceed in a civilised and proper way. We will make totally sure that she is completely well before we bring her here.

'Miss Fielder was found lying on the floor of her hotel room, as was the body of a man calling himself Eugene Preston. Also lying there was the pistol with which he had been killed. For your information the only fingerprints on the weapon were those of Miss Fielder.

'I must point out that you are here voluntarily and that if you need a drink or to visit the gents at any time during our discussions we will have a break for you to do so. And you may, of course, consult your lawyer at any time if you wish to do so. Before we begin may I have your full name, occupation, nationality and permanent address and your temporary address in Switzerland. I'll take those one by one, you have your passport with you? Good. Thank you.'

The Inspector's English was impeccable and with Jacob and the lawyer present there should be no problems on that score. Lewis began to answer his questions in a matter of fact way, it was going to take some time and he so wanted to see Elizabeth. He was questioned about the reasons for the visit to Basel, why Elizabeth had come and about his relationship with her. He was open and told them that they lived together, that she was carrying his child and that they planned to marry once he and Ruth had been able to obtain a divorce.

Yes, he knew the deceased, Eugene Preston. He was a customer, a very good one who had brought a substantial amount of business to his firm. They had first met in February the previous year. Preston had introduced Elizabeth to him when his secretary, Vera, had been ... when she had been killed by a hit and run driver. To Lewis, telling the story in a Basel police station, her death sounded far more sinister than it had ever done before, as if wherever he went there were murders.

No, he did not consider Eugene Preston a rival for Elizabeth's affections. He certainly had nothing against him. At this point the lawyer intervened and the Inspector re-phrased a question. Lewis replied that Preston was a good and respected customer with whom relations were most cordial. No, they had never had any arguments about Elizabeth or about anything else. Elizabeth had never spoken of Preston except as a cousin and, of course, as a customer.

On Sunday evening he had been with his friend Jacob Gold and his wife at their home in Allschwil after a day in the Alps. His own wife Ruth and his son Michael had been there as well. Yes, Ruth was the child's mother. He was becoming weary with the interrogation, with having this man delving into his life and relationships before an audience. The note taking irritated him as did the knowledge that the interview was being recorded on disc.

The questioning then took a new and disturbing turn. Did Lewis have any knowledge of the identity of the American man with whom Elizabeth had spent the whole of Sunday and with whom she had had dinner at *Die Drei Könige*? Lewis felt sick, he felt betrayed. What had she been doing in his absence? He replied mildly that he had no idea. The man's description did not suggest anyone he knew.

The questions that followed were even more surprising and disconcerting. Lewis answered them all quietly but he felt numb. If only they would go away and leave him alone. But he knew that if he wanted to see Elizabeth he had to co-operate with the Inspector. He longed for bed, for sleep, for oblivion and yet he knew that he would not be able to sleep that night. He had had some shocks in his lifetime, this was by far the worst. No, he had no reason to doubt the identity of Elizabeth. He believed that she was British - a citizen of the United Kingdom as he insisted in putting it to the Inspector - and that she had spent a large part of her life in the USA and Canada. No, he had no reason to think that she was a Russian. It was all becoming too fantastic, Michael's Third World War seemed commonplace beside what was being told him here in the Basel Central Police Station in the form of questions. The same went for Preston, he had thought he was a Canadian, certainly not a Russian.

Inspector Burkharter looked through his notes and had a whispered conversation with has colleague. He looked at the lawyer, 'I have to put this question to your client, it is essential that I should do so.' He turned back to Lewis, 'Herr Lewis, did you have any involvement in the murder of the man known as Eugene Preston.'

'None whatsoever.'

'Did you have any knowledge that Elizabeth Fielder intended to murder the said Eugene Preston?'

'None whatsoever.'

That will be all for now, Herr Lewis. I am most grateful for your assistance this evening and wish you as enjoyable a carnival as circumstances permit. You will, of course, remain here in Switzerland until we no longer need your assistance. I will hold your passport, my colleague Jörg will give you a receipt for it.'

'You seem good at issuing receipts! My son was given one for our video camera this afternoon by one of your people and now I'm to get one for my passport. You can't film the carnival with a receipt or travel the world on one.' He sounded offended, he *was* offended, though he didn't quite know why this was. Perhaps it was the feeling of being a captive in a foreign land.

The Inspector commiserated with him, 'Sadly not Herr Lewis, sadly not.'

'And I can see Elizabeth Fielder? I do feel with our relationship that I am entitled to see her and be sure that the welfare of our child has not been impaired by what she has experienced.'

The Inspector thought for a moment, 'I have been pondering that for a while and can see no reason why you should not visit her in the *Universitätsspital* and do so. But a woman member of my staff will be present throughout the meeting and she will tell you how you must conduct yourself towards Miss Fielder. It is my intention to bring a formal charge of murder tomorrow or as soon as the hospital indicates that she is well enough. In addition there may be other charges, our enquiries on these other matters are continuing. I am very sorry that this has happened during your visit to us. You are always most welcome as a businessman and as a tourist.'

'Though without a passport!'

'Indeed you are temporarily without a passport but it is in good hands - unlike the ladies and your son this afternoon. While you were on your way here I was able to see your son's amazing film of the proceedings this afternoon. I am sorry that events are crowding in on you and your family, and your family Doktor Gold as well. I must wish you goodnight.'

Lewis looked at his watch. It was 10.47 p.m. and they had not finished yet. Behind him Jacob was in discussion with the lawyer. Jacob lent forward and put his hand on Lewis' shoulder, 'I am really sorry about all this, Peter. It's a muddle from beginning to end. Our lawyer friend tells me that he has a colleague outside who will be present when you see Elizabeth. I know you can do without an audience for the meeting but it is in her best interests to have legal representation.' Lewis nodded, what after all was one more for the show?

***

They drove in silence to the *Universitätsspital* and were shown to a private room. An armed woman police officer guarded the door and another was posted inside the room. Jacob waited outside while the second lawyer accompanied Lewis into the room. There was silence for a moment. Their eyes met and each saw in the other weariness, sadness, hurt and longing. He saw that she had been crying. She saw a man who had had the stuffing knocked out of him, who had had a shock that had stopped him in his tracks.

'Elizabeth.'

'Peter.'

Once again there was a silence in which each was conscious of the hurts of the other and in which, despite themselves, the police woman and the lawyer wished they were not intruding.

The silence was broken by the lawyer who explained his rôle and advised Elizabeth to take care about what she said to Lewis so as not to incriminate herself. He would be available the next morning to speak with her in complete privacy about her situation and about any charges that the police might be bringing against her. Lewis explained that the lawyer came on the recommendation of the law firm who were used by Jacob's laboratory for their business and that he himself had a separate lawyer. She accepted the lawyer's services and the conversation continued.

'Peter, I'm sorry that this has happened and that it's hurt you. Yes, I can see that you are very badly hurt. They tell me I shot Vladimir - Eugene to you and the rest of the world – I can't understand it - the whole thing is fuzzy. I know I've got the mother and father of all headaches, it seems I hit my head on a table or something, but I just can't focus on what happened.'

Lewis was not going to tell her tonight about what Inspector Burkharter had said on the subject of fingerprints on the weapon. But all he could manage was, 'It must all be a mistake, Elizabeth ... it must be.'

'Peter what have they told you?'

'Enough to turn my hair gray, Elizabeth, I'm afraid. Eugene, or whatever you call him dead in your room with a bullet through his brain and you concussed on the floor with the offending gun beside you.'

'I'm bitterly sorry he's dead - Vladimir wasn't a bad guy at heart.'

'And the young American who spent the day with you and dined with you at *Die Drei Könige*?' This was something that Lewis couldn't let go without an explanation.

'This is hard to explain, Peter, but try to believe me! I met him, Sam Charles, at dinner on Saturday, it was busy and we had to share a table at the *Hotel International*. I told him that I was going to the mountains by train the next day and invited him to come. I just wanted someone to talk to after all the tension that we've experienced. No Peter, honestly I wasn't looking for someone else. I'm yours and I'm carrying our child. By the way they tell me that there appears to be no discernible damage to the foetus and, despite the bruising to my head, there's no brain damage. To go back to Sam Charles, he was like you in this way - he was the sort of man who would never take advantage of a woman. You are an English gentleman. He was an American gentleman. I trusted him as I trust you and he didn't let me down, just as you would never let me down.' Despite her situation she suddenly exuded confidence and Peter caught the fragrance of her perfume. Deep down he felt a slight lifting of his spirits, it wasn't totally helpless. He knew without a shadow of doubt that she trusted him implicitly but could he retain his trust in her. He knew he would once have trusted her with his life – but now could he still do so?

'And Elizabeth, who *are* you? It seems that Eugene was Vladimir. Who are *you*? And why aren't you - I don't know how to put it, I'm tired and I'm getting confused - why aren't you Elizabeth Fielder? When we marry I would like to know who it really is that I'm marrying!' And he said to himself, '*When?* Can it really be *when* rather than *if?*' For his trust and confidence in her had been shattered.

His eye had caught the little *Fasnacht* drummer badge on the lapel of her jacket which was on a chair beside the bed. He had pinned it there only two days ago when they had last been together. He remembered his comment to Jacob and the others that morning about the man who had convinced the police of his identity as a Basler by playing the drum. If only Elizabeth could establish who she was as simply and as surely! And drum rolls could be a call to action or accompany the march to the scaffold - now he was becoming too melodramatic - he would do all he could for her to mitigate the sentence she risked if she were tried for Eugene's killing. To him the drum was issuing a summons to action on her behalf, he couldn't desert her now but he had no idea of the final outcome, of their future together.

'Peter, it's a long story and it will have to keep for the moment. It won't help to rush and I'll tell you all of it when I can. Just keep trusting me and we'll sort it out. The one thing that spoiled my happiness over the last few months was having to act a part and pretend to be someone else. I just want to be me, to be myself, and to be with you! My

real name is Lizaveta Feldman ... and I *am* Russian.'
Tears were running down her face and the others in the room again wished they could slip out and leave the couple to themselves. Lewis got up, walked around the bed and took Elizabeth's hand. He knelt and kissed her and she felt his tears on her cheek. The woman officer kept her eye on them, she was not having anything passed to her prisoner and she would make sure with a thorough search afterwards, but she was prepared to bend the rules for once and, after all, it was the first day of *Fasnacht*.

A couple of minutes later Lewis felt a hand on his shoulder, it was the woman officer, 'The evening is getting rather late Herr Lewis. If you want to go home tonight rather than tomorrow we had better finish now.'

Elizabeth gave him one more kiss and took her leave, 'Good night Peter. Thanks for coming to my aid in this mess. Before you came, do you know what I was saying to myself? Well it was something from Petrarch:

"Pace non trovo, e non ho da far guerra." '

She turned to the woman officer and the lawyer, 'You Swiss all speak Italian don't you. Can you translate?' Both declined, the lawyer suggesting that Mediaeval Italian was beyond him. Elizabeth who was increasing in confidence as the minutes ticked past threw back her head and laughed, 'The English translation is:

"I can't find peace and don't know how to fight."

'Coming here tonight you've brought me some hope, Peter!' She kissed him and the officer led him to the door.

'Good night, Elizabeth. Seeing you has done me a world of good. By the way, Ruth, Michael and Paula Gold were kidnapped this afternoon and then rescued.'

'What carnival goings on?'

'No, It was for real. They gave Paula a knock out jab -

the police here are investigating – we're keeping them too busy for comfort.'

'They're OK though?'

'They're fine.'

'Good, goodnight Peter.'

'Goodnight Elizabeth. I hope they let me see you tomorrow.' Talking about the kidnapping had seemed almost like reporting a day on the beach, it paled into insignificance beside the murder charge hanging over her head.

Jacob was waiting outside the room and they prepared to leave.

'I caught a glimpse of her as you left, Peter, she looked tired.'

'She's high at the moment. I hope she doesn't come down with too much of a bump when she views her situation in the cold light of day. She perked up when she saw me, though there's nothing I can do to get her out of here. She can't remember killing the fellow. It may be the result of her concussion. It looks as though something hit her hard on the head. Thanks for arranging the lawyers for both of us. What time is it? Five past midnight? We'll have been on the go for nearly twenty two hours, it feels more like two hundred and twenty two!'

'I will find a taxi to take us back to Allschwil. You do not want to spend the night here!'

'Not unless I'm with Elizabeth!' His emotions were in a state of complete turmoil – he loved her but he was conscious of having been so badly deceived. She must have been planted on him. And then it dawned on him that Vera's demise had almost certainly been something other than a coincidence.

Chapter 31

Monday 17th February 1997, 3.40 p.m.

The *Fasnacht* Carnival, kidnapping, foreign armies, and murder were not the only things exercising the minds of the Basel Police that evening. Another disturbing incident had taken place which struck at things held most dear by all good Swiss, who know very well on which side their bread is buttered. There was much to discuss in the canteen at the Central Police Station that night.

But first we need to go back to Sam and the things that kept him busy after he had left the ambulance at the *Universitätsspital* at 3.40 p.m. Dressed as a harlequin he was as inconspicuous in Basel at *Fasnacht* as he would have been in a business suit in the City of London. There was no need to rush, his team would be still on the road taking the captive Russians to a large farmhouse in the Simmental, beyond Spiez. There they would be interrogated. He would join them that evening so that the next day he could speak with Dr Svyatoslav Gordeyev. After that his part in the action would be over and he would return home via London to await the debriefing. But next he had to call at the *Bahnhof SBB*, the main railway station. He deposited the briefcase in the Left Luggage, noted the number of the ticket and then headed for the bookstall near the main entrance to the station. He had been there two days before and knew what he was looking for. Good, the poster on the side of the stall advertising a German scandal sheet was still loose at the bottom left hand corner. He bought the *Basler Zeitung* and moved back to the poster. Leaning against the kiosk he read the paper while he slipped the Left Luggage ticket under the edge of the poster and secured it with Blu-tack. His gloves ensured that no finger prints were left behind.

He moved off and began to search the paper for news of Elizabeth. On the first day of Fasnacht news of any other kind has to fight for space in the local press. On page two he found the item for which he was looking, it was headed, **"Canadian Man Shot Dead in Basel Hotel: English Woman Held by Police"**. The report apart from naming the hotel and giving the time the police were called did not add much to the headline, except for one significant phrase, "Basel Police are anxious to interview an American man believed to have spent the day with the woman and to have dined with her at *Die Drei Könige* on the evening of the shooting." A not very specific description of the American followed. Again he knew that these events must have been the direct outcome of his diversion for Eugene with Anna. For two days Sam's scheme had stoked up Eugene's sexual frustration and then he had attempted to take it out on Elizabeth. Sam felt sorrow, guilt and anger. Why hadn't he just got on with the operation without embroidering it in this way? He was personally responsible for Elizabeth's predicament. He had been seen with her at the *Hotel International*, on the Rigi and at *Die Drei Könige* and the police wanted to interview him. He hoped that his purported departure for Hamburg would throw them off his scent. Nevertheless he must be out of Switzerland as soon as possible. He should be gone by tomorrow evening at the latest. He would take the train through the Gotthard into Ticino, the southern Canton and cross the border into Italy, they were likely to be more casual there than in other parts of Switzerland. From there he would fly to London to see Alan Winters and then fly on to Tel Aviv.

He folded the newspaper and put it in his pocket. Although there was no danger of being recognised with his mask and carnival suit he had no wish to linger. Within twenty minutes he was at the apartment and waiting for a telephone call from his Number Two.

At six o'clock the call come. They were all safely settled in their new accommodation, the afternoon's exercises had given them nothing worse than a few bruises and aching limbs and their guests were as happy as one could hope for. Grigor had been encouraged to speak to his friend in Bern on the telephone. He had spoken very well and very clearly, exactly as they had asked him to do, they of course had wanted to keep the telephone bill down and hadn't encouraged him to chatter on. The friend from Bern would be on the train suggested by Grigor and would arrive at Basel at 19h59 that evening and he understood what he had to do.

Two hours would allow the Police sufficient time to make their arrangements. Sam left the apartment and walked to the public telephone a block away. He called the number he had been given and asked for an extension. A young and enthusiastic police officer replied. Sam read him a short statement in German, including details of the Left Luggage ticket number, asked him if he had fully understood, read it again and hung up. It was a pity that he wouldn't be able to see the fun for himself. At the apartment he completed his packing and at six twenty five he was on his way to join the others in their country retreat.

***

The train with the Second Secretary from the Russian

Embassy in Bern arrived at Basel SBB Station at one minute after eight. He felt conspicuous but there was no reason to worry, he knew that. He circled the bookstall and located the poster. He stopped beside it to tie a shoe lace and as he stood up fumbled under the edge of the poster. Good there was something there! He placed it in his pocket and walked off looking for the Left Luggage. It took him three minutes to find it and one minute for the attendant to find the briefcase. He had time to kill before the 21h01 back to Bern, there was an earlier train but the 21h01 had a restaurant car and his eating arrangements had been messed up by the visit to Basel.

He needed a drink, not in the Station Buffet, he would try the *Hotel Euler*, it was suitably upmarket for someone like himself. As he made his way towards the station exit and the *Hotel Euler* he was stopped by a plain clothes policeman and escorted to a car waiting outside the station. The policeman and his colleagues refused to believe his claim to be a diplomat – 'They all say that don't they, sir?' - and took him to the Central Police Station where the briefcase was opened and copies of bank statements for members of the Swiss Council of State and other prominent citizens were found. They were never able to understand his comment, made on arrival at the police station, that the drug wasn't dangerous. The documents were of some considerable interest to the police and Swiss Security who had also joined the welcoming party for the unfortunate Second Secretary. He did not enjoy the showing of the video film of his progress through the station a little earlier that evening.

At midnight, a while after Lewis had left the Central Police Station, the Russian Ambassador arrived to collect his errant member of staff. The film taken by their security cameras of him arriving in his official limousine was one which the Basel Police treasured but quickly impounded in case it should fall into the wrong hands. After all the matter was very confidential and should never be allowed to reach the press. The Ambassador had spent a most unpleasant evening with Swiss Government officials in Bern and they had insisted that he should go to Basel in person to collect the Second Secretary. He was to have some very rough months ahead, with flak coming at him both from Bern and Moscow. Flak also flew between the Kremlin and the SVR HQ for quite some time.

Chapter 32

Tuesday 18th February 1997

Fasnacht Tuesday is for the children, with their procession in the afternoon. The other attraction is in the *Münsterplatz* where the lanterns of the adult *cliques* are parked outside the cathedral, available for all to view. That was where Paula, having recovered surprisingly well from her experience the day before, took Michael to see them. She was anxious to keep him occupied while Peter and Ruth decided how to respond to the situation.

'We've got to find the lantern that wasn't complete when we saw it in the parade, Aunty Paula.' He had borrowed a video camera from her husband and was deciding which of around 200 lanterns to record. Paula had a hard task explaining the significance of the *cliques' sujets,* some of which defeated her completely. With others there were bystanders who gave an explanation or ventured a guess.

They took a break at a refreshment tent there in the *Münsterplatz* and Michael, who had been somewhat subdued throughout the afternoon, began to quiz Paula, 'Aunty Paula, something awful has happened, hasn't it? Mum said it was to do with Dad's Elizabeth, something about being in trouble with the police.'

Peter Lewis had been given a sleeping tablet by Jacob the night before and had surfaced in a bleary, shell-shocked condition just before Paula and Michael had set off for the city, so he had been unable to converse sensibly with Michael.

Paula had been expecting his question and did her best, 'You will have to get the details from your Mum and Dad, Michael. What I can say is that *they* are not in trouble but they are very upset. Elizabeth, has problems,

Michael, that's certain. But I cannot tell you more. Your Mum and Dad are going to tell you about it this evening so you will know then.'

'I hope they lock her up for ever, don't you Aunt Paula?'

'Michael, I know it has been very difficult for you and you can tell *me* just what you feel, but your Dad is very upset and you must help him by being very careful about what you say.'

'But I hate her Aunty, I really hate her.'

Paula was beginning to sweat, she wanted to pour oil on troubled waters and not make things worse for them all. 'Michael, I know it's hard for you to like Elizabeth and I am not going to ask you to do that. But you must look after your Father. I know you love him and that you will want to help him. If something awful happened to *you,* what would Peter do?'

'He'd look after me, I know that.'

'Well, Michael, that is what you have to do for him! He really is going to need your help. I think you will know what has happened by this evening. They want you to know.'

The tram stop was crowded with young families returning from the afternoon parade - even the toddlers in push-chairs were dressed for carnival costumes. After a short wait they boarded the tram to Allschwil. When they had taken their seats Michael had a further question, 'Aunty Paula, the news-sheet for the *Basler Zeitung* says, *"Fasnachts Mord bei Hotel International,"* isn't that where Elizabeth is staying?'

'Yes it is, Michael.'

'And she hasn't been murdered?'

'No.'

'Is she a murderer, Aunty Paula?'

'Keep you voice low, Michael. ……….. I think that is what they are accusing her of.'

Michael was silent for the rest of the journey. He was aware of very conflicting emotions as he tried to grasp the significance of the news. Kidnapping and murder weren't what you normally experienced on holiday!

***

Ruth and Jacob accompanied Lewis to Elizabeth's lawyer who insisted on seeing Lewis alone. He outlined the charges that were likely to be brought. In response to Lewis' question, 'Who is she, then?' He sketched out what Elizabeth had told him of her work for the Russian SVR and the KGB before it.

'What did they want with me?'

'Nothing with you directly. It was a drug from your friend Doktor Jacob Gold's laboratory that they were after. It is likely, very likely that Paula Gold together with your wife and son were going to be used yesterday afternoon to persuade the laboratory to hand over the drug. The Russians' efforts were, it seems, frustrated by someone else although the police are desperately anxious to know whom to thank for the intervention - to thank or to charge with many crimes if they can catch them! Another coffee Mr Lewis? I am not surprised that you are shaken by these events - they are extraordinary. I will be frank with you, most of a lawyer's life is spent with dull and routine matters, tedious contracts which have to be completely accurate and leave nothing out, dull crimes by dull people and so on. When a case like this comes along it is like a breath of fresh air to a jaded advocate! Miss Fielder will have the very best of my attention: I owe it to her as a client and I owe it to my own reputation.'

'But what gave the police the idea that Elizabeth and Eugene weren't who they claimed to be?'

'My understanding is that he had in his pocket some draft notes for a letter to the Headquarters of the SVR, a plea to be allowed to remain in England and stressing the work he was in process of doing there. As for my client, Miss Fielder, or rather Lizaveta Feldman, as we're all going to get used to calling her, she was saying odd things when she returned to consciousness and one of the police officers recorded it on a pocket machine. By itself it would, perhaps, not have been significant but, with the discovery of the letter in the deceased's pocket, questions were put to her and she admitted to her true identity. It is not an offence for a member of the SVR to visit our country so long as they behave themselves. So it is a question of what the lady was doing and of the significance of her meetings with the Young American. She says his name was Sam Charles but the Swiss Immigration authority has no one of that name on its computers. My task will be to protest her innocence of any illegal activities on Swiss soil but as she came here on false papers that may not be easy. I am not sure that I should be telling you these things, Mr Lewis, but my client insisted that I should be completely open and you do not look like a Russian spymaster or even a British one, at any rate you do not resemble Alec Guinness or rather George Smiley, they are one and the same person, don't you think? Oh yes, there was one other point. Doktor Jacob Gold will be paying any of the fees for the defence of the lady so far as they are not met from official Swiss sources.'

Lewis was already beyond thinking about spymasters or legal bills. He thanked the advocate, Herr Vogel - yes he had the same name as the fallen bishop - everyone reminded him of that! - and retreated to rejoin Ruth and Jacob. The latter saw that they wished to be alone and said he would wait for them at the car. A shaken Peter Lewis related to his wife what he had just been told and received her promise of total silence about what he had passed on. She wondered aloud about what the British papers might print, she would telephone his office in Kilburn and tell them not to answer any questions about Elizabeth or about Peter. They would also have to tell Michael before he heard in some other way. And it would be as well to tell him to be quiet about his film of World War Three. Despite everything his description of the previous afternoon's events made them laugh.

Lewis looked at his wife, 'Thanks for being with me in all this. I need you Ruth, I really need you!'

'We all need one another, Peter, and we'll both stand by Elizabeth.'

***

Peter Lewis and Ruth arrived at the *Universitätsspital* and waited outside Elizabeth's room. The armed police guard had been maintained but with two different female officers. A telephone call to the Central Police Station before their departure had obtained permission for the visit but with stringent rules about contact and with a prohibition on giving anything to Elizabeth.

'I want you to see her Ruth and give me your opinion of how she is.'

'Once you have seen her on your own, Peter. I don't want to make things difficult.'

He nodded and went into the room. Elizabeth opened her eyes and attempted a tired smile.

'Hello, Peter. Thanks for coming again, it really is good

to see you.'

'What am I supposed to call you? Is it Elizabeth or is it Lizaveta?'

'*Elizabeth*, Peter – all the elements of the Elizabeth you know are here – I had hoped to leave Lizaveta behind. But we can't go into all that now, though we will in good time. I'm still muzzy and confused, I've got a really thick head. The hospital say it's shock and concussion. I seem to have fallen and struck my head on the hotel furniture. I'm racking my brain to work out what happened. They tell me what they found in the room: me on the floor with a badly bruised head and Vladimir – yes, that's his real name – dead on the floor, killed by a pistol shot. I know it sounds like evasion to say that I don't know what happened – I *think* he was trying to rape me and maybe kidnap me but I don't know for sure and that baffles me.'

'What do the hospital say, Elizabeth. Have they done tests and all that?'

'Scans, Peter, they've scanned my brain and my foetus – our foetus, and they don't think there are any problems there – they've taken samples, blood and urine, they've had me connected to a monitor. This is Switzerland they're nothing if not thorough – I'm not sure who's paying the bill!'

'What next, Elizabeth?'

'The hospital have more or less finished with me. Tomorrow they will call – that's the Basel Police – and take me to the Public Prosecutor's Office and prison, I believe it's near the railway station, Peter.'

He would never forget the previous evening's visit to the Central Police Station, no doubt the Prosecutor's Office would be very much like the Police Station.

She continued, 'They intend to charge me with Vladimir's murder and possibly some other offences and then lock me up in the *Untersuchungsgefängnis*, which seems to be their long name for the remand prison. The police woman told me it was a new jail, but whether that makes being locked up any better … I suppose it does.' She closed her eyes and was quiet for a while, the exertion had tired her. She was drained physically and emotionally. After a while she opened her eyes, 'Peter, I really am sorry for all this hurt. I don't know whether it helps or makes things worse,' she paused, 'I love you Peter, good, kind Peter. I should never have got you into such a muddle, never.'

'I think I still love you, Elizabeth but I'm confused, very confused.' He wept and then sat quietly holding her hand.

He felt a hand on his shoulder and, expecting to see one of the police officers calling time on the visit, he was surprised to find Ruth standing beside him. She bent and kissed Elizabeth on the forehead, 'Elizabeth, this is devastating. I've never known a situation like it! I believe you are a good and honourable woman, I don't believe you are a murderess. There must be something we don't know about all this. What ever can I say to help? Only this, Peter and I will stand by you and the baby – rest assured of that – we won't abandon you, Elizabeth.'

She assured Elizabeth that Peter would come to see her as long as the police held his passport and after he was able to return home he would fly out to Basel each weekend.

***

Sam waited for Dr Gordeyev to be brought into the barn. He remembered Alan Winters taking him aside at the final briefing for a private word. 'If you get a chance to put a bullet through his brain don't hesitate to do so! He was at the *Serbsky* and has a vile record of cruelty, all in the name of medical science, of course. Get him to talk about the work he did there at *Kropotkinskii Street*, Moscow when he was working under Dr Daniel Luntz. You know of Luntz? No? He was a KGB Colonel, an odd sort of label for the head of a psychiatric institution! But you know of the place's reputation? If you were a dissenter making a nuisance of yourself they very quickly labelled you a paranoid schizophrenic. They drugged you with things like *Aminazin* which brings shock and depression, skin sores and the destruction of the memory. The medication was to make you ill and not to cure, though they told the world the contrary! Well if you get a chance put down that swine Gordeyev and make it a cleaner world, then do so, don't hesitate Sam!'

Sam also remembered Gordeyev's speech to Eugene and Grigor three days earlier on how the Serbsky had kept dissidents in check.

The minutes ticked by and an old man was escorted into the barn by one of Sam's men and given a seat facing Sam at an old garden table. He didn't need guarding and the two men were left together.

Sam looked across the table at a man who had prematurely aged and clearly did not have much longer on this earth. From what he had been told he knew he should have no sympathy for the man, and yet ... 'Dr Gordeyev, would you like a cup of tea of coffee? Tea? And how do you like it? OK I'll get them to bring one.' Despite all that Sam had been told of the man he was just that, a man, and Sam was more interested in what had led him to use his scientific knowledge to harm and oppress, than in inflicting pain on top of his present discomfort. He had decided to probe whether Gordeyev had any regrets and whether he showed any signs of repentance – Sam had tried to find a non-religious word but could not.

'And to conclude, how do you summarise your life Dr Gordeyev?'

'You are some sort of therapist, Mr Charles, or perhaps a priest, or both?'

'Perhaps and perhaps not.'

'Technically, Mr Charles, a life of achievement, as to humanity an abject failure. This afternoon you have shown humanity and kindness: you have behaved as a gentleman and this has shamed me.'

'You told me at the beginning that you have only a couple of months left. I think that it is good that you have faced up to the balance sheet of life, Dr Gordeyev. Many people never do.' Sam stood up and Gordeyev rose to face him. Sam thought for a moment, he took Gordeyev's hand and shook it. 'You will be home very soon, Doctor, I trust your remaining days will not be too uncomfortable.'

Gordeyev nodded, 'And that is what I hope. Goodbye Mr Charles, never lose your humanity.'

Sam Kagan stood in the empty room and reflected on the last year's work. His task was done, tomorrow he would head for home with some of his questions about the operation still unanswered and with a burden of guilt over Elizabeth's plight.

***

Michael was waiting for Peter and Ruth on their return to Allschwil. They hung up their coats and scarves and shepherded him into the lounge.

Peter began. 'Michael, I know yesterday afternoon was a fantastic adventure and, as there seem to be no lasting ill effects for Paula, we can laugh about it. Another very unusual thing happened on Sunday night or perhaps on Monday morning. While we were out on the streets in the city centre for *Moorgestraich*, Elizabeth was lying unconscious on her hotel room floor. She had either fallen and struck her head a severe blow or been hit on the head with some weapon. You've met Elizabeth's cousin Eugene at the warehouse, haven't you? Well ... he was also on the floor, not unconscious but dead with a bullet through his head.'

Lewis found it was getting too difficult and Ruth took over, 'Your Dad and I are sure there must be an explanation but the Basel Police are going to charge Elizabeth with,' she paused to steady her voice, 'with murder, Michael. This has been a time of shocks and surprises and there are two more I'm afraid. Both Elizabeth and Eugene were Russian Security Agents.'

'Spies, Mum?' Michael had been getting more and more uptight, as much from watching his parents and absorbing their unease as from what he was being told, and, whether to ease the tension or just to have something to say, blurted out, 'Is she a Russian 007?'

Ruth didn't know whether to laugh or cry. Peter had no doubt: he began to weep quietly.

'Dad, don't.' True to form Michael showed his dislike for displays of emotion. 'I'm sorry. I didn't mean to laugh, it's just that everything is so fantastic I can't guess what the boys at school will think.'

'And, Michael, that's one of the reasons we are telling you all this and not hiding anything. The papers are going to get hold of the story and your chums will know. They will read all about it and there will be things they read that aren't true. What the papers don't know they will invent, some of them anyway, and it's possible that your photo will greet you from the front page of some of them.'

Peter broke in, 'What would you do if a photographer tried to snap you outside the school?'

'I'd knock his camera out of his hands,' came the confident reply, 'and probably kick him as well.'

Peter and Ruth were impressed at his show of spirit. Ruth took over, 'Just keep what you know and what you have seen to yourself, Michael. No word to anyone but us and, if necessary, the Basel Police. Anything you say is likely to get distorted and make things even more difficult. Understood?'

'Understood, Mum. And ... Dad, I'm sorry.' He hugged them both.

Chapter 33

Tuesday 11th March 1997

The interview was almost over. They were in the dining room of the apartment in West Hampstead. They had arranged to meet there when he called on Lewis at his office. He had introduced himself as Brown from Security and produced some sort of identification. By then Lewis was somewhat punch-drunk and beyond caring, the ID produced to him could have been made up but he supposed the fellow was genuine. He had come with someone from the Special Branch and Lewis was a little more impressed by him and accepted Brown on the strength of the impression made by his companion. Both had been slightly scruffy with shabby raincoats and somehow they had fitted Lewis' idea of what the breed would look like. Either Security or child molesters was his thought. Lewis had insisted that he would say nothing without having his solicitor present and Brown had given his grudging agreement to this. Punch-drunk or not, Lewis had snapped back, 'You see me with him or you don't see me at all. If I don't wish to speak to you I won't. You see me on my terms or not at all.'

Brown had responded wearily, 'Bring him along then if you must and we will meet at the apartment, the one you lived in with her. I have powers to search the place, of course.'

Lewis had responded bitterly, 'Which you have done already, *of course*.' Neither empathised with the other and Lewis had not looked forward to the interview with any enthusiasm.

Now it was almost over. He had sweated under Brown's

questioning for over two hours, uncomfortable about this intrusion into his private affairs, and had insisted on regular comfort breaks. He had continued replying to a question whenever Brown had tried to move on to the another before he had finished his reply to the last. Lewis had been determined, for dignity's sake, to keep some sort of control over the proceedings and move at the pace *he* wished.

'... and it's a question I must put to you once again, Mr Lewis. Did you have any reason to believe that this woman, known as Elizabeth Fielder, was working for Russian Intelligence? Think carefully, it's important.'

'I've told you before that I hadn't the slightest idea of any connection and I'm not going to bloody well tell you again. I've answered quite enough questions for one afternoon and that's it!'

Brown shrugged his shoulders, 'If you don't mind my saying so, Sir, you are fortunate that this didn't take place during the Cold War. If it had you might well be facing serious charges.'

Lewis rose to his feet, paused for a moment and spoke very quietly, 'And you Mr Brown are not so lucky. My solicitor John Evans will be making a formal complaint to your organisation about your manner. We will await your copy of the notes of today's meeting to make sure that they are accurate but in the mean time a complaint will be sent. I would like your business card or whatever you call it from your outfit. Thanks, John will take it. Now off you go, You've had enough of our time and I've had enough of you.'

Brown made his way to the door. 'I'm sorry you're upset, Sir. I understand the stress you're under but I may have further questions as our enquiries progress. Of course if you don't agree the notes I've made it's the word of one of us against the other, we've covered a lot of ground and memory isn't perfect.'

'No Mr Brown memory isn't perfect, neither yours nor mine. That's why we've taped the interview to ensure that there's an accurate record. Oh, didn't you know that? I must have forgotten to tell you. Have a safe journey home and don't talk to any strangers, you never know which country they might be working for.' He closed the door on him, returned to the sitting room and sank into a chair. 'John, I really could have done without this! It's been traumatic with all that's happened and then to have to deal with the likes of him!'

'I'll get you a coffee or would you prefer something stronger? OK coffee it is. You did well, Peter, especially at the end. He wasn't a happy man when he left. He misjudged you, thought that the stuffing had been knocked out of you by the events in Basel. To tell the truth I enjoyed the way you sent him away with a flea in his ear.'

Lewis sat waiting for the coffee. Outside it was a drab day. He had risen to the challenge and was elated at his performance but he knew that the elation wouldn't last.

They finished their coffee and Evans took his leave, 'I'll have that tape transcribed tomorrow and let you have the typescript. Oh yes, don't worry I'll have several copies made of the tape itself tonight and leave them in different locations, just in case anyone should want to get their hands on the recording! By the way how does all this affect your divorce proceedings or should I leave that question for the time being? OK, I'll put a note in my diary to talk to you about it in a month or so. Look after yourself Peter and don't let it get you down. You did say that Ruth would be collecting you? Right, see you in a day or so with the transcript. I'll let myself out.'

Lewis looked at his watch. Four twenty five and just over half an hour to go before Ruth was due. He took the cups back to the kitchen, washed them and put them away. He was tempted to sweep the floor but didn't. He poured the half empty carton of milk down the drain, there was no point in putting it into the fridge. Still half an hour to go. He ought to get out of the place, the memories were too painful. But he couldn't bring himself to leave. He wandered round the apartment aimlessly. He had come back to earth with a bump, it hadn't taken long. The adrenaline had ceased to flow and he felt well and truly down.

He opened the wardrobe door in the bedroom and took out her turquoise evening gown. He caught the smell of her perfume. Was it only a couple of months ago that she had worn it for their "alternative Christmas" celebration? It seemed like a lifetime away. Then he had felt himself to be the most fortunate man on earth. And now? There was at the same time numbness and an aching - nothing else save an awful tiredness. He had no idea how he was going to get through the next few months. He couldn't face the idea of work. Meeting people was beyond him after what the newspapers had printed about himself and Elizabeth. He laid the dress on the bed, it had been their bed. He turned to the window. Her tray of cacti was there and one had a few flowers, an early flowering perhaps, a few cream blooms. He found a sharp knife in the kitchen and returned to remove a bloom, he didn't know why, and put it carefully into his wallet. The knife had to be washed and put away, she wouldn't have left anything like that around. He closed the door of the kitchen and returned to the sitting room. There were still twenty minutes to go.

Lewis sat down on the sofa and looked at the piano. He

was where he had sat the evening she had first played the Steinway, the night when he had been lost for words to describe the intensity of his emotions. The night when she had told him that she was carrying their child. And he now knew where the idea of an "alternative Christmas" had come from. How long before he had to get the piano and the other things out of the apartment to make way for the next occupant? He wondered who the landlord might be and when the notice to quit for non-payment of rent would come. Would he come here again before he had to clear the place? He didn't know. He was tempted to put a CD on the hi-fi but knew he couldn't bear it.

And this was where he had sat with Elizabeth the previous June, when he had visited the apartment for the first time after the concert at the Wigmore Hall. He remembered the feeling he had experienced that night of something new and wonderful stirring within him. That night had been his introduction to Chopin's music. She had insisted that he couldn't go until he had heard Rubinstein's rendering of the final piece from the recital. What had she said about it? He didn't have to work to extract it from his memory. It came with complete clarity, "All conflicts resolved." So did his reply, "Yes, if only life were like that!" He felt loss, he felt betrayed and yet he still loved her. At one and the same time he both condemned her and forgave her. He knew that she had been caught up in something that prevented her from being open with him about her identity and activities. That softened the sense of having been deceived, though it did not remove it. He did not know what to think or how to respond to a situation that had overwhelmed him - a situation that had overwhelmed them both.

A vase of flowers caught his attention. He had given them to her just four weeks ago, a dozen red roses. The vase was dry, the foliage withered and the petals lay on the table and on the floor. Tears came to his eyes.

Restless, he went to the window and looked out at the gray March day. Life was drab, he could see nothing ahead but pain. It would be one day of hurt after another - days, weeks and months of unremitting pain. He had lost her and there was also Michael. Fortunately his problems showed some signs of lessening, but would they ever go away? - especially after the reports in the papers. ... He looked down through the bare branches of the trees, struggling against their urban environment. It was hardly any time ago that he had been looking out impatiently, waiting for the piano to arrive as her surprise present. He opened the window and looked down, there was nothing for him to look forward to, nothing to delight him any more. The apartment was empty and silent. He looked down. It would be a quick way to go. He thought he was high enough to make a decent job of it.

Fifty yards along the road Ruth and Michael sat in the Volvo waiting for Lewis to appear at the entrance to the block. They were deep in conversation on something to do with Michael's homework when Ruth looked through the car windscreen and saw the apartment window open and her husband's face appear. Afterwards she said that she hadn't analysed the situation, she had simply known instinctively what he was about to do. 'Out Michael and go with me, forget about locking the car!'

They stood on the pavement below the window and looked up. Lewis looked down at them as if they had suddenly appeared from Outer Space.

'Peter just stay there where you are! Don't attempt to move! Now throw the keys down and we will come up to you.' She turned to Michael, 'Make sure you catch the things when he throws them!' She looked up again, 'Michael will catch them. Right Peter throw them down.' There was a pause that seemed an age, then Lewis fumbled in his pocket and threw the keys out. 'Please God don't let us lose them!' She was never sure whether she said it aloud or not. She watched them on their way straight into Michael's hands. Never would he take a more important catch. She breathed a sigh of relief. 'OK Michael you keep him talking. Anything you like as long as you hold his attention! Football, Tolkien's orcs or anything else. Just keep him talking!'

The apartment was on the top floor and she would be able to guess which one it was or at any rate find which lock yielded to the key. Calmly she looked up, 'I'm on my way, Peter. I won't be long.' She walked to the door and tried the keys, her shaking hands made it difficult but on the second attempt she succeeded. Once inside she fled up the stairs, she daren't risk the lift, and reached the top. She had no doubt about the door to the apartment and saw the name card "Fielder/Lewis" and to her surprise she found herself wondering what was on the card outside Elizabeth's present abode. Suddenly she was composed and able to open the door without fumbling. In the hallway she had to decide on which was the door to the room facing the street. She guessed correctly, opened the door and saw him there by the open window. He turned towards her looking desperately sad, "like a walking corpse" she told a friend long afterwards, which in a sense he was.

'Peter!' She came slowly towards him, took him by the hand and led him away from the window. For a moment she left him and returned to the window. 'OK Michael, everything is all right. That was a great catch just now, we're proud of you. Here catch the keys again, let yourself in, find the kitchen and wait until I come through to you.' She watched him make the catch, closed the window, locked it and returned to her husband. 'Peter we love you, let us help you.' She held him close to her. There was a moment of silence and stillness. Then he began to sob, his body convulsed. In the room where he had wept tears of joy a few weeks before he now wept tears of sorrow and hurt. His present sadness and past sadnesses and hurts welled up and came to the surface at last.

Elizabeth had asked him of his parents, 'Did you grieve for them, Peter?' and he had replied, 'I know that I should have.' He was now repairing that omission and others, things repressed over the years were coming to the surface. For Peter Lewis a long healing process was beginning.

He looked at his wife and between sobs whispered, 'She's carrying our child, Ruth, there in jail.'

'Well we've just got to see what we can do for her and your child, Peter. We won't abandon any of you.'

Ruth held him close and wept with him. He was going to need a lot of help and support but she was going to give it to him. And Michael could give help as well as receive it. She remembered that he was in the kitchen. They all needed to be together. She called him, 'Michael, your Dad and I need you.'

The afternoon's proceedings had been picked up by Sam's bugs but, as his team had cleared out of their apartment around the corner the previous day, there was no one to receive the illicit transmission. After a year of giving it special attention, foreign Intelligence Agencies had lost interest in the apartment and its occupants and had moved on to pastures new.

***

Lizaveta sat in her cell in the *Untersuchungsgefängnis* in Basel glad that she didn't have to share with anyone else. She needed her space, particularly in her present situation. There was much that she would have to think through. Not that she kept herself separate from the other women in the wing, she was getting them to teach her German and, with her first efforts in that tongue, she was doing what she could to help them. Like the homeless at the Christmas dinner in London much had happened to set them on the course that had brought them here.

She had deep concerns for two other people: for poor, kind Peter and for her mother. Of all the ways for Peter to discover her true identity she could not think of a worse one. What she might have explained, what she should have told him early on, with careful and gentle explanations had been announced to the world in the most lurid way imaginable. And Peter had had to contend with the world's press. She was carrying his child. She didn't know how the press had got news of that, probably through money paid to someone at the hospital, she supposed. It had given the British tabloids just the lurid headline they specialised in, "British businessman fathers love-child by Russian spy". She felt for Michael, how had he coped with the ragging he must have faced at school? And then there was her mother, what pressures were they putting on her and with Lizaveta unable to send her money – they could hardly be paying her salary any more – her mother's pension, even if they were still paying it, would hardly suffice.

And she deeply regretted the fate of Vladimir, though the precise events of that evening were blurred, made out of focus by the concussion she had suffered from the blow to her head. All she could suppose was that he must have been trying to rape her. For all his faults she had not forgotten the good times together, even though at others he had been a Georgian bastard!

Yet despite all this she was not utterly cast down, though she found it hard to know why. Perhaps it was something to do with the postcard, with the view from the Rigi, that had arrived that day with a Bern postmark saying simply:

"Elizabeth, you are not forgotten. Don't lose hope. Sam".

Chapter 34

Wednesday 19th March 1997

To the north the late afternoon sun, glinting on the snows of Mount Hermon, reminded Sam of his day among the Swiss mountains. His thoughts returned to Elizabeth and her situation, thoughts which were never very far from his mind. He knew that she had been charged with the murder of Vladimir and with a number of offences against the integrity of the Swiss state. His people in Bern would keep him informed of developments, but he did not expect Swiss legal processes to move more quickly than the law did elsewhere. His feeling of guilt at her predicament and at the fate of her colleague did not lessen as the days passed. It was a month since he had left Switzerland for an uneventful journey via Italy to London and then home, on an El Al flight, to Tel Aviv. There had been nothing remarkable about the flight: security had been tight as usual, he preferred an extra hour at Heathrow to the risk of sweating for days in a hijacked aircraft, parked on some Middle Eastern or North African airport, or of being turned into aerial mincemeat by a bomb. The passengers had been the usual mix of Jews and Christian Gentiles and he was always strangely reassured, at take off and landing, by the sight of black hatted Chassidim bobbing in prayer while Christian monks and nuns said their rosaries.

From Ben Gurion Airport he had taken the bus to Tiberias, on Lake Kinneret, and from there another bus to the *kibbutz* in the Upper Galilee. All had been quiet in the area for a while, though there had been loss of life in the Security Zone, in Southern Lebanon, where Hizballah had recently taken to killing IDF troops with roadside bombs disguised as rocks. Their new ploy was a difficult one to counter and, as a former member of the Golani Brigade, it brought a tingle to his spine. Life was precious, such meaningless acts of violence and hatred, whether perpetrated by Hizballah here in the north or by the likes of Goldberg and Friedman against the Palestinians in Hebron, were becoming more and more repugnant to him.

Now that he was back home he was wearing his knitted *kippah*, the one he had worn on military service. Back home - there were a number of homes so far as Sam was concerned and this highlighted some of the tensions in his life. There were principally two, he was Sam Kagan of *Kibbutz Baruch*, Upper Galilee, Israel and Sam Kagan of Brooklyn, New York, though he also had the *nom de guerre* of Sam Charles when working in Europe. Very different worlds - but he belonged to one as much as to the others. In their different ways they had helped to form him and shape his life and thinking, though the main influence in that direction had always been his father. Which was why he stood in the small burial ground of the *kibbutz* beside the graves of his parents.

In life his parents, and particularly his father, had had a profound influence on him. In death his father had caused Sam's career to make an abrupt change in direction. It had been the main factor in his decision to join Mossad or, to give the organisation its full title, The Central Institute for Intelligence and Special Missions. They had spotted him in 1982 while he was serving in the IDF and approached him as a possible recruit. His gifts of leadership and his coolness in danger had impressed them - while on duty in Southern Lebanon he had led his patrol out of an ambush and then organised them to give cover as he went back and brought out a wounded colleague. Such qualities allied to a first rate brain - his Masters degree from the Technion, Haifa was in Electronics and Computing - would make him eminently suitable for the Institute's work. The approach had been very flattering but he had already made up his mind to train as a rabbi and would not be swayed from this. He had declined and been told that if he ever felt differently he should get in touch with their Headquarters in Tel Aviv. He had not expected to take up the offer but things had turned out differently.

On a day in early June 1985, while Sam was studying in Jerusalem, his father David had been in the workshop at the *kibbutz* repairing a tractor when the building was hit by a *Katyusha* rocket, fired at random from over the border. He had died instantly in a pile of rubble and debris, a kindly man, a stranger to malice or prejudice of any kind, who had always got on well with the people of the area whether Jew, Palestinian or Druse. For Sam it had been a profound shock and a painful loss but at first he had overcome it and continued with his studies. Indeed he had completed the studies and received ordination, taking a post that combined teaching at the Hebrew University of Jerusalem with the pastoral care of his students.

It had been in 1987, when his mother Hadassah had died from a heart attack, that he had become fully aware of the degree of the anger burning deep down within him. He had felt guilt at the bitterness, knowing that his father would have been the first to tell him to take control of his feelings and to refrain from a blanket hatred of Arabs and Russians. But Sam Kagan was not David Kagan. In so many ways he was his father's son but his was not naturally a gentle, forgiving spirit. He longed for vengeance on those who had killed his father - Hizballah who had fired the rocket and the Russians who had supplied them - perhaps vengeance is not the right word, he longed for justice to be done. His feelings of bitterness and guilt caused him to do two things. He resigned from his rabbinic post and he contacted the Institute. It was typical of Sam that he did them in that order rather than waiting to be sure that he had a new post before giving up the old one. His decisiveness had been rewarded and he was now into his tenth year as a Mossad agent. Most of his time had been spent working for Branch C of the Collections Department in London, Paris and Marseilles.

Eighteen months ago he had been transferred to *Metsada*, the clandestine combat branch, for the Basel operation. Tomorrow morning he would be back there in Tel Aviv for the debriefing. Besides the mess that he had got Elizabeth into, there were aspects of the operation that still puzzled him. He would be interested to hear at the next morning's debriefing the full details of what they had achieved. But now it was time for other things:

"Hear, O Israel, the Lord is our God, the Lord is One."

"In the palm of your hand
you hold our souls
which we entrust to you;
the souls of the living
and the souls of the dead.
In the palm of your hand
you lovingly hold
the divine spirit of all things living.
To you, O Lord,
O God of truth,
I commit now the spirit that is within me.
Heavenly Father,

your name alone is holy,
you are unchanging
and your kingdom is eternal;
you will reign over us for ever. Amen."

The evening prayer over, he placed a small stone on the grave and turned to go back to the *kibbutz*. At the burial ground's entrance he paused and leant on the gate. Despite all the tensions, despite his present worries and his visit to the grave of his parents, he was aware that this was a place to which he responded from the depths of his being. To one side was a memorial to the victims of the Holocaust. "Never again!" - that was a cry he could re-echo wholeheartedly. If anyone tried to push him and his people into the Mediterranean he would be one of the many who would fight to the death to stop it. But there was a better way, a way of talking and compromise, of give and take. You must negotiate from strength and not from weakness but you *must* negotiate. He had seen the slums of Gaza, he had seen the frustration of young Palestinians locked out of their Universities at Bir Zeit, Hebron and elsewhere. You could not build peace on that sort of foundation.

He had wept when Rabin had been murdered, murdered by one of his own people. He had feared for the nation. After the destruction of Jerusalem by the Romans, 1900 years ago, a group of rabbis and their disciples had met at Yavneh. "Why was the second temple destroyed?" someone had asked. Someone else had responded, "Because of blind hatred." Not the hatred of Roman for Jew and Jew for Roman but the hatred of Jew for Jew! And now Netanyahu had continued on the same path of negotiation and compromise that Rabin and Peres had taken, though he claimed to be driving a harder bargain.

"Bibi is good for the Jews." It had been an election slogan of Habad, the Lubavitchers, a Chassidic group based in Brooklyn - he knew them well, Mia his fiancée came from a Lubavitcher family. Would Bibi be good for the Jews and for the other inhabitants of the land, for all Abraham's children? Only time would tell. Sam looked north towards Hermon. How his father had loved the view. He felt grateful that his father had been able to enjoy the land and the life of the *kibbutz* for fifteen years from their arrival from Brooklyn in 1970. How different it was from the native Poland of David Kagan's parents and from the urban sprawl of New York City!

The temperature had dropped quickly in a few minutes. He was hungry after a busy day in the *kibbutz* workshop that had replaced the one where his father had died. It was always good to get your hands dirty and keep the old machinery going. There was the pleasure of being part of a team and of working in harmony with nature, of producing bananas, grain and other food for your fellows. It was a pity that the *kibbutz* movement was in financial difficulties and heavily in debt. Perhaps it had pioneered and had had its day? The thought hurt, it seemed like a betrayal of the pioneers who had cleared the rocks from the land and made it fertile for the good of the members of the *kibbutz* and for the good of their people. His father would have felt let down. Sam wondered whether he ought to rejoin the *kibbutz* once he had finished at Mossad, whenever that might be. He was hungry and made his way to his brother's house for dinner. Once the members of the *kibbutz* had all eaten together in the *kibbutz* dining hall, but that was in the past and now almost all the members ate at home. Privatisation began in small ways.

***

The next morning he borrowed his brother's car and started early so as to be at Headquarters in Tel Aviv before 10.30 hours. There was a light mist as he made for the main road at Kiryat Shmona. On the way he had to wait for several minutes as Druse herdsmen led a flock of several hundred goats across the road. In the cold morning air their breaths were like steam and Sam took pleasure from the scene. Apart from his car and the paved road little had changed in four thousand years. Some things endured untouched by time. Others were as transient as the morning mist which would soon yield to the warmth of the morning sun. He still felt the fascination of his work with Mossad and he was curious about the details of the outcome of Operation Basel Formula. But he also felt the pull of a simpler life, one at harmony with nature. While he was at Tel Aviv he would book a meeting with Personnel and discuss what plans they had for his future.

Sam looked around the table, they were almost all present. Typically it would be those from just along the corridor who would be the last to arrive. At the centre of the table sat the Deputy Chief of Mossad. On his left sat Alan Winters, smoking one of his Turkish cigarettes. On his right was a woman official from a section within the Ministry of Foreign Affairs, a survivor of *Lekem*, the Scientific Affairs Liaison Bureau of the Defence Ministry which had officially shut up shop after the failure of its efforts to run Jonathan Pollard as a spy in US Naval Intelligence. Her organisation might have a shadowy existence but she herself was of a substantial bulk that suggested a compulsive eater. Sam had been placed facing them on the other side of the table. A variety of officials from within Mossad made up the rest of the cast. Sam had spent long enough in the premises to know the faces, if not the names of most of those present. The premises had a Spartan feel about them, it was not the sort of place to make you want to linger and the company was not, except possibly for Winters, such as Sam would choose to share a desert island with him. The Deputy Chief finished his conversation with Winters, who stubbed out his cigarette, and the meeting began.

'Thank you all for being here this morning, it was very kind of you to come.' No one knew whether he was naturally given to an exaggerated politeness or whether it was a form of sarcasm that he had developed. It was safer to treat it as the former and smile your thanks. If you crossed him there were some mighty unpleasant spots in the world which were waiting for the talents which "only you, you must understand, have got and for which we are extremely grateful." He looked around the table, 'It appears that we are all here so I will first congratulate all those who were involved in the operation on its highly successful conclusion. As you will find shortly the operation achieved considerably more than had been expected. Alan will now give his report to us and I would mention that he has been able to update it with information we received from Moscow sources late yesterday afternoon.'

'Thank you for your words of congratulation to those involved in the operation. I am delighted to add my own thanks to them. In particular may I thank Sam for the highly efficient way he ran his side of things and for one or two of his ideas which enhanced the effect of our efforts. The first of those ideas was to use one of our women, Anna wasn't it Sam? Yes Anna. To use her to disturb the Russian Number 1, Vladimir, by playing on his sexual frustration. The outcome was that he attempted to rape the woman Elizabeth and got a bullet in the brain in return. This alerted the Swiss police to the existence of Russian espionage on their soil - Sam's friend Vladimir had in his pocket the draft of a letter to his HQ making a plea to be allowed to stay in England and continue his activities there, he had been stupid enough to write it in Russian and there was little doubt about the intended destination of the letter. This has upset the Swiss and no doubt they will let the British know, the knowledge will not endear the "new" Russia to the Swiss or the British. The woman is held by the Swiss police on murder and other charges and again the publicity of her trial will not be to the liking of Russian security. Just one thing Sam, we were fortunate that the SVR team in Basel had a good Number 2 in Grigor. If he had not had a cool nerve he might have called the operation off after Vladimir's decease and that would have been a waste of much of our effort. Still they did go ahead and that's what counts.

'Sam's other piece of ingenuity was the briefcase in the Basel Railway Station Left Luggage office. We have gathered details of the bank accounts of some of the Swiss top brass over a long period and they have been of some considerable interest to us. They could be useful for bargaining, I won't say blackmail, if an episode like that of the Alfred Frauenknecht case arose again. You younger folk won't remember, but he was caught in 1969 collecting some of the plans for the Swiss version of the French Mirage III jet fighter from the Sulzer Brothers fighter division in Winterthur, Switzerland. However earlier batches of plans had got through to us and as a result of his success we had the *Kfir* fighter which was invaluable in the 1973 Yom Kippur War.

'That Swiss venture was a happy and fruitful collaboration between our friends in the sadly defunct *Lekem* and ourselves.' He nodded to the solitary woman present, the representative of the Ministry of Foreign Affairs, 'Hanna here represents what was left after *Lekem* ran into trouble and had to be pruned drastically, one might say Pollarded.' He had struggled to render the pun in Hebrew but it was met with silence and he knew at once that he had misjudged the mood. Perhaps, as he spent so much time in London, he was out of touch with Israeli feeling and especially with such feeling within the Intelligence community. He hurried on, 'Sam's idea of returning copies of some of the bank statements using the Russians as our messenger boys, so that *they* would get the credit for the research, was masterly. It has upset relations between Switzerland and Russia, between the Kremlin and the SVR. And the Swiss banks have a lot of egg on their faces, which is something that we can enjoy at the moment when they are somewhat unwilling participants in the hunt for lost Jewish assets and Nazi gold!' This was appreciated by his audience. He relaxed again and prepared to tell them of the results of the main operation.

'Operation Basel Formula was set up with a number of objects in view. We worked on a need-to-know basis and those involved only knew about matters which directly concerned them and the effectiveness of their part in the overall plan. Even Sam did not know all the ramifications of the operation and I can see that he's all ears to discover what the final stages involved. I will take the points one by one and work from the headings that I have prepared. If the projector could be switched on, please. Thank, you. We will go through the points in order.' There was some moving of chairs. 'You can all see? Good I will start:

'1. Tying Down SVR Resources. You will be aware that the SVR committed a number of their agents to the operation for a long period. The couple in London, Eugene and Elizabeth, or Vladimir and Lizaveta as they were in reality, were tied down there for a whole year plus the time that they spent getting used to the place. Then there was the man the SVR planted in the Basel laboratory, Heinrich Nussbaum who was originally one of Marcus Wollf's people from the DDR. He was technically qualified and it was necessary to keep him from direct contact with the work on the drug while at the same time ensuring that enough information reached him in oblique ways to keep his masters happy. At a crucial stage, in December, he went absent without leave and took with him not the secrets of the drug but instead the wife of Bernhardt Sussmeyer the boss of the lab. They are still missing so far as I know. They have also lost Vladimir to an early grave and Lizaveta to the Swiss police.

'**2. Updating Ourselves on the Working Methods of the SVR.** Over the period of a year we have been able to observe the workings of an SVR unit and update our knowledge of their *modus operandi*. I will not bore you with the detail, besides the analysis is still going on. Suffice to say that their standards were not particularly impressive. This may have more to do with the personality of the late Vladimir than with inherent weakness in their system, though a tightly run system should have monitored his performance more closely.' There were murmurs of agreement from round the table. Sam noticed that it was the desk-bound monitors of the field officers who were showing their support for the idea.

'**3. Giving Free Publicity to Russia and the SVR.** It is all too easy for our political masters, here in Israel and elsewhere to think that Russia under Yeltsin is no longer a threat. That is not so and I do not need to remind you of the fragility of Yeltsin's health. The young shoot of liberty is in danger of frost damage in a country which, whether under the Tsar of All the Russias or Lenin and his successors, never knew a democratic regime. By this operation we have reminded the world that the Russians are active in places like Switzerland and the British government is by now no doubt aware that something has been going on in London. Governments will be aware that trade and commercial secrets are among the targets of the SVR.' There were signs that some in the room were becoming bored at Winters' lecture but as he moved to his next point he once more had their full attention.

'4. Operation Basel Formula was a Vital Part of the Test Programme of the Drug. I expect that most of you assumed that the Basel operation was mounted to protect a small Swiss laboratory, involved in the development and testing of drugs, from the depredations of the Russian wolf. To protect an important drug from Russian pillage.'

The unwary nodded, the more streetwise waited for him to continue.

'The drug does exist but it was developed here in Haifa at the Technion, where the initial testing was done. What were needed were not further laboratory tests on guinea pigs - or, so they tell me, on rats - but tests on suitable humans. Perhaps I should explain the effects of the drug concerned. They were well set out by Dr Svyatoslav Gordeyev, formerly of the Serbsky Institute, Moscow, at a meeting with Grigor, the SVR's Number 2 in the operation, on the Sunday morning. Is that right Sam? Good. We have a transcript of what he said and I will pass around copies.'

There had been mutterings at his mention of the Serbsky and Winters now responded to this. 'I did tell Sam, only semi-humourously, that he was to put a bullet through the brain of the man from the Serbsky.'

Sam took his cue, 'He was an old man, tired out, in pain and almost at death's door. He was best left to the Almighty.'

'Thank you Sam. So if you have digested the transcript of Gordeyev's comments you will see that the drug was a conditioning agent, one that our people at the Technion believed to be both gentle and effective. Sam and his team had their fun at the Basel *Fasnacht* carnival and collected together seven members of the SVR team, remember the other three were not available - one was in a Basel mortuary, the girl was in the Basel police station and the East German was, I assume, frolicking somewhere with his boss' wife. The seven were taken to the Simmental, we couldn't run to the cost of accommodation in Gstaad so we stopped short and entertained them in a remote farmhouse with a secure basement. That was the point at which you took your leave of them, wasn't it Sam?

'Sam's team stayed to maintain security and a second team took over contact with our Russian guests. This group was made up of people with psychiatric training , people who had treated patients suffering from a variety of personality disorders or with delusions. Oh yes, I should mention that Sam's team and the psychiatric team were all with American backgrounds. They spoke impeccable American English, if such a thing is possible. No Hebrew was spoken by any of our people on any occasion during the Basel operation and the Simmental house party. There was nothing about either group that would have led to any of our guests discovering who were the providers of the warm hospitality they were receiving. They would clearly have believed that we were the CIA and indeed that was what we ultimately told them.

'The drug developed by the Technion is colourless and tasteless. Given in water or other drinks it is impossible to detect. The patient treated with the drug becomes susceptible to the advice and guidance of those treating him, though in this case there was nothing to suggest to the Russians that they were patients. By using a group of SVR agents we were testing it on people who, because of their commitment, personalities and training, would be extremely hard to condition. If the drug worked on them it was likely to work on almost anyone. They were being conditioned and trained to respond to the stimulus of the American Dollar rather than love of the Russian Motherland or fear of their SVR masters. They were told, of course, to deny any agreement with the CIA and they were given a variety of tasks to do for the CIA. From our contacts at Langley and from local knowledge we were able to compile a list of some of their agents in Moscow, Russians who have been useful in the past but were by now almost on the retired list and expendable. There is no evidence that their identity has been compromised to the SVR by their people who returned from Basel, but we will monitor the situation over the coming months.

'At the end of a week our seven guests were sent on their way and went home to Russia. Sam has referred to Gordeyev's health and he needed two of the others to help him travel. They all got back home a month ago and the exciting part of my report concerns developments since them.'

They were all quiet, he had them eating out of his hand. He looked at Sam but his face betrayed nothing beyond intense concentration.

'We are fortunate to have effective sources of information within the SVR and as a result we have been able to establish how our seven guests have fared since their return home. One great stroke of luck for us was that this was not purely the project of the SVR, they were working on behalf of commercial interests who, it seems, have Mafiya links. In the old days we could have expected the KGB to conduct a very rigorous interrogation of any of its agents who might have been in the hands of the CIA and who might have been turned by them. Now the SVR pussyfoots around by comparison. The Russian Mafiya know better and they treated the escapade of the seven with extreme suspicion. They suspected that they, or at any rate some of them, had got their hands on the drug and the papers relating to it and that they had sold them to the Americans. Their revenge was hard: they took the seven, or I should say the six because Gordeyev had died within a few days of reaching home, they took the six apart - I really mean that! They took them to within an inch of their lives and then beyond. Not even with their dying breaths did they divulge anything that they had been told. We were extremely fortunate to have such a thorough test for the drug and it came through with flying colours. I believe that, in engineering, components are tested to destruction: in the case of Operation Basel Formula the SVR personnel were tested to destruction. We have even been supplied, through one of our people in Moscow who has contacts with the Mafiya, with a video recording of the interrogation of Grigor. If you would switch on the machine Noam ... '

Sam was on his feet and the eyes of all those around the table were on him. His intervention was spoken about long afterwards in the ranks of Mossad. The two things that made an indelible impression on his audience were the quiet intensity of his delivery, which was without a hint of histrionics, and the fact that he included himself in the denunciation he delivered.

'As this operation progressed I became more and more aware of the feeling that there was something about it that was peculiar. You, Alan, have complimented me on the side-shows that I devised, but I have come to regret the one which so tantalised Vladimir and led to his attempted rape of Elizabeth, his death and her arrest. However it has had the beneficial effect that Vladimir had a quick death, rather than being "taken apart bit by bit", and Elizabeth has, so far, escaped the attentions of the SVR and its Mafiya friends.

'I am appalled that we have received with such enthusiasm news of the testing to destruction of *"the human guinea pigs"* and that we are now preparing to watch a video recording of the process. In addition, you were prepared to endanger CIA agents in Moscow who had risked their lives for the West in the past. If our work has so hardened us to other people then we ought to give serious consideration to doing something to restore our humanity and take ourselves elsewhere - for a while at least!'

There was total silence in the room and Noam stood

frozen by the video recorder.

'A little earlier, Alan, you referred to the success of the *Kfir* fighter in the *Yom Kippur War*. We do well to be grateful to those who won that war for our safety and security with such brilliance and devotion. But with actions like the present, in which I with others have had a guilty part, we bring dishonour to Israel and to Mossad. We do ill to remember the *Yom Kippur War* and not *Yom Kippur* itself. Let me remind you and myself of part of one of the prayers for that day:

> "We have abused and betrayed. We are cruel.
> We have destroyed and embittered other people's lives.
> We were false to ourselves.
> We have gossiped about others and hated them.
> We have insulted and jeered. We have killed. We have lied.
> We have misled others and neglected them.
> We were obstinate. We have perverted and quarrelled.
> We have robbed and stolen.
> We have transgressed through unkindness.
> We have been both violent and weak.
> We have practised extortion.
> We have yielded to wrong desires, our zeal was misplaced."

'What I say to all of you I say to myself, *"our zeal was misplaced."* There is a precept in the Torah, *"Justice and only justice, you shall follow that you may inherit the land which the Lord your God gives you."* If we wish this land to be secure for ourselves and for our children's children we have to do better than this!'

Sam turned to the Deputy Chief, 'I am sorry sir, but I do not think that I can make any further contribution that will be useful to your proceedings. May I have your permission to leave?'

'Yes, Sam, I do feel that that would be the appropriate action at this stage. You will see me later? I will be here until late this evening.'

Sam hesitated for a moment. There was no point in dragging things out, he would get it done that day. 'This evening then. At six o'clock?'

With that he was gone and silence reigned in the conference room. Winters looked at the Deputy Chief for guidance. His answer came, 'We will adjourn until one o'clock. And, please, gentlemen and madam, keep to yourselves what has been said here this morning. I have no need to tell you that in any case.' The room emptied quickly and he turned to Winters, 'Lunch in my office, wind up the meeting as quickly as you can this afternoon and then your thoughts on what to do about Sam Kagan.'

***

Sam went straight to his car and headed for Jerusalem. He needed to clarify his thoughts. He drove down the Jaffa road and round the Old City to the Dung Gate. He found a place among the tourist buses and parked. 'Quiet today?' he exchanged the time of day with the young IDF soldier on duty at the gate to the Western Wall Plaza.

'Yes quiet, tomorrow it's Hebron and you never can tell where it's going to come from there.'

'Best of luck, I survived several stints in Hebron. That was some years ago. Let's hope it improves.'

Sam crossed the Plaza, washed his hands and walked to the Wall. The sight of the old stones moved him to tears. What must it have been like being with the IDF units when they took it, the *Kotel*, in 1973 and heard the *Shofar* - the ram's horn - blown. A memorable *Yom Kippur* indeed. A half an hour later he returned to his car. It was just after one thirty. That was about right for his plans for the afternoon.

He drove past Mount Herzl and was struck by the irony

of the Mossad operation having been located in Basel, the city where Herzl had organised the first Zionist Congress in 1897, 100 years ago. And to think that at various stages they had debated Uganda or South America as locations for a Jewish homeland! Mount Herzl where Rabin's body lay buried, a victim of one of his own people, a victim of "blind hatred".

He drove through the gates of *Yad Vashem*, the Holocaust Memorial, - heavy iron gates with their pattern of harsh and jagged thorns - and parked the car in the shade of the trees. After a bottle of orange juice in the cafeteria he walked the length of the "Avenue of the Righteousness Among the Gentiles". The carob trees provided shade from the sun which, even in mid-March, was hot. He was glad the Avenue was there, it was a reminder to him and other Jews that, despite the evil perpetrated against them by many peoples over many centuries, by no means all the *Goyim* were their enemies, to believe otherwise was the road to national paranoia. At the "Wall of Remembrance" he paused and renewed acquaintance with Nathan Rappaport's statue to the "Warsaw Ghetto Uprising" and his relief plaque, *"The Last March"*, with its depiction of a Jewish community with their Rabbi being marched to the Death Camps. There was something about the plaque that moved him deeply whenever he saw it, the horror of death and persecution for ordinary folk and the understatement of the might of Nazi force with the military helmets and bayonets just visible above the heads of the victims being led to the slaughter.

He paused for prayer in the "Hall of Remembrance". The "Eternal Flame" burned in its broken-shaped bronze cup and the name "Treblinka" stood out among the infamous names of the other death camps on the floor - it was where most of his parents' relations had perished. From the dark he returned to the sunshine and set off for the "Valley of Destroyed Communities" and for the next hour and a half he wandered there, walking, sitting and thinking. He made no new decisions but he confirmed in his mind decisions he had already made.

***

Back at Mossad Headquarters he had a sandwich and a drink and chatted with an acquaintance about the fortunes of Maccabi, Tel Aviv. For the next half hour he read the *New York Times* and at ten minutes to six he knocked at the door of the Deputy Chief's PA and announced his arrival.

At ten past six Sam was shown into the Deputy Chief's office. Elaborate apologies for the delay were proffered, he'd just taken a telephone call from the Ministry of Foreign Affairs that had gone on for nearly a half an hour but, as it had been someone close to David Levy, the Minister, and as it had concerned something that was worrying the Americans, he hadn't been able to cut him short. He was sorry to inconvenience Sam and sorry that Sam had been upset by Alan Winters at the meeting that morning.

Sam raised an eyebrow and sniffed, 'I'd hazard a guess that Alan has been within close range of your room for a substantial part of the afternoon. He's like the Cheshire Cat which vanished but left its grin: he vanishes but leaves an enduring aroma of Turkish cigarettes!'

'Ten out of ten for observation, Sam. You've worked the anger out of your system with a good walk this afternoon?'

'I've been back to basics. The Western Wall and *Yad Vashem*. I wanted to be sure that my decision was the right one. I'm sure of it and so I'm giving you my resignation. No doubt Personnel will be able to tell me how to word the letter and let me know about my pension and that sort of thing.'

'You shouldn't do anything like this in haste, Sam. You

know we value your work for the Institute very highly. You're tired and you need a break. Things are not too busy here at the moment - except for me, of course - take a couple of months' leave, work out your inhibitions on the *kibbutz* or see that fiancée of yours, better still marry her! Alan told me that the Russian girl - Elizabeth was it? - was having an effect on you. He mentioned that you had spent one evening and the next day with her - he didn't refer to it in front of the others at the debriefing, of course - that was unwise of you and might have led to trouble, especially as it was on the eve of the action in Basel and there would have been real difficulty if you had been out of action on the Monday.'

'The reason for my resignation is to be free to try to get Elizabeth out of her Swiss jail. I've made up my mind on the matter and you won't budge me. It could be useful to you, she might well have information that the CIA or the FBI would appreciate and it always helps to be able to chalk up Brownie points with them. I promise I'll take care not to compromise Israel or the Institute by my actions, I'll travel on my American passport but, and here I'm coming to you cap in hand, I may - I almost certainly will - need a variety of forged papers, passports, driving licences and that sort of thing that the Documents Section turns out, nothing that could be traced back to here, of course. And you can take the cost out of my pension.'

'After what you've achieved for us over the years I think we can run to the expense of a few forgeries. I can see that you won't be dissuaded from your intentions. Just let me say that if you ever want to come back you will always be welcome and if you would like to give lectures on a freelance basis to our new recruits we would be delighted to have the benefit of your experience and wisdom - you might even have a shot at "The Morality of Intelligence Work" or something of that sort.'

Sam rose, 'I'll wish you well, sir. We're sure to meet sometime.'

'Just hold on a minute, Sam' He disappeared through the door behind his desk and returned two or three minutes later. 'The *Memuneh* will see you before you go. He's spent the afternoon with Netanyahu discussing a paper on Syria and the Golan, almost in your *kibbutz's* backyard isn't it?'

At five to seven that evening Sam Kagan shook hands with General Danny Yatom, the *Memuneh* or Patriarch, the Head of Mossad, and left Headquarters. Once more he headed up the road to Jerusalem. He would spend the night with Noam Chazan, an old friend from the IDF and now a singer and entertainer at the Khan Club. Tomorrow he would return to the Upper Galilee and commence planning.

***

Sam Kagan had now but one object in life - to get Elizabeth out of her Swiss jail. He had no real idea of how to do it, he had no idea of how she would react if he were able to restore her freedom. None of that mattered, he had only one task before him and he would be devoting all his thought and energy to it. Whatever it took and however it had to be done, he *would* get Elizabeth out and set her free.

And what next?

How is Sam to secure Elizabeth's freedom and will his infatuation with her meet fulfilment?

How will Ruth cope with Peter's breakdown and Michael's problems?

What future awaits Elizabeth and Peter's child - "the love-child of the London businessman and the Russian spy"?

The story continues with Part 2 of The Basel Trilogy – The Basel Exodus

Due out shortly!

About the Author

Born 21 August 1939, Plymouth, Devon, UK. Secondary education at Plymouth College.

Working life with HM Customs and Excise (on purchase tax in north and west London and at a distillery in Dagenham) and then with the Inland Revenue, including five years at the Special Investigations Section, dealing with tax avoidance and also tax evasion cases, followed by spells as District Inspector in charge of tax offices in Willesden (north-west London), Dalston (north-east London) and finally Paignton, Devon.

From 1960 to 1962 did National Service in the RAF, servicing V-bomber navigation and bombing radar equipment, mainly at Marham, Norfolk.

Married to Jennifer with a son (in Australia) and a daughter (in the UK) and five very sporty grandsons.

Interests: politics, music, history, theology (Christian and Jewish), travel, railways and photography (which two often combine).

Published on Kindle 2015: *The Basel Formula (Part 1 of The Basel Trilogy)*.
Shortly due for publication: Parts 2 & 3, *The Basel Exodus* and *The Basel Account*.

Also in the pipeline, an unconnected novel: *O Château, O Seasons!*

Apart from Moscow he has visited all the locations

featured in these novels.

His book of railway photographs, *Plymouth Steam 1954 to 1963* was published in 1984

Made in the USA
Charleston, SC
03 September 2016